W9-AYG-973

TRAPPED BY A KILLER

Julia goes absolutely still at the sound of a muffled thump.

She waits, poised, listening. For a long time there's nothing but silence.

Deciding it must have been her imagination, or perhaps a cat prowling around the cellar door, Julia uneasily begins to scrape clumps of stain from the wooden dresser.

Minutes later, a more distinct sound reaches her ears: a floorboard creaking overhead, on the first floor of the house.

"Dulcie?" Julia drops the scraper and hurries toward the stairway. She warned Dulcie not to try to come down the flight of stairs by herself.

At the bottom of the steep, cobweb-draped stairway leading out of the cellar, Julia stops short, looking up in disbelief. The angled double doors at the top of the stairs are closed.

Fighting back an urge of panic, Julia swiftly mounts the stairs.

It must have been the wind. Except . . .

What wind? It's a beautiful, calm day. There's not even a breeze. And if the wind closed the doors, wouldn't I have heard them banging shut?

As she nears the top of the steps, Julia hurriedly reaches overhead to push open the doors. But they don't budge.

Reality sinks in, and with it, numbing terror. Somebody has latched the doors from the outside, imprisoning Julia in the musty cellar. . . .

Books by Wendy Corsi Staub

Published by Kensington Publishing Corporation

IN THE BLINK OF AN EYE

Wendy Corsi Staub

ZEBRA BOOKS
KENSINGTON PUBLISHING CORP.
http://www.kensingtonbooks.com

ZEBRA BOOKS are published by

Kensington Publishing Corp.
850 Third Avenue
New York, NY 10022

Copyright © 2002, 2009 by Wendy Corsi Staub

All rights reserved. No part of this book may be reproduced in any form or by any means without the prior written consent of the Publisher, excepting brief quotes used in reviews.

If you purchased this book without a cover you should be aware that this book is stolen property. It was reported as "unsold and destroyed" to the Publisher and neither the Author nor the Publisher has received any payment for this "stripped book."

All Kensington titles, imprints, and distributed lines are available at special quantity discounts for bulk purchases for sales promotion, premiums, fund-raising, educational, or institutional use.

Special book excerpts or customized printings can also be created to fit specific needs. For details, write or phone the office of the Kensington Special Sales Manager: Attn. Special Sales Department. Kensington Publishing Corp., 850 Third Avenue, New York, NY 10022. Phone: 1-800-221-2647.

Zebra and the Z logo Reg. U.S. Pat. & TM Off.

ISBN-13: 978-1-4201-0688-6
ISBN-10: 1-4201-0688-0

First Pinnacle Mass-Market Printing: March 2002
First Zebra Mass-Market Printing: April 2009

10   9   8   7

Printed in the United States of America

For Suzanne Muldowney Schmidt,
who became my friend on our first day of kindergarten,
and who will be my friend forever
—With love and fond memories from "Wendell"

And, as always, for my three guys:
Mark, Morgan, and Brody

ACKNOWLEDGMENTS

First, I must acknowledge two people whose friendship I treasure: my incredible editor, John Scognamiglio, and my terrific agent, Laura Blake Peterson. Without you guys, this book wouldn't be in print. I would also like to thank the following people who graciously—and some, unwittingly—aided in the research and inspiration for this book: Frances Bennett of New York Ghost Chapter; Bonita Cable, Rick Genett, Christian Nova, Susan Glasier, Gretchen Clark Lazarony, Sesla Skowronski, Patty Lillis, who brought through my dearly departed in vivid detail; and others at Lily Dale who preferred not to be mentioned by name. Thanks to dynamic Doug Mendini and his marketing staff for the advance vote of confidence; to my cherished friend and fellow author Beverly Beaver for being a one-woman writer's support system; to the amazing Joan Scott for keeping my little ones out of my office; to Kim Powell, Suzanne Schmidt, and Stacey Staub for cheerfully accompanying me on various ghostly missions. I also must voice my deepest gratitude to my husband, for playing editorial consultant and providing valuable feedback on the manuscript-in-progress; and my family, who patiently endured a rainy April afternoon on the shores of Cassadaga Lake in search of those last few details to make it real—thanks, Mom, Grandma T, Scooter, Lisa, Hannah Rae, Leo, and of course, seasoned researchers Morgan and Brody. Finally, I have to thank my Aunt Mickey, for ultimately validating what I already knew was real.

Prologue

Halloween night, fifteen years ago
Lily Dale, New York

"Okay, one more house and then we're done." Julia Garrity teeters across the small patch of wet lawn, her heels sinking into the damp earth.

"Three more," Kristin Shuttleworth amends, walking several steps ahead. "I didn't even get any Milk Duds yet and they're my favorite."

"*One*," Julia insists. "I mean it, Kristin. That's it for me. You can keep going on your own if you want."

"That would be stupid. My costume doesn't make sense without you, Jul. I need you. Please."

Kristin is very good at pleading. Most of the time, she can talk Julia into just about anything. But tonight, Julia shakes her head. She's had it with this whole scene.

For one thing, at fourteen, they're getting too old to be trick-or-treating, free Milk Duds or not. For another, Julia's feet are killing her in her mother's pointy old satin pumps. She can't wait to change into sneakers and jeans and wash this gunk off her face.

Why the heck did she ever let Kristin convince her to dress up as the female half of a bridal couple?

Kristin, as the groom, gets to wear her father's old tuxedo and a pair of flat, comfortable black shoes. Her long blond hair is tucked beneath a black top hat, and only a fake mustache mars her pretty face.

Meanwhile, Julia is decked out in a long white gown with a train that she keeps tripping over, her vision obscured by multiple layers of illusion. The veil is attached to a tiara, which is pinned to the teased brunette wig that conceals Julia's mop of boyish brown hair. The wig—and full makeup—was Kristin's idea, to make Julia look more feminine.

"If I'm so masculine, why can't I be the groom?" Julia had asked grumpily when they were getting dressed.

"Because my mother doesn't have a wedding dress I can wear. She had on some crazy short, psychedelic hippie dress when she married my dad in that freaky flower child ceremony," Kristin pointed out impatiently.

True. Not that Julia's mother has a wedding dress, either, having never married Julia's father, whoever—and wherever—he is.

Kristin continues, "And your grandmother is freaked enough as it is about us borrowing her gown for a costume. She definitely wouldn't want me to be the one wearing it."

True, again. Julia's grandmother isn't crazy about Kristin. And Julia's mother, who is usually laid-back when it comes to parenting, can't stand her. She thinks Kristin's a bad influence.

Julia can understand why. Strong-willed Kristin, who smokes and curses and never studies, isn't the kind of girl parents like. But she's a loyal friend, and she's loads of fun. She's adventurous where Julia is cautious, outgoing where Julia is reserved. A teacher once said the biggest difference between them is that Julia tries to avoid making waves, while Kristin thrives on rocking the boat.

That might be the biggest difference, but it's far from the only one.

Often mistaken as being much younger than her fourteen years, Julia is an athletic but petite freckle-faced, jean-clad tomboy—not unattractive, but she certainly doesn't turn heads the way leggy, slim Kristin does.

Kristin's wide-set eyes, high cheekbones, and full mouth are striking even without makeup, though she hasn't been in public without it since sixth grade. Naturally, she's thrilled when strangers assume she's several years older. She even recently started dating college guys from the state university a few miles away in Fredonia. They all think she's eighteen or nineteen.

Of course her parents have no idea what Kristin is up to. Julia can't help worrying that she's going to get herself into trouble one of these days, but her self-assured friend never seems to waste a moment on apprehension as she slap-dashes her way through life.

Kristin is so utterly opposite in temperament and appearance that even Julia herself sometimes finds it hard to believe that they're still so close. But there aren't many girls their own age in a community the size of Lily Dale, with only a handful of year-round families. They've been basically thrown together since they were toddlers, and for all Kristin's faults, Julia loves her like the sister she never had—and will never have, judging by the way her mother goes through men. It doesn't look as if she's ever going to find one she likes and settle down.

"Come on, Jul, let's go," Kristin says, striding up narrow Summer Street, her plastic orange pumpkin swinging from her hand. "Looks like the Biddles are home."

Julia hesitates, glancing at the two-story Victorian cottage ahead. "I don't think we should go to their place, Kristin."

"Why not?" Kristin doesn't even break her stride. "It's not like we have a lot to choose from, Jul."

She has a point. Most of the homes in Lily Dale are deserted at this time of year, windows covered with plywood, owners settled far from the harsh winds and snows that batter western New York from October until April.

But Rupert and Nanette Biddle, like the Garritys and the Shuttleworths, have always stayed in town. Though they tend to keep to themselves, they seem friendly in a distant sort of way when Julia sees them at Assembly services.

"Their porch light isn't on," Julia points out. "And we've never gone trick-or-treating here before."

"There's a first time for everything," is Kristin's glib reply. She's already halfway up the steps.

Julia sighs, following her friend as the wind gusts off nearby Cassadaga Lake. Dry leaves scuttle along the gravel walk and a chorus of wind chimes tinkles forlornly on the breeze. As she climbs the steps Julia gathers her train in one hand and grasps the wooden railing with the other, wobbling in her shoes, her dress whipping precariously around her ankles. Above her head, suspended from an ornately carved bracket that matches the scrolled trim lining the porch eaves, a wooden sign sways in the wind.

RUPERT BIDDLE, REGISTERED MEDIUM.

A floorboard creaks beneath Julia's weight as she crosses the porch to join Kristin, who is already reaching for the antique doorbell.

Like most of the other cottages in Lily Dale, this place is probably a hundred years old. But Rupert Biddle is one of the more successful mediums in the Spiritualist Assembly, and his home is one of the few that have been restored to its former pristine state. No peeling paint, missing spindles, or lopsided shutters here.

None at the Shuttleworths' home a few blocks away, either. Kristin's father, Anson, is a nationally renowned psychic medium whose fame has grown considerably ever since he helped the police up in Buffalo track down the bodies of several children who were murdered by a serial killer almost three years ago. He's just published a book about that experience.

Kristin doesn't like to talk about that, or about her father in general.

Nor does she waste much breath discussing her older half brother, Edward, who lives down in Jamestown with his mother, Anson's first wife. Julia remembers him coming around more often when they were younger, but he doesn't anymore. Kristin once mentioned in passing that he'd had a big blowout with her mother, Iris. Julia sometimes forgets he even exists, and it certainly seems as though Kristin is an only child, the way her parents dote on her.

Julia is an only child, too. But her mother is far too busy and self-involved to dote. Nor will she discuss the circumstances of Julia's birth. Even Grandma, who lives with them, won't reveal her father's identity—if Grandma even knows. Julia figures it's possible that she doesn't. And whenever she asks Grandma about it, Grandma says that she shouldn't concern herself with that. She tells Julia how lucky she is to have a mother and grandmother who love her.

Not that Julia doesn't feel lucky, but—

Footsteps sound on the other side of the Biddles' tall front door with its frosted oval beveled-glass window. As it opens, an overhead globe is switched on from inside, flooding the porch with light.

Nanette Biddle, an attractive middle-aged woman whose blond hair is perpetually tucked back into a neat bun, stands there looking surprised.

"Trick or treat," Kristin announces cheerfully, thrusting her plastic pumpkin forward.

"It's Halloween!" Mrs. Biddle replies, as though she hadn't realized it until just now. "You both look adorable! I'm so sorry, girls, I don't have anything ready . . ."

Julia squirms, wanting to tell her to forget it. But Kristin stands her ground expectantly, so Julia follows her lead as usual.

"Why don't you come in?" Mrs. Biddle suggests. "Rupert isn't home, but I think he bought some candy bars when he went up to Tops the other day. I'll see if I can find them. You deserve a treat with those costumes. I wish I had a camera!"

She holds the door open for them.

Julia steps over the threshold and looks around as Mrs. Biddle closes it behind them, saying, "I don't want to let the draft in. It's chilly out there tonight, isn't it?"

Julia politely murmurs that it is. Kristin says nothing. She isn't the type to make small talk with adults.

"I'll be right back, girls," Mrs. Biddle says, disappearing toward the back of the house.

Julia looks around, curious. She's always wondered whether this house is as pretty inside as it is out.

They're standing in a high-ceilinged stair hall. To the immediate right of the front door is a pair of closed French doors. Beside them, between two massive, carved newel posts, three wide, curved bottom steps lead up to a landing, and a long flight continues from there to the second floor, rising between a spindled railing on the open side and dark-paneled wainscoting along the wall.

Immediately to the left of the front door is an archway that opens to a shadowy dining room. Straight ahead, a short hallway leads past the stairs to what must be the kitchen. Julia can hear Mrs. Biddle opening and closing cabinets there.

The walls of the hall are covered in maroon and gold striped paper. Overhead, a frosted amber-colored glass bowl-shaped antique light fixture is suspended from three chains that meet at the center of a scrolled plaster oval on the ceiling. There is a crystal vase of white flowers on the small telephone table beside the stairs, and healthy potted plants are everywhere. The hardwood floors gleam. Every strand of fringe on the oriental area rug is aligned as perfectly as if somebody has combed it.

"Nice, huh?" Julia whispers to Kristin, struck by the contrast to the cluttered, rickety lakefront cottage she shares with her mother and Grandma.

Kristin doesn't reply.

Julia turns to see that her friend, wearing an odd expression, has retreated a few steps, her back pressed against the closed door.

"What's wrong, Kristin?"

It's as though she doesn't even hear, Julia realizes.

Kristin's big blue eyes are fixed on something over Julia's shoulder, on the stairs.

Julia quickly turns to see what it is.

The stairway is empty.

"Jul . . ." Her voice a strangled whisper, Kristin is touching her arm, *grabbing* her arm.

"What is it, Kristin? What's wrong?"

"Do you see her, Julia?"

"Who?" Julia looks around, thinking she must be talking about Mrs. Biddle.

But Mrs. Biddle is still in the kitchen.

Kristin is still staring at the stairway.

And the stairway is still vacant.

"Do I see who?" Julia asks, fear slithering over her.

Kristin, wide-eyed, shakes her head slowly, letting go of Julia's arm.

"I couldn't find the candy bars, girls," Mrs. Biddle says, reappearing, "but I do have some Oreos, and I put some into sandwich baggies for each of—"

She breaks off suddenly just as Julia hears a commotion behind her and feels a cold breeze on her neck.

She turns to see that Kristin has thrown the door open and is rushing out of the house as though she's running for her life.

"My goodness, what's wrong with your friend?" Mrs. Biddle asks.

Julia's heart is pounding. "I don't know," she tells her, moving toward the door. "I'd better go find out."

But she never does.

When she finally catches up with Kristin on the front steps of the Shuttleworths' house three blocks away, Kristin, strangely quiet, refuses to talk about what happened to her inside the Biddle house.

In the weeks that follow, Kristin grows increasingly withdrawn. She doesn't want to help Julia bake pumpkin pies for Thanksgiving, as they usually do, and she turns down a rare invitation to go Christmas shopping at the Galleria Mall up in Buffalo with Julia and her grandmother. Every day after school, she only wants to go home—alone.

When her father's book becomes an overnight best-seller and he decides that their family will spend the rest of that winter in Florida, Kristin clearly isn't upset to be leaving Lily Dale behind.

In fact, she almost seems relieved when she gives Julia one last hug and disappears into the black stretch limo taking her family to the Buffalo airport.

With the money from Anson's book and subsequent television appearances, the Shuttleworths soon buy a big house on the beach near Boca Raton. After this, they will spend only summers in Lily Dale. Julia and Kristin will reestablish their friendship every June, and say good-bye every August.

They will never again discuss what Kristin saw—and Julia didn't—in the Biddle house that Halloween night.

In time, Julia's memory of that night will fade, only to be nudged back into her consciousness more than a decade later, when she hears that Rupert and Nanette Biddle have sold their house to Kristin's mother, the newly widowed Iris Shuttleworth.

Kristin, long absent from Julia's life and by then living on the West Coast with her boyfriend and young daughter, will make a final appearance in Lily Dale to help her mother move into the new home.

She will arrive her beautiful, breezy self to stay with her mother in the Victorian house at Ten Summer Street.

She will grow increasingly subdued, visibly troubled as the days wear on.

She will leave in a coffin.

Chapter One

The present
Long Beach, California

"Daddy!"

Instantly awakened by the shrill cry, Paine Landry sits straight up in bed. Was it real?

The room is illuminated in the bluish glow from the television and moonlight spilling through the open window. Sheer white curtains billow slightly.

Somewhere, a faucet drips.

Palm fronds rustle in the warm June breeze.

A chirpy has-been sitcom actress hawks an incredibly complicated plastic food storage system on a television infomercial.

Paine feels for the television remote on the rumpled quilt

and presses POWER, silencing her, plunging the room into darkness.

He listens, unsettled, certain he heard it, unless—

"Daddy!"

Dulcie.

He bolts out of bed and rushes across the shadowy bedroom and down the short hall, shoving open the door to his daughter's room. Enough moonlight filters through the drawn blinds for him to make out Dulcie huddled in bed, knees drawn up to her chest, arms wrapped around them.

"What is it?" Paine strides over to take his daughter into his arms. "Did you have a nightmare?"

Dulcie's body is trembling. "Not a nightmare . . ."

"What happened?"

"Gram's here."

It takes a moment for Paine to grasp her words. Then, relieved, he laughs. "Dulcie, you were dreaming. Gram isn't here. She's back East, and it's the middle of the night."

"No, she's here."

"It was a dream," Paine repeats, again hearing the steady dripping of the faucet in the bathroom down the hall. He keeps forgetting to call the landlord about that. He'll do it first thing in the morning.

"Daddy," Dulcie says, almost frantically, feeling around in front of her, finding and clutching at Paine's T-shirt. "I'm not lying, Daddy. I saw her."

The last three words are faint.

A chill slithers over him. "You *saw* her?"

Dulcie nods, her sightless eyes focused on a spot over his shoulder. "I don't know how it happened, Daddy, but I was lying here in bed, and a sound woke me up. I thought it was the wind but then it was more like a whisper. And I saw Gram's face, standing over me. She was smiling."

It was just a dream, Paine tells himself, biting down on

his lower lip. *Just a dream. It has nothing to do with Kristin . . .*

Or what happened three years ago.

"Was that all? You saw her smiling?" Paine asks his daughter softly, his tone carefully neutral. He strokes Dulcie's tousled blond hair, his fingers automatically lacing through the strands, gently untangling them.

"She talked to me."

"What did she say?"

"She said she loves me. She called me Dulcinea, like she always does. And then she said that she has to go away."

Paine's hand involuntarily jerks toward his mouth, yanking Dulcie's hair in the process.

"Owww!"

"I'm sorry, baby," he murmurs, his heart pounding. "That's all she said?"

"Uh-huh. And then she disappeared. How did she get here, Daddy? Where did she go?"

"I don't know," Paine answers—truthfully to the first question.

As for the second . . .

He might know the answer.

But he hopes to God that he's wrong.

The sun is shining on Lily Dale for a change as Julia walks swiftly up Summer Street carrying a bunch of deep purple Dutch irises she just picked from the meager patch beside her back door a few blocks away. After a rainy May and a cooler than usual start to June, she almost gave up hope that seasonal weather will ever arrive, but here it is at last.

Later she'll go home and change into shorts, she decides, uncomfortably warm in the jeans and sweatshirt that have pretty much been her uniform for the last nine months. Her short, thick brown hair is damp with sweat around her forehead and at the nape of her neck.

"Hi, Julia!"

Startled by the voice, she turns to see Pilar Velazquez hurrying toward her across the small lawn of the pretty blue and white house at Eight Summer Street.

"Pilar! You must have brought the sun with you from Alabama!" Julia reaches up to return the much taller older woman's embrace. "How was your winter?"

"Wonderful. I visited my son Peter in September—did I tell you he's stationed in Japan?"

"No—that must have been a fascinating trip."

"It was. I even tried sushi—it wasn't bad!"

"Well, there are plenty of fish in Cassadaga Lake," Julia points out with a grin. "Dig in!"

Pilar makes a face. "Think I'll pass. Anyway, Julia, when I got down to Mobile in October, Christina and Tom had a surprise for me. They had spent all last summer having an apartment built over their garage for me. Now I don't have to live in their guest room nine months a year."

"That's great." Julia knows that Pilar has had a rough transition ever since she lost her husband Raul to cancer a few years ago. She finally sold her house back in her Ohio hometown and now spends winters with her daughter and son-in-law in Alabama.

"I wasn't sure I'd be seeing you again this summer," Julia tells her. "I thought you might decide to stay down South." That's what her own mother does now, leaving Julia to live alone year-round in the house where she grew up.

"Oh, I'll keep coming back here to work—at least for a few more seasons," Pilar assures her, adding, as a U-Haul rumbles past, "Guess I'm not the only one."

The small village is indeed stirring to life this morning beneath the welcome blue sky. After months of deserted silence, cars roll through the narrow maze of gravelly streets, well shaded by the leafy branches of towering old trees. People call out to each other, delighted to see familiar faces again. Plywood is pried from the windows of turn-of-the-century cottages; dogs bark; children play.

"Where are you off to?" Pilar asks Julia, eying the purple bouquet in her hand.

"I'm bringing these flowers to Iris."

"She's back from Florida?"

Julia nods. "She got in last week. She mentioned the other day that it's ironic she wouldn't even recognize the flower she's named after, and I told her I'd bring her some from my garden now that the blossoms are open, so she'll know what an iris looks like."

"Iris is no gardener," Pilar says with a laugh, bending to scoop her purring cat into her arms. As she strokes its fur she adds, "I'll bet Nan Biddle can't bear to come by her old house and see the way Iris has let all her perennial beds get overrun with weeds. And she never even bothers to put in annuals."

Julia's smile fades. "Actually, Nan hasn't been out and about much this spring, Pilar."

"Oh, no. Don't tell me she's getting worse?"

"That's what I hear. Myra Nixon told me she hasn't even made it to the last few healing services." Though Nan has been battling metastatic breast cancer for several years now, Julia has often seen her around, usually wearing a hat or turban, and, more recently, leaning on her husband's arm. But she hasn't glimpsed her at all since before Easter, and the latest news isn't encouraging.

Julia's friend Lorraine Kingsley, who lives a few doors down from the Biddles, said that Rupert has been spending more and more time alone in the yard, sitting in a chair, brooding. Everybody in Lily Dale knows that Rupert and Nan are utterly devoted to each other. It's heartbreaking to imagine him being left alone.

"I'll call Rupert as soon as I settle in," Pilar says, her dark eyes shadowed. "That poor man. I know what it's like to be in his shoes. And Nan isn't much older than Raul was when he died."

Julia lays a comforting hand on her arm. "I'm sure Rupert will welcome the support. I actually don't really know the Biddles very well and I don't want to intrude, but if there's anything you think I can do, let me know."

"I will. And tell Iris I'll be dropping by later for coffee. We've got a lot of catching up to do."

"Good luck unpacking." Julia leaves Pilar thoughtfully petting her cat and cuts across the small front lawn to the house she'll probably always consider the Biddle place, even though it's been three years now since Rupert and Nan sold it to Iris.

As she walks up the steps she notices that they're starting to sag badly, and one of the spindles is missing on the porch rail. If Rupert Biddle is inclined to think about anything other than Nan's declining health, he must be dismayed at the way Iris has neglected not just the garden, but the house itself.

Maybe if things were different . . .

But even if Iris hadn't tragically lost Kristin within days of moving into this place, she isn't prone to spending much time on appearances. Not her own, and not her house's. She doesn't care what people think.

Funny, because Kristin was always the opposite. She was beautiful, and she knew it. She looks so much like Iris, who shares her bone structure and big blue eyes. But while earthy Iris never bothered with makeup or even a blow-dryer, Kristin spent a lot of time on her looks. Back in junior high, her goal was to become a model. She had amended that to actress by the time she reached high school, and she was on her way to accomplishing that when she died. She had merely done summer stock theater productions and a handful of television commercials in Los Angeles, but Julia always thought that was only the beginning. So did Iris.

While Kristin was alive, Julia was never particularly close to her friend's mother. In fact, both Kristin's parents tended to keep their distance from her. Julia figured that although they doted on Kristin, they simply weren't that interested in other kids. Especially Anson Shuttleworth. Whenever Julia was around their house, he pretty much stayed out of the way, mostly in his office doing "paperwork," according to Kristin.

Years later, in the days after Kristin disappeared, before her body was found, Julia felt compelled to stay with Iris around the clock. There was no one else. Most of the Shuttleworths' friends were in Florida. And though Iris had repeatedly tried to reach Edward, Kristin's stepbrother, who still lived in Jamestown, he didn't turn up until the funeral.

So, when Iris's worst fears were confirmed, Julia was the one who called Kristin's live-in boyfriend, Paine Landry, in California with the news. She was the one who took charge of the funeral arrangements. And she was the one who comforted Kristin's three-year-old daughter when both Iris and Paine were overcome by their own grief in the gloomy days after Kristin was buried.

These past few years, she has become what Iris affectionately refers to as her "summer daughter." She looks out for Iris during her annual three months at Lily Dale, and they keep in touch by telephone during the winters, when Iris is back in Florida. Julia misses her when she's gone. More than she misses her own mother, if the truth be told.

Now, as Julia rings the doorbell, the memory of a chilly Halloween night fifteen years ago flits into her mind.

Something happened to Kristin in the few moments she was inside this house.

Kristin's words echo back to her.

Do you see her, Julia?

Who, Kristin? Who did you see? What happened to change you that night?

Or maybe it wasn't that night that changed Kristin. Maybe it was the move to Florida, and maybe in Julia's mind that's mixed up with what happened here on Halloween. She's no longer sure.

But she does believe that Kristin saw something here fifteen years ago.

And that when she came back to help her mother move in, she might have seen something again.

That's the only possible explanation for the strange changes in Kristin's personality.

After all, Julia picked her up from the Buffalo airport upon her arrival from L.A., and spent several hours with her before dropping her off at the house on Summer Street.

In that time, Kristin seemed to be her old carefree self, aside from the sadness that came over her when she discussed Dulcie's recent illness and the subsequent loss of her vision. Julia suspected that Kristin's visit back East wasn't so much to help her mother with the move as it was an effort to get away, even briefly, from the stress of having a newly disabled child.

But that was normal, being concerned about your child, and needing a reprieve.

What didn't seem normal was the haunted expression in Kristin's eyes when Julia saw her again the day after her arrival. It didn't show up fleetingly, as did her concern about Dulcie. No, this was an intense apprehension that emanated from Kristin's core—the same mood Julia had sensed that night in the Biddles' stair hall.

A few days after her arrival in Lily Dale—a few days after the aura of dread came to permanently roost in her beautiful blue eyes—Kristin was dead.

Her death was officially ruled an accidental drowning. And most of the time, Julia believes that.

Most of the time.

Where is Iris? she wonders belatedly, trying unsuccessfully to peer through the opaque glass of the oval window. Iris usually answers the door right away.

Julia checks her watch. It's only a little past eight—too early for Iris to be out. The official season hasn't yet started, and Lily Dale's sparse businesses—a small cafeteria, library, and a few shops—won't open until later this morning.

Iris can't have left the village because the ancient VW Bug she keeps in Lily Dale is parked on the gravel driveway beside the house.

Worry has begun to filter through Julia's vague curiosity about her friend's whereabouts.

She transfers the bouquet to her left hand and knocks on the door, loudly.

Maybe she's gone for a walk, she speculates, but quickly dismisses the idea. Not sedentary, overweight Iris, who often laughingly says that her motto in life is "why stand when you can sit?" She only walks when Pilar drags her along.

Okay, well, maybe she's in the tub.

But that's her nighttime ritual. Iris is a creature of habit. She once told Julia that a long bath always relaxes her before going to bed. It wouldn't make sense for her to take one first thing in the morning. And she can't be taking a shower. There's no nozzle above the old claw-foot bathtub.

"Iris?" Julia calls after a few more disconcerting

moments of silence, even as she realizes that Iris probably won't hear her because the windows are closed.

Wouldn't Iris have opened them this morning?

Wouldn't she have raised the shades?

"Iris?" Julia's voice is higher pitched than usual, taking on an edge of panic.

Still no answer.

Julia hesitates, her hand pressed against her mouth as she ponders the situation. She glances over at Pilar's house next door, but the older woman is nowhere to be seen.

What should I do?

I can't just leave. Something is wrong. I can feel it.

Her trepidation mounting, Julia bends to take a key from beneath the rubber doormat at her feet.

The phone rings just as Paine is stepping out of the shower. Grabbing a towel, he hurriedly rubs it over his body as he strides across the hall into the bedroom to answer it. He glances at the clock on the bedside table as he reaches for the receiver. It's only seven-thirty. Who would be calling at this hour of the morning?

"Hello?"

"Is this Paine Landry?"

"Yes . . ."

The caller's voice is female, and vaguely familiar. It takes only a moment for him to place it. When he does, his breath catches in his throat.

Until now, he's forgotten about Dulcie waking him in the wee hours. But the unsettling incident instantly rushes back at him, along with the disturbing memory of another phone call three years ago—a call that began just as this one is beginning.

"This is Julia Garrity. From Lily Dale—"

"I know where you're from," he says tersely, sitting on the rumpled bed, the towel falling to his feet unheeded.

I know where you're from . . . and I know why you're calling.

"I—I don't know how to say this. I'm so sorry to have to be the one to tell you . . ."

He waits.

He prepares.

He knows what she's going to say; yet still, when he hears the words, utter disbelief swoops in to claim him, momentarily stealing his breath, his voice.

"Paine, it's Iris. I found her this morning. She's dead."

Five minutes later, Julia hangs up the telephone. Her legs nearly giving way beneath her, she sinks shakily into the chair beside the desk in Iris's small second-floor study and buries her tear-swollen face in her hands.

It's been more than two hours, but she can't stop reliving what happened. Describing it in the stilted conversation with Paine Landry didn't help to calm her frazzled nerves.

Again, she envisions the gruesome scene she discovered in the bathroom down the hall.

Iris, facedown in the full bathtub, her naked body dangling over the edge, her legs sprawled across the tile floor behind her.

Julia knew instinctively that she was dead even before she touched her hard flesh.

A freak accident, the paramedics said. She must have slipped on the wet tile as she was getting into her bath. She fell forward, hit her head on the edge of the tub. Unconscious, she toppled face-first into the water and drowned.

A freak accident.

Drowned.

Just like Kristin.

Julia's hands flutter to her lap, then back to her face. She's trembling, her entire body quaking at the unimaginable horror of Iris's death, and Kristin's death before hers.

Her breath is shallow, audible. The only other sound in the room—in the house—is the antique clock ticking loudly in the parlor at the foot of the stairs.

The old house is empty now, after the flurry of activity that kicked into motion when Julia ran shrieking from the house.

It was Pilar who dialed 911.

And it was Pilar who accompanied Iris—Iris's *body,* Julia amends—when they took her away. Somebody had to go, and somebody had to stay behind, to call Paine and tell him that his daughter's grandmother was dead.

Of course Julia volunteered. Pilar, after all, is a virtual stranger to Paine and Dulcie.

So is Julia, really. She only met them once, when they came east for Kristin's memorial service. They were all so caught up in raw grief during the week they were here that she barely remembers speaking to Paine, who spent most of the time silent, remote, lost in anguish.

But Dulcie . . .

Julia bonded with Dulcie during those muggy, gray August days.

Her heart tightens at the memory of Kristin's beautiful child—a child who was blinded as a toddler after a harrowing bout with meningitis.

So much tragedy in one family.

And now this.

The phone call was as difficult as she had expected. His voice tight with emotion, Paine promised Julia that he and Dulcie would be here as soon as they could. When he asked her about funeral arrangements, Julia pointed out that he would most likely be in charge of that. After all, Dulcie is Iris's only descendent, aside from her stepson Edward. As far as Julia knows, Iris hasn't seen him in the three years since he showed up, stone-faced and distant, for Kristin's memorial service.

Suddenly weary, Julia leans her head against the high, upholstered back of the chair, her eyes closed.

Then she feels it.

Startled, she picks up her head, poised, listening.

She isn't alone in the house.

There is nothing to hear. No rush of sound, no distorted snatch of a voice.

Yet the presence is here, around her, tangible.

Her eyes still closed, she concentrates, struggling to make contact.

Who are you?

Iris?

Kristin?

Who is it? Who's here?

The energy is gone as swiftly as it made itself known.

Shaken, Julia rises from the chair and makes her way quickly down the stairs and out the front door, instinctively needing to get away—before it comes back.

Chapter Two

"How much further, Daddy?"

Paine glances at Dulcie, curled up in the backseat of the rental car, a braille storybook open on her lap. He notices that her pigtails are uneven. He'd tried to do them as her baby-sitter back home does, but a big loop of hair is sticking out near her ear.

"Only a few miles now, I think," Paine tells her as they leave behind the bustling stretch of Route 60 in Fredonia, a small college town perched in the southwesternmost corner of New York. This is where they got off the interstate, and even the unremarkable strip-mall sprawl is a welcome change from hundreds of miles of freeway driving.

Only nobody calls it the "freeway" here in the East, Paine reminds himself. Yesterday, a service station attendant and a motel desk clerk corrected him about that. Here, it's called the thruway.

"Okay, tell me everything you see, Daddy."

He smiles at Dulcie's familiar command—smiles at her innate bossiness, inherited from her mother, and at her insatiable thirst to know what's going on around her.

When she was younger, she was satisfied with broad descriptions: *there's a red barn* or *the sky is blue with a few white clouds*. Now, at six, she wants him to paint verbal pictures that are as detailed as possible. *How big is the barn? Does it have windows? How many windows? Are there horses and cows? How many clouds, Daddy? What are their shapes?*

When he isn't with her, he finds himself noticing the most intricate aspects of ordinary things, just as he does when he's being her eyes. Sometimes he catches himself scrutinizing strangers: subconsciously counting the rings on a woman's fingers or noticing the color of the stripes in a man's tie.

"Daddy?"

He smiles, clears his throat. "We're heading south, and we just passed through what looks like the last busy intersection on the fast-food strip—Arby's, McDonald's, Wendy's."

"Wal-Mart, too?"

"How'd you know that?"

"Because there's always a Wal-Mart. In every town we've stopped in, wherever that other stuff is, there's a Wal-Mart."

Nothing escapes Dulcie's attention. Nothing. He smiles, thinking, as always, that she's an incredible kid. So much like her mother.

Oh, Kristin. If only you could see her . . .

If only he could believe that she could, that her life didn't end that traumatic day three years ago. That the essence of the woman he cherished still exists somewhere. That she's with him and their daughter, and always will be.

But that's religious crap. Kristin never bought into it, and neither does he. As far as he's concerned, when you're dead, you're dead. Gone. Buried. Forever.

"Go on, Daddy." In the rearview mirror, he sees Dulcie settling back, her face tilted toward the window as though she's looking through it.

He swallows the bitter grief swelling from his gut, forcing an upbeat tone into his voice. "Now the road is two lanes instead of four, and it's opening up more. I see hills ahead— we're climbing. And there's farmland—lots of corn, and it's as high as an elephant's eye."

"Huh?"

"Never mind, Dulc." He smiles faintly to himself.

The corn is as high as an elephant's eye . . .

Lyrics from the song "Oh, What a Beautiful Morning" in the Rodgers and Hammerstein musical *Oklahoma*. Paine performed it in summer stock at Chautauqua a full decade ago when he first met Kristin. He played Curly. Kristin was Ado Annie.

"Why am I always cast as the slut?" she only half jokingly asked the director at that point, having previously played Aldonza in *Man of La Mancha* and Mary Magdalene in *Jesus Christ, Superstar*.

"What else, Daddy?"

Dulcie's voice launches him back to the present.

"There are grape vineyards"—he glances from left to right—"and produce stands and two-story frame houses. Some of them have barns."

"Nice houses?"

"Some are," he says, looking around as he gently presses the brake. "Some of them have nice yards with wooden tubs of flowers and flags and picnic tables. But a few are kind of shabby, with rusty piles of junk everywhere."

"Why are we slowing down?"

"Because there's a semi in front of us that's only going

about thirty miles an hour, and I can't see around it to pass on this slope.''

He's a cautious driver. Kristin wasn't. Being in her passenger seat was like riding the Scrambler at the county fair when he was a kid. You just closed your eyes and held on for dear life while you were jerked this way and that with nonchalant Kristin at the wheel.

She was so incredibly reckless on the road that he braced himself whenever she was late coming home from her late-night waitressing job in Santa Monica. Terrible images would run through his head: what it would be like to open the door to a somber-faced police officer who had come to tell him she'd been in a fatal wreck.

How many times did he imagine the blow of losing her before it really happened?

But when her time came, weeks after her twenty-sixth birthday, it wasn't a car accident. That was as shocking for him to absorb as her death itself.

He had never imagined her drowning.

Even now, three years later, he can't quite accept it. Whenever the unwelcome, horrific visions barge into his head— *Kristin, panicking, arms thrashing, going under, opening her mouth to breathe, inhaling water, no air, water, water, suffocating*—he shoves them away. The only way he can deal with what had happened is to focus on the big picture— *Kristin is gone forever*—and ignore the details.

Details.

Back to Dulcie.

''There are trees all around us, on both sides of the road, Dulc,'' he says, forcing his gaze to the blur of scenery as the truck in front of him picks up speed at the crest of the hill. He accelerates, glancing in the rearview mirror to see if there's traffic behind him. Nothing. He's not used to this kind of driving. Two-lane road, rural setting, no congestion

. . . what a pleasure after so many years on the feverish L.A. freeways.

He rises a bit in the seat to glimpse his own reflection in the mirror and barely recognizes the man there. His unruly dark hair needs a trim. His blue eyes are edged by a faint network of wrinkles that aren't there from smiling. What Kristin used to call his "pretty boy" face is shadowed with under-eye trenches and sparse patches of stubble—he hasn't bothered to shave in the ten days since he got the phone call about Iris's death. Maybe he won't shave until he goes home.

Nah.

Paine never could grow a beard. He tried when he landed the role of Tevye back in college. It came in laughably patchy, and after a few weeks, the director, Dr. Netzer, ordered him in front of the entire cast to shave it. Netzer wanted him to wear a fake beard but, still smarting from the humiliation, Paine insisted on playing Tevye bare-faced. It wasn't his finest performance.

Dulcie's voice interrupts his thoughts again. "What kind of trees are there, Daddy? Palm trees?"

He smiles. She is truly a child of southern California, her sun-streaked long hair and golden skin testimony to long days at the beach. But those days are over for awhile.

Dulcie's been shivering ever since they left the blistering heartland heat and crossed into Pennsylvania earlier this morning.

Though he was born and raised in California, Paine did spend that one summer at the conservatory theater at nearby Chautauqua, so he wasn't necessarily expecting to be greeted in western New York with balmy temperatures and blue skies. Yet nor did he recall that late June in the eastern Great Lakes region can feel more like April, maybe March. The sky is weighted with dense gray clouds and the temperature can't be above the mid-fifties.

"Definitely no palm trees here," he tells Dulcie. "There are maples, and oaks, and pines, and I don't know what else—you know I'm not good at trees."

She grins. "You're not good at flowers, either. Not like Margaret."

Margaret is the woman back in L.A. who baby-sits for Dulcie while he's working one of his three jobs. In between auditions, he bartends for a Beverly Hill caterer, he takes classified ads for the L.A. *Weekly*, and he teaches a night class in television commercial acting at a community college. Oh, and once in a great while, he actually acts, too. Sometimes. Just in commercials and industrials. His greatest claim to fame is being Ben Affleck's stand-in for a few weeks right after Dulcie was born.

Money has always been tight. Sometimes so tight that he can't afford to pay Margaret. But she always understands. Her oldest son is an actor, too. He wasn't always as successful as he is now, playing a supporting role in a new Broadway musical.

He glances at Dulcie again in the rearview mirror and sees that her grin has given way to a wistful expression.

"Thinking about Margaret?" he asks.

"I miss her already. She was coming to New York, too. Why couldn't she drive with us instead of flying?"

"For one thing, she's uncomfortable in the car because of her arthritis. And for another, she's going to the opposite end of the state."

He's explained this before, even showing her on the map—tiny Lily Dale in the lower left corner of New York State and sprawling New York City on the lower right—with more than four hundred miles in between them, according to the scale.

He goes on patiently, "Margaret's going to visit her son and her grandchildren for a few weeks. After the memorial service, and when we're done taking care of Gram's house, we'll go back home and so will she."

"You promise?"

"I promise." He doesn't intend to stay here longer than necessary, even though he doesn't start teaching his class again until late in August, and the caterer and the L.A. *Weekly* are flexible about letting him take time off.

"Knock, knock, Daddy."

He grins, glad to be off the subject. Dulcie is into knock, knocks lately. He's heard all of hers a zillion times, but he always manages to react with hilarity. He's an actor, after all. "Who's there?"

"Ach."

"Ach who?"

"Gesundheit!"

They laugh together.

Then Dulcie asks, "What does 'taking care of Gram's house' mean?"

Paine purses his lips, glad she can't see his face. "I'm not sure, Dulcie. Her lawyer says she's left the place to you. But we can't live there."

"I don't want to." She pauses. "Why can't we?"

He takes a deep breath. "It's complicated."

He knows Dulcie has no memory of their last trip to Lily Dale, for her mother's funeral. How can he explain to a six-year-old, without scaring the hell out of her, that this isn't a regular town? Better not to try. At least, not now.

"Hey, there's a sign," he says instead. "Lily Dale, Next Right. We're almost there. Bet you're ready to get out of this car."

"Uh-huh."

He looks over his shoulder at her and sees her lower lip trembling. "What's wrong, Dulcie?"

"I want to go home."

"Dulc—"

"I just want to go home, Daddy. Please."

"We will, Dulcie. Just as soon as we—"

"I don't want to be here. This is where Mommy died. And Gram, too. It's a bad place, Daddy. Please. I'm scared."

With a sick feeling in his stomach, he pulls over to the shoulder and puts the car into park. Then he leans into the backseat and wraps his daughter in his arms.

"It'll be okay, Dulcie. Maybe being here will make you feel closer to Mommy. And to Gram. They didn't just die here. They lived here."

She says nothing, her slender little body quaking in his embrace.

"Listen, Dulcie, this is where Mommy spent her summers, growing up. She used to talk about how beautiful it is here."

That's a stretch. *Beautiful* is not a word Kristin used to describe Lily Dale.

Paine goes on, "You were too young to remember being here the last time."

He doesn't remember much of that trip either. He was too paralyzed by sorrow to grasp anything. This visit is different. He truly liked Iris, but her sudden death hasn't ripped his heart out or left a gaping hole in his life. This time, unlike last, he's capable of coping.

"We've got to do this, Dulcie," he says quietly. "You and me, together. For Gram. And for Mommy."

She doesn't reply. When he looks at her he sees that her jaw is set resolutely.

He puts the car into DRIVE again and pulls back onto the highway. Moments later, coming into the run-down farming town of Cassadaga, he makes a right-hand turn onto Dale Drive. There's another sign.

LILY DALE, 1 MILE.

Okay. Almost there. Then everything will be better.

After all, it's been an endless trip. They left home a full week ago today, Thursday. His old Honda has 125,000 miles on it already, so he splurged on a car rental. Maybe he'll trade in this midsize sedan for a truck to drive back—if Iris's house has anything worth bringing with them. From what he vaguely remembers, he doubts it. Iris was a self-proclaimed pack rat, and she loved old things.

Paine doesn't love old things, and the last thing he needs is to cart a load of junk cross-country. But you never know. Maybe there are valuable antiques. Or maybe Dulcie will want to keep some of it. She's just a kid, but it's technically her inheritance—her last link to Kristin and Iris.

He recalls a conversation he and Iris once had, about the estate she inherited when Anson died. There wasn't as much money as she expected. Apparently, he'd made some poor investments in the years since he'd become a successful medium, and there was far more debt than Iris realized. When she settled his affairs, in the end, all that was left was the house—and the insubstantial royalty money from his books, which still comes trickling in twice a year.

Iris told Paine that it was no big deal, really. That she certainly didn't marry Anson for his money in the first place—not that he had much then, either. She told Paine that she and Anson fell madly in love at a time when he was coming out of a bitter first marriage, and she was lonely and beginning to wonder if she would ever find Mr. Right. She also mentioned that she didn't regret marrying Anson, but hinted that their early years together were rocky.

"But we stayed together," Iris said contentedly. "That's

what you do when you're married. We made it to the end—until death did us part.''

Now everything they had belongs to Dulcie. It isn't a fortune, but it will help. That's for sure. Paine intends to put the money from the royalties and the house sale away for Dulcie, for college. He's always wondered how he'll afford to send her.

Thank you, Iris, he says silently.

The road winds past a few small houses. Then tiny Cassadaga Lake appears on the left, its gray, choppy waters lapping at the grassy shore mere yards from the road.

That's where Kristin drowned.

Kristin, who couldn't swim.

Kristin, who lived recklessly in a lot of ways, but knew her limits and feared the water.

So what the hell was she doing alone in a rowboat in the middle of the night without a life jacket?

He'll never know.

The first time he was here, he was too shocked by her death to speculate about the circumstances. But over the past three years, as his grief ebbed, he's spent more time wondering.

Now, as he glances out at the water, full-blown doubt and confusion threaten to take hold. He fends off the troubling thoughts that assail him, needing to get through one thing at a time.

One death at a time.

And for now, it's Iris.

Grimly, he keeps going, grateful for Dulcie's silence.

They pass a quaint country restaurant called Lazzaroni's Lakeside on the right and, on the left, a sprawling white clapboard building with long porches and a sign that reads LEOLYN HOTEL.

Directly opposite, the road widens abruptly at the entrance gate to the village.

He slows the car, recalling the staggering pain of his last journey to Lily Dale.

"Are we there, Daddy?"

"Yes." His voice is hoarse.

Oh, Kristin. What happened to you here?

"What do you see, Daddy?"

He clears his throat. "A little white gatehouse, with a boy inside."

"A little kid?" She sounds surprised, so hopeful that he wonders if there will be kids here, kids she can play with. Kids who will be kind to a motherless little blind girl.

"Actually, he's a teenager, Dulcie."

"Oh." Then, "What's he doing?"

"Remember I told you this is a private community? So you have to pass through the gate to get in and out. His job is to let us in."

"What else do you see?"

He doesn't want to tell her. Not yet.

He just stares at the sign that reads WELCOME TO LILY DALE, LARGEST CENTER IN THE WORLD FOR THE RELIGION OF SPIRITUALISM.

"Rupert!"

Nan's voice, urgent, is stronger than it has been for days, blasting over the small white receiver on the rolltop desk in front of him. The baby monitor is Pilar's idea. Their former neighbor had bought it to use when her young grandchildren visited her, but suggested that Rupert borrow it now that Nan is virtually confined to her bed. This way, he's never out of earshot if she needs him—and she does need him, more and more frequently.

"I'm coming," he calls, running his hand through his shock of white hair as he rises from his swivel-bottomed leather chair. He hurriedly puts aside his checkbook and the stack of monthly bills and glances at the clock. It's nearly five-thirty; time to start dinner—after he tends to Nan, of course.

He makes his way through the quiet, orderly house to the small back bedroom adjacent to the kitchen.

There, lying in the hospital bed he rented for her months before it became necessary, his wife is propped against several pillows. Though he spends almost every waking hour at her side, he is struck anew by the drastic recent changes in her appearance. Some part of him clings stubbornly to the image of Nan before cancer had ravaged her, leaving her body shriveled and skeletal, her nearly bald head concealed by a turban, her face swollen from the drugs that can't save her now.

Nobody has come right out and told him how far gone she is. But he suspects.

No . . .

He *knows*.

"What do you need?" he asks gently, walking over to the bed and touching her thin arm through the blanket.

"The bathroom," she says weakly.

"Emergency?"

She nods.

He reaches for the walker near the bed. It would be far more efficient to carry her than to allow the painstaking excursion across the room and around the corner into the small half bath off the kitchen. He longs to haul her into his arms the way he used to so many years ago; then out of playfulness and not bitter necessity.

He takes care of himself, and these aging bones are strong. Strong enough to lift her—or so he keeps telling himself, and her. But she won't listen. She's stubborn. She needs to do this—all of this—on her own terms.

He helps Nan out of bed and into her robe that hangs on a hook behind the door. Not the pink cotton summer robe she's always worn at this time of year, but a newly purchased dark-colored fleece one. Despite its weight, he suspects that it fails to keep her warm enough on a day like today. After less than a week's reprieve of summerlike weather, today again feels more like autumn than June. The windows are closed and he won't be surprised if the furnace kicks on tonight.

Rupert has never minded the harsh climate of western New York, choosing not to leave Lily Dale in September with almost everyone else. He and Nan have always stayed on, cozy together through the snowy winter months, preferring the forced isolation, really, to the more temperate but fleeting warm-weather season when Lily Dale is packed with tourists.

But now, seeing her thin shoulders shiver, he wonders if it might have been good for Nan to spend some time in the southern sun.

Maybe in September—

No. It's too late for that now.

Nan is restless, yes.

But she doesn't want to go South.

She wants to go home.

"You okay?" He holds her elbows for a moment to steady her as she grips the walker.

"I'm fine." She offers him a wan smile that breaks his heart. "When do I see Doctor Klauber again?"

"Saturday. Day after tomorrow."

"Good."

No. Not good. Rupert doesn't want to hear what the oncologist has to say.

They begin the tedious journey toward the doorway, Rupert a step behind her, his hands outstretched, hovering at her hips, to catch her if she sways. Her walker thumps rhythmically on the hardwood floor.

"One good thing about this house—you don't have to climb steps," he comments, for something to say. He instantly regrets it, unable to see her expression from his position, but sensing her dismay.

It's been just over three years now since they moved from the house where they lived the better part of the last four decades. If it were up to Rupert, they would never have moved, but he'd done it for Nan, thinking it was best.

When the rigorous chemotherapy had weakened her hipbones a few years back, she struggled to make it up and down the stairs several times daily. Rupert couldn't stand to watch her suffer, and finally decided it would be best to move to a smaller, single-level home. Within a year of their move to this one, on Green Street, Nan had two hip replacements. The surgery bought her more quality time. She was able to get around more easily until her health began seriously failing just after the new year.

Nan desperately misses their old place; still calls it home, unable to adjust to this one-level lakefront house. She never did feel comfortable in the master bedroom where Rupert now sleeps alone in their full-size bed for the first time in their married life.

Moving her to a different bedroom was her oncologist's idea, not his. But of course Dr. Klauber was right. The master bedroom is much farther from the front and back doors.

It's hard enough as it is for her to cover the short distance from the back bedroom to the driveway, and she refuses to let him rent a wheelchair and install a ramp at the back door.

Partly, he suspects, because she can't face the harsh reality that her health is rapidly, and irrevocably, deteriorating. But also because the ramp would mean they're here to stay.

Until this summer, he's assumed that they are.

Now, in the wake of Iris Shuttleworth's sudden death, their old place—a rattletrap Victorian several blocks away, on Summer Street in the heart of the village—stands vacant once again.

Should he tell Nan his idea? He's tempted to blurt it out— to give her something to look forward to, maybe something to fight for.

But no. He can't tell her. Not until he knows for certain. And he won't, not until after Iris's granddaughter and her father arrive from California. They should be here any day now, according to Howard Menkin, the attorney for the Shuttleworth estate. Then Rupert will approach the young man—who isn't even Iris's son-in-law, because he had never married Kristin Shuttleworth—and see about the house.

Paine Landry is an outsider. Why would he want to settle in a remote lakeside village devoted to clairvoyance and psychic phenomena?

Of course he won't.

If all goes as planned, he'll turn over Iris's cottage to Rupert, and he can bring Nan home to die. He only hopes Paine Landry doesn't take long to make up his mind, because he knows in his heart that Nan doesn't have much more time.

"You okay?" he asks her around a lump in his throat as she inches the walker forward.

"I'm fine."

No, she isn't.

Everything hinges on a stranger's decision. *Everything*.

He only hopes Paine Landry makes the right one.

* * *

As Julia steps onto the porch of her small cottage, a bell tolls loudly, reverberating through the village.

Knowing instantly what the chime means, she turns to glance up at the sky. Sure enough, gray clouds that have hung low over the lake all afternoon now look threatening. The bell signals that the regular five-thirty services will be held in the auditorium instead of in the usual spot, at Inspiration Stump. The secluded spiritual retreat sits at the very edge of the community, surrounded by the towering trees of Leolyn Woods. There, the audience assembles along rows of park benches in the open air. Facing them, a handful of mediums gather beside the historic tree stump now encased in cement to protect it from the harsh western New York elements.

On days like today, however, services are held in the antique auditorium nearby. It's a shorter walk for Julia, but she prefers the more reverent outdoor setting to channel the fragments of spirit voices that fade in and out of her head like a wavering radio frequency on the verge of being consumed by static.

She has been a practicing psychic medium for almost a decade now, having passed the rigorous requirements necessary to become registered at Lily Dale.

There was a time, when she was growing up, when she thought she would ultimately leave this place. Just as Kristin swore she would never end up in her father's profession, Julia never expected to follow in her mother's and her grandmother's footsteps to become a medium.

When she was in high school, facing the grim reality that her mother couldn't possibly afford to send her to a four-year university, she had taken secretarial classes, thinking that she could maybe move to Buffalo—or even New York

City, and work for one of those rich businessmen you see in the movies.

After graduation, with that goal still in mind, she had attended Jamestown Business College. But gradually, the voices in her head—the voices that had always been there on some level, she later realized—became louder, demanding to be heard. It was Grandma who, when Julia finally confided in her, explained what was happening—and what to do about it. Grandma said Julia had a gift, and that she shouldn't throw it away.

So, she learned shorthand and computer skills by day.

And by night, under her proud grandmother's tutelage, she developed her talent for communicating with dead people.

As it turned out, it is her calling. And once she got used to it as a profession rather than a hobby, she realized that it's like any other job. It has its bad points, but it certainly has more good—most importantly, that Julia is able to help people. The part of her that has always needed to nurture others is almost entirely fulfilled by the nature of mediumship.

The only part of her that isn't fulfilled, in fact, is the part that remains restless after all these years—still dreaming that there might be more to life than this shabby little lakefront community that is, like Hollywood, a one-industry town.

When Kristin was here three years ago, and Julia was pumping her for exciting stories of life in L.A., she had insisted that it wasn't the least bit glamorous once you got used to it. Acting was just a job, like any other job.

Being a medium is the same for Julia. How can it not be, when she grew up in a family of mediums and lives in a town dedicated to spiritualism?

She enjoys her life, and if she spends the rest of it right here where it started, in this gated community on the shore of Cassadaga Lake, she will probably be content.

It would be nice not to spend it alone, though. Now that Grandma has been dead for almost two years and Mom is retired in Florida, Julia can't help feeling lonely. Especially during the long winters.

She figures the time will come when she heads South with the others as soon as September rolls around. But she isn't ready for that yet. She has always liked the change of seasons, the snow, the icy gray days when you don't feel guilty curling up on the couch with a book from morning until night.

Not that she enjoys that kind of weather in June.

She inserts her ancient key into the front door lock and turns it, then, shivering in the unseasonal chill, buttons a red cardigan over the long floral-print dress that drapes her petite frame. Descending the three steps from the porch, she notices that the small patches of grass on either side of the walk need mowing, and the sign that dangles on a chain from the peeling white post near the street is askew. She straightens it.

JULIA GARRITY, REGISTERED MEDIUM

Julia starts down the narrow, tree-shaded street lined with close-set gingerbread cottages similar to hers, many fronted by signs that announce the spiritual counselors in residence. All of the homes display classic 1880s architecture: pillared porches with spindled rails; ornately carved wooden over-hangs; fish-scale shingles; bull's-eye windows under the eaves. Some are in good repair, freshly painted in authentic colors, their tiny yards green and immaculate, bordered by neat flower beds and dotted with birdbaths and benches. A few—like Julia's—show their age. Blistered paint, sagging steps, rotting wood.

The town bell chimes again as Julia reaches the end of the street, where it intersects with Cleveland Avenue, Lily Dale's closest claim to a main drag. A trio of tourist types are on the corner, consulting the visitor's pamphlet. One of them, a grossly overweight woman wearing a straining purple polyester pants set and a black windbreaker, turns to Julia.

Huffing slightly, her face florid as though it were ninety degrees out instead of barely sixty, she says, "Excuse me, do you know where Inspiration Stump is?"

"It's down that way, along a path," Julia tells her, pointing vaguely to the left. "But the services have been moved to the auditorium because it looks like it might rain. That's what the bell means."

"Where's the auditorium?"

Julia points to where the historic white wooden building is visible ahead. She considers, then dismisses, an offer to escort them. It isn't far, and she's headed to the same destination. But she isn't in the mood to chat with strangers. Iris's death less than two weeks ago still hangs heavily over her.

Julia notices the camera slung over the woman's chubby arm, and a gold ring—a wedding band?—on a chain around her neck.

A younger woman with her asks, "So what happens at these services? People just show up and the fortune-tellers do their thing?"

Julia wearily summons her patience, reminding herself that the summer season will soon be under way and she'll have to do this often now that Lily Dale is overrun with outsiders. Most of them uneducated about the community's origins, and more than a few are skeptics.

"Mediums aren't fortune-tellers," Julia explains.

"So it isn't like a seance?" asks the purple-clad woman, obviously disappointed. "I was hoping to contact my husband. A friend of mine was here and she said—"

The obese younger man with them interrupts. "Ma, get

it through your head: you ain't gonna contact Dad. This is just a waste of money.''

"It was only six bucks each to get in the gate," says the girl, obviously his sister. "And she paid for all of us, so what do you care?"

He rolls his eyes and looks at Julia. "You ever met one of them mediums?"

"A few." As she speaks, she hears something.

Her mind's voice, a garbled rush of sound. She automatically focuses, straining to interpret it.

"So you think this stuff is real?" the guy is saying.

"What I think doesn't matter. You'll have to make up your own mind," she says, mentally dismissing the intruding spirit voice as she hurries away, toward the auditorium.

"What do you think? Do you want to go over there and sit in on the readings?" Kent Gilman asks, pointing at the auditorium in the distance.

Standing beside him on the porch of the peeling two-story clapboard-sided Summer Street Hotel, beneath fluttering American and Canadian flags, Miranda Cleary follows his gaze. A steady stream of people, the vast majority of them middle-aged women traveling in twosomes and threesomes, files through the auditorium door.

Miranda shakes her head, shifting her heavy blue canvas tote bag to the opposite shoulder and wondering if she should run back upstairs for a jacket. It feels chillier out here than it did when they checked in a little while ago, and the clouds overhead look ominous. She makes a mental note to pick up a local paper and check the weather report.

"We can skip the readings for now," she tells Kent. "I'd love to see the mediums in action, but according to the brochure, there are sessions every day. Right now I'd rather use the last few hours of daylight to check out the lay of the land so we'll be acclimated tonight.''

"Sounds good.'' Kent nods and raises his hand, indicating the steps in an *after you* gesture. "Let's go.''

Miranda hesitates. "Do you think I need a jacket? It's pretty cool out here.''

"You can wear my sweater if you get cold.''

"But what if *you* get cold?''

"This is just for show.'' Kent motions at the pumpkin-colored cardigan tied around his shoulders, a perfect complement to his pale yellow polo shirt and khaki shorts. "You know I'm always warm.''

That's certainly true. Their biggest arguments, since becoming roommates two years ago, have been over the thermostat setting.

Miranda glances at the sweater. "I don't know, Kent . . . That color will clash with my hair.''

"And your freckles. But who's going to see you here? A bunch of fashion victim tourists and maybe, if we're lucky, a couple of ghosts. And if by any chance a potential Mr. Right appears, remember, eight percent of men are color-blind. Maybe he'll be one of them.''

Miranda grins. "Okay, then let's get going.'' She adds, with a shiver, "And hand over the sweater now. There's a breeze coming off the lake.''

Kent obliges, holding her bag as she shrugs into the sweater. It's soft and luxurious, deliciously scented with Kent's designer aftershave. She raises the cotton to her nose and inhales deeply.

"Don't worry, I just took a shower,'' Kent says, watching her.

"It's not that. It smells great. Michael used to wear this cologne.''

"Really? Then remind me to toss the bottle into the trash when we get back upstairs."

She rolls her eyes. There's certainly no love lost between Kent and her ex. Michael's blatant homophobia didn't help matters much.

She buttons the sweater. It fits almost perfectly, as she and Kent are almost the same height. And weight, she thinks ruefully, with a glance down at her ample hips. Hopefully she won't stretch out the waistband.

"We're burning daylight, Miranda," Kent says impatiently.

"Oh, please, look who's talking. Didn't I just spend a half hour waiting for you to decide which pair of hiking boots to wear?"

"I still think the Timberlands would have looked better."

"But they give you blisters," she points out as they descend to the tree-shaded street.

"Sometimes pain is beauty, Miranda." He hesitates, glancing in both directions. "Right or left?"

"Which way is more interesting? You're the one who's been here before."

"It doesn't really matter. The whole place is interesting," he tells her, and gestures to the right. "Let's go that way first."

Miranda feels around inside the bag to make sure she put in a few extra rolls of 800-speed film. They aren't beginning the investigation until much later, after dark, but in this line of work it's best to be prepared for anything at any time. Which is why, in addition to her 35mm camera and film, the bag also contains a notebook and pens, a digital camera, an audiotape recorder, a thermal scanner, and a compass to record shifts in magnetic fields.

Kent is lugging a video camera with a tripod, an EMF meter, a motion sensor, and a Trifield Natural Meter.

Tonight, when they get down to business, they'll be wearing their khaki photographer's vests with clips and pockets for the rest of their equipment, including an infrared night scope, flashlights with extra batteries, lanterns, candles and matches, a first-aid kit, and a cell phone in case of an emergency. Miranda hasn't encountered one since she started investigating paranormal activity almost a decade ago, but when you're prowling around remote locations in the dead of night, you never know what might happen.

They set off down Summer Street, heading away from the busy commons area and auditorium.

They only arrived in Lily Dale an hour earlier, having risen at dawn to make the nine-hour drive from Boston in Kent's aging Jeep. This is their first stop on a summer-long paranormal research tour that will take them to the West Coast and back on a carefully mapped route. With any luck, their findings will yield them enough material for a book collaboration. Not that either of them is an experienced author, but spiritualism seems to be a hot topic at the dawn of the new millennium. With any luck, they'll earn enough money from an advance and royalties to quit their day jobs and become full-time paranormal investigators.

"This place is charming," Miranda says, reaching up to shove a strand of rust-colored hair from her eyes. As usual, she's pulled her unruly shoulder-length mop back with a hastily fastened barrette at the nape of her neck; as usual, the wiry curls are desperate to escape confinement.

"Yeah, charming in broad daylight," Kent agrees. "But tonight, we'll see what pops out of all this frilly gingerbread woodwork."

"If the rain holds off. Because I feel it coming," she says, as the wind gusts, rustling the leaves overhead.

"So do I. We should pick up a newspaper and check the weather report."

"You read my mind," she says with a smile.

She and Kent have been working together for several years now, as founding members of the New England Ghost Society. They had originally been introduced to each other by an elderly widow, Mrs. Bird, who was convinced that (A) her sprawling ancestral home harbored spirits, and (B) Miranda and Kent would make a good couple.

She was wrong on both counts.

Despite numerous nocturnal visits to the supposedly haunted Back Bay Town House, Miranda never found anything other than a lonely old lady desperate for company and the opportunity to regale someone with tales about her family's colorful past.

When Miranda finally concluded that her client's home was free of supernatural activity, the disappointed Mrs. Bird swiftly rebounded into a matchmaking mode. She insisted that Miranda come to lunch one day at her Commonwealth Avenue home to meet a fellow paranormal investigator who had also recently proclaimed the house free of spirits.

Miranda went along with the blind date with minimum reluctance. At that point, she was still trying to work things out with her ex-husband, but she figured it couldn't hurt to meet someone who shared her interest in psychic phenomena.

Michael certainly didn't share the interest. In fact, that was part of the reason their marriage had foundered. The other part had to do with a buxom female bartender named Cassie, who later became the new Mrs. Cleary before the ink was dry on the divorce papers.

But as Miranda keeps assuring Kent and her therapist, she's long over Michael. Meanwhile, she remains grateful to Mrs. Bird—now dearly departed—for the introduction to Kent.

Miranda's first thought, upon meeting him, was that he

isn't her type. Tall, lanky, bespectacled and bearded, he has an owlish, scholarly look. Miranda, the youngest child in a large, fun-loving Irish-Catholic family, has always been attracted to rowdy, redheaded, green-eyed men like her ex. A lot of good that has done her—but she still can't seem to help herself, even now, despite Kent's constant warnings to steer clear of blarney-spouting good-time Charlies—and Patricks and Seans.

Miranda's second thought—after realizing at that long-ago luncheon that she wasn't the least bit attracted to Kent Gilman—was that apparently, the feeling was mutual.

Miranda's oldest brother, Declan, had abandoned the seminary in favor of a live-in relationship with another man, and she had met enough of their friends over the years to pick up on the signals Kent Gilman was sending across Mrs. Bird's damask-covered, candlelit table. Clearly, Miranda noted, this particular man wasn't interested in dating women.

She later learned that he, too, was merely humoring the hopeful Mrs. Bird, who to her dying day believed that her ploy was a success and that Miranda and Kent were partners in more than just ghost busting.

And no wonder. They are definitely soul mates—just not the romantic kind.

They now share an apartment in a two-family house in south Boston, within blocks of Miranda's family home. They're both educators—Miranda a fourth grade teacher in the city's public school system; Kent an instructor at a local community college. And they both have a crush on their downstairs neighbor, a rugged personal trainer who seems to have no idea that either of them even exists.

Then there's their part-time work as certified ghost hunters. During the school year, they limit their activity to occasional weekend investigations at the request of home owners who are convinced, as Mrs. Bird was, that their houses are haunted. But during the summer months, Miranda and Kent have taken on more complex projects.

Last year, they spent all of July on Nantucket, documenting paranormal activity at a local whaling museum at the request of the curators.

The summer before, Miranda and Kent spent most of their time on the Cape, investigating haunted centuries-old cemeteries.

The cross-country tour is Miranda's idea. In the wake of another shattered romance—this one with her sister Maureen's husband's cousin, Tom—she's anxious to get out of the old neighborhood for a while and lick her wounds.

The book is Kent's idea. Like countless academics before him, he originally intended to become a writer. As far as he's concerned, a coauthored nonfiction parapsychology title is a stepping stone to the great American novel.

"Check out that cottage garden," Kent comments, as they pass a pretty blue house fronted, like most on the block, by a medium's shingle. "I would love to do something like that in front of our place."

"Kent, we live in a rental," Miranda points out, glancing at the colorful beds of blooms in front of the porch. "Besides, we travel in the summer. You aren't around to take care of a garden."

"A cottage garden is basically carefree, Miranda. It's supposed to look cluttered and chaotic, filled with cosmos and sweet peas and morning glory vines . . ."

As he continues talking about flowers, quoting a horticultural article he read in a recent issue of *Martha Stewart Living*, Miranda's gaze shifts to the next house on the block.

There is no medium's shingle here. Nor is there a garden, unless you count the few dandelions dotting the overgrown grass in front of the porch. Someone has taken care to paint the place in period colors—dark yellow with maroon and green trim—but the paint isn't fresh. An atmosphere of abandonment hovers about the place.

Abandonment, and something else.

Miranda stops walking, her practiced eye drawn to a sweeping tree tucked into the small backyard, in a patch of lawn just behind the porch.

"What's the matter?" Kent asks, stopping beside her and following her stare.

"That tree," Miranda says. "There's something about it."

"It's not a tree," Kent informs her. "It's almost two stories high, but technically, it's a shrub. A lilac."

As he speaks, car tires crunch on gravel behind them.

Miranda turns to see a red sedan pulling up at the curb in front of the house. She glimpses a handsome, dark-haired man at the wheel and a small blond child in the back seat. The car has California plates.

"Come on, Miranda," Kent says.

She looks again at the towering lilac branches.

A chill steals over her, despite the weight of Kent's sweater.

"I want to come back here later," she tells Kent in a low voice. "There's something about that tree."

"Shrub," he corrects.

"Whatever. We need to check that out."

"Just the shrub? Or the whole yard? Or the house? Because we'll need to get permission from the owners if you want to—"

"I know, I know," she says impatiently, cutting him off.

Of course she knows how it works. They can't just go trespassing on private property in the middle of the night.

She glances back up at the Victorian structure, and then at the newcomers, who don't appear to notice her as they prepare to get out of the car.

"Let's go," Miranda tells Kent with a shiver. "We'll come back after dark and see if anything's happening by that tree."

Something tells her they won't be disappointed.

Chapter Three

The house is more ramshackle than Paine remembers.

So ramshackle that even passers-by seem to stop and stare, like the couple that is now strolling off down the street. They're weighed down with camera equipment, which can only mean one thing: they're tourists.

That isn't surprising. The Lily Dale season is almost under way, and the small community is already filled with outsiders, just as it was the last time he was here.

As Paine stands looking up at the house his daughter has inherited, he wonders what Kristin thought of the place when she visited her mother here three years ago. He knows that for most of Kristin's life, her parents lived in a bigger Lily Dale home. When she couldn't convince her widowed mother to give up spending her summers here, she had talked her into selling the larger home.

But Paine recalls her being upset when Iris called to say

she'd bought a new place. When he'd questioned her about the conversation, Kristin had simply said she knew the house her mother had bought and she didn't like it.

Now Paine can see why. The two-story frame house is hardly Kristin's style—she favored sleek modern architecture.

"I don't like it here," Dulcie says, beside him. Her small hand is warm in his, and he squeezes her fingers reassuringly.

"It's going to be okay, Dulcie," he tells her, summoning a confidence he doesn't feel. "You're going to love the house. It's like something out of a fairy tale."

Or a ghost story.

A cold breeze stirs the towering maples overhead.

"Tell me," she says tersely, shivering from the chill, removing her hand from his and jamming it, with her other one, into the front pockets of her jeans.

With a pang of guilt, he notices a threadbare spot on her knee, and that the sleeves of her red Gap Kids sweatshirt are too short. She's worn nothing but shorts and T-shirts for months, but she'll need warmer clothes here, despite the fact that it's summer, and apparently she's outgrown hers. He'll have to take her shopping—if there's any place to shop, that is. Looks to him as if Lily Dale is smack in the middle of nowhere. Well, there's always the Wal-Mart about ten miles back. All she needs are a few pairs of Levi's and—

"Daddy," Dulcie prods. "Tell me."

He takes a deep breath. "Okay, the house is painted a dark yellow shade, with maroon and dark green trim. Sounds awful, but looks nice. I bet it's historically accurate." He seems to remember Kristin mentioning something about the place being restored by the previous residents. "There are porches upstairs and down at the front of the house—porches with railings and spindles and lots of carved wood. There are only two windows in front on the first two floors, one on either side of the doors that lead to the porches. No shutters. The third-floor attic is shaped like a triangle, and there are scalloped shingles on that section, and there's a round window up at the top.''

She nods. Her eyes are closed, as they always are when he gives her descriptions. He wonders, as he often does, what she's envisioning—how close her mental image is to reality. Hopefully not too close, in this case.

He doesn't tell her about the drooping foliage poking forlornly from the hanging pots on the porch, or the too-tall patch of weed-ridden lawn that fronts the house like a fringe of overgrown bangs. Anyway, he can take care of all that— spruce things up, eliminate that woebegone, abandoned ambience that hovers about the place.

Somehow, until now, he had been picturing something completely different, having convinced himself that the dreary blur of images he had retained from his first visit were tainted by his own mourning.

Ever since he got the phone call about Iris's death and decided to come back to Lily Dale with Dulcie, his errant mind had conjured something bright and sun-washed and cheerful, a cozy lakefront cottage with screen doors, blooming window boxes, a flagstone path. The kind of home you might find in some other Victorian vacation spot—Oak Bluffs on Martha's Vineyard, or Cape May, New Jersey. Even nearby Chautauqua Institution, where he and Kristin met doing summer stock a decade ago.

All the trappings of a summer resort town are here in Lily Dale—kids on bikes, small boutiques, a bandstand and gazebo, a playground, a beach.

But there's something else, too.

Maybe it's the gloomy weather.

Maybe it's the sorrowful cause of this repeat visit.

Whatever the reason, Paine senses that there is a distinctly funereal aura about this ancient Queen Anne in the heart of this strange, secluded village obsessed with supernatural communication.

Oh, well. He's stuck here for at least the next month or two. He'll go through Iris's stuff, unload the property on the first interested person who comes along, and then he and Dulcie will hit the road headed back West, where they belong.

"Come on, Dulcie, let's go inside," Paine says, putting a hand on her shoulder and taking a step forward.

She doesn't move.

Her face is tilted up, toward the house.

"Dulcie."

"I don't want to," she says on a sob, and presses a hand against her mouth.

"Oh, Dulcie . . ." Paine crouches beside her and pulls her close. "I know. I miss Gram, too." Not that they had seen Iris more than a half dozen times since Dulcie had been born.

"No," she says in a small voice. "It's not that. I mean, I miss her, but . . . it's not that."

A prickle runs down Paine's spine when he sees her uneasy expression.

He thinks back to that night more than a week ago, at home, when she awakened in the middle of the night saying Iris had been in her room . . .

And three years ago, when she was little more than a toddler, yet old enough to articulate to him in no uncertain terms that her mommy—who was back East, helping Iris settle into the new house—had come into her room in the middle of the night.

Paine went along with it, assuming it was nothing more than wishful thinking by a little girl who missed her mother.

Even when Dulcie told him what Kristin supposedly

said—"I love you, Dulcie, but I have to leave you now"—
he didn't think twice about it. After all, that was pretty much
Kristin's parting message to their daughter that last day at
LAX, when she embraced Dulcie at the gate. Only that time,
there was something tacked on the end—"I'll be home as
soon as I can."

There was no such postscript to the supposedly imaginary
message Dulcie reported to him.

Hours later, Iris had called. Kristin was missing. Iris told
him not to come East, certain her daughter was inexplicably
headed back home to California and Paine and Dulcie.

But she wasn't.

Days later, amidst a nightmarish blur of waiting and worrying and wondering, Paine got the other call. The one from
Julia Garrity, reporting that Kristin's lifeless, bloated body
had floated to the surface of Cassadaga Lake, identified
only by the clothing she had been wearing the night she
disappeared.

Numbed by shock and grief, Paine broke the news to
Dulcie as gently as he could.

It was she who comforted him, patting his back as he
sobbed. "It's okay, Daddy. I told you. She had to leave us.
But she loves us."

Of course Dulcie's vision of Kristin was a coincidental
dream.

And so was her vision of Iris on the night she had died.

Paine chooses to believe that, because not believing it
would mean that he believes in something else.

Something utterly far-fetched.

"Come on, Dulcie," he says grimly. "We don't have a
choice. It's going to rain. Let's go inside."

This time, she doesn't protest. He takes her hand and
together, they walk up the front steps and across the porch.
He glimpses a green VW parked at the back of the driveway.

Iris's car. That, too, now belongs to Dulcie. Maybe—if it has less mileage than his own car— they'll keep it, drive it back home. No. It's ancient. It'll never make the trip. He'll have to sell it. So many decisions to be made . . .

A musty scent hovers around the house. It's pungent, but not unpleasant. Like dry old wood, Paine thinks as he bends to lift a corner of the fraying mat in front of the door.

A key is there, just as Howard Menkin said it would be. It's supposed to fit the locks on both the front and back doors.

Hiding a key under a mat seems to Paine like something someone would do in a vintage Frank Capra film, but Howard had insisted people do it all the time in Lily Dale.

The door is heavy and old-fashioned, dark wood with three vertical inset panels in the bottom and a large oval pane of beveled frosted glass in the top half. He turns the tarnished brass knob with more effort than he'd expected and pushes it open, peering into the space beyond.

"It's okay, Dulc, come on," he says, squeezing her hand.

Together they step over the threshold. They're in a foyer. The walls are covered in striped paper, the colors impossible to discern in the dim light. Paine feels for a switch beside the door. His fingers encounter a raised plate. He turns to see that it's an antique wall switch with two vertically stacked round black buttons, the top one protruding, the other depressed. He presses the top in and the bottom one promptly pops out as an overhead light fixture illuminates.

"Interesting," he mutters.

"What's interesting, Daddy?"

"I never saw a light switch like this. It's an old, old house, Dulcie."

"I can feel it," she says, her voice hushed. "Tell me about it."

"We're in the foyer. There's a stairway leading up—a

really beautiful stairway with lots of carved wood and a banister with spindles and big round newel posts at the bottom. Looks like the kitchen is straight ahead, and on the left there's a dining room with a fireplace, and there are double French doors over here to the right . . ." He tugs on one, pulling it open. "Oh, it's a parlor. There's lots of furniture, and it's definitely not modern. A dark green sofa with a curving back and high arms, a couple of matching chairs, floor lamps with fringed shades . . ."

Definitely not his style. That's okay. They can sell the stuff. Maybe it's worth something.

"There's pretty rose-colored wallpaper," he informs Dulcie. "It's textured. Here, feel it."

He guides her hand to the wall beside the door, letting her run her fingers over the velvety brocade as he describes the rest of the vaguely familiar room for her. "There are tall windows covered in heavy maroon drapes with tassels, and there's a fireplace. Lots of framed pictures on the mantel."

"Pictures of who?"

He lets go of her hand and steps closer. "They're mostly family pictures. Iris, and your grandfather, and your mother," he says, fighting to keep the emotion out of his voice.

He picks up a photo of Kristin that he's never seen before—an enlarged snapshot of her on a beach somewhere. It's most likely Florida, definitely not here. White sand and palm trees. She looks about seventeen—flashing her dimples, blue-eyed and gorgeous, her long, pale hair blowing back from her face.

He sets down the photo and glances at the one next to it. It's a posed shot, diagonally stamped *Olan Mills* in gold script lettering. Paine smiles faintly. When he was growing up back in California, his mother used to take him to Olan

Mills studios for pictures, too. This photo shows a little boy awkwardly holding an infant on his lap. He recognizes the baby as Kristin and realizes that the boy must be Edward, her older half brother, Anson's son from an earlier marriage. Kristin and her parents were estranged from him for years, and Paine knows little about the situation, other than that it was bitter and Kristin didn't like to talk about him. He remembers Julia telling him after the funeral that Edward had been there, among the hundreds of mourners, but Paine didn't meet him.

Now he wonders fleetingly why Iris kept this photo of him on the mantel. Had she reestablished contact with Edward in recent years? Or has it been here all along? He doesn't remember it from the first visit—but then, what *does* he remember? Only soul-searing heartache.

"What are you doing, Daddy?" Dulcie asks.

"Just looking around." He returns the photo to its place on the dusty mantel and looks around at the cluttered book-shelves, tables, cabinets. "This room is full of knickknacks, Dulcie. The whole house is. Looks like we've got our work cut out for us."

"And now, I'd like to introduce our next medium, Ms. Julia Garrity. She's our youngest medium in residence this season, and she was raised right here in Lily Dale as a spiritualist. Julia?"

Along with the handful of other mediums, including her friend Lorraine, she had been leaning against a low platform to the right of the stage, beside the open door that led outside. Now she strides across the room to the head of the wide aisle between the rows of wooden seats.

She takes a deep breath, exhales slowly, and looks out at the audience, scanning their faces with practiced scrutiny.

She barely notices the outside sounds drifting through the big rectangular open-air gaps in the wooden walls—voices of passersby, children playing in the park across the way, cars crunching slowly along a nearby street.

While waiting for her turn, she intended to begin by selecting an elderly woman in the center of the section on the right. Julia is certain she's made a connection with the woman's dead husband, or perhaps her brother.

But now Julia's gaze falls on the overweight woman in the purple polyester, the one she'd seen on the street. The woman is looking back at her with incredulous recognition, obviously surprised to see her here, among the mediums.

Julia sees that a haze of energy is beside her, vaguely human in form. She closes her eyes, again hearing the fleeting surge of sound in her mind. This time it's almost intelligible. She expertly strains to hear it again. The spirit obliges. The message is repeated, even more clearly this time.

She opens her eyes. "I need to go to the lady in the back, on the far aisle," she announces. "The lady in the purple top. Yes, you. I'm getting a name that sounds like Louis, or something similar."

"Lucas!" the woman cries out. "Oh, my God."

Julia tilts her head and closes her eyes again. *Lucas?* Yes, that's it.

The spirit is giving her more information. It comes via her own mental voice, but the contact isn't always presented in that manner. Sometimes the spirits come through sounding like themselves—detached voices speaking in Julia's head. Usually, their words are somewhat garbled, but occasionally they're surprisingly intelligible, allowing her to make out fragments of one-sided conversation. The strangeness of this sensation has long since worn off.

Sometimes Julia gets actual visions to accompany the voices, but more often the communication is strictly clairaudient. Funny how, when directly translated, the word means "clear hearing." But for the most part, what Julia hears is fuzzy at best.

After carefully listening to her mind's voice, she tells her rapt subject, "Lucas is giving me the number six. This is symbolic. Either something happened in June, the sixth month, or on the sixth of a different month . . . ?"

The woman is shaking her head, disappointment apparent in her eyes. Glancing at her companions, Julia sees that the daughter's expression mirrors the mother's, and that the son's face is smug.

"Think about it," Julia says, ignoring the son, hearing the unmistakable whisper in her mind once again. "He wants me to refer to 'six,' and it's—"

"Oh!" The woman claps her hand over her mouth. "He's been gone six years. Is that it?"

"It might be."

"But what does he mean by this? What is he trying to tell me?"

"It's most likely his way of validating his presence to you." Julia frowns as the spirit comes through again.

She concentrates on Lucas's energy, allowing it to seep into her, listening intently to what he's trying to say.

Chairs creak. People cough. In the back of the auditorium, somebody sneezes. Several voices whisper, "Bless you."

Julia tunes out the distractions. *Lucas. Lucas. What are you trying to tell me?*

"Are you having trouble with your hand?" she asks finally, and the woman gasps.

"Is that what he told you?"

"I'm not sure. I'm getting something about a hand, and I'm feeling his concern for you."

"My wrist has been bothering me for days," the woman

tells her, waving her left arm in the air. "I don't know why. I thought maybe it was just the damp weather."

Julia shakes her head, feeling Lucas's urgency. "You need to have it checked out," she says firmly. "It could be something more serious."

Alarm crosses the woman's face. "Is there something really wrong with me? Is that what he told you? Is it like a warning?"

"Just know that he's concerned and you should have it looked at."

"What else is he saying? Is he all right where he is?"

In the decade Julia's been doing readings, she has come to understand that this is the most important information she can give to someone whose loved one has passed to spirit. People need to be reassured not just that their relative still exists someplace, but that the person is at peace.

"Know that he's just fine," she tells the woman with a smile.

"Is that what he said?"

Julia nods. It's easier than trying to explain the intangible.

People tend to assume that the messages she gets from the other side come through with the clarity of a long-distance telephone call. The reality is that most of the time communicating with the spirit world is like talking on a cell phone during a terrible storm, with a poor connection that keeps fading in and out and static that almost drowns out the few things that do come through.

Thanks to years of experience, Julia can usually interpret the merest whisperings of information. She knows instinctively when a spirit is troubled and when it's at peace.

Luckily Lucas falls into the latter category. They don't always.

She jostles that thought away, hearing something else.

"Do you know somebody by the name of Carla or Charlotte or . . ." She pauses, listening. "Or Charlie?"

"That's him. He's our son!" the woman blurts, grabbing his arm.

"Charlie, your father has a message for you," Julia says. "It means nothing to me, but it might mean something to you. He's saying . . ." Another pause. Then, certain she's got it right, she says, "He's saying something about the swing. He's saying 'sorry for the swing' or 'sorry about the swing.' Does that make sense?"

The mother cries out. Tears stream down her cheeks.

Charlie's face is ashen. His gaping stare is all the evidence Julia needs to know that she's hit home.

"Daddy was pushing Charlie on a tire swing when we were kids," his sister speaks up emotionally, her hand clasped against her heart. "He was pushing him really high, and Charlie started screaming for him to stop. Then he fell off and broke his leg. Daddy always felt real bad about that."

"I can't believe this," the mother says, clinging to her son's arm. "This is just . . . is there anything else?"

Julia shakes her head, feeling the energy starting to pull back. "Just know that he's okay and that he comes to you with love."

She redirects her attention to the white-haired old woman in the middle of the room.

"I need to come to the lady there in the pink sweater . . . no," she says to a hopeful, similar-looking woman in the row ahead, whose sweater is really more of a peach shade. "No, the lady right there, in the glasses. Your husband has gone to spirit, hasn't he?"

The woman's jaw drops. "Yes, he has. How did you know?"

It could have been a lucky guess based on the woman's age, but it isn't.

There are plenty of phonies in this profession, some of them incredibly convincing. If you do enough readings, you eventually learn to interpret not just the stirring of sounds and images from the other side, but the body language and other details surrounding the people you're reading.

Julia suspects that she could come up with a fairly convincing reading based on nothing more concrete than her own intuition or a series of speculations. But that's not what she's about. When the energy isn't there, she doesn't fake it.

This time, it's there.

She smiles at the old woman. "Okay, then I believe it's your husband who's coming through. Is his name Henry?"

"Yes!"

Bingo. Julia's next try was going to be Harry. She's getting a strong *H* sound at the beginning, and the *ee* sound at the end, but what's in between is slurred.

She proceeds with the reading, and when she's through, the old woman thanks her with tears in her eyes.

The moderator calls the next medium to the front of the stage. Julia retreats, drained. As she once again leans against the platform by the door, she glances outside to see if the rain has started yet.

It hasn't.

But there's an unfamiliar red car parked in front of Iris Shuttleworth's house across the green, on Summer Street, and the shades have been lifted on the windows beyond the porch for the first time in weeks.

Julia knows what that means.

Kristin's daughter has come home to Lily Dale at last.

* * *

"Knock, knock, Daddy," Dulcie says, seated at the small round kitchen table.

"Who's there?"

"Boo."

"Boo who?"

"Don't cry, it's only me," she says with a giggle.

Paine laughs. Hard. As though it's the first time he's heard that one. He laughs as he's laughed at all of her rusty knock, knocks for the past half hour.

"Somebody's coming, Daddy," Dulcie says.

"You know what, Dulc? Why don't we lay off the knock, knocks for a bit because it's hard for me to concen—"

"No, I mean really. Somebody's coming. I hear footsteps."

"Footsteps?" Paine turns off the water at the scarred porcelain kitchen sink where he'd been scrubbing his hands. He's been in the house little more than an hour and already he's filthy. All he's been doing is wiping away cobwebs, throwing away stale food, and opening windows in an effort to air out the musty rooms.

"Don't you hear that?" Dulcie asks. "Footsteps on the porch."

He frowns. The house is silent, the only sound the wind and rain outside the open window above the sink. He's about to tell Dulcie she was wrong when he hears the faint sound of a creaking board.

Then, sure enough, somebody knocks at the front door.

"You don't miss a trick, do you?" He should have known she wasn't hearing things. He's become accustomed to Dulcie picking up sounds before he does. Her pediatrician told him that when a person loses sight, the other senses become more acutely developed to compensate.

Dulcie smiles and pops another raisin into her mouth from a box he'd found in the cupboard—pretty much the only thing that was edible there.

"I'll be right back," he tells her, wiping his hands on a paper towel from the nearly empty roll on a spindle above the sink.

He crosses the foyer toward the door, seeing the outline of a person through the oval glass. He assumes that it's Howard.

But when he opens the door, he finds a woman standing there. Behind her, sheets of rain fall past the porch overhang, pattering softly on the overgrown lawn.

She's unusual-looking, all angles from head to toe—a sleek, geometric short haircut, jutting cheekbones, a sharply defined jawline. Long, skinny neck atop a long, skinny body with long, skinny limbs. Her hair, eyes, skin, and clothing are varying shades of brown. She's smiling at him, and he finds himself smiling back.

"Paine? I live next door. Pilar Velazquez. We met before, when you were here . . ."

Trying to place her, he shakes his head. "I'm sorry, I don't—"

"That's understandable." She holds out a plate covered in plastic wrap. "These aren't homemade—I don't bake. That was just one of the things Iris and I had in common. But they're from an excellent bakery, the Upper Crust over in Fredonia. I know kids like chocolate."

He realizes that she's looking past him, and he turns to see Dulcie in the kitchen doorway. She's holding on to the wall, and her clouded blue eyes are focused high on the wall to his right.

He glances sharply at Pilar to see her reaction to Dulcie's blindness.

There is none. No shock. More importantly, no pity.

"This is Dulcie," he announces, deciding he likes Pilar Velazquez. He takes the plate from her.

"Hello, Dulcie," she says gently, wearing that same smile. "I brought some treats. They're called chocolate volcanos—they're rich little chocolate cakes. They have frosting, and a cherry on top, but no nuts. I don't know many kids your age who like nuts."

"I don't." The corners of Dulcie's mouth curve slightly upward. "But I like chocolate, and I'm starving. All Daddy could find in the cupboard was raisins."

"Sounds like raisins don't rank much above nuts with you, huh, Dulcie?" Pilar turns to him. "I'm so sorry about your . . ." She hesitates only slightly. ". . . about Iris."

"Thank you." He likes her even more. He knows she'd started to say mother-in-law. That's okay. If it were up to him, Iris would have been his mother-in-law and Kristin would have been his wife.

If it were up to him, he'd be back in Los Angeles right now, walking on the sunny beach with Dulcie riding on his shoulders and Kristin by his side.

"Have you made any plans for the funeral yet?" Pilar asks.

"Not yet. Iris's will specified that she wanted to be cremated, and for her ashes to be scattered over the lake here." The lake where her daughter drowned. Did she put that in the will before or after Kristin's death? He didn't think to ask when Howard Menkin told him about it. "I thought maybe I could set up some kind of memorial service. Maybe next week."

"That would be good. Lots of people will want to come. Iris had so many friends."

He gives a tight nod, uncomfortable.

"Well, I know you're busy. I just wanted to tell you that

I'm right next door if you need me,'' Pilar says, and gestures. ''On that side. In the blue house.''

He realizes which house she means. He noticed it on his second trip in from the car, when he'd brought Dulcie some of her braille books to keep her busy while he cleaned up a bit. Actually, it wasn't the house he noticed, as much as it was the shingle hanging out front. It read PILAR VELAZQUEZ, REGISTERED MEDIUM, he remembers belatedly—and with a twinge of disappointment.

He doesn't know why it bothers him that she's one of *them,* but it does.

''And if you need any help with anything, don't hesitate to call me,'' Pilar goes on. ''I'm home most of the time.''

''Thank you.''

He wishes she would go, but she starts talking about Iris again. Saying she was absolutely stunned by her friend's death, and that she's going to miss her terribly.

''Iris and I walk down to the lake and back every day when we're here in the summers,'' Pilar tells him. ''I make her do it. She needs—*needed* the exercise. She used to grumble, but she always came along. I'll have to walk alone now, and I—''

She breaks off abruptly when Dulcie makes a startled sound.

Paine spins around. ''What's wrong?''

''There's somebody in the kitchen,'' his daughter says, feeling her way toward him along the foyer wall.

He strides toward her, explaining to Pilar, ''She always hears things before I do. She heard you on the porch before you even knocked. It must be Howard Menkin. He's supposed to . . .''

He trails off, looking into the kitchen.

The room is empty.

The only sound in the house is the rain falling against

the roof two stories up, and the clock ticking at the foot of the stairs.

"There's nobody there, Dulcie."

"Yes, there is."

"Did you hear somebody?"

"I thought—I just . . . I just . . ." She shakes her head, swallowing hard. "I guess I was wrong."

He turns back to Pilar.

And catches her looking at his daughter with a peculiar, thoughtful expression.

Chapter Four

"How's your wine? Too dry?"

Julia's almost forgotten about the goblet in front of her. "Oh, it's very good." She takes a sip.

"You're quiet tonight," Andy Doyle observes, his green eyes on her. "Is everything all right?"

"Everything's good," she says, smiling at the good-looking russet-haired man across the small table.

Good. That word again. Things are not good. The wine *is* too dry, but that's the least of what's on her mind.

They're at Lazzaroni's, a surprisingly—for this area—upscale restaurant with an espresso bar, just outside the village gates.

On a cool, rainy night like this she'd prefer to be home in sweatpants with a good book or a Blockbuster rental.

But the food here is excellent, Andy's fun, and maybe this will take her mind off Iris—and Kristin, she thinks, forcing her gaze away from the wide, rain-splattered window and the gray lake waters beyond.

"How did it go today?" she asks Andy, noticing how handsome he is in the soft glow of the low-hanging cone-shaped lamp that hovers over the table.

"It went well. I have some interesting students."

A fellow medium, he's giving a series of workshops on past-life regression this week, his first back at Lily Dale, where he's spent the last few summers. The rest of the year he travels around the country, teaching and lecturing on parapsychology.

Julia first met him the night she was out with Kristin during her final visit. The two of them had stopped for a few drinks at the White Horse Tavern in Cassadaga on the way back to Lily Dale. Andy had only been in the area for a few days at that point, but Julia recognized him as he approached them, having seen his photo in the Lily Dale workshop guide for the upcoming season.

She initially assumed it was beautiful Kristin whose presence lured him over, and she was probably right. It was Kristin whom Andy flirted with that night, and Kristin's number he requested. Julia fought back the old jealousy that threatened to bubble up, and bit back her disapproval when Kristin told him where she was staying, and that she would love to see him again.

Julia shouldn't have been surprised. The Kristin she knew wasn't the type who would let motherhood—and a live-in boyfriend—stand in the way of a good time.

After Andy left, Julia asked Kristin straight out if she was free to see other people. Kristin shrugged and pointed out that she wasn't married. When Julia asked her why not, Kristin said glibly, "If it were up to Paine, we would be."

So it was Kristin who didn't want to make the commitment, not even after having a child.

The following week, after her death, when Julia met Paine, she couldn't shake the memory of Kristin flirting with Andy. She saw the unmistakable devotion in Paine's grief-stricken eyes, and she wondered how well he knew Kristin. Did he believe she was faithful to him?

Well, was she?

Julia has no idea, even now. She can't bring herself to ask Andy whether he ever connected with her friend after that night at the White Horse Tavern. He attended the memorial service along with nearly everyone else in Lily Dale, but had seemed no more sorrowful than the others.

For her part, Julia knew him only casually until last July, when, to her surprise, he asked her out.

He isn't her usual type. Her last few relationships—none of them serious—have been with men who are more reserved and who don't share, or even understand, her profession. Andy is good-looking, flirtatious, and self-assured, and she finds it liberating to be involved with another medium, somebody who doesn't regard her with curiosity or, far worse, skepticism.

They dated casually throughout last August, and then he left. They didn't see each other at all during the winter months, and he rarely called. She e-mailed him a few times but his replies were always belated, and invariably brief.

At first that bothered her. She had really thought their relationship might lead somewhere. But as the months went by and their contact diminished, Andy faded from her awareness . . . only to resurface last week in the grim aftermath of Iris's death.

Julia didn't intend to get involved with him again this summer. Yet when she bumped into him over at the Shur-Fine supermarket in Cassadaga on the day after Iris died and he asked her to join him for a drink, she found herself saying yes.

Maybe she just needs somebody to talk to about what had happened. Or maybe it's more than that, because she has found herself attracted to him all over again. This is the third night they've been together.

"Did you decide whether you're going to order the fish or the pasta special?" he asks, and she realizes she's fallen into silence again.

"The pasta sounds good. I'll have that."

"Julia, are you sure you're all right? You're not yourself."

"I'm just not very good company tonight."

"What's up?" He pours more Heineken into his mug. "Are you thinking about Iris again?"

She nods and looks out at the rapidly darkening sky. She should have stopped at Iris's to see Paine and Dulcie. Why didn't she? She meant to do it. She even walked over to the house after the service. But she passed it by, unable to bring herself to see them yet, telling herself that she just isn't ready to mourn Iris anew.

But is that really why she didn't stop?

Or is it that she doesn't want to be in that house again?

She hasn't been back since the day Iris died—the day she felt somebody hovering nearby as she sat alone in the study. It wasn't a malevolent presence. And of course, she isn't frightened by spirits. How can she be, in her line of work?

But something definitely happened to Kristin that night long ago.

Kristin is dead.

Now Iris is dead.

And Julia can't help but be afraid of whatever—whoever—lurks in the house at Ten Summer Street.

"Want to talk about it, Julia?" Andy is asking.

She looks at him blankly. She has never discussed Kristin with him, even now that her mother has died.

"About Iris," he prods.

"No. I'd rather not," she says abruptly, then adds, "Sorry."

"It's okay. Just thought I could help."

"You can. Entertain me. Tell me about your seminar students. Anyone interesting?"

"Got all night?" He grins and drinks some beer. Then he begins talking, and it's a welcome distraction. They place their order, begin their appetizers.

She's nearly finished her tomato-basil vinaigrette when the door beyond the bar at the far end of the room opens and two newcomers blow in with a gust of wet wind.

Julia, facing in that direction, glances idly at them. The man's familiar, finely chiseled face grabs and holds her attention.

Paine.

He's tall and incredibly good-looking, more so than she remembers, with his tanned skin, unruly dark hair that brushes his collar, and a broad-shouldered build. He's simply dressed in jeans, a flannel shirt, and a denim jacket. His rakish charm is enhanced by a growth of dark stubble on his cheeks. When his gaze flicks around the dining room and momentarily collides with Julia's, she realizes she's staring.

She hurriedly shifts her gaze to the child with him, and finds herself staring at the identical image of Kristin.

"Do you want to try my crab cakes?" Andy is asking.

She shakes her head, dragging her attention back to him.

Buttering another roll from the basket between them, Andy is telling her about the new lures he just bought for an early morning fishing trip he's planning first thing tomorrow.

Julia nods as though she's listening intently, struggling to grasp the fact that Kristin's daughter and her—her significant other, Paine—are mere feet away. She has to go to them, but, caught off guard, she isn't ready.

She sneaks another peek past Andy's shoulder as the hostess comes forward to greet them. Julia is struck anew by Dulcie's resemblance to Kristin, even more impressive now that she's older. The lovely face, the long, flaxen hair, or even the defiant way she shakes off her father's arm as he tries to help her take off her red windbreaker . . .

The child is definitely Kristin revisited.

Julia swallows hard over a massive lump in her throat as the hostess leads them out of her line of vision.

"Nan?" Pilar asks in a near whisper, leaning toward the bed.

There's no reply. Her friend's eyes are closed, and her breathing is quieter, less labored. Satisfied that she's asleep, Pilar closes the paperback romance novel she was reading aloud.

Knowing Nan has always loved romances, Pilar bought her a couple last week in Wal-Mart. Yesterday when she visited, she noticed that they were still stacked neatly on the bedside table, spines unbroken.

Realizing that her friend has become too weak to even hold them propped up in bed, she promised to come back tonight to read aloud.

Pilar's personal taste leans toward biographies and historic nonfiction, but she can see why the simple contemporary love stories, with their predictable happy endings, are a comfort to Nan.

With a sigh she puts the book aside, rises, and tucks the heavy down comforter more snugly around her friend's shrunken body. She notices that even in slumber, Nan's face isn't at peace. Her features seem slightly contorted, as if in pain.

Pilar pauses in the doorway and looks back at the sleeping woman in the bed, then glances around the room. For the first time, she's struck by its simplicity—just the hospital bed, a small table and chair beside it, the bureau, and a television. The walls are white, the two windows covered in drawn white Venetian blinds, the hardwood floor bare now that Rupert moved the area rug aside so Nan won't trip. There isn't much to look at—no vases of flowers or artwork or family pictures.

She understands that this is merely a spare bedroom— that the master suite is on the other end of the house. But now that it's sadly clear Nan won't be moving back there, it won't hurt to make this room a little more homey.

Pilar decides to bring a bouquet of roses from her cutting garden on her next visit, and to talk to Rupert about what else they can do to cheer things up.

She closes the door quietly behind her, then gives a start when she finds Rupert standing right there, in the small hallway that opens into the kitchen. He has an unnerving way of moving silently around the house. Before she got sick, Nan used to tease him about sneaking up on her.

"Is she asleep?" Beyond his horn-rimmed glasses, his sharp gray eyes are concerned.

Pilar nods. "I made sure the monitor is on. Where's the receiver?"

Rupert pulls it halfway out of his pocket. "I keep it with me all the time now, in case she needs me." He walks into the kitchen with the stride of a decades-younger man. Pilar isn't sure of his exact age, but she's fairly certain he's past sixty.

She follows him, watching him fill a copper teakettle at the stainless steel sink. The kitchen is sleek and modern, as is the rest of the interior of the cottage. It was built in the mid-nineties, after the Victorian on the site had burned to the ground.

"Can I offer you a cup of tea?" Rupert asks, placing the kettle on the gas stove top and turning on the flame. "I'm going to make some for Nan. I'm afraid I only have herbal . . . keep meaning to get to the store for the regular caffeinated kind, but . . ."

"No, thank you." Pilar leans against the polished oak table as he opens one of the streamlined white cabinets and takes out a box of Celestial Seasonings.

She hesitates, not certain whether she's about to overstep her neighborly bounds.

Then, still uncertain, she begins, "Listen, Rupert, if you want to go out and do your grocery shopping—or even if you just need to get out for a little while—I can stay here for a few hours and watch her."

He shakes his head. "Not on a night like this," he says, glancing at the blackness beyond the nearby window. "It's storming like a son of a bitch out there. Let me give you a ride home, Pilar."

"No, don't leave her."

"You only live two minutes from here. I'd be right back."

"She might wake up and need you. And you're right, I only live two minutes from here. I have my umbrella. I'll walk. But, Rupert . . ."

"What's the matter?" He opens the stainless steel refrigerator, takes out a carton of milk, puts it on the glossy black granite countertop.

"I'm just . . . worried."

"Well, so am I," he says gruffly, not looking at her.

"No, not just about Nan. About you, too. Rupert, I've been in your shoes. I know how hard it is."

It's been over five years since she nursed Raul through

the final stages of lung cancer, but she hasn't forgotten the mind-numbing grief and exhaustion.

"You need more help," she tells Rupert.

"You're doing enough, Pilar. You have your work, and the season's about to start—"

"No, I wasn't talking about my help." Catching the look on his face, she quickly adds, "It's not that I don't want to help you, Rupert. Of course I do. But I'm busy with readings at this time of year and I'm going away next week. My daughter and her husband are giving me a cruise for my birthday."

"That'll be nice."

"I suppose it will." In truth, she wishes the cruise could be postponed until September, after the Lily Dale season is over, but by then the grandkids will be back in school. Christina and Tom refuse to wait to take the cruise until Christmas, and insist that it won't hurt Pilar to take a week away from Lily Dale in the summer. It's not so much that her finances will suffer if she leaves—Raul's foresight in taking out a large life insurance policy earlier in their marriage left her well off enough so that she could probably get away with not working at all. But she can't help feeling reluctant to interrupt the pleasant, familiar rhythm of the fleeting season, which will officially be under way with opening day at the end of the month.

"Anyway, Rupert," she goes on, back to the matter at hand, "you need more support—not just physically. Emotionally, too. Don't you think it's time you called Katherine?"

For a moment he's motionless, but his eyes have hardened.

And when he moves—toward the stove, turning his back on her—she realizes what she's done. She's said the wrong thing—the most wrong thing you can say to somebody nursing their loved one through a terminal illness. She, of all people, should have known better. She should have sensed that he doesn't want it to be time for that yet. He's not ready to summon their daughter for the bedside deathwatch.

And maybe it isn't time yet. It will be, soon enough.

"I only meant that it would probably be good to have her around the house, Rupert," Pilar says softly, steepling her fingers in front of her, pressing them against her nose, watching him closely. "And I'd think she'd want to be here with you."

"Katherine doesn't visit during the summer," Rupert tells her stiffly. "It's too busy here. She likes to come off-season."

"I know." Pilar has never met Katherine, who lives somewhere on Long Island. Nan had once shown her a few snapshots of her as a child, but she doesn't speak often of her daughter.

Still, even if they're not close, Pilar would think Katherine would want to know the seriousness of her mother's situation.

Stay out of it.

The message in her head has come from Raul.

Pilar is startled to hear it. She rarely makes contact with her husband, but when she does, it's usually unexpectedly, like this. It never happens when she's consciously trying, which is typical of their relationship. When he was alive, Raul would often tune her out, absorbed—or pretending to be—in newspapers or ball games.

She doesn't blame him. She can be a nag. She knows it.

Stay out of it?

How like him. She finds herself smiling, but quickly straightens her mouth as Rupert turns toward her again.

"I'll send for Katherine when the time comes," he says firmly. "But it's not time yet."

"I know, Rupert. I only thought she could help you, so

you won't have to bear this alone. I know I couldn't have done it, when I—when Raul was sick. If I hadn't had Peter and Christina there with me—''

"I'm all right," Rupert cuts in. He reaches into a cupboard and takes out a mug, slamming it onto the counter.

Pilar has never seen him this way. But then, she's spent little time alone with Rupert. Nan is the one she befriended, the one with whom she had bonded through all the seasons they were neighbors on Summer Street, despite the fact that they didn't have much in common aside from the fence that separated their yards.

"Are you sure you don't want some tea?" Rupert asks, facing the cupboard, his hand still cupping the mug he just banged on the counter.

"No, thank you." Pilar reaches for the yellow raincoat she'd draped over a kitchen chair earlier. "I really should get home. Tell Nan I'll come again tomorrow night, or Saturday."

"I will." Rupert leaves the mug and walks with her through the shadowy dining room and living room toward the front door.

The house is too dark and quiet, Pilar thinks. At home, she has a habit of turning on lamps and televisions and radios in deserted rooms—a routine that began long before she was widowed.

But since losing Raul, she leaves the living-room light on and the TV tuned to *The Tonight Show* when she goes upstairs to bed at night. Raul was a night owl, unlike her, and he always liked to watch Jay Leno. Pilar finds it easier to go to sleep listening to the familiar sounds of the late-night talk show. Sometimes she pretends that Raul is still down there, on his end of the couch, his feet propped on the coffee table.

She realizes, as she glances around the Biddles' living

room, that they don't even have a television in here. It surprises her. She's never noticed it before—not that she ever spent much time in their home until Nan got sick. Even when they were living next door to her, Pilar rarely visited them.

But Nan has always been an avid gardener, and whenever Pilar saw her in the yard they'd chat over the fence. Sometimes Pilar would invite Nan for lemonade on the porch, but not often. What with Stump services, giving private readings, Assembly activities, and sitting in on workshops, her summer days are invariably too busy for socializing.

"It was nice of you to come and read to Nan," Rupert says.

"I'm happy to do it."

They've arrived in the front hall. He opens the door for her.

Outside, the rain is still coming down hard.

If he offers her a ride again, she'll take it, Pilar thinks as she looks out into the storm.

But he doesn't offer again.

Clearly, her unthinking comment about calling Katherine jarred him out of denial, and he hasn't yet forgiven her. Nor has she forgiven herself. She has nothing but empathy for the man.

"Good night, Rupert." She puts her hood up and zips her coat, stepping out onto the front step.

"Good night," he calls over the rain. "Get home safely."

He closes the door.

She puts up her umbrella and splashes toward the street lamps. Normally, she enjoys an evening stroll through the sleepy village, when lamplight spills from the turn-of-the-century homes and you hear the sound of quiet voices and creaking gliders on porches.

But tonight's chill rain gives her the strange sense that summer is drawing to a close, rather than just beginning.

June is always her favorite month of the year—the start of another busy season at Lily Dale. But this June, nothing is the same. Things haven't been right here since Raul died, and now with Iris gone, and Nan so sick, everything is changing.

Maybe, Pilar muses as she heads down Green Street, she *should* give up on Lily Dale, just as she did on the Iowa hometown where she and Raul had raised their family.

Neither of them was born in Cedar Bend. Pilar was raised in Cleveland, and Raul in Dayton, where Pilar eventually moved to attend college. They met after she graduated, when she was still trying to figure out what to do with her degree in English literature. Soon after they married, Raul took a management job with a large midwestern utility company. They settled in leafy Cedar Bend on the shore of Lake Erie, a place that felt like home for the next three decades—until Pilar was left alone there.

But Lily Dale is different from Cedar Bend.

Though the people here come and go, the essence of the place remains intact. Nowhere else in the world is there a community of people who understand Pilar's gift—people who not only respect it, but many of whom share it.

Pilar spent her growing-up years concealing her spiritual talents from her Roman Catholic parents and grandparents, who were convinced mediumship was the devil's work. She didn't share her capabilities with Raul, either, until well into their marriage. But Raul, bless him, understood. He encouraged her to read up on the subject of spiritualism, and to nurture her talent. He accompanied her on the four-hour drive up to Lily Dale for her first psychic seminar while their kids—Christina and her brother Peter—were away at summer camp. Later, when Raul's company offered early retirement, he took it. That was when they bought the summer place in Lily Dale and Pilar earnestly began training as a medium. By then, Christina was in college and Peter was in the navy, stationed overseas.

Renewed contentment courses through Pilar as she turns the final corner and spies her place ahead. The two-story blue house, with its mansard roof and wide front porch, is reassuringly lit up inside and out, the proverbial beacon in the storm.

As she quickens her pace, hurrying toward it, Pilar notices that the Shuttleworth place next door is dark. When Paine had asked her earlier where he and his daughter could get a decent meal, she'd suggested Lazzaroni's. There isn't much to choose from within the Lily Dale grounds, and coming from Los Angeles, he probably won't even blink at the pricey menu.

They must be at dinner, Pilar thinks as she passes the dark, obviously empty house.

Suddenly remembering something, she pauses in her tracks despite the pouring rain.

She's been so busy worrying about Nan that she hasn't allowed herself to consider the incident involving Iris's little granddaughter.

But now, as she looks up at the house, she wonders if her hunch is correct.

Dulcie was momentarily convinced that there was somebody in the kitchen.

Paine checked and said nobody was there.

Either the little girl was hearing things . . .

Or somebody was there.

Somebody Paine isn't capable of seeing.

* * *

"Paine Landry?"

Startled, he glances up from the three torn sugar packets in his hand, about to pour the contents into a steaming cup of coffee.

A young woman stands beside him. Her thick brown hair is cut boyishly short, framing attractive features that are enhanced by only a touch of lip gloss and a soft smudge of liner rimming her big brown eyes. She's wearing trim khaki pants with a slouchy beige fisherman's sweater.

How does she know my name? On the heels of the question, the only possible answer pops into Paine's head.

"Julia?"

Kristin's friend nods, flashing a brief, tight smile. "I wasn't sure you'd remember me. I know we spoke on the phone the other day, but it's been a long time since . . ."

"Yeah," he says uncomfortably when she trails off. "It's been a long time."

Not so long that he shouldn't have recognized the woman who had been a constant presence in those terrible days here at Lily Dale. But there are so many details he doesn't remember—details he must have blocked out. Anything to get past the initial, debilitating stage of grief.

"You must be Dulcie," Julia says gently, crouching beside his daughter's seat across the small table, and touching her sleeve. "I can't believe how grown up you are. I haven't seen you since you were a little toddler."

"Are you Mommy's friend?" Dulcie asks, spoon poised above her bowl of ice cream.

"Yes," Julia says, looking as pleased at the unexpected recollection as Paine is startled.

"Do you remember Julia, Dulcie?" he asks.

"Not really. But Gram used to tell me about her when she visited. She told me about the silly things my mom and

Julia used to do when they were little girls. And she said Julia took care of me when Mommy died."

Paine's gaze collides with Julia's. Caught off guard by the intense sadness in her brown eyes, he looks away.

Kristin rarely spoke of her girlhood friend, and he knows they didn't see each other much in the past two decades. Yet Julia picked up Kristin at the airport on that last visit, and she stood staunchly by Iris in the days after Kristin's disappearance. She was a comfort to Dulcie, too, Paine recalls with sudden clarity.

Memories pop back to him.

Julia sprawled on the floor of Iris's living room with Dulcie, guiding the little girl's fumbling hands through the assembly of a simple jigsaw puzzle . . .

Julia sitting on the front porch cuddling Dulcie on her lap as the house filled with strangers after the funeral . . .

Julia wiping Dulcie's mouth and hands after a drippy chocolate ice cream cone . . .

"Thank you," he says abruptly.

"Thank *me?*" She appears confused. "For what?"

"For helping me and Iris with Dulcie back then. At the time, I was so distracted that I never quite realized what you were doing for her—and then I never had the chance to talk to you again."

She looks flustered. "It was . . . it was fine. I didn't mind at all. In fact, I loved spending time with her."

"What did we do together?" Dulcie asks. "Gram told me that you took me to the beach."

"I did," Julia says, mildly surprised, as though she's forgotten all about it until now. "It's not much of a beach here by the lake, though. You kept asking me why there wasn't lots of soft sand to walk in like there is on the beach back home. Here, it's mainly grass. And gravel mixed in with the sand. It hurt your feet."

"Gravel?"

"Little rocks," Paine explains to Dulcie.

Simultaneously, Julia says, "Little stones."

They smile at each other.

Julia tells Dulcie, "We picked up lots of gravel. You wanted to collect it. You liked the smoothest, roundest ones."

"Now I collect shells."

"There are probably lots of those on the beach back in California."

"Haven't you ever been there, Julia?" Dulcie asks.

"No."

"You should come and visit us sometime," Dulcie offers with the innocent enthusiasm of a child who has no idea that this last connection to her mother's past has been severed with Iris's death.

After all, Paine notes, there is no reason for Julia to keep in touch with them, really. No reason for Dulcie to see her ever again. Not after this. Not with Iris gone, too.

Paine is struck by an inexplicable pang of loss, yet . . .

Why? Here is a woman he hasn't thought about in the past three years—a woman he barely noticed on the one tragic occasion they did meet. Yet for some reason, he finds himself wanting to chime in with Dulcie's suggestion that Julia come visit.

"Maybe I will," Julia says lightly.

"Knock, knock."

"Who's there?" Julia says it simultaneously with Paine.

"No, Daddy, I was knocking for Julia," Dulcie says.

He holds up his hands with a grin. "Sorry. Julia, it's all yours."

"Who's there?" Julia repeats.

"Dewey."

"Dewey who?"

"Dewey have to go to bed? I'm not even tired!"

Julia's laugh is genuine.

Paine fights the impulse to hug her.

A man comes up behind her, still in the process of tucking a credit card back into his wallet. "We're all set," he tells Julia, and flashes a curious look at Paine.

"Thanks, Andy. These are old friends of mine. Paine Landry and Dulcie, who is Kristin's—"

"Daughter. I figured." Andy's gaze rests on Dulcie, whose unseeing eyes are focused in the direction of Julia's voice.

Paine tells himself the other man's curious expression is natural. And when Andy offers him a perfunctory handshake, he tells himself that he's just imagining tension in the brief grasp.

Then Andy announces, "I met Kristin when she was here that summer, before . . ."

As his words trail off meaningfully, an inexplicable apprehension seeps into Paine.

"Really? How did you meet?" he asks Andy, his voice level. "Through Julia?"

"Actually, I met Julia and Kristin at the same time," Andy tells Paine. "They had stopped in at a bar down the road for a drink the night Kristin flew in from L.A. I happened to be there, and I introduced myself."

His hands are tucked into the pockets of his khaki pants, and he rocks back on his heels in what should be a casual posture. Yet Paine reads something brazen into his tone.

"Andy is well known in the field of parapsychology," Julia says—as if that means anything to Paine. "He travels and gives workshops. He's in residence at Lily Dale again this summer."

Paine acknowledges this with a tight nod of his head as Dulcie asks, "What's parapsychology?"

"It's the study of things we can't quite understand," Julia tells her.

"That's not exactly it." Andy takes a breath, apparently about to launch into a more complicated explanation.

Julia cuts him off. "We should let you get back to your coffee and dessert before Dulcie's ice cream turns into soup."

"I like it that way," Dulcie says, stirring the melting contents of her bowl. "But you should come over to our house and visit. Can she, Daddy?"

"Sure, whenever," Paine says noncommittally.

"No, tonight. Please? We just got here and we're lonely in our house."

That's news to Paine. After all, the two of them have been on their own for three years now, and Dulcie has never talked about being lonely before.

Then again, this is a strange place. And if he's feeling unsettled about being in the house where Iris so recently died, it can't be easy on Dulcie, either.

"Why don't you come back with us?" he suggests—mostly to Julia, though he assumes Andy is part of the deal. He wouldn't mind some adult company, after endless days on the road with only Dulcie and the tape deck for company. "I'm sure I saw an unopened can of Maxwell House in Iris's cupboard, and one of the neighbors brought over some cupcakes from a bakery."

"Chocolate volcanos," Dulcie corrects him. "You can try them. They're really good."

"Chocolate volcanos? Pilar next door must have brought those," Julia says. "Am I right?"

Paine nods. "How did you know?"

"Her sweet tooth is even bigger than Iris's used to be. And she's always buying chocolate pastries from the Upper

Crust bakery over in Fredonia. I've had those chocolate volcanos, Dulcie. They're delicious.''

"Do you want to come over and have one, then?" Dulcie asks eagerly.

"That would be nice," Julia says unexpectedly, and adds, mostly to Paine, "In fact, since I'm pretty familiar with Iris's house—I always keep an eye on the place when she's not here—I can help you get settled by showing you some of the quirky things you might not have noticed."

"Actually, Howard Menkin stopped by earlier," Paine begins.

"Did you say Howard?" Dulcie cuts in. "Knock, knock."

Paine sighs. "Dulcie . . ."

"Who's there?" Julia asks.

"Howard."

"I bet it's not Howard Menkin," Julia says, and Paine smiles. "So, Howard who?"

"Howard I know?" Dulcie erupts in a fit of giggles.

Julia joins in.

Paine can't help himself. He laughs, too.

He notices Julia's friend barely cracks a smile.

Getting back to his earlier subject, Paine tells Julia, "*Anyway,* Howard showed me a few things—like how to work the thermostat in case we need to adjust the heat. I never expected it to be this cold here in June."

Julia smiles. "Around here, July is pretty much the only month that you can count on not having the furnace kick on. Did Howard show you how to get into the basement? I know that old furnace is pretty temperamental. You might have to go down and kick some sense into it if it acts up later."

"He said something about that. I haven't had a chance to look for the stairway yet and I didn't see one."

"That's because it's outside, around the side yard, behind the big lilac tree. There's no basement access from inside the house."

"That's strange," Paine comments, checking on Dulcie, who is contentedly lapping up her ice cream.

"Not so strange for a vintage Victorian, really. And old houses aren't known for convenience. Like I said, yours has plenty of quirks. They all do, around here."

Andy has been silent during the exchange. Now Paine catches him glancing at his watch. He looks up and meets Paine's gaze.

Something flickers in his eyes and is gone before Paine can figure out what it was.

"Would you like anything else, sir?" the waitress asks Paine, popping up beside the table.

"No, thank you. Just the check." While she tallies it on her pad, Paine looks expectantly at Julia. "So you'll come back for a little while, then, for coffee?"

"That sounds good to me, but—what do you think, Andy?"

"I'm going to take a rain check," he says easily. "I've got to be up before dawn to go fishing. Why don't you go, Julia?"

She seems a bit surprised by the suggestion. After a moment's hesitation, she glances at Dulcie, and nods. "I think I will. It's still early."

"You might as well ride back with Paine, then," Andy says, sneaking another glance at his watch as he slips his arms into the sleeves of his lightweight navy jacket.

The waitress hands the check to Paine, then gives Dulcie a little nudge. "Looks like you're enjoying your ice cream, huh, sweetie? Come back again."

"We will," Dulcie promises.

It's good to see her smile, Paine thinks, watching her

fumble on the back of her chair for the red windbreaker. He reaches across to help her, but Julia is already there, helping her find it. He's impressed by the way she simply places the jacket in Dulcie's hands, allowing the little girl to put it on, as though she instinctively senses Dulcie's fiercely independent streak and that she wants to do things for herself despite her disability.

Paine hands the waitress his Visa card.

"Thank you, sir. I'll be right back. Pretty little girl you've got there."

"I guess I'll head out, then," Andy announces as the waitress departs. "I'll see you tomorrow night, Julia. Don't forget—the movies."

"I won't forget."

"Nice meeting you, Paine."

"You, too," Paine murmurs, wondering whether Julia and Andy are a long-term couple.

Something tells him they're not. Maybe it's the almost awkward way he bends to give her a peck on the cheek before he leaves. Julia turns her head toward him, as though uncertain about where he's aiming, and his kiss lands on a wisp of short hair at her temple.

Then Andy's gone, and Paine is signing the credit card slip, and the three of them are heading for the door. Dulcie walks between them, with Paine's hand on her shoulder, guiding her through the restaurant.

Paine looks over at Julia. She's looking at him, too. Suddenly uncomfortable, he tries to think of something to say.

He settles on, "So you're going to spill all the old house's secrets to me, huh?"

She nods, but she doesn't smile. "There's actually something else I'd like to talk to you about, too."

"There is? What—"

"Later," she says, with a slight nod toward Dulcie.

Paine immediately senses that it's about Kristin.

His heart beats faster as the three of them head out into the wind-driven rain.

Chapter Five

Hair still damp from her shivery shower, Miranda flops down on the bed in Kent's room. Hers is across the hall, a sparsely decorated rectangle containing only the basics. So is his, but Kent has somehow made his temporary lodging homey.

The single wide windowsill has become a makeshift bookshelf lined with novels and parapsychology books. His plump down pillow from his bed back home, tucked into a cheerful Ralph Lauren plaid pillowcase, is propped at the head of the bed. On the scarred dresser top, in a half-filled water glass, is the wildflower bouquet he picked by the lake earlier, the petals still glistening with raindrops. Beside the makeshift vase is a collection of toiletries that includes several glass bottles of expensive cologne.

"Did you really throw away the bottle of cologne you

had on this afternoon?'' Miranda asks, not spotting it on the dresser.

"Of course. If Mike wears the same stuff, it's lost its allure for me.''

"Oh, come on, Kent. That's ridiculous.''

"Hey, careful, my glasses are there,'' Kent says, reaching out to snatch them from the range of Miranda's elbow as she rolls onto her stomach and props her chin in her hand.

"I wish it would stop raining, damn it!'' She tilts her head, listening to the steady dripping on the roof.

They never launch an investigation unless the weather is clear. Rain or snow interferes with their equipment.

"Relax! It has to let up sooner or later.'' Standing in front of an old picture-sized wall mirror, Kent removes his contact lenses.

"The forecast says later. Much later.''

"Well, we're not on a strict schedule. If we have to, we'll wait to go out tomorrow night.''

"I know, but I'm feeling claustrophobic,'' Miranda complains, sitting up and walking over to the closed window. She presses her face against the pane, staring out into the darkness.

"Don't get any ideas. I have no desire to do the duck thing again.''

"I know. We did enough sloshing around out there this afternoon.'' Miranda had hoped that a long shower would help warm her up after that, but the old hotel only has one shared bathroom on the floor, and by the time it was free, the hot water was gone.

She turns away from the window, slaps her hands against her thighs, and exhales through puffed cheeks. "Looks like we've got an evening to kill, Kent. What do you want to do? Are you hungry?''

"Nope. Still stuffed from that cheeseburger at the snack bar."

"So am I. I think I brought a deck of cards," she offers.

"No, thanks. You cheat." Kent pops his right contact lens into the vial and twists the top on, then grabs his glasses.

"I don't cheat!" Miranda protests, going back to the bed and plopping down again.

"Yes, you do." He sits on the bed beside her and pats the mattress. "This bed is lumpy."

"Is it?" She lies back. "Not worse than mine at home. But then, I'm no Princess and the Pea, unlike you, so—"

"Hey, who are you calling princess?" He swats her arm.

Miranda laughs and rolls onto her back. She studies the network of cracks in the water-stained ceiling. It's dry now, but it's not hard to imagine the old plaster springing a few leaks if this rain keeps up.

She supposes the hotel is suited to Lily Dale's generally shabby, rudimentary ambience. But back in Boston as they were planning the trip, when Kent described their lodging to her, she found herself picturing more of a quaint, cozy bed-and-breakfast. The reality is reminiscent of a Depression-era rooming house.

"So what's the plan for later?" Kent, sprawled beside her on his back, has his elbows bent and hands tucked beneath his neck. "Or tomorrow, if the weather doesn't break tonight?"

"First, I want to go back to Inspiration Stump. Since that's where the mediums spend a lot of time doing readings, it makes sense that we might find some activity there."

He nods. "What about that house on Summer Street?"

"You mean the one with the lilac tree? And don't tell me it's a shrub, because I'm not the least bit interested in horticulture. Yeah, I definitely want to go back there."

"I figured. Why?"

She shrugs. "It's just a feeling."

He accepts that without question.

They've both been in this business long enough to trust each other's hunches.

Yet neither of them has extrasensory abilities. Their mission is strictly to conduct scientific research, collecting data that isn't visible or audible without the equipment they tote with them. At least, not to those who aren't gifted mediums.

But experience has taught both Miranda and Kent how and where to look for the spirits who are willing to communicate, and whose energy will come through most effectively.

It happens randomly, really. During an investigation, Miranda is sometimes struck by the sense that she should point her video camera in a certain direction, or she impulsively knows to spend more time in a certain room. When that happens, she's often rewarded with vivid documentation—stark video footage of darting orbs or ectoplasm, snatches of disembodied voices on tape.

Miranda is convinced, after a drizzly afternoon poking around the narrow, tree-shaded streets, that Kent was right about this place. Lily Dale will prove to be fertile ground for their research.

And no site captivates her more than the tree in the overgrown yard of that forlorn house at Ten Summer Street.

"How do you take your coffee?" Paine asks as the old-fashioned stainless steel Farberware percolator sputters on the blue Corian countertop.

Julia looks up from the book she's reading to Dulcie. It's Maurice Sendak's *Where the Wild Things Are*, one of Dulcie's favorite stories. It's a classic, but Julia has somehow never read this fanciful tale of mischievous little Max, sent to his room without supper, where his imagination takes over and he courageously sails off on an adventure.

"I take my coffee with milk ... if you have it," Julia adds, remembering that Paine probably hasn't had time to set up housekeeping yet.

It's strange—Iris's kitchen without its usual lived-in aura. When she was alive, every surface was cluttered. Perhaps less so in the winter months, when she was living hundreds of miles away. Yet, while most summer residents cleaned out their homes before abandoning them for the season, when Iris left, her place remained perpetually pervaded with *stuff*. Stacks of magazines and catalogues, needlepoint projects she was planning to get back to the following summer, recipes she had clipped—mainly desserts, of course, and most of them chocolate. Not that Iris ever baked. But she was always talking about how she'd learn how, someday.

Now she never will.

Julia swallows hard.

Paine has been here less than a day, but already he's rid the kitchen of more than just perishables. Resentment stirs inside Julia, though she knows he has a right to make changes. Iris is gone. The house is his and Dulcie's.

At least for now. She can't imagine them staying in Lily Dale.

"You're in luck. I do happen to have milk," Paine is saying. "Dulcie and I went out to get some basics over at that Shur-Fine supermarket in Cassadaga. She drinks a lot of milk."

"Somehow I knew that," Julia says, noticing the faint milk mustache above the little girl's upper lip.

"And Daddy eats lots of potato chips," Dulcie says, with a grin.

"I didn't realize potato chips were considered a basic

item." Julia spies a jumbo-sized bag of Ruffles peeking through a cupboard door that's slightly ajar.

"They're a basic in our pantry," Paine tells her. "So is sugar . . . and I just realized I forgot to buy it."

"Doesn't Iris have some in the cupboard somewhere?" *Present tense,* Julia realizes belatedly. *Stop that.*

But she can't get used to talking about her friend as though she's gone.

It was different when Kristin died. Probably because after so many years of estrangement, Julia had already taken to thinking of her in past tense.

"Iris did have a whole canister full of sugar," Paine tells her, "but ants had gotten to it. I dumped it. In fact, I dumped a lot of stuff."

Yeah. I noticed.

Aloud she says only, "It's okay. I don't take any in my coffee."

"I do."

Yes. She remembers seeing him tearing open several pack-ets back at the restaurant. That was when she had worked up the nerve to approach him, knowing that it was now or never, with Andy paying the check and ready to leave.

"Julia, can you finish reading the story?" Dulcie prods, pouting a little.

"Sure. I'm sorry I got sidetracked, Dulcie."

"Oh, don't worry about her," Paine says lightly. "It's not as if she doesn't know how it ends. I read it to her almost every night before bed."

"Yeah, and he describes the illustrations after he reads what's on each page, not *before* he reads, like you do, Julia."

"I'm sorry," Julia says again. "I'll do it your daddy's way."

"I like your way better," she says shyly. "Then I can picture what it looks like while I hear what's happening."

Julia is struck by a flood of affection for the little girl. It's all she can do not to impulsively give her a hug. She doesn't know how Dulcie would react to that now, at her age. When Julia last knew her, as a toddler who had just lost her mother, she had willingly curled up in Julia's arms.

"Julia?" Dulcie nudges again, but she's unsuccessfully stifling a yawn.

"Right after this, it's bedtime, Dulc," Paine warns, taking the carton of milk from the fridge.

Bedtime? That will leave Julia alone with Paine.

She finds herself slowing the pace as she works her way through Max's adventures in the land of the Wild Things, postponing the conclusion and the inevitable departure of the sleepy little girl.

Julia was never alone with Paine the last time they met. What will they talk about?

Kristin.

That's what they'll talk about. What else do they have in common? And anyway, she needs to bring up the nagging doubts about Kristin's death—doubts that have surfaced to haunt her now that Iris, too, has met a tragic end.

Paine pours two cups of coffee.

Then, grumbling about holes in the screens, he grabs a plastic fly swatter and goes after a moth that's darting around the overhead light.

Julia turns the pages, struggling to capture aloud for Dulcie Maurice Sendak's incredible illustrations of big-eyed beasts with gap-toothed grins in a bewitching twilight forest, and Max, who coronates himself only to become lonely for home and his mom.

Dulcie likes to run her fingertips over the dog-eared pages, almost as though the flowing artwork can seep into her through the alternative sense of touch. Julia notices that she never places her hands over the type, as if she senses precisely where the print is on the pages and knows to avoid blocking it. She lovingly caresses the pages that have no text as Julia tells her about the pictures.

When the book is finished, and little Max has found his way back to his room with a hot supper waiting, Julia swallows hard. "No wonder you love this book, Dulcie. It's a wonderful story."

"I sleep with it under my pillow every night," Dulcie confides. "Sometimes, I pretend that I'm Max."

Paine scoops his daughter from her chair and cradles her snugly in his arms. "Tell Julia good night, Dulcie."

"Good night, Julia," Dulcie says around a yawn. "Will you come back tomorrow?"

"I'll come back again," Julia promises, handing her the book.

"Tomorrow?"

Julia smiles, touched. "Maybe."

"I'll be back down in a few minutes," Paine tells her.

Julia leans back in her chair, her hands cupped around the hot mug of coffee Paine has set before her with the warning that it might be too strong. He's used to his automatic drip coffeemaker, not a percolator.

She hears the stairs creaking, then footsteps overhead and water running in the bathroom.

She closes her eyes to block out an image of Iris, dead, in front of the tub.

Oh, hell. She doesn't want to be here.

She should have said no when Paine asked her to come back. And she would have, except . . .

Dulcie.

Julia can't help being drawn to Kristin's daughter, not merely out of pity or curiosity, but some innate sense of concern. Maybe it's because of the intensely emotional time they spent together that summer—or maybe because Dulcie is a part of Kristin, and Kristin will always be a part of Julia.

As she sits in the silent kitchen, eyes closed, she becomes aware of little sounds. The last of the rain, plopping steadily on the tin roof above the back entryway. Paine's weight groaning the old floorboards above. The antique clock chiming the hour in the front hall.

She strains for some other sound—for some hint, audible or not, that she isn't alone in the room. Yet she knows instinctively that this time, there will be nothing. She doesn't feel the presence that was here before, the day Iris died. Nor does she want to.

Now, though she's half waiting for the energy to make itself known once again, she isn't willing to accept the distraction. It's hard enough, just being here in Iris's house without the familiar disarray. Without Iris herself.

Her death is still a shock. So, three years later, is Kristin's.

Julia muses at the cruelty of fate. Both mother and daughter died in Lily Dale, though neither lived here full-time. Both died in tragic accidents. Both deaths occurred at this time of year.

The macabre coincidence strikes Julia anew, along with another wave of uneasiness.

"Katherine. . . ."

Seated in the bedside chair, Rupert looks up from his newspaper, startled by the sound of Nan's voice. Her head is turned away, facing toward the window.

"Nan?" He leans toward the bed, touching her shoulder, feeling her protruding bones despite the layers of clothing and blankets. "Are you awake?"

No reply.

He rises and walks to the foot of the bed, peering at her

face in the lamplight. Her eyes are closed, her lips parted, almost slack.

"Nan?"

No. She's asleep. She must be dreaming.

As he returns to his seat, a faint groan escapes her.

"Nan? Darling, what is it?"

Is she in pain? Rupert looks at his watch. It isn't time yet for another dose of morphine.

"Katherine," she moans, her voice ragged.

"No, Nan." He goes to sit beside her, brushing back from her face what little hair hasn't been ravaged by the chemotherapy. "I'm here, darling. Rupert is here. I'll take care of you."

Her eyelids flutter, as though she's making an effort to return to consciousness. But she swiftly gives up, sinking further into the sleep that comes more frequently now, yet is anything but peaceful. Her breathing is labored, testimony to the malignant cells that have invaded her lungs, multiplying, lingering, in a slow strangulation that nobody can stop. Not Nan. Not the doctors. Not Rupert.

Helpless, he turns away, walking toward the window. He parts the curtains to look out into the night. He can see nothing past the rain streaming down the glass.

Don't you think it's time you called Katherine?

Damn Pilar for coming here, for suggesting that.

Did she say something about it to Nan? Is that why their daughter's name is suddenly on her lips? Does she sense that it's time . . . ?

"No!" Rupert's voice shatters the silence.

His wife doesn't stir.

No. He won't let Nan go. Not yet.

He stares vacantly at the flooded pane.

Pilar was kind to come here and read to Nan. And she was only trying to give him helpful advice.

But what does she know?

She thinks she's been in his shoes. She thinks she understands his pain.

She doesn't understand anything.

If only she would stay away. If only everyone would stay away, and leave Rupert alone with Nan.

If only they could go home.

"We will, Nan," he says aloud, his voice hushed this time as he turns to look at her. "I'll bring you home. I promise. First thing tomorrow, I'll talk to Paine Landry."

Finally, Julia hears Paine's heavy footsteps creaking back down the stairs.

"Is Dulcie all tucked in?" she asks as he comes back into the room wearing a distinct frown.

"She made me sit with her until she fell asleep. That's why it took so long. Did you know there's no shower head on that old bathtub?" he asks abruptly.

Yes, of course she knows. She knows the bathtub too well. Can't stop seeing it in her mind.

Paine catches the look on her face. "I'm sorry, I didn't mean to bring up—"

"It's okay."

But it isn't. Will she ever hear anyone mention the word *bathtub* again without being blindsided by a gruesome vision?

She tells Paine, "Iris didn't take showers."

"What about the people who lived here before? You can't tell me that nobody in this town has ever heard of a shower."

The way he says it—*this town*—sends a fresh ripple of dislike rumbling through her. Ever since she connected with him at the restaurant, she's sensed an air of contempt about him. He obviously doesn't like it here. Whether that has to do with the old-fashioned, no-frills surroundings or with the issue of spiritualism isn't clear—nor does it matter. Not to her.

Lily Dale is her home.

If he doesn't like it here, he should leave.

"Some of us actually do take showers," she says icily. "I can't speak for the Biddles."

"The Biddles?"

"The family that owned the house before Iris did. You can ask them about it when you run into them. And you will," she adds ominously. "This is a small town."

Meaning, he'd better watch his step. He can't go around slinging veiled insults about the place and its people without the locals picking up on his disdain.

He takes his own cup of coffee from the counter and sits down across the small wooden table. Apparently her warning has escaped him because he says, with the tone and expression of a classic skeptic, "So you're a medium."

She nods stiffly.

"Will it offend you if I say I don't believe in that?"

"You're an actor, right?" she shoots back.

He nods, looking bemused.

"Will it offend you if I say I don't believe in *that?*"

"What I do is different, Julia."

"It's your career. Mediumship is mine." She looks moodily down at her coffee. She's had better. Much better. He's made it bitter. Too strong.

"I'm sorry."

Surprised, she looks up from her cup, momentarily thinking he's talking about the coffee.

She isn't expecting an apology about his skepticism.

"I can't help it," he tells her. "I guess I'm just too practical. I never believe anything unless I can see it."

"Really? It's a good thing Dulcie doesn't think that way."

The second the words are out of her mouth she wishes she could take them back.

Yet, strangely, he doesn't seem insulted. In fact, he almost sounds impressed when he says, "Good point. But Dulcie's cut from a different cloth than I am. Than Kristin, too. She's more like . . . I don't know. Just not like us," he says quietly.

Julia senses that he was about to say Dulcie is more like Iris. Something stopped him. Perhaps the fact that he doesn't—didn't, she corrects herself grimly—know Iris very well. She only visited them in California a handful of times. But Julia is aware that she was always writing letters to Dulcie, and sending gifts, and calling.

"So Dulcie isn't a born skeptic?" Julia asks Paine. "Does she believe in spirits?"

"And Wild Things, and God, and fairies, and leprechauns. You name it," he says with a smile.

"How do you suppose that happened?" she asks dryly.

"You got me. My father's a levelheaded banker. My mother's a pragmatic accountant. They weren't big on whimsy. Santa Claus and the tooth fairy never came. We never went to church."

"So you were raised agnostic?"

"Atheist," he corrects. "I doubt any of Dulcie's spirituality or other creative beliefs came through my bloodline. Must have been Kristin's side."

"You realize that Iris wasn't a medium, right?"

"But she believed in them."

Julia nods. "Her husband was an incredibly gifted, world-famous spiritualist. But then, you must know that."

"I do."

"And you think he was a fake?"

Paine takes a sip of his coffee and makes a face. "It needs sugar."

"I don't think that would help."

He smiles.

So does she. Yet she asks again, "You think Anson Shuttleworth was a fake, Paine?"

"I don't know what to tell you, Julia. I don't believe that people can communicate with the dead. I think there are a lot of people out there taking advantage of widows who are desperate to talk to their husbands, and parents who need to connect with lost children . . ."

"You're right, Paine."

He raises an eyebrow at her.

"There are plenty of fakes. More than a hundred years ago, with the birth of spiritualism, con artists went to great lengths to trick people during seances. They still do. But there have always been legitimate mediums, too. People who choose to use their gift to help others—and to make a living. There are also lots of genuine mediums who never put their gift to use. They simply choose not to acknowledge it—just like Kristin."

"*What?*"

"I said, there *are* fakes, but—"

"No. What did you say about Kristin?"

"That Kristin apparently chose not to acknowledge her gift?"

"*What* gift?"

It dawns on Julia then.

He doesn't know.

Didn't Kristin ever tell him?

Perplexed, Julia thinks back to their childhood. To that Halloween night when Kristin saw something—someone—in the Biddle house.

Could that have been the only clairvoyant experience she ever had?

Julia finds that impossible to believe.

But Kristin lived with this man for years.

They had a child together.

Why would she keep something like that from him?

"Julia . . . ?" Paine is waiting, watching her.

"I'm sorry," she says. "I just assumed that Kristin was . . ."

"A medium? No. Like I said before, she was like me. She didn't believe in any of that stuff."

Did he say that earlier? He must have. Julia hadn't realized what he meant when he said Dulcie was different.

Now the implication sinks in.

Dulcie is different.

Dulcie, quite possibly, has a gift.

A gift she won't know what to do with, unless somebody helps her. Somebody who understands. The way Grandma helped Julia.

"I didn't know that," Julia murmurs, realizing Paine has stopped talking and is waiting for her to say something. "Kristin and I never really talked about it, so—you must have known that we never really had much contact as adults. I don't know why I thought I knew anything about her."

"She was a hard person to know," Paine says quietly. "Sometimes even I wonder how well I knew her."

Julia looks into his clouded eyes, wondering what he means by that.

"Did Iris ever tell you why Kristin and I weren't married, Julia?"

"Iris? No, she never told me why." Uncomfortable to be discussing something so intensely personal with a man she barely knows, Julia senses that he needs to talk about it. Maybe not even necessarily with her. But she happens to be here. And she'll listen.

"It was because Kristin didn't want to be anyone's wife," Paine says simply.

Selfish.

It's the first word that pops into Julia's head.

Kristin could be selfish.

She was so many other things, too . . . had so many traits that made her infinitely likeable. But her own needs always came first.

How like her, to prefer to live her life solo, free to walk out on this man if the mood struck her. And what about their daughter?

Julia doesn't know what to say, other than, "That does sound like Kristin. But I knew her mainly as a rebellious kid."

"I doubt she changed all that much over the years. She was reckless and carefree, and she was hell-bent on staying that way."

"Even after having Dulcie?"

"*Especially* after having Dulcie. It was as if she wanted to prove that she wasn't going to get stuck in a conventional life. She refused to consider marrying me and being a full-time mom . . ."

I know, Paine. She told me.

But Julia doesn't tell him what Kristin told her that night three years ago about her relationship with Paine. It would feel wrong, somehow—like a betrayal.

"She wanted to keep acting, and working, too—she was a waitress. Not that she had any choice, Julia. I mean . . . I've never made much money. But that wasn't what stopped her from marrying me."

"And it wasn't that she didn't love you enough, either," she muses, remembering the way Kristin's eyes lit up when she spoke of Paine and Dulcie.

"Did Kristin tell you that, Julia?"

"No," she says hastily. "But I doubt that she would have stayed with you for so long, or had the baby, if she didn't love you."

He turns his head away. "She didn't want the baby. When

she found out she was pregnant, she—she fell apart. She kept calling the baby 'it.' She kept talking about having to make a choice. . . .''

"And you talked her into having the baby?"

He doesn't answer that directly. Instead he sits forward in his chair, looks at her again. "Have you ever seen the musical *Man of La Mancha*?"

"No."

He takes a moment to make his point, his thoughts obviously drifting, a faint smile on his face.

"I met Kristin in summer stock when we were both just out of college. We were at Chautauqua Institution. Do you know where that is?"

"Of course." The summer colony is as world-renowned for the arts as Lily Dale is for spiritualism. It's less than a half hour's drive from here, and Julia does recall that Kristin was enrolled in a summer theater program there years ago, after they had drifted out of touch. During Kristin's few visits to Lily Dale that summer to visit Iris and Anson, Julia glimpsed her from a distance, sun-bleached hair, tanned and gorgeous. She remembers being awed as ever by the aura of glamour about her, and being too intimidated to approach her.

"The first show we were cast in together was *Man of La Mancha*," Paine tells her. "I played Don Quixote, the male lead. Kristin was the female lead. Aldonza. I'm not going to get into the whole plot, but the point is, Don Quixote was in love with his dream girl."

"Aldonza?"

"No. Dulcinea."

Dulcinea.

It's Dulcie's full name. Iris always called her that.

"Don Quixote saw Dulcinea in Aldonza," Paine explains. As if that makes sense.

"What?" Julia doesn't get it. She can feel Paine's impatience—that he wants her to understand. That this is important.

"Dulcinea is only a vision—a figment of Don Quixote's imagination—but he's convinced that she exists." Paine sips his coffee, barely seeming to notice the bitterness now. "That was how I felt when I found out Kristin was pregnant, Julia. Even though she was calling the baby 'it,' and telling me that she wasn't sure if she would terminate the pregnancy, I knew that she wouldn't. I knew the baby was a girl . . ." He swallows hard, his voice hoarse when he continues, ". . . and that she would be born, and that not only would I cherish her, but Kristin would, too. It was *my* vision."

"So you named her Dulcinea." Something stirs inside Julia. She doesn't want to find this man appealing. He's a stranger. He's a skeptic. He belonged to Kristin—still so obviously belongs to Kristin.

Yet she can't help being drawn to him.

"I never thought it would end up like this, though," Paine says, a ragged edge in his voice, as he bends his head and runs a distracted hand through the wavy hair above his forehead. "I never thought she would lose her sight, or that we would lose Kristin . . ."

"I know." Julia takes a deep breath, not wanting to add to his heartache, yet unable to keep it back any longer. "Paine, about Kristin's death . . . is there the slightest chance, in your mind, that it wasn't an accident?"

His head jerks upward. "Why do you ask?"

"I just never believed she'd go out on the water at night."

After a long pause, he says slowly, "She couldn't swim."

"I know. Iris says it didn't matter—that she was reckless and she might have been drinking. But she was always so afraid of the water when we were kids. And even when she came back to visit, that last time, I invited her to go sailing on Chautauqua Lake with a few friends of mine. She said no way—that she had never learned to swim. I remember it so clearly—I was teasing her about it. Telling her that I could get her some of those swimmies—you know, those blow-up things that kids wear on their arms . . .''

Paine leans so close to Julia that she can smell the coffee on his breath. "What are you saying, Julia?"

"That the more I think about it, the more positive I am that Kristin would never have willingly gone out on a boat alone at night."

"Are you saying that somebody was with her? Somebody talked her into going? Or that somebody—"

"I don't know."

"Oh, hell." He buries his face in his hands. "I didn't want to go there, Julia. You know? I've been trying, ever since it happened, to get past it. But I can't. Something happened to her when she was here. Something led her to go out on the lake at night."

"Or someone."

"Or someone." Paine exhales heavily. "You were one of the last people to see her alive, Julia. You know more than I do about what she was up to when she was here."

"But I don't, Paine. Not really. She closed herself off to me," she says reluctantly. "Something changed between the time I picked her up at the airport, and the next time I saw her. By then, she was acting strange. Withdrawn."

Paine narrows his eyes. "Do you think . . . was she on something?"

"*On* something?" Julia echoes. "You mean . . . drugs?"

He sighs. "She had a problem in the past. Years ago. Before Dulcie."

"I had no idea. Iris never told—"

"Iris never knew. Kristin didn't want her to know, even after it was over. And it was pretty bad, while it lasted. She left me. She went to live with a low-life dealer she had gotten tangled up with. But I couldn't let go of her. I kept trying to help her. Finally, it worked. She came back. She went into rehab.''

Julia nods slowly. ''I can see her getting caught up in the drug scene. She always seemed so restless, when we were younger. Like she was looking for an escape.''

''Exactly. And for a long time, I thought it was me that she was trying to escape. But now I don't think so. I think it was something else. Maybe she didn't even understand it herself.''

They fall into an uneasy silence.

The rain has picked up again outside, pattering noisily on the roof as the wind gusts, stirring the branches above.

Again, Julia remembers the presence in the upstairs study the day Iris died. Again, her mind drifts back to what happened to Kristin here on that Halloween night.

She has to tell him about it. Maybe he knows something, too. Something Kristin told him about this house.

She ignores the nagging voice that reminds her that Paine didn't know about Kristin's gift.

She ignores the possibility that she herself might have been mistaken about it—that perhaps Kristin had no psychic ability.

''Paine—'' Julia begins.

He cuts her off, his contemplative mood abruptly giving way again to derision. ''Wait a second, Julia. Before we get even further off the subject, let me ask you one thing. Because this is really bugging me.''

''What is it?'' she asks warily.

''If you really can communicate with the dead, why are you asking *me* what happened to Kristin? Why don't you just ask her what the hell she was doing out on the water that night? Ask her whether it was an accident, damn it.''

She clamps her mouth closed. *He's angry,* she reminds herself. *He's a skeptic. And he's still grieving.*

And so is Julia. For Kristin. For Iris. Doesn't he think that she would do everything in her power to help find out what happened to them?

No. He doesn't think that. Because he doesn't believe she's legitimate.

"I would if I could, Paine," she manages to say levelly, collecting her whirling thoughts, regaining her composure. "But it doesn't work that way. I can't just tune in a specific spirit like it's . . . like it's a radio station."

"Well, have you tried making contact with her?"

For someone who doesn't believe, he suddenly sounds more earnest than cynical.

"Have I *tried?* Not necessarily. But I'm open to the energy, Paine. And hers hasn't come through." She chooses her words carefully, not wanting to come across as too New Agey, alienating him even further.

"So you're saying you can contact other spirits—strangers' spirits. When somebody's paying you. But you can't contact—"

"You know what? I have to go," she says curtly, standing. "It's getting late."

He doesn't respond.

Julia carries her cup to the sink, dumps the acrid coffee into the drain, and turns on the tap to rinse it. She is swept by a sudden, vivid memory of Iris standing in this very spot, laughing, chattering above the running water. Her eyes sting with tears. She wishes Paine would vanish and leave her alone with her grief.

Damn him.

Why did he have to ask her about it—about the one thing she's wondered herself, many times, these past three years?

She was telling the truth about not being able to tune in

a specific spirit. She's been in this line of work long enough to have confirmed that there are limits to her miraculous ability. That most spirit energy is weak, and that it takes a tremendous force for those who are able to come through.

Yet she's made contact with other people she's lost. How can it be possible that Kristin, so powerful a force in life, hasn't made herself known in death?

There are only two viable explanations.

It's because Kristin isn't able.

Or because Kristin isn't willing.

Neither possibility sits well with Julia.

Dulcie's eyes snap open.

Is it morning?

Snuggled cozily beneath the weight of her quilt, she strains to hear the usual telltale sounds—chirping birds, Daddy's footsteps, water running, traffic passing.

She can hear only rain and wind.

She remembers, then. She isn't in her familiar bed in the Long Beach apartment. She's in Gram's house in Lily Dale, in one of the upstairs bedrooms.

She lies still, searching for the usual clues that will tell her whether it's time to get up.

She yawns, still tired—but that doesn't mean anything. Dulcie loves to sleep late. Back home, Margaret always calls her ''sleepyhead.''

She misses Margaret. Daddy says it won't be long before they're back home in California again, with Margaret there to take care of Dulcie. She doesn't want to think about that, though. However much she longs for Margaret and home, being in Lily Dale is an adventure.

And Dulcie feels closer to Gram when she's here. And to Mommy.

Concentrate, she reminds herself, and goes back to silently, motionlessly searching for clues to the time. There isn't much to go by.

She notes that this room can't be very big—she can feel that the walls are close around her.

A damp, mildewy smell hovers in the air. Daddy said it's a "cottage" smell, and that they can open all the windows when it warms up in a day or two.

The rain patters loudly on the roof overhead.

It was raining when she fell asleep, with Daddy sitting at her side.

Is it still night? Has she only been asleep a little while? Maybe Julia is still downstairs with Daddy.

Dulcie considers climbing out of bed and feeling her way out of her room to find out. But that could be dangerous. She doesn't know this house yet; doesn't know where the walls and doorways are, or how many steps there are from her bed to the stairs. Daddy said for her to call him if she needs to get up to use the bathroom.

She doesn't need to use the bathroom.

That's not what woke her.

But something did. What was it?

Dulcie concentrates.

Gradually, she remembers that she was having a dream. It comes back to her in fragments now—something about being on a beach, picking up shells. Julia was there.

Dulcie smiles faintly. She likes Julia. She feels safe when Julia is nearby.

She feels safe when Daddy is nearby, too.

That's why she asked him to sit with her until she fell asleep. It isn't that she's afraid, exactly—more that she's a little nervous, being in a strange house. The house where her grandmother died.

It's sad, about Gram. Dulcie will miss her. Even though

she lived far away, she always let Dulcie know that she cared about her.

Not like Dulcie's other grandparents, Daddy's mother and father. Grandma and Grandpa Landry only live an hour away, but Dulcie and Daddy hardly ever see them, and when they do visit, it isn't much fun. They never hug and kiss anybody, the way Iris did. They act as though they feel sorry for Dulcie, and they talk about her as if she isn't even there—as if she's deaf, rather than—

Dulcie realizes suddenly that she isn't alone in the room.

She can feel weight sloping the mattress near her legs. Oh—so Daddy is still here. It's not morning after all. She must have drifted off to sleep for only a few seconds.

And Julia must be getting tired of waiting down in the kitchen for him.

"You can go downstairs now, Daddy," Dulcie tells him. "I'll be fine."

The room is silent.

"Daddy?"

Silence.

But the weight on the mattress is gone. She didn't hear creaking bedsprings or feel the slightest movement, but it's gone.

Dulcie sits up, feeling around at the foot of the bed.

She feels only the quilt, and the extra pillow Daddy said was there in case she needed it.

Dulcie slowly lies back down, listening to the storm outside. She could have sworn Daddy was here with her. She felt him sitting there.

Well, she felt *someone* sitting there.

She doesn't feel it anymore . . . but she did. She definitely did.

Could it have been Julia?

But why wouldn't she have said anything? Would she—

could she—have snuck out of the room just now without Dulcie hearing her?

Hmm.

Daddy says Dulcie hears everything.

She yawns deeply.

Maybe it was her imagination.

Maybe nobody was here with her.

Maybe somebody was. But who?

Sleepy, she tucks a hand under her pillow, feeling for her book. She likes to keep *Where the Wild Things Are* under her pillow. Her fingers brush against the familiar rectangle, and she is instantly reassured, thinking of Max and his magical journey.

Another yawn sweeps over her.

She's pretty certain that it's no longer evening. Nor is it morning. It must be the middle of the night.

She might as well go back to sleep. But in the morning, she'll remember to ask Daddy whether he or Julia snuck back in to sit on her bed after she was asleep.

Chapter Six

"Jules?"

Julia cries out, nearly losing her balance on top of the ladder as she catches sight of a figure below.

"Lorraine! You scared me!"

"Sorry. I knocked. Your stereo is so loud I knew you wouldn't hear it. Good thing you never lock your door."

The stereo *is* loud. There's nothing like blasting an old Rolling Stones album to erase a foul mood. And Julia has been in a foul mood ever since last night's encounter with Paine Landry. It's compounded by the realization this morning that her kitchen ceiling is leaking. Badly. Everywhere.

"What are you doing up there, Jules?"

"One guess, Lorraine."

Her friend glances at the various buckets, pans, and bowls Julia has set out to catch the drips. "Oh. The ceiling again?"

"It's much worse this time." The ladder teeters as Julia

climbs down. It, like everything she owns—including the house itself—is ancient and rickety. "I've got to do something about the roof before the whole thing collapses."

"I thought you said you got an estimate last summer and it would cost a fortune to replace it."

"It *will* cost a fortune."

"Can you afford it?"

Julia thinks about the savings account she opened last year over at Lakeshore Savings and Loan in Fredonia. She made only that one initial deposit—the money her grandmother left her in her will. It isn't much—and it's all she has, besides the house, which she owns with her mother. But she doesn't have a choice.

"I'll *have* to afford it," she tells Lorraine.

"I'd float you a loan if I could, but I'm tapped out, as usual," Lorraine says. More than a decade older than Julia and recently divorced from Bruce, her deadbeat ex-husband, she struggles to pay college tuition for her two daughters.

Julia notices that Lorraine's short, curly brown hair is damp despite the umbrella in her hand, and her fine-featured face is flushed as if from exertion, though it's a mere two-minute walk from her house to Julia's.

While Julia is clad in jeans and a long-sleeved T-shirt, Lorraine has on a lightweight, sleeveless cotton romper—in fact, it's one she borrowed from Julia last summer. They're the same size, and Lorraine is forever raiding Julia's closet and forgetting to return things.

"Has it warmed up outside?" Julia glances at the gray scene through the window as she folds the stepladder and leans it against the worn laminate countertop. The world beyond the glass looks drippy and dreary.

"It's disgusting. Warm and humid. The rain is supposed to stop any minute now, and the sun is supposedly going to shine, but don't get your hopes up. Hey, by the way, I heard you left Lazzaroni's with Kristin's boyfriend and daughter last night.''

"You're kidding." Julia lowers the volume on the stereo. "The news is out already? Who told you that?"

"Myra said Ted saw you there."

That figures. Myra Nixon's husband Ted is even more of a busybody than his wife is.

"I went back to Iris's with Paine to show him a few things he might not know about the house," Julia acknowledges, even as she realizes that she never did get around to showing Paine where to find the basement steps, or how to open the closet door in the master bedroom that sticks when it's humid.

Well, he'll have to figure things out for himself.

"How's the little girl doing, now that she's lost her grandmother too?" Lorraine asks sympathetically.

"She's hanging in there." Julia feels a pang for Dulcie. She promised the child that she'd come back to visit. Eventually, she'll have to. It will mean putting up with Paine again, but she can't break her promise. Not when Dulcie looked so hopeful.

"How about the boyfriend?" Lorraine pulls out one of the mismatched chairs at the small, scarred wooden table and plops down.

"Paine is still bitter about what happened to Kristin," Julia says, moving a half-full bucket a few inches across the worn linoleum floor, to better position it beneath a steady drip overhead. "I can't help feeling sorry for him. He's been through a lot. So has Dulcie."

"Dulcie is the little girl? Now there's an unusual name."

Julia finds herself telling Lorraine about Dulcinea in *Man of La Mancha*. And about Kristin not wanting to get married. And about Paine being a skeptic.

"I can respect a difference of opinion, but he's very

irritating.'' Julia paces, too edgy to sit at the table with Lorraine. ''He's so irritating that I keep thinking I should stay as far away from him as possible. But . . .''

She falls silent, picturing Dulcie's face.

''But you won't stay away,'' Lorraine says, watching her.

Julia smiles. ''Is that a prediction?'' Lorraine, of course, is a medium. One of the best in Lily Dale.

''It's a commonsense observation. You feel like they need you, don't you?''

''I feel like Dulcie needs me. Paine could do without me. Hell, he obviously could do without Lily Dale and everyone in it.''

''Kristin's feelings about this place must have rubbed off on him, then?''

''Maybe. The thing is . . .'' Julia shakes her head, pondering. ''I don't know exactly what Kristin felt about Lily Dale. All I know is that once she left, she never seemed to look back. I almost get the impression that she spent her whole life trying to stay away from here.''

''Why?''

Julia opens her mouth to tell Lorraine about the Halloween experience in the Biddle house. Before she can speak, the phone rings.

She sighs. Now that the season is almost under way, it's probably somebody wanting to schedule an appointment for a reading. Considering the pricey home-improvement project she's facing, she should be aggressively drumming up as much business as possible, but suddenly, she's not in the mood to work.

As Julia walks toward the phone on the wall beside the back door, Lorraine pushes her chair back and stands.

''Stay,'' Julia tells her, reaching for the receiver. ''I'll make us some coffee.''

She can use a decent cup after that awful brew Paine served her last night.

"No, that's okay. I just stopped by to find out what happened last night. I've got to get home. Mrs. Hanover is coming for a reading in fifteen minutes."

Mrs. Hanover, a wealthy widow from Buffalo, is one of Lorraine's weekly clients. Julia has her share of regulars, too. But luckily, she hasn't scheduled any appointments today. She's free to spend the next few hours dealing with the soggy kitchen and her own thoughts about the Shuttleworths, Paine, and Dulcie. Tonight, of course, she has that date with Andy. They're going to see the new Julia Roberts romantic comedy that's playing over in Fredonia.

"I'll talk to you later," she tells Lorraine, who waves on her way out as Julia lifts the receiver with a businesslike "Julia Garrity speaking."

"Julia. How are you?"

Terrific. It's the last person in the world she wants to talk to when she's in this kind of mood. If only she had let the machine get the call. Too late now. She's trapped.

"Hi, Mom. I'm great, thanks."

She doesn't want to ask in return, but she knows it's expected—and knows her mother will tell her regardless. So she takes a deep breath, sinks into a wobbly chair at the table, and reluctantly vollies the question back. "How are you?"

Naturally, Deborah Garrity is anything but fine. She launches into a detailed chronicle of the past few days. Julia barely listens, murmuring "mmm-hmm" or "oh, no" often enough to hold up her end of the conversation.

She marvels, as always, that her mother doesn't seem to notice that she's doing all of the talking. But then, that's how Deborah likes it.

Julia is swept by a wave of longing for her grandmother,

the only other human on the face of the earth who understood how it is with Mom and who willingly, if helplessly, shared the burden of listening to her. Now Julia must tolerate her mother single-handedly. Thank goodness it's a long-distance relationship now—much easier than when Mom and Julia were sharing a roof, and Mom was forever cornering Julia with her run-on commentary and complaints.

It only became unbearable after Grandma passed away, leaving Julia alone with Mom. Before that, Julia and Grandma used to exchange secret glances behind Deborah's back, bound by mutual exasperation tempered with affection for the complicated, self-absorbed woman who had so little in common with either of them.

Granted, as a working medium, Deborah does share her mother's and her daughter's occupation. But Julia is convinced that she doesn't share their gift. Whatever slight psychic intuition Deborah might have inherited from Grandma at birth has long since given way to a shrewdly efficient ability to provide clients with surprisingly accurate readings based on nothing more than expert guesswork and luck.

Yes, her mother is, in all likelihood, one of the frauds Paine Landry considers universal and so despises—a fake who, in her shady proficiency, has contributed toward diminishing the profession's credibility.

Julia has never confronted her mother with her suspicions. Of course, Deborah would only deny it. Or maybe, with her characteristic narcissism, she's convinced herself that she's done nothing wrong. After all, she had quite a following in Lily Dale, and does now in Florida. Her clients seem satisfied.

A knock on the door allows Julia to cut the phone call short, but it takes three attempts before she successfully interrupts her mother. She manages to hang up with a hasty, insincere promise to call back later.

As she hurries through the small living room to the door, she wonders, fleetingly, if the visitor could possibly be Paine. The ludicrous thought is promptly banished, even before she sees the two strangers standing on her porch. Both middle-aged women are clutching the familiar pamphlet-sized Lily Dale visitor's guides and both are wearing pastel sun visors, shorts sets, and anxious, expectant expressions.

"We saw your sign out front," one of them says. "We've never been here before and we were wondering if you could do readings for us."

Julia hesitates.

Normally, she takes walk-in appointments if she's not busy. And she does have to worry about replacing the roof and kitchen ceiling. She can be nearly a hundred dollars richer an hour from now if she agrees to read these women.

This morning, though, she'd rather be alone with her thoughts. About Paine and Dulcie. And Iris. And Kristin.

Or would she?

You're not going to talk me into going sailing, Julia. I never did learn how to swim.

Bulldozing the disturbing memory from her mind, she holds the door open for her visitors with a decisive "Come on in."

"Okay, Dulc, one more step and you'll be down," Paine says, guiding his daughter's hand along the polished wooden railing. Her foot, clad in a white sneaker, feels its way to the edge of the stair tread and over the edge.

"Great! You made it," he says, behind her, his hands on her shoulders.

"Can you go back up and check one more time for my book, Daddy?"

"Let's go into the kitchen and get some breakfast first," he suggests. He needs to get the phone and call his voice mail back home, just in case his agent has left a message about one of the auditions he had before he left.

"But I need my book."

"We'll look for it again later." He's already checked everywhere it can possibly be—under the bed, in the crevices between the mattress and the wall, among the sheets and blankets. She insists that she put *Where the Wild Things Are* under her pillow last night as always when he tucked her in, but he's certain she must have forgotten. Dulcie is certainly a creature of habit, but she was exhausted, and distracted by Julia's presence, and in a strange house.

"Don't worry, Dulc, it'll turn up. Let's go eat. We bought Lucky Charms yesterday, remember?"

"But there's no sugar to put on them."

"Lucky Charms are sweet enough without sugar." Paine wonders how he's ever going to undo all the bad habits Dulcie's picked up from him over the years. Luckily, dumping piles of sugar on presweetened cereal is about the worst of his habits.

Kristin had more than her share, though. From not wearing a seat belt to . . . well, to the drugs. There's no telling what kind of influence she'd have been on Dulcie, had she lived.

"Daddy?"

"Hmmm?" Paine is steering her toward the kitchen. After breakfast, they'll head to the nearest hardware store for a shower head. Splashing warm water on his face at the bathroom sink just now didn't do the trick. He won't feel fully awake until he's immersed himself under a hot spray and scrubbed himself clean. He'll shave, too, he decides, rubbing the itchy stubble on his cheeks.

"Were you in my room last night, Daddy?"

"I sure was. Remember? I promised I wouldn't leave till you fell asleep, and I didn't." He makes a mental note to pick up some wire mesh to repair the screens, too. The last thing he needs is an indoor mosquito or fly infestation.

"No, not when I went to bed," Dulcie says. "Were you in there later?"

"Yup. I tucked you in before I went to bed. You were sound asleep."

"Oh." Dulcie's tone is thoughtful.

Coming into the kitchen, he half expects to see her missing book sitting in the middle of the kitchen table. But all that's there is a circular milky brown stain where his and Julia's coffee cups sat. He was too exhausted to sponge it away before going up to bed.

"Okay, here we are." He pulls out a chair for Dulcie. It's the one Julia vacated last night, when she left before he had a chance to ask her any more three-year-old nagging questions.

As though she's read his mind, Dulcie asks, "When will Julia come back? Did you invite her over for lunch?"

"For lunch?" he echoes, not sure whether to smile or frown. "No, I didn't, Dulc. We have a lot to do today."

"I want Julia to come over."

"Maybe tomorrow," he says vaguely. "She's busy."

Dulcie sits heavily in the chair and scowls. "Doing what?"

Taking hard-earned cash from people who believe she can talk to their dead relatives.

He skirts the question, picking up the phone and dialing his voice mail number. "We're busy too, Dulcie. We have to run some errands . . ."

He frowns. No new messages. Well, what was he

expecting? He didn't really expect a call-back from the latest round of auditions.

"What kind of errands, Daddy?"

He hangs up the phone. "We're going to buy some stuff for the house, and we're going to pick up some new clothes for you."

"I want Julia to come shopping with us."

"Not today. Knock, knock," Paine says to distract her.

"Who's there?" she asks halfheartedly, and adds, "I hope it's Julia."

Rolling his eyes, Paine says, "Oswald."

"Oswald who?

"Oswald my gum."

Dulcie frowns. "I don't get it."

"Oswald—sounds like I swallowed. I swallowed my gum," he explains patiently.

"Is Oswald a name?"

"Never mind, Dulc." He pours cereal into a pair of chipped Fiestaware bowls, splashes in some milk, and sets the bright yellow bowl in front of her. "There you go. There are lots of marshmallows in there, so dig in."

She picks up her spoon. "Are you sure I was asleep when you tucked me in last night, Daddy?"

"Sound asleep." He plucks a small yellow moon from the blue bowl as he carries it to the table.

"Oh."

Paine picks up his spoon, and notices that Dulcie's is still poised over her bowl.

"What's wrong, Dulc?"

"Did you sit on my bed when you tucked me in?"

"No, I sat on your bed when you were falling asleep." He looks up at her. Familiar guilt seeps in as he notices traces of last night's milk mustache still hovering above her lip.

He was so caught up in the search for her missing book that he forgot to help her wash her face and brush her teeth upstairs. And he'll have to remember to comb her tousled hair and pull it back into a ponytail later, before they leave. Margaret always does those things for her. He realizes with a pang that he isn't a very good replacement for Dulcie's beloved baby-sitter. Nor for her mother.

Kristin might not have been the most maternal woman he'd ever known, but she was great at mother-daughter things like hair combing and clothes shopping. She was always brushing and braiding Dulcie's long hair, and dressing her up in pretty clothes. She even used to paint Dulcie's little fingernails when she did her own.

"Did Julia come up to my room before she left?" Dulcie asks.

Christ. Julia *again*.

It doesn't take a child psychologist to figure out that Dulcie has latched on to Julia as a female role model in Margaret's absence. Paine sighs. This is going to go on all day if he doesn't put a stop to it.

"No, Dulcie, Julia didn't come into your room before she left, and she can't—"

"Are you sure?" Dulcie interrupts.

"Trust me, I'm sure." He personally watched Julia leave after a curt good-bye and her repeated assurance that she'd be fine walking the few short blocks to her house alone. He tried not to worry about her, but found himself filled with doubt as she splashed out the door and down the street without an umbrella to protect her from the downpour.

"Because I thought she was sitting on my bed."

"She wasn't."

"Are you *sure?*" Dulcie asks again.

Paine's initial frustration with her persistence gives way

to apprehension when he catches the worried look on Dulcie's face. A chill creeps over him.

"Why do you keep asking, Dulcie?"

"I thought somebody was there. Sitting on my bed."

"I told you, I was—"

"It was later. You weren't there. I woke up, and I thought . . ."

"Maybe you were dreaming," he suggests, when she trails off.

"No. I was dreaming *before* it happened, and I dreamed again *after,* but that part wasn't a dream. Somebody was there."

"Like when you thought Gram came to you that night . . . the night she died?" Paine asks, fighting to keep a tremor from his voice.

"Kind of like that," Dulcie says matter-of-factly. "Except, this wasn't Gram. It was someone else."

"You thought it might be me? Or Julia?"

"I thought so. But just because you were the only other ones in the house with me." Dulcie shakes her head. "Maybe it was somebody else. I don't know who."

"Don't be afraid, Dulcie. It was probably just a dream."

"It wasn't a dream, and I'm not afraid," she says matter-of-factly, spooning some cereal into her mouth.

No. She isn't *afraid,* Paine thinks, watching her.

But I am.

It isn't easy, getting Nan from her bed to the car. Rupert can't help but acknowledge that a wheelchair and a ramp would be an enormous help. Finally, he settles his wife in the passenger's seat and tucks a fleece blanket around her thin, shivering frame.

A wheelchair . . .

A ramp . . .

But how many more times will Nan leave the house?

She wanted him to cancel the appointment with the oncologist this morning. He would have gladly agreed, if it weren't for her breathing. It's becoming increasingly hard for her to take air into her lungs. On her last visit, Dr. Klauber suggested getting an oxygen tank set up for her at home. She refused. Now, Rupert suspects, it has become a necessity.

The doctor also pulled Rupert aside and suggested—not for the first time—that he look into getting hospice care for Nan at home. But that's out of the question. Rupert doesn't want anyone taking care of his wife but him. He's been doing it since he met Nan when she was only fifteen, and he'll do it until . . .

Till death do us part.

"Are you okay?" Rupert asks, flashing an artificial smile and giving the blanket a final tuck beneath her fragile knee.

She merely nods, looking too exhausted to speak.

He goes back to lock the door, wishing fervently that this were the house on Summer Street. It isn't helping either of them, going through this traumatic experience in a place that doesn't feel like home. Not the way the old house did, right from the start.

He thinks back over the years, picturing Nan there, young and healthy, baking in the big old-fashioned kitchen, puttering in her garden—and Katherine, underfoot, or sailing on the swing he rigged for her in one of the big old trees in the yard . . .

"Rupert?"

"Yes?" He turns to see Nan in the car, with the door still open as he left it.

"I'm so chilly. Can you please hurry?"

"I'm sorry." He fits his key into the lock, gives it a twist, and dashes back across the patch of gravel drive. After planting a gentle kiss on her turban-covered head, he closes her door before going around to the driver's side.

Rupert drives slowly through the Lily Dale streets, mindful of the increased pedestrian traffic that indicates the season's imminent commencement. The rain has stopped at last, and the clouds have scattered just enough to reveal a sliver of sun. The rays filter almost eerily through the lingering mist, glistening on the water droplets that still cling to leafy branches overhead.

He hesitates before turning down Summer Street, one of the many possible routes leading to the main gate. This isn't the quickest way, and they have a fifteen-minute drive to the doctor's office in Dunkirk.

But maybe Iris's granddaughter and her father have arrived. He forgot to ask Pilar about it last night in his haste to get her out the door.

Sure enough, when the house comes into view, an unfamiliar car with California plates sits at the curb in front.

They're here.

He sighs in relief, glancing at Nan. She, too, is looking at the house.

Rupert follows her gaze. The only sign that the place is occupied is that the windows facing the street are raised to let the fresh air in.

Fool. Doesn't he realize those screens are full of holes?
Eccentric Iris never minded an occasional fly buzzing around, but any sane human being would repair them before opening the windows at this time of year.

"It's so beautiful," Nan says softly.

He turns to see her wincing as she turns her head to keep the house in view as they drive slowly by.

Beautiful?

That, it isn't. Iris let the place go all to hell in the three years since they moved out. But Rupert will have it whipped into shape in a few days. He's already making plans: he'll cut and fertilize the grass, and repaint the trim, and fill the window boxes with blooming annuals . . .

Nan makes a slight sound, a cross between a sigh and a moan, turning her head again toward her own window as they round the corner.

He doesn't need to see her face to know that the merest movement contorts her features in pain, or that she's wearing a wistful expression, thinking about the old house.

As soon as they get back from Dr. Klauber's office, he'll settle Nan at home. Then he'll waste no time getting back over to Ten Summer Street to talk to the young man from California. Of course he'll be relieved to have an interested buyer knocking at his door. It will save him the trouble of finding a Realtor, listing the house, showing it. And then there's the fact that he is restricted by the Lily Dale Assembly from selling the home to anyone who isn't a member of the Assembly.

Rupert is.

And he's prepared to write Paine Landry a check today, even if it means using every last penny of his retirement investments. All that matters is that he bring Nan home before it's too late.

"Hello, Myra?" Pilar clamps the phone to her ear with her shoulder and carries her empty coffee cup and cereal bowl to the white porcelain sink. "It's Pilar. How are you?"

"Pilar! Welcome back. I heard you brought chocolate pastries to Iris's little blind granddaughter. That was so sweet of you."

News travels quickly in Lily Dale, particularly when Myra is on the sending or receiving end. Since buying a summer cottage in Lily Dale a good twenty years ago, she hasn't missed much that's happened here within the gates. She isn't a medium, nor is her husband, Ted, but between the two of them, they have a hand in just about everything that happens in the community.

"Yes, I stopped over there to say hello yesterday," Pilar says briefly. "After all, I'm right next door."

"I can't believe I haven't run into you since you've been back. How was your winter in Alabama?"

"Milder than my winters were in Cedar Bend, that's for sure. How have you been?"

"I can't complain, although I think this was the first and last winter we're going to spend here in Lily Dale. We stayed thinking we'd take up skiing, but we didn't go once. Next year, I think we'll head to Florida again," Myra says. "Ted and I had a nasty bout with the flu that lasted for weeks. But we've generally been healthy lately, thank God."

It's the perfect segue. Pilar seizes it. "Speaking of health, I was over at Nan's last night. She isn't doing well. I'm so worried."

"So am I. The poor thing. She's fading fast."

"It broke my heart, seeing her that way."

"I don't know how Rupert does it, day in, day out. He wants to care for her himself, but Ted and I were just saying the other night that she should be in a hospital in her condition. Rupert won't hear of it."

"Maybe their daughter should get involved," Pilar suggests, rinsing the cup and bowl and reaching for the Palmolive.

"Katherine? Yes, she probably should. I suppose Rupert keeps her informed."

"When was the last time she visited?" Pilar squirts some of the thick green liquid onto a sponge. Too much. Suds quickly explode in the sink beneath the running water.

"Let's see . . . over the Easter holiday. She was here when

Ted and I were on our golf trip in South Carolina. And I heard she was here for Christmas, too—that was when we had the flu. We've both made up our minds to get flu shots next year.''

Pilar artfully steers the conversation back on track, attempting to rinse the soap suds down the drain. The white fluff only seems to multiply, filling the sink with bubbly clouds. "I wonder if Katherine plans to come back soon. I'd love to talk to her about getting hospice care. Rupert and Nan don't have to go through this alone, but I can't seem to get that across to him."

"Oh, Pilar, you know that Rupert can be a stubborn old S.O.B.," Myra says.

"Well, I've been in his shoes," Pilar tells her, swallowing hard and looking out the window above the sink. Framed with cheerful blue gingham curtains, it faces her small, tidy yard with its vibrant raised flower beds Raul built and helped her to plant with perennials many summers ago. The colorful petals glisten with raindrops.

Raindrops.

Teardrops.

Pilar lifts her shoulder, wiping her suddenly brimming eyes across the top of her cap sleeve.

"I know you've been there, Pilar." Myra is sympathetic. "You understand what he's going through more than anybody."

"It's hard to think clearly when your world is falling apart around you. You resent anybody who tells you what you don't want to hear. But somebody has to."

"I know."

"I'm worried about Rupert. And about Nan. And about their daughter. She should be here. I wonder if Rupert has even told her what's going on. Something tells me that he's afraid to admit it to anyone."

"Well, Katherine will see for herself when she comes back—only I don't know when that will be. You know she doesn't like to be here in the summer. She doesn't like the crowds."

Pilar does recall Nan having mentioned something about that. "If she isn't planning to come back for a few months, she's going to be too late. Nan doesn't have long. You wouldn't happen to know how I can get in touch with Katherine, Myra, would you?"

"All I know is that she lives near New York City. She's been there ever since Rupert and Nan sent her away to boarding school there when she was a teenager. I've never even met her."

"Boarding school?" This is the first Pilar has heard of that. "Why? Weren't they satisfied with the local school system?"

"I heard it was more that they wanted to get Katherine away from the boy she was seeing at the time."

"Was he a troublemaker?"

"I guess so."

Pilar thinks about her own children.

She thinks about the time Peter, usually an excellent student, started receiving Cs and Ds. Pilar and Raul suspected that he was smoking pot, but he kept lying about it until he was caught doing it at school. He was threatened with expulsion—which scared him straight, thank God.

She thinks about the time Christina fell in with a bad crowd in high school, and started dating a tattooed high-school dropout with a drunk-driving conviction on his record. Raul threatened to send her away to a Catholic boarding school just to get her away from him. Luckily, Christina came to her senses before they reached that point and broke up with the boy on her own.

Apparently, Katherine Biddle didn't.

"Are you thinking of calling Katherine and telling her what's going on?" Myra asks.

"I don't know," Pilar says slowly. "I just think Rupert is in denial. He needs support. His daughter should be here— for his sake, and for her own."

She finishes rinsing her breakfast dishes and sets them in the drain board to dry.

"I might be able to find out how to reach her if I ask around," Myra offers.

"Do that. But please be subtle about it, Myra." Pilar runs more water into the sink, intently watching the last of the suds swirl and disappear down the drain. "I don't want it getting back to Rupert. He won't understand that I'm only trying to help."

She carries the cordless phone back to the living room and places it back in its cradle on the end table beneath the picture window, right beside a framed photograph of Raul. The lump she held back moments earlier rises again in her throat, threatening to escape in a sob.

She forces herself to look away from his smiling face, out the window, where a movement catches her eye. Somebody is walking up the front steps of Iris's house next door.

It's Julia, Pilar realizes, recognizing the petite figure. She watches her friend knock on the front door. It opens almost immediately. Handsome Paine Landry stands on the threshold, looking uncertain. Yet it's clear from the way he immediately holds the door open that he was expecting her.

A smile curves Pilar's lips.

She watches until Julia steps inside and Paine closes the door after her.

"Where's Dulcie?" Julia asks Paine, stepping into the entry hall.

"She's upstairs in her room sorting beads. Her baby-sitter back home taught her how to string them to make jewelry. I'll get her in a minute. She isn't expecting you."

"She isn't? But I thought that was why you called and asked me to—"

"Yes, that's partly why. I mean, that Dulcie wants to see you," Paine says in a low voice. "But that's not the only reason I asked you to come over. Something she said this morning bothered me and I thought maybe you'd know what—"

"Daddy? Who are you talking to?" Dulcie calls from overhead.

"Geez. She hears everything. It's like she has bionic ears. I'll talk to you about this later," Paine whispers. Aloud, he says, "It's Julia, Dulcie. She's stopped by to visit."

"Julia!" A floorboard creaks upstairs, followed by an explosive clattering, rolling sound and a wail.

"Oh, no, I dropped my beads."

"Don't move, Dulcie. I'm coming." Paine is already halfway up the steps.

Julia frowns, looking after him.

When he called her just as she was finishing her readings for the two walk-ins, he simply asked if she could come over for a half hour because Dulcie was asking about her. Naturally, she said yes for Dulcie's sake.

Apparently, there's more to his request. What could Dulcie possibly have said to him this morning that would make it necessary for him to summon Julia?

She hears them upstairs, talking, moving around, picking up the beads. Should she go up and help?

When Iris was here, Julia wandered the house freely. Now she quickly dismisses the idea of going upstairs as too presumptuous.

Instead, she goes into the living room and idly glances at the photos on the mantel, waiting.

Restless.

Wondering—

And then it happens.

The temperature seems to drop instantaneously, sending goose bumps over her bare arms.

A rush of energy saturates the room, not seeping in but swooping, and with it comes an eruption of sound. It evaporates so swiftly that Julia isn't certain what she heard— perhaps a scream, a blast of music, possibly both.

Tense, she holds her breath, willing further contact even as she feels the energy pulling rapidly away, like a train speeding off around a bend.

Then it's gone entirely, and Paine and Dulcie are chatting on the stairway.

"Julia! Thanks for coming to see me," Dulcie calls. "I have lots of good knock, knock jokes for you."

Unwilling to share with them what just happened, Julia forces her body into action. She moves toward their voices, smiling, reaching out to give Dulcie a quick hug as she feels her way from the bottom step to the floor, with Paine gripping her arm.

"Dulcie has quite a project for later, too," Paine says, holding up a large plastic bag filled with beads. "She has to sort these all over again."

"Maybe I can help you, Dulcie," Julia offers, her voice far steadier than she feels. "How do you do it?"

"Each color has a different shape. Like, the blue ones have little raised ridges in the middle, and the red ones are smooth. That's how I know which is which. I can make you a bracelet, Julia, if you want."

Pushing aside the troubling incident in the living room, Julia says, "That would be wonderful."

Dulcie grins. "Are you going to come with us to the store?"

"To the store?" Julia looks at Paine.

"We have a few errands to run. I thought we could go a little bit later, but if you feel like taking a ride with us now, maybe you can come along and show us where to shop."

"Shop? Around here? There aren't many places," Julia says. "The nearest mall is down in Jamestown."

"I don't need a mall. I just have to get some stuff for the house. And Dulcie needs some clothes."

Julia looks down at the little girl, who's wearing ill-fitting pink shorts and an orange T-shirt that doesn't match. Knowing what Kristin would have thought of the outfit, Julia says, "I'm sure we can find a few things that would look nice on you at T.J. Maxx, Dulcie. There's one over in Dunkirk."

"Is there a bookstore there, too?"

"Sure. The Book Nook is right down the road from T.J. Maxx."

"Good. Because I lost *Where the Wild Things Are* last night."

"But I just read it to you," Julia says. "Didn't you take it with you up to bed?"

"She sleeps with it under her pillow," Paine says. "I'm sure it must have slipped behind her bed. It'll turn up later."

Julia glances at Dulcie, who doesn't look so certain. She seems troubled.

"You don't think it's somewhere in your room, Dulcie?" Julia asks.

The answer is prompt, accompanied by a stubborn chin-lift. "No."

"Then where can it be, Dulcie?" Paine's tone makes it clear they've been through this before, yet he sounds more concerned than exasperated.

"I don't know. Unless whoever was in my room took it. But why would they do that?"

Paine's head snaps around, and Julia is caught off guard by the intensity in his gaze when it meets hers. It takes a moment for her to connect the stark worry in his eyes to Dulcie's words.

"Whoever was in your room?" Julia echoes slowly, looking from Dulcie to Paine. "What do you mean, Dulcie?"

"I think somebody came in last night and sat on my bed while I was sleeping. Daddy says it wasn't you or him. I don't know who it was," she adds with an almost casual shrug.

Alarmed, Julia stares at Paine. He raises his eyebrows at her in return. This, clearly, is the reason he called her.

"Did you hear anything, Dulcie?" Julia asks. "Footsteps, or somebody's voice, or . . ."

A scream.

A burst of music.

"No. I didn't hear anything like that. Why?"

"I just . . . wondered."

"Why did you wonder that?"

"Because sometimes—" Julia breaks off as Paine shoots her a warning look that clearly says, *Drop it. Don't scare her.*

There's a pause.

Dulcie asks, "Can we go shopping now?"

"In a few minutes, Dulcie," Paine says. "Why don't you sit at the kitchen table and start sorting your beads again while Julia shows me where the basement is? I need to check the boiler."

"Can I come with you guys?"

"The stairs are so steep, Dulcie, almost like a ladder," Julia says hastily.

"We'll be right back," Paine adds, guiding her to the

kitchen and pulling out a chair for her. "Sit right here and work on your beads."

"I can't wait till you start working on my new bracelet." Julia pats Dulcie's hair, noticing that it needs to be combed. She wonders if it would be out of place to offer to help her with it. She finds herself longing to straighten the silky blond tangles, to smooth them beneath her fingertips as she did in that fleeting interlude when she knew Dulcie as a toddler. The little girl would snuggle into her lap and lean her cheek against Julia's heart, seeming to take comfort in having her hair brushed and braided.

"Okay, Julia, come on. Where's the basement stairway?" Paine asks, turning to her with an expectant expression.

She leads the way to the back door, asking, "Have you decided what to do about a memorial service for Iris yet?"

"Actually, I just made some calls to set that up. It's going to be next week. Thurday morning, at Assembly Hall. Afterward, I'm going to have somebody scatter her ashes over the lake. That's what she specified in her will."

"You're not going to do it yourself?"

Paine gives her a look. "I have no desire to go out on that lake in a boat, Julia."

Because of Kristin.

She can understand that. But . . .

"Who's going to scatter the ashes, Paine?"

"Do you want to do it, Julia?"

She nods slowly. "Yes. I think it should be someone who . . ." She clears her throat, choked up.

"Someone who cared about her," he says quietly, nodding. "You should do it. Thursday, after the service. I can make arrangements for a boat to—"

"No, it's okay. I'll find somebody to take me out on the lake."

"That would be good."

They're in the yard now. Julia notices that the sun has finally made an appearance. The air is thick with heat and moisture, tinged with the scent of wet earth and long grass and flowers. A fat bee buzzes lazily at the blooming magnolia tree beside the door, hovering above a dewy pink bloom.

"It's humid," Paine comments. "I should change."

She nods, glancing at his jeans and rumpled long-sleeved light blue chambray shirt that exactly matches the shade of his eyes. He has yet to shave, and his glossy dark hair is as tousled as Dulcie's.

Both father and daughter clearly need looking after.

Well, Paine will certainly find someone to fill the emptiness in their lives when he's ready. Men who look like him don't stay single longer than they want to.

"Why are you looking at me like that?" he asks, running a careless hand through his hair, shoving it back from his face. "You're thinking I need a haircut, right?"

"No! No, I just . . ." Realizing she's been staring, she turns away. Her face grows hot. "The basement stairs are over here."

She leads him around the corner of the house, just behind the front porch. There, in the shade of the lilac's leafy branches, a pair of sloping horizontal wooden doors jut out from the stone foundation.

Julia reaches down to pull them open.

Paine brushes past her. "Get back, I'll do that."

Thrown off by his nearness—the faint masculine smell of him—she steps aside. How did Kristin resist marrying this beautiful man who was so crazy about her?

Paine tugs on the doors, first one and then the other, opening them to reveal a steep, narrow stairway leading downward into cobweb-shrouded blackness.

"Is there a light down there?" he asks, looking dubious.

"I think so."

He wrinkles his nose and starts down the steps, looking up at her. "You coming?"

She nods.

"Good. I need to talk to you," he says softly. "Where Dulcie can't overhear us."

Julia gingerly climbs down the ancient steps into the cellar. The air is clammy here; chilly, almost, and it smells like mud and mildew. She's only been down here a few times, with Iris, who never liked to venture below ground alone.

In a far corner of the windowless room, beneath the bare overhead bulb, is an old dresser she recognizes.

"Iris was going to refinish that for me," she says, walking across the dirt floor and running her fingers across the dusty wood. "It's so dark, and I told her I would like it if it were a lighter stain. She said she could strip it."

"She meant to give it to you?"

Julia nods. "I've been using my grandmother's bureau since the drawers warped in mine. But Gram was into moth-balls, and all my clothes end up smelling that way. Like an old lady in her Sunday best, Iris used to say."

She smiles at the memory.

"Well, you can still have it, if you want," Paine offers, poking around, his back to her. "In fact, if there's anything else you want, help yourself. I'm going to have to unload a lot of this stuff."

"Won't Dulcie want to keep some mementos of her grand-mother? And of Kristin? I'm pretty sure Iris still kept some of her dolls and things up in the attic, to give to Dulcie when she's older."

"I'll have to go through it all," Paine says with a sigh. He turns back to her. "Listen, I don't want to leave her alone up there for long. I just need to tell you about a few strange things that have happened with her."

"What kind of strange things?"

"I'm not saying they mean anything, or that I believe anything," he says, raising a hand as if to hold her at bay. "I just need to know how to deal with them, because if there is anything at all to your medium stuff—and I'm not anywhere near convinced there is—I don't want her to turn out all screwed up."

Julia quells her resentment over his skepticism. He's entitled to his opinion. At least he came to her for help—and that's the important thing. Helping Dulcie.

"You think Dulcie is sensitive to paranormal experiences," she says evenly. "Is that it?"

She expects some kind of disclaimer, or at the very least, a heaping dose of sarcasm, but he only nods, throwing up his hands helplessly.

"When she said there was someone in her room . . ." He shakes his head. "I would write it off as a dream, except that it's happened before."

"When?"

"The night Iris died. The night Kristin died. Those are the most memorable experiences, and there's more to it—I won't go into detail now. But there have been other times, too. Once in a while, when she's alone, I've caught her talking to people who aren't there, Julia. Looking at people who aren't there. I want to believe it's just her imagination, but there's something so . . . odd about it. I mean, she's *blind,* Julia. She can't see what I see. How can she see what I can't?"

She hesitates, searching for the right words, words that won't further alienate him. "I can't explain that, Paine. How can I see what other people can't see? How can I hear what other people can't hear? I don't know. It's a gift. Maybe Dulcie has the gift." She closes her mouth, not letting anything more, anything about Kristin, spill forth.

Instead, measuring her next words carefully, Julia says,

"I've felt a strong presence in this house, Paine. It could be that Dulcie feels it too."

"A ghost?"

She nods. "If that's what you want to call it."

"What do *you* call it?"

She studies him. He seems receptive, yet she knows his cynicism can't be far below the surface.

"I call it energy." She takes a deep breath, explains, "It's the energy of someone who's passed."

"Do you feel it now? Here?"

"No."

"When? Where?"

"It comes and goes." She doesn't want to alarm him. Doesn't want to tell him that the presence she's felt in this house is troubled.

He's silent for a few moments.

At last he asks, "Can it be Kristin? Can she be haunting this place? Or . . . haunting Dulcie?"

Haunting. Another folklorish term she prefers not to use.

She lets it go by, saying only, "I don't know, Paine. It might be Kristin. I don't sense that it is. But the few times I've felt it have been so rushed—whoever was here was gone before I could tell more."

He just looks at her, his eyes burning into hers. "I won't lie to you. A big part of me thinks this is just a bunch of bullshit. I've never believed in any of it. When you're dead, you're dead—that's what I think. And when Iris came to visit, she knew enough not to raise the topic. But . . . I'm worried about Dulcie, and I don't know what's going on with her. I don't want her to be . . ." He trails off.

"She doesn't seem frightened." Julia runs her fingertips along the oak dresser's carved scrollwork, brushing away the dust and shreds of cobwebs.

"She isn't frightened. But . . ." Paine exhales heavily.

"Look, I sure as hell don't want to stay here. I don't even want to be here a second longer than I have to. The sooner I clean this place out and get back home, the better. But it's not going to happen overnight. And I don't have anyone else to ask . . ."

Julia waits, standing still, her fingertips resting on the old wooden dresser. She knows what he's going to say. And she knows how she'll respond.

"Can you sort of spend some time here, Julia? With her? Just in case she'll open up to you about . . . anything that's happening?"

Julia thinks about the season that's just beginning. This time of year is insanely busy. She needs to work. And her roof is shot. Everything at home is shot. There are hundreds of household tasks she could be doing in what little free time she has.

Then there's Andy. Who knows where that's leading?

"I know you're busy, and you have a life," Paine says, and she realizes that he's watching her. Waiting for an answer. "I wouldn't ask if I thought there was somewhere else I could turn. But there's stuff I have to get done around here, and it would be nice to have someone to keep her company once in a while. She needs more than me. Not just now, but all the time. Back home we have her sitter. Here, there's just me. She really likes you, Julia."

"I know. I feel the same way about her. She's very sweet."

She pictures Dulcie's little-girl face. It melds in her mind with Kristin's little-girl face, the Kristin she had known so long ago, and loved.

Kristin, who saw something in this house and never got over it.

Kristin, who came back here only once . . . and died.

A stab of fear—fear for Dulcie—takes hold in Julia.

"It's fine. I'll help you," she tells Paine decisively, just as she knew she would. "When I'm not busy working, I'll try to spend some time with her. I'll try to see what's going on with her."

"Good. Thank you so much, Julia. I don't know what to do for you in return—except give you that dresser. And anything else you want. Like I told you—"

"I know. You're going to unload it," she says flatly

"Well, what else can I do? Cart it all the way across the country?"

"What about the house?"

"I'm going to sell it as soon as possible. Although who in their right mind would want to buy this place is beyond me."

"Hello?" Rupert calls through the screen door for the third time. He knocks yet again, certain there's somebody home. The red rental car is parked at the curb.

There is no reply.

Maybe they're out walking, exploring the village. Or down at the beach, now that the warm sun has burnt away the clouds.

Hell. Rupert needs to talk to the man now. He's waited long enough.

But what's he supposed to do? Comb the streets of Lily Dale, looking for Paine Landry and his daughter?

Damn it.

He should have come earlier.

But he couldn't.

Before the endless wait at the pharmacy for refills on all the usual drugs, including morphine, there was the doctor's appointment . . .

He shuts that out, not wanting to think about the somber

expression in Dr. Klauber's eyes as he examined Nan, nor the pity in his receptionist's kindly tone when Rupert told her they wouldn't be needing to schedule another appointment this time.

Dr. Klauber was ordering an oxygen tank for Nan's room at home. He said there was no need to bring her back to the office. The fifteen-minute drive to Dunkirk was too hard on her now.

"But then . . . when will I see you again?" Nan asked Dr. Klauber in her halting, labored voice.

Dr. Klauber didn't answer her.

Rupert supposes he should resent the doctor for that— for the way he looked past Nan, addressing only Rupert.

But he doesn't resent Dr. Klauber. He doesn't want anything spelled out for him, and certainly not for Nan.

Dr. Klauber tactfully mentioned that Rupert could bring her to the hospital if he'd like—that she might be most comfortable there, and that Dr. Klauber would then be able to see her when he made his rounds.

Rupert saw the expression in Nan's weary eyes when she heard that. He quickly assured the doctor that she would be perfectly comfortable at home.

And she will . . .

In *this* home, at Ten Summer Street.

Rupert raises his hand to knock again, frustrated, knowing it will be futile, but—

And then he sees her, there, through the screen. Framed in the familiar doorway at the end of the hall leading to the kitchen.

For a moment, years drop away and he's certain that it's Katherine standing there. His beloved little towheaded daughter.

He half expects to hear her giggling voice greeting him, to see Nan coming out of the kitchen behind her . . .

But it's all wrong.

The little girl's eyes are as blue as Katherine's were, but hers are oddly empty and unfocused.

Her hair is too yellow, too long, too loose.

Her clothes are too modern.

Nan always had Katherine in dresses, or full skirts and blouses, and short socks with lace edging, and white or black little-girl shoes with straps . . .

This isn't Katherine.

This isn't his house.

Katherine isn't here, and Nan isn't here.

"Who's there?" the little girl asks, standing absolutely still in the doorway, her hands outstretched to clutch the frame, her sightless eyes tilted in his direction.

Rupert realizes that she knows he's here; she must have heard his knock and his voice. She senses him now, though she can't see him.

Where the hell is her father?

Has he left her alone?

What kind of parent would do that?

Doesn't he realize the world is a treacherous place?

Rupert studies the child for a long moment.

He's about to call out to reassure her when she does something strange. Something that sends a chill down his spine.

Her head snaps suddenly to the left, toward the base of the stairs—as though she's heard something, or glimpsed movement from the corner of her eye.

But she can't see.

And there is nothing to hear, or the sound would have reached Rupert's ears, too.

"Are you the person who was in my room last night?" she asks abruptly, still facing the empty stairway.

Silence.

Rupert holds his breath, watching.

"Well, why did you take my book? Where did you put it?"

Dread steals over Rupert as he watches the bizarre one-sided exchange.

"It isn't funny," the child says. "Stop laughing. Stop it. I'm going to tell my daddy about you."

The little girl's expression changes then. Even from yards away, with these old eyes, in the dim light of the hall, Rupert can see the flicker of fear in her vacant blue eyes.

"Why not?" the little girl asks the invisible visitor. "Who are you? Are you my mom?"

Rupert holds his breath, his hands clenched tightly at his sides.

"Wait, come back!" the little girl cries out suddenly, letting go of the door frame and stepping forward. Her hands flail in front of her as she feels for something to guide her way. There is nothing.

She takes another step forward, feeling blindly, fumbling, stranded helplessly in the middle of an unfamiliar room.

Again, she calls, "Come back!"

Rupert backs away silently, descending the porch steps without a sound, his heart racing madly as he hurriedly strides away.

"Geez, what's up with him?" Kent mutters to Miranda as the old man brushes by them, hurrying off down Summer Street and disappearing around the corner onto Cleveland Avenue.

"Who knows? Maybe he saw a ghost."

Kent chuckles. "Then we're in luck. Did you notice where he was coming from?"

"Of course. Should we check it out now, or wait until

later?'' Miranda is clutching a white piece of paper in her hand, repeatedly rolling it into a tube between her palms and unrolling it again.

"Will you quit doing that?'' Kent snatches it from her. "It's getting all wrinkled. We didn't bring that many copies with us.''

"We brought plenty. And if we get low, we can always photocopy it,'' Miranda points out.

"Yeah, at a nickel a copy. That's a waste of money.''

Miranda sighs, thinking it's probably going to be a long summer. The trip with Kent seemed like such a good idea when they were back in Boston, and she was nursing her broken heart, desperate to get out of town. Now she wonders if she might not have been better off doing a weekend beachfront rental in Scituate with some of her friends instead of trekking across the country looking for ghosts. It would certainly be more relaxing.

She glances up at the house that so intrigued her yesterday. Again, she feels a prickle of interest. There's something here. She dismisses thoughts of lying on the beach and tells Kent, "Let's knock and see if somebody's home. There's a car parked out front and it looks like the inside door is open.''

"Sounds good.'' He carefully tucks the sheet of paper into his shoulder bag and they pick up their pace.

As they near the house, Miranda spots movement near the lilac tree beyond the porch. A man and a woman are emerging from a cellar stairway beside the foundation. The man she recognizes from yesterday—the one who drove up in the red car with the little girl.

Miranda nudges Kent, who nods and says in a low voice, "Come on, before they go into the house.''

"Excuse me,'' Miranda calls, walking swiftly toward the attractive dark-haired couple. They look up, startled.

"Can we talk to you about your house for a moment?" Kent asks, boldly crossing onto the overgrown lawn.

Miranda follows, noticing that the woman seems uncertain and looks at the man, waiting for him to respond.

"What about the house?" the man asks, folding his arms across his chest with an expectant stare.

He's beautiful, Miranda thinks, fixated on his perfect features. *Too beautiful. Not my type . . . and apparently, I'm not his.*

She drags her attention to the brunette at his side, finding her petite and utterly perky-looking. Kind of like that actress Kent likes so much—Sandra Bullock. A far cry from sturdy Miranda, with her wiry red hair and freckles and extra padding at the hips and thighs.

"We're scientific researchers in the field of paranormal studies," Kent says with practiced efficiency, after introducing both himself and Miranda. "We're conducting an investigation here in Lily Dale and we'd like access to your property later tonight."

The man is scowling even before Kent is finished speaking, which is when he promptly shakes his head. "I have a young child. I can't have people in the house late at night when she's trying to sleep."

"We wouldn't need to come inside," Miranda speaks up, addressing the woman, who doesn't seem to share her counterpart's inhospitable attitude. "We have a release form that explains the investigation process—show them, Kent."

Kent begins reaching into his bag as the man says, "Don't bother. I'm not interested in knowing more."

Miranda persists gently, "But we'd just like to take a look around the yard—maybe take some pictures and use some of our equipment to measure—"

"No," the man cuts in flatly, not even bothering to consult his wife. "Absolutely not."

Miranda bristles, reminded of her ex-husband. Like this brusque stranger, Michael seemed to think he was the sole spokesperson of the family.

"You wouldn't even have to know we're here," Miranda says, turning to the woman, sensing that she's far more receptive to their request. "We do this sort of thing all the time and we're always careful not to disturb anything—or anyone."

"I'm sure you are," the woman says with a faint smile. "But it's not up to me."

"Obviously not." Kent's tone is huffy. "Come on, Miranda."

"If you change your mind, we're staying at the hotel right down the street," Miranda calls over her shoulder.

She hears the man mutter, "Trust me, I won't change my mind."

"What an asshole," Kent says. "I should have known somebody who looks like that would be a close-minded asshole."

"Now that's open-minded." Miranda shakes her head at him. "You should have let me do the talking right from the start. You came on too strong. You know we have better luck when we take a more subtle approach, Kent."

"This is Lily Dale," he says stubbornly. "I figured people would be more receptive here."

"So did I." Miranda looks back over her shoulder.

The spot where the couple was standing, beneath the branches of the lilac tree, is now vacant.

Or so it appears.

There's something there, Miranda thinks, shaking her head. She's almost certain of it.

There's something there, and without the owner's permission, they're not going to be able to check it out.

"Let's try again tomorrow," she tells Kent.

"Are you kidding? He's a lost cause. There are plenty of other active spots around here, Miranda."

"I'm sure there are, but—"

"Okay, here we go," Kent says with an exaggerated sigh. "Another Miranda obsession in the making."

"I am not obsessed."

"You are always obsessed. You are an obsessive personality. You told me yourself that your therapist helped you figure that out."

That's true. Miranda makes a mental note never again to rehash her therapy sessions with Kent.

"Forget about the damn shrub, Miranda."

She sighs. "I'll try, Kent."

But it's not going to be easy.

She casts a last longing look over her shoulder.

Chapter Seven

"Thank you, Julia," Dulcie says shyly from the backseat of the car as Paine starts the engine.

"Your dad's the one who bought everything," Julia points out, turning to see Dulcie happily clutching two big plastic shopping bags bursting with new clothing.

"Thanks, Daddy," Dulcie says dutifully. "And you too, Julia. Because you're the one who helped me pick the stuff out."

"You did a good job," Paine says, glancing into the rearview mirror as he backs out of the parking spot in front of T.J. Maxx. "I never know what to buy for her."

"She's going to look adorable in those blue and white capri pants," Julia says. "Don't forget to wear the sandals we bought at Wal-Mart with them, and the blue top, too, Dulcie. It matches your eyes perfectly."

"I won't forget. But if I do, you can remind me, Julia."

Julia says nothing to that. Ever since they left Lily Dale a few hours ago to do some shopping here in Dunkirk and Fredonia, she's been trying to think of a way to back out of her promise to Paine. It isn't that she doesn't want to spend time with Dulcie, because she does—more than ever. Clearly, the child craves female affection.

But ever since those paranormal researchers waylaid Julia and Paine in the yard, he's been in a brooding, contemplative mood. Granted, he's been perfectly polite to Julia, and grateful for her input in the matter of Dulcie's wardrobe. But she can't help remembering his bitter cynicism last night, his contempt for Lily Dale and everyone in it.

The more Julia considers his earlier request for help with Dulcie, the more certain she is that she has enough headaches right now without complicating her life further. She would be better off steering clear of him until he and Dulcie leave. Hopefully, that will be soon—although Paine did spend quite a bit of time and money in the hardware department over at Wal-Mart earlier.

He bought a shower head, and some tools, and everything he'll need to repair the old screens. He even bought some furniture stripper so that Julia can refinish the old dresser in Iris's basement. He picked it up while she was in the shoe department with Dulcie, helping the little girl find sandals and sneakers.

Julia's thoughts keep drifting back to the expression that crossed Paine's face when he wheeled his full cart over to where they were, and found out Dulcie's old shoes were a full size too small.

He looked momentarily devastated—as though he had made some awful, irrevocable error.

Julia found herself wanting to pull him aside and tell him not to beat himself up over it—that he's clearly trying to be a good father. That he *is* a good father, in the ways that really count.

So Dulcie outgrew her shoes. So her part isn't even and her pigtails are lopsided and her fingernails need to be trimmed. So what?

Julia looks out the window. From here, she can glimpse the sign for the movieplex where she and Andy are going to see that Julia Roberts film tonight. Now she wishes she didn't say yes when he suggested it last night over dinner. She tells herself that's because she'd rather see the movie some other time—like on video, in the comfort of her own living room, instead of crammed into an uncomfortable seat in a crummy, no-frills cinema.

But she realizes that's not the only reason she doesn't want to go tonight.

It's Andy.

The voice is familiar, Julia realizes, tuning into the energy that sweeps over her. She can feel her grandmother with her. Telling her that she doesn't want to see Andy.

And suddenly, it isn't clear whether the reluctance is coming from within Julia herself, or fed to her by Grandma's energy.

This wouldn't be the first time Grandma has barged into her thoughts to voice an opinion. Once, when Julia was trying on sweaters down at the mall in Jamestown, she clearly felt Grandma pushing her to get the red one, when blue is more in keeping with Julia's understated style.

Grandma always went for bright colors. That incident amused Julia.

This one doesn't.

Does Grandma have something against Andy?

"No, Daddy," Dulcie calls out abruptly from the backseat as Paine stops at the intersection at the edge of the parking lot and turns the steering wheel back toward Route 60.

"No, what?" he asks, surprised.

Julia glances into the backseat and sees that Dulcie is shaking her head adamantly. "Don't turn back toward Lily Dale. There's a bookstore the other way. Remember?"

"The Book Nook," Julia says, marveling at the little girl's ability to perceive not just the slight movement of the wheel, but the direction they should be facing. She tells Paine, "I told her earlier that it's in a shopping plaza just down the road in the opposite direction."

"It's getting late, Dulcie," Paine says, looking at the digital clock on the dashboard. It's almost five. They've been shopping for several hours now. "I'm sure we'll find your book at home if we look again."

"No." Dulcie shakes her head stubbornly. "It's gone."

"It can't be gone."

"Well, it is."

Julia glances from father to daughter, noting the similarity in their suddenly tense posture and willfully set chins. She thought Dulcie was the image of Kristin, but for the first time she vividly sees Paine in her, too.

"Dulcie, that's impossible," Paine says. "The book can't be gone."

"It is. It's not in the house."

"How do you know?"

"I just do."

"That's ridiculous."

"No, it isn't. I know it's gone because—"

She breaks off.

Paine glances into the rearview mirror at his daughter's face. Julia turns her head to see Dulcie's arms folded resolutely, as they were before. But this time, her expression isn't just obstinate. Her blue eyes are troubled.

"How do you know it's gone, Dulcie?" Julia asks softly.

"I just do." Dulcie turns away, toward the window.

Paine says nothing. But he spins the steering wheel to the right, pulling out of the parking lot toward the shopping plaza.

Two minutes later, the three of them are walking into the cozy Book Nook. As before, Paine escorts Dulcie, his hand on her arm. He told Julia earlier that she's been taught to use a cane, but doesn't like to, especially in public. Apparently, there are cruel kids back home who teased her about it at some point.

Julia's heart aches at the thought of what this sweet child has been through. From her disability to the wrenching loss of her mother—and now Iris's death. It isn't fair.

I can't abandon her, Julia thinks. No, she's going to keep her word to Paine. She's going to be there for Dulcie for as long as she's in Lily Dale.

They stop just inside the front door, beside a display marked LOCAL INTEREST. Paine looks at Julia expectantly. "Do you want to . . . ?"

"The children's books are back this way," Julia says, touching Dulcie's arm. "Come on, sweetie. I'll bring you."

"I'm going to check the home-improvement section," Paine tells them, releasing his grasp on his daughter. "I'll meet you by the register in a few minutes."

Julia leads Dulcie to a wide aisle along one end of the store, where the shelves are crammed with children's books. It doesn't take long for them to find a new copy of *Where the Wild Things Are*. Julia selects several other books that she loved as a child.

The two of them sit cross-legged on the carpeted floor, and Julia reads them to Dulcie, remembering to provide plenty of description for each illustration.

"I'm going to buy these for you, Dulcie," she says when she's finished the third book.

"You will? That would be great, Julia! Will you come over and read them to me again?"

"Sure."

"When?"

Julia hesitates. "Oh, I'll be around, Dulcie. I'll pop in."

"Maybe we can go down to the beach again, too," Dulcie suggests, clutching the familiar Maurice Sendak book against her chest. "And Daddy says there's a playground at Lily Dale. Will you take me there?"

"Sure," Julia says again, this time with a smile.

"Maybe I'll come, too."

Julia turns to see Paine behind them. She realizes he must have been there for a while, watching them.

The tight expression he's worn all afternoon has eased a bit, and when he smiles at her, she senses that he's more relaxed now.

"Are you ready to hit the road, ladies?" he asks, bending to help Dulcie to her feet.

"All set." Julia spies several books in his hand. "Looks like you found some reading material yourself."

He nods, but she notices that he shifts the volumes so that the spines are turned down.

It isn't until the cashier is bagging his purchase that Julia glimpses the titles. One book is on furniture restoration. The other is a history of spiritualism.

The phone rings inside just as Pilar finishes coiling the garden hose around its metal holder beneath the open kitchen window. She hurries in to answer it, leaving behind the dripping patch of garden and the lengthening rays of sunlight reaching over the back fence. It might be Christina wanting to talk about next week. Pilar is flying to New York in a few days to meet her daughter and son-in-law for their cruise, which leaves from Manhattan and will take them down the coast and into the Caribbean.

But when she picks up the phone, it isn't Christina's voice on the other end.

"Myra!"

"Did I catch you at a bad time, Pilar? You sound breathless."

"I was outside in the garden and I hurried to catch the phone." Pilar runs water at the sink, scrubbing the soil from her hands and beneath her fingernails.

"Speaking of gardens, have you seen Iris's yard? Maybe you can go next door in your spare time and weed out the beds. They're an eyesore."

"I don't think her son-in-law would appreciate my trespassing like that, Myra."

"Oh, he isn't her son-in-law, Pilar. Didn't you know Kristin never married him? They had the little girl out of wedlock."

"Did they really?" Pilar murmurs as though it's news to her. She shakes her head as she dries her hands and pumps lavender-scented hand lotion into her palm. She begins rubbing it into both hands with a circular motion, noticing that her bare arms have turned a deeper shade of mocha in the past few hours. Thanks to her Latin blood, her skin rarely burns, but that doesn't mean she's any less likely to get more wrinkles—or melanoma. She should really have remembered to put on sunscreen. And she'll need plenty for the cruise. She makes a mental note to pick up more in town before she leaves for New York.

"Anyway, Pilar," Myra is saying, "the reason I'm calling is to tell you that I've been asking around about Katherine Biddle, and nobody knows how to get in touch with her. I hear that she's somewhere in the New York City area, but nobody knows exactly where. Maybe you should talk to Rupert again about it."

"I hate to do that. I don't want to hurt him again by implying anything. Maybe I should just drop it."

"I don't think you should, Pilar. I was walking by the Biddles' earlier and I saw a van there. They were carrying oxygen equipment into the house. Nan doesn't have much longer, Pilar. Don't you think her daughter should be at her bedside when she passes?"

"That's not up to me or you to decide, Myra."

"Well, maybe I'll have a word with Rupert if I see him tomorrow at the worship service. Or at the healing service at noon. He and Nan were going regularly, but I haven't seen them lately."

Nan's beyond healing, Pilar thinks sadly, absently pumping another dollop of pale purple lotion into her already moist hands.

She realizes what she's done and wipes it off on a paper towel, about to hang up the phone when Myra says, "I just thought of one more thing you might want to try, Pilar."

"What's that?"

"Katherine's old flame—the troublemaker I told you about earlier?"

"Yes?"

"He's a farmer. Somebody mentioned that he still lives around here—I think over in Sinclairville. Maybe he knows how to reach Katherine."

"I doubt it," Pilar says. "If Rupert and Nan went to all that trouble, sending her to boarding school to get her away from him, they probably lost touch."

"Probably. He married somebody else years ago. But you never know."

"No," Pilar muses, "you never do. You wouldn't happen to know his name, would you, Myra?"

"Can I bring you some tea, Nan?" Rupert asks, poking his head into the shadowy back bedroom and finding his wife awake.

She shakes her head, her eyes meeting his. They are huge in her sunken face, and full of fear. He finds it hard not to stare at the clear plastic tubes disappearing into her nostrils, and the oxygen equipment newly ensconced beside the bed. It surprised him, how quickly the medical van arrived, and how quickly they set things up and then left again.

Nan seems to be resting better now. She's been sleeping for the past hour, more peacefully than she has recently, though her breathing is still noisy and labored. Rupert realizes he was hoping the oxygen would work miracles. It hasn't.

"Are you sure? I bought more of that blackberry tea you used to like—the one they haven't had over at Shur-Fine lately."

"No . . . thanks . . ."

Rupert notices that the sun has set beyond the window. He goes over and reaches for the cord to lower the blinds, gazing out over the lake, where a shimmering path of waning pink sunlight glistens on the water.

A lump rises in his throat.

How many sunsets over the lake has he shared with Nan?

How many does she have left?

How many will he witness alone, longing for the woman he's loved from the moment he laid eyes on her when she was merely fifteen?

She was a beautiful girl, with thick golden hair in a pompadour high above her forehead, the way all the girls used to wear it then. She had a tiny waist, emphasized by the full skirts and broad-shouldered blouses that were so in style in those years after the war. The New Look, they called it. All the girls in their Bronx neighborhood were wearing it, but Rupert only had eyes for Nan.

He was in his early twenties, but he didn't tell her that. Not at first. There was a lot he didn't tell her. She had enough to worry about, the oldest daughter in an impoverished household with eight children and a widowed mother.

It was so easy for Rupert—who had also been born in poverty—to spoil her. He knew from experience how much any treat was appreciated when you had nothing.

Nan's face always lit up when he gave her something, even if it was the smallest of gifts—a pack of chewing gum, a bouquet of daisies. He took great pleasure in making her smile.

He still does.

Swallowing hard, Rupert lowers the white Venetian blinds and turns away from the window.

He reaches past the bottles of medication and the baby monitor on the nightstand and switches on a bedside lamp.

"I have to go out for a short time, Nan," he says reluctantly. "Will you be all right alone?"

She barely nods.

He senses her fear.

She's worried that something will happen while he's gone. To her.

Nothing will happen, Nan. You'll be here when I get back. Just as you always have been.

"I'll be right home again," he promises. "Fifteen minutes."

He considers that. How long can it possibly take? Paine Landry will most likely be grateful for the offer.

"Maybe only ten minutes," he amends, and walks swiftly to the door.

Leaning against a streetlight with a cigarette between his lips, Edward Shuttleworth feels in the back pocket of his jeans for a book of matches he's certain he picked up earlier, at the White Horse Tavern. It isn't there.

He reaches into the other back pocket, then checks both his front pockets and the one on his gray T-shirt. Nothing.

He curses softly, wondering how the hell he managed to leave the car without a light. It's parked back on Dale Drive outside the grounds, and he's not in the mood to hike all the way back through Leolyn Woods before he can smoke a freaking cigarette.

He removes the pack again from its usual place in the turned-up sleeve of his T-shirt, takes the butt from his mouth, and slides it back in with the others. Only three left. He'll stop for more on the way back to Jamestown.

Edward sighs, frustrated by the wasted trip. Twenty miles' worth of gasoline—no, forty round-trip—and all for nothing. That piece-of-shit car of his is a real gas guzzler, too. Not like that little red rental job parked a few yards away, at the curb in front of his stepmother's house.

He arrived here twenty minutes ago, just as the guy and his kid were getting out of it, loaded down with packages.

Lousy timing.

Or maybe it was lucky timing.

After all, if he had arrived a few minutes earlier, he'd have been inside when they came home.

They would have caught him off guard.

They might even have seen him.

Well, not the kid, he cracks to himself, his thin lips tilting into a smirk. She's never going to see him, or anything else, for that matter.

When he saw them go into the house, he backed up to this streetlight and stood watching, thinking they might just drop off the packages and leave again. But after they disappeared into the house, lights went on, one after another, downstairs and up.

Yeah, they're staying put for a while.

Well, he can come back tomorrow.

No, not tomorrow. Tomorrow he's working a paving job down in Bradford. It's a Sunday—time and a half.

So he'll come back Monday. With any luck, the place will be empty.

If it isn't—well, he'll figure out what to do then.

Sitting cross-legged on the floor of her room, Dulcie carefully places an oblong bead—a purple one—into the compartment with the other purple beads. She has a lot of sorting to do before she can start on that bracelet for Julia. She's decided to make a necklace, too—if she has enough beads. If she doesn't, maybe they can buy more at Wal-Mart. Unless Margaret buys them at a special store back home. Maybe the beads at Wal-Mart all have smooth edges.

She reaches for another bead and runs her fingertips over it. This one has a raised ridge around the middle.

Blue.

She can hear Daddy in the bathroom down the hall. She keeps hearing a clanking sound, like a metal tool banging against a metal pipe, and he's been swearing a lot. Sometimes he does it under his breath, but other times he does it right out loud. She hears everything anyway.

He's trying to put a shower head over the bathtub.

Another bead.

Smooth and round.

Red.

"Dulc, I have to go down to the basement to see if I can find a different wrench," Daddy calls, his feet already descending the stairs. "I'll be back in a second."

"Okay."

An oval bead.

Green.

A flat-topped bead.

Gold.

Dulcie looks up suddenly. Someone is in the room.

"Daddy?"

But it isn't him. She didn't hear his footsteps coming back up the stairs.

She didn't hear anything at all.

It's just a sense that she isn't alone.

"Who's there?"

An image flits into her mind. A face. So pretty . . .

Dulcie remembers faces. Dimly, but they're there. Stored in her memory. When Daddy reads to her or describes things to her, those memories of her distant, sighted days help her mind to see what he's seeing.

She remembers colors, too.

Now, her eyes squeezed tightly shut, she zeroes in on the picture her mind's eye has conjured.

Blue eyes . . .

Light yellow hair . . .

"Is that you?" she asks aloud, addressing the presence. "Am I seeing you?"

Yes.

The answer is little more than a whisper inside Dulcie's head.

This is how it always happens. This is what happened that night in her room, when Gram was there.

And earlier, when she was in the kitchen and Daddy and Julia were in the cellar. At first, she was certain she had heard someone knocking on the door, and a man's voice calling out. But when she found her way to the hallway, she realized someone was inside the house. By the stairs. And it wasn't a man.

It was a woman. Or a girl.

Whoever it was had stolen Dulcie's book. Whoever it was thought that was funny. The laughter echoes in Dulcie's head again—or maybe she's hearing it now. Maybe whoever is here with her in her room is still laughing about that.

Then, with a sudden chill, Dulcie realizes it isn't laughter after all.

Somebody is crying. Hard, and loud. The way Dulcie cried when Daddy told her Gram was dead.

She can see the pretty face with the light hair. And tears are coming out of those big blue eyes. They're so sad.

"What's the matter?" Dulcie asks, reaching out in front of her, waving her arms, thinking she might encounter a person.

There's nothing but emptiness.

Yet the room isn't empty.

She's still here.

Crying.

Frightened.

Dulcie can feel her fear.

Goose bumps pop up on her own bare arms below the short sleeves of the new summer top Julia helped her pick out. Dulcie hugs herself, rocking back and forth, afraid.

Not for herself.

For *her*.

Now there are words in Dulcie's head along with the pitiful wails. Words that are screamed in a shrill, panicky voice.

No!

Stop!

Help!

There is music, too. Faint at first, but it seems to grow louder with the shrieks, until it explodes in Dulcie's head along with one piercing scream . . .

Only to be silenced abruptly.

"I'm back, Dulcie," Daddy calls, and she hears his heavy footsteps on the stairs once again.

She opens her mouth, struggling to find her voice.

"Dulcie?" He sounds worried. She hears him coming down the hall, toward her room.

"I'm fine," she calls back to him.

"How's it going with the beads?" he asks, nearer now. Not muffled. She knows that he's poking his head in the doorway.

"Okay."

"I can't find the right kind of wrench. Looks like I won't be able to take a shower again tomorrow. I have to go back to Wal-Mart."

Dulcie tries to focus on what Daddy's saying. "But I thought you said we were going to go for a ride to that place where you used to live."

"Chautauqua. I did say that, didn't I?"

"You said Julia can come, too. Remember? And she said she will."

"I know. But she has to go to her church first. So you and I will find a hardware store first thing in the morning.

Then we'll come back here and get Julia and go to Chautauqua. Okay?''

"Okay."

"Finish your beads and then we'll find something to eat for dinner. Maybe I can boil some elbow macaroni. We have butter to put on it. And then it'll be bedtime. It's getting late."

Dulcie nods.

She doesn't want to go to bed.

Because sooner or later, *she's* going to come back.

It isn't that Dulcie's afraid of her.

No.

Remembering the aura of fear, and the crying, and the screams, Dulcie realizes that she's afraid *for* her.

Rummaging through the cluttered wooden pantry cupboard beside the humming refrigerator, whose door he just closed in frustration, Lincoln Reynolds can't find a thing to eat. What is all this stuff, anyway?

He surveys the shelves, stooping his six-foot-four frame to see the lower few. Canned vegetables and soup. Cereal. A box of crackers that's been open for months and has just crumbs left in the bottom. And countless cylindrical plastic bottles filled with spices and herbs—not the brands that cost four bucks in Shur-Fine, but the cheap kind that are only ninety-nine cents over at Wal-Mart.

In this household, there never has been money to spare on brand names.

Lincoln begins taking the containers down one by one, lining them up on the scarred red laminate countertop. There are three open containers of oregano. Two of cinnamon. And what the heck is cream of tartar? A waste of space, that's what it is.

What does he need all this stuff for, anyway? He never cooks, unless you count warming a can of chicken noodle soup or chili on the old gas stove. Corinne was the one who did all the cooking. She even made chicken soup and chili from scratch. Said it was cheaper that way.

Lincoln rubs his tired eyes, realizing that she's been gone almost a year and he hasn't even cleaned out the cupboards yet.

Hasn't got used to doing the grocery shopping yet, either. That's why there's nothing good to eat at nine o'clock on a Saturday night when that take-out pizza he ate for dinner has long since been replaced with an unsatisfied rumbling in the pit of his oversize stomach.

He's hungry, damn it.

He could go for some of those chocolate snack cakes Corinne used to buy him. Or some peanut butter smeared on crackers. Or a bag of chips.

Lincoln glances again at the row of spices on the countertop, then crosses the room and takes the plastic trash container from the cupboard beneath the sink. He carries it over, positions it under the counter, and with one movement, sweeps all the spices and herbs into it.

There.

Now at least he'll have room to fill the cupboard with snacks. If he can afford to buy them, the next time he makes a trip over to the supermarket in Cassadaga.

He doesn't like to go there very often. Even now, after all these years of living a few miles down the road, in Sinclairville, going into Cassadaga brings back memories he'd rather keep buried.

Memories of Kathy.

Lincoln scowls and looks down at the trash basket, now brimming with discarded plastic bottles he'll never use.

Not without a woman around the house.

Lincoln liked being married. It felt natural, having a wife.

They never were able to have a family. They wanted children. They tried to have children. But it just didn't happen. Back then, when he and Corinne were first married, things were different than they are now. Now you hear about people going to special doctors, and having tests, and going to all sorts of crazy extremes to have babies.

Back then, there were no test tubes or sperm or egg donors. At least, not that Lincoln and Corinne ever heard. Even if there had been options, they wouldn't have been able to afford fancy medical treatments. Hell, they barely would have been able to swing baby shoes and formula if they were fortunate enough to conceive a child.

But they weren't.

They simply accepted their childless state and moved on, financially unable to adopt, either. That wouldn't be the same anyway, Corinne thought. She wanted a baby of their own, or no baby at all.

It wasn't as though they had to dwell on their situation. There was always too much to keep them busy, so that they fell into bed, exhausted, every night after sundown and dragged themselves out every morning with the rooster's crow at the first light of dawn.

It wasn't easy, running the farm Lincoln had inherited from his parents. But he and Corinne managed to squeak by, as his parents had. They made a good team.

A better team than he and Kathy would have made.

That's what he's spent the last few decades trying to convince himself.

Sometimes it worked.

Sometimes it didn't.

Sometimes he wondered what would have happened if Kathy didn't leave him the way she did.

Standing in the farmhouse kitchen, still clutching the brimming garbage can against his chest, Lincoln Reynolds shakes his gray head as a familiar sense of fury seeps into him.

"Do you want popcorn?" Andy asks, his hand on Julia's elbow as they edge forward to the head of the line to buy their tickets for the movie.

"Hmm?"

"Popcorn? Do you want some?"

Julia glances up at Andy. She notes that he's still wearing his sunglasses. He does that a lot, she realizes. Wears his sunglasses inside, like a movie star who doesn't want to be recognized. For some reason, that irritates her.

She focuses on the question. Her stomach is empty— there was no time to eat after Paine and Dulcie dropped her off. She had to make several phone calls about the roof, and then her mother called back . . .

"Julia?"

"Popcorn? Sure. I'm starving."

Andy nods and steps up to the ticket window as the spot in front of it is vacated.

Julia watches him uneasily.

I shouldn't be here.

At least, that's the feeling she's had ever since Andy turned up on her porch a half hour ago—along with a palpable energy Julia recognized right away as belonging to her grandmother.

She's certain now that Grandma didn't want her to go out with Andy tonight.

So why didn't she heed the spiritual warning?

Because it was too late to come up with an excuse, once Andy was there, wearing a nice green shirt and an expectant expression.

What was I supposed to say? I've changed my mind? I suddenly have a headache?

He would know she was making excuses. His feelings would be hurt. He might never ask her out again.

So, here she is.

"Let's get the popcorn fast," Andy says, finally taking off the sunglasses and putting them into the leather case.

He hands their just-purchased tickets to the sullen-looking teenaged boy stationed at the glass door leading into the theater. There's a huge line at the snack counter, and the two girls working it seem to be moving in slow motion.

Andy checks his watch. "The movie starts in two minutes."

"It's okay. We don't have to get popcorn," Julia tells him.

"I thought you were starving."

"I seem to have lost my appetite," she says truthfully.

Andy glances quizzically at her, then shrugs and leads the way down the corridor.

Paine hears the knock on the door just as he dumps a teaspoon of salt into the pan full of water he's just set on the stove to boil.

"Somebody's here. I'll be right back, Dulcie," he tells his daughter, who is sitting at the kitchen table with her beads. She insisted on bringing them downstairs, saying she wants to finish sorting them so that she can get started tonight on the bracelet she plans to make for Julia.

"Maybe Julia is here," Dulcie says hopefully.

Paine suppresses a smile. "No, she had a date tonight, Dulcie, remember?"

"Maybe she canceled."

As he heads for the hall, Paine wonders if those two crazy ghost busters have come back to bug him.

But an old man stands on the other side of the screen door. "Paine Landry?"

There's an impatient air about him, as though he has an urgent message.

"Yeah, that's me." Paine comes to a halt in front of the door. The stranger's weathered face is handsome, topped by thick, white hair and marked, behind a pair of horn-rimmed glasses, with a pair of piercing eyes that are precisely the shade of the rocks that line the lake shore.

He looks like my father, Paine realizes. Sounds like him, too, when he speaks with a no-nonsense air.

"I'm Rupert Biddle. I used to own this house."

The first thought that flits into Paine's mind is, *So you're the one who doesn't believe in modern plumbing.*

Maybe the old man can help him make sense of the pipes in the wall compartment above the tub. Paine isn't the least bit handy, and he wasn't able to make heads or tails of the shower-head installation, appropriate wrench or not.

"Mr. Biddle. Come in." He unlatches the screen and opens the door.

"I can't stay. I only wanted to speak with you for a few minutes."

Something tells Paine this isn't a welcome-to-the-neighborhood visit, as Pilar's was.

"Would you like to come into the living room and sit down?"

"No. Thank you. I'll just say what I have to say and then get home to my wife. She's—not well."

"I'm sorry."

Rupert Biddle doesn't meet Paine's gaze. His eyes are shifting around the entrance hall, taking in the wallpaper, the decor, and probably the cobwebs that dangle from high in the corners of the crown molding.

"I won't waste your time or mine, Mr. Landry. We both know that although Iris bequeathed this house to your daughter, you are restricted by the Lily Dale bylaws from selling it to someone who isn't an Assembly member."

"I was aware of that, yes."

"Good. Of course, I'm a member of the Assembly. And I want to buy this house, Mr. Landry. Immediately, if possible."

It isn't what he says so much as the way he says it. Paine balks at the stern tone. Rupert Biddle sounds as if he's giving an order, not making an offer.

He sounds like my father, Paine thinks again.

How many times did Dad speak to Paine this way? Especially when the subject was Kristin.

I want you to get rid of her, Paine. She's bad news.

I want you to find a decent girl and settle down.

I want you to tell Kristin to have an abortion. Don't worry. I'll pay for it.

I want . . .

"I want to move in before the week is out," Rupert Biddle goes on.

"That would be impossible," Paine tells him, even as he wonders what the hell it is he's doing.

This man could be the answer to his fondest wish. He's offering to take the house off Paine's hands and spare him the trouble of selling it.

No.

He isn't offering.

He's telling Paine what to do.

Just as Dad tried to tell Paine what to do.

If Paine had listened to him, he wouldn't have Dulcie.

"I fully intend to sell the house to a member of the

Assembly at some point, Mr. Biddle,'' Paine says. ''Probably soon. But not this week.''

''Why not? You're not planning on staying, so why stick around here?''

''My daughter and I have to go through Iris's things. There will be mementos Dulcie will want to keep, of her grandmother, and of her mother.''

''Kristin. Yes. I'm sorry about that,'' Rupert says belatedly. Is his sympathy genuine, or a ploy to get his way? ''And I'm sorry about your more recent loss as well. Iris.''

Paine nods stiffly. ''My daughter is very upset about it.''

''I'm sure she is.'' Rupert takes a deep breath. ''It can't be helping that she's being made to stay here, in this house, Mr. Landry. The sooner you pack things up and leave Lily Dale, the sooner you can both begin to heal.''

Paine finds himself fighting back a grin despite the grim subject. ''Mr. Biddle, you just told me you want the house back as soon as possible. Obviously, your reasons for wanting us out of here have nothing to do with my daughter's ability to recover from her grief.''

''I won't argue with you there.'' Rupert Biddle's stone-cold eyes meet Paine's. ''This was my house for more than forty years. I never should have sold it to Iris. Now that she's gone, and you have no use for it, I want it back. Please, Mr. Landry.''

The last three words feel tacked on. As though the man is pulling out all stops to get what he wants, even if it means trying to appear civil.

Something about him rubs Paine the wrong way.

He's too much like Paine's father.

Feeling like a stubborn little boy, Paine lifts his chin, looks pointedly at the door, telling Rupert Biddle, ''I'm not interested in discussing this with you now. Maybe in a week or two, when I've had the chance to go through some of Iris's things—''

"It will be too late then," Rupert cuts in.

Startled, Paine shifts his gaze to the old man. There is an unsettling air of desperation about him. Why the urgency?

"Look, Mr. Biddle, I've got a little girl in there who's up way past her bedtime. I've got to feed her and get her settled. I can't talk to you about this now. Please don't push me."

Rupert Biddle looks at him for a long moment, as though he wants to say something else.

But he doesn't.

He simply nods and walks to the door.

Paine follows and holds it open for him.

The old man steps out onto the porch and turns around again.

Paine expects him to make one last appeal, but he doesn't. His gray gaze drifts past Paine, coming to rest on something behind him.

Paine realizes that he's staring thoughtfully at the stairway. Rather, at the foot of the stairs, a spot just between the two newel posts.

Then, wearing a cryptic expression, Rupert Biddle gives the slightest nod before turning and walking off into the night.

"Don't be afraid. We won't hurt you." Kent's low, gentle voice drifts to Miranda and she turns to see him aiming his infrared night scope in the direction of a low-hanging willow tree in Leolyn Woods.

It's close to midnight and the streets of the tiny nineteenth-century village are deserted, aside from the occasional sound of car tires crunching in the distance. They chose this spot more because they were intrigued by the ominous painted wooden sign nearby—DO NOT ENTER LEOLYN WOODS DURING WINDY OR STORMY WEATHER—than because they were drawn by any particular sense of psychic activity here. Tonight the weather is clear, though an occasional breeze rustles the branches overhead.

They've been out here almost an hour, and so far, Miranda's equipment has registered nothing. But now, apparently, Kent is on to something.

"What's going on over there, Kent?" Miranda asks quietly, picking her way toward him through the damp undergrowth, careful to step past the tripod where the digital video camera is taping.

He doesn't reply, just motions for her to come closer. As she reaches his side, a tone alerts her to glance down at the Trifield meter in her hand. The needle is swaying wildly to the right, meaning it has sensed some kind of magnetic field ahead of them.

Miranda leans over Kent's shoulder and looks at the screen of his scope. "What have you got?"

"Ecto," he replies. "It's really nice."

Yes. On the scope, Miranda can clearly see the ectoplasm drifting a few feet above the ground, beneath the willow's sweeping fronds. Invisible with the naked eye, the shapeless blob drifts in front of them. Sometimes a face takes shape in ectoplasm, but not this time.

"We won't hurt you," Kent calls out again. He's a big believer in reassuring the spirits.

Miranda is more apt to go quietly about her work, still uncertain, after all these years of working together, whether Kent's attempts at verbal communication serve more as a distraction than the intended encouragement.

Miranda steps back to the camera and looks down at the screen. The ectoplasm is visible there, too. As she gazes at it, a silver orb shoots into the frame, crossing it and then disappearing.

"We've got some orbs, too," Miranda calls softly to Kent as another glowing ring of light darts onto the screen. This one is brighter, meaning the energy is stronger.

She reaches into the pocket of her khaki vest, the kind professional photographers wear. Her small, whirring audiotape recorder is nearing the end of the cassette. Swiftly, she pops it out and replaces it with a fresh tape, then presses RECORD again.

She and Kent have never heard ghostly sounds live, with their own ears. But occasionally, when they play back the audiotapes after a session, they hear something.

Sometimes it's a voice—fleeting, but with discernable words or phrases.

They've heard other sounds, too. Footsteps, creaking, snatches of music, even the whir of invisible appliances. Once, investigating a haunted oceanfront cemetery on Cape Cod, they clearly heard the clanging bell of a ship on the recording, though there had been no such sound during the investigation. They later learned that years ago, a ferry dock was located not far from the cemetery.

Staring down at the camera, watching the orbs flit playfully among the trees, Miranda finds herself thinking of this afternoon's encounter with the residents of the house on Summer Street. Wistfully, she wonders what the equipment would be registering at this moment if she and Kent were standing in that yard, beside the lilac tree.

The owner was clearly resistant to letting them find out.

Some people are like that. And Miranda is usually capable of accepting their refusal to allow her and Kent to conduct an investigation on private property.

But this time, she doesn't want to let go so easily.

You're an obsessive personality, Miranda.

Well, so what?

Damn Kent, anyway. Her therapist, too.

She isn't going to leave Lily Dale without finding out what's going on by that tree.

With or without the owner's permission.

Chapter Eight

Coming to a stop at the edge of rectangular Bestor Plaza at the heart of Chautauqua Institution, Paine feels the years falling away.

"Are you okay, Daddy?" Dulcie asks, beside him.

"I'm fine . . ." He clears his throat, hard. "It's just the way I remembered it. My God. Nothing here has changed in ten years."

"Nothing here has changed in more than a hundred years, Paine."

He glances at Julia to see her smiling. She's right about that. Time has truly stood still here. Aside from bicycles, virtually the only traffic in the grounds is pedestrian, with visitors' cars relegated to the massive parking lot across the highway from the gate.

Here, three blocks in from the entrance along a brick-paved avenue, is an old-fashioned colonnade lined with shops and offices. The green is dotted with towering old trees, green park benches, and turn-of-the-century street lamps with circular white globes. A post office lies straight ahead, with a bookstore on the basement level, and a four-story wooden-frame hotel looms directly behind them. Bright impatiens spill over in beds and planters, and neatly clipped hedges rim a tall granite monument.

The lone hint that the setting is closer to the turn of the twenty-first century than the twentieth is in the modern clothing worn by the people who stroll along the wide, tree-sheltered brick paths or sprawl on benches that dot the manicured grass. Here and there, artists stand intently at easels, and the sound of somebody playing piano scales drifts faintly from one of the small wooden cabinlike practice studios back by the gate.

"Should we take a walk down to the lake?" Julia asks, turning her gaze ahead to the maze of narrow streets beyond the bookstore, where the terrain slopes downhill toward the waterfront. There is no sun today; nor is there rain. The sky is a milky backdrop overhead, and there is no breeze to stir the leafy branches overhead.

"Yes, let's go down there!" Dulcie says eagerly, bouncing a little in the bright white canvas sneakers she and Julia picked out yesterday. "Maybe there are shells here."

"There are," Paine murmurs, remembering. Shells. The small beach. Kristin.

He sighs and looks around, trying to blink away the images that haunt him.

Like Lily Dale, this gated Victorian town is perched at the edge of a picturesque lake, nestled in the rolling western New York countryside. Bow-shaped Chautauqua Lake is far larger than Cassadaga Lake, and its namesake community is far larger than Lily Dale. It's also much more upscale. Wealthy residents of Pittsburgh and Cleveland and New

York City summer here, sailing and golfing by day, enjoying nightly concerts in the vast amphitheater and soaking up the cultural atmosphere. In addition to the summer theater, Chautauqua has its own ballet and opera companies, its own symphony.

The charming streets are crowded with gingerbread cottages and wood-frame boardinghouses, many in the distinctive Chautauqua architecture that stacks three and sometimes four balconies on top of each other.

Paine remembers that he was curious about the balconies when he first arrived here, and somebody told him that in this part of the country, summer is fleeting. Locals want to spend as much time as possible outdoors. Walking through the streets of Chautauqua on summer nights, even terribly humid or rainy nights, Paine soon grew used to the sounds that floated from nearly every porch: creaking gliders, laughter and chatter, radios tuned to ball games or chamber music.

"You know what, Dulcie?" Julia's voice snaps Paine out of his reverie. "There's a miniature replica of the Holy Land down by the lake. You'll be able to feel the hills and walk over them and I'll describe it to you."

Palestine Park. Paine recalls it well. Recalls walking down there with Kristin after dark one summer night, when the sun was sinking low in the west and there was a soft breeze off the water and the air was scented with roses. They sat on a bench watching two little girls romp over the low knolls of the reproduced Holy Land, laughing when the children snuck Tootsie Rolls out of their grandmother's pockets as she dozed on a nearby bench.

Gradually, Paine recalls, the sun set and the little girls and their grandmother left. The full moon hung plump and low in the starry sky over the lake and the crickets began to hum, and Paine put his arms around Kristin, pulled her close, and kissed her for the first time.

"I want to see the Holy Land. Let's go. Come on, Daddy!"

Paine looks down at Dulcie, eagerly tugging his arm.

He clears his throat, but when he speaks his words are hoarse anyway. "You two can go down there. I'm going to take a walk over to the residence hall where I lived when I was in the conservatory theater here."

He can feel Julia's eyes on him, studying him. "Come on, Dulcie. We'll catch up with your dad in a little while."

He half expects Dulcie to protest, but she gives a happy little skip, lets go of Paine and clutches Julia's arm, and chirps, "Okay, let's go."

I should have known better than to think she might miss me, Paine thinks, watching the two of them walk away after agreeing to meet him by the amphitheater in half an hour.

Of course Dulcie is thrilled to have Julia all to herself. Julia is all she talked about all morning. The whole drive from Lily Dale to Fredonia, the entire time the two of them were eating breakfast over at the Bob Evans restaurant on Route 60; all the while they were in Wal-Mart looking for a new wrench, and then on the drive back to Lily Dale.

Julia this, and Julia that. More Julia than knock, knock jokes, for which he should have been grateful, but . . .

Paine wonders again if he should be discouraging his daughter and Julia from spending time together, rather than encouraging it. But he can't seem to help himself. It's a pleasure—a relief, really—to have some female help with Dulcie now that they're so far from home and Margaret is away.

That isn't the only reason you asked Julia to stick around, he reminds himself. But that other reason was ridiculous. Here, in the broad light of day, far from Iris's creaky old house and the book on spiritualism he read late into the night, Paine can't quite believe that he almost believed Dulcie was communicating with ghosts—or that he needs Julia around to help her deal with it.

No, all Julia can help her with is picking out clothes and braiding her hair, which she did the moment she showed up to meet them after her worship service earlier. She asked Paine if he minded, first.

Of course he didn't. He had just moments earlier been studying Dulcie's hair that was still matted—he had forgotten to comb it before it dried after her morning bath—and wondering what he was going to do about it. Having Julia step in with a brush and deftly weaving fingers was a godsend.

Paine sighs and turns away from Bestor Plaza. He doesn't want to think about Julia now.

He doesn't want to think about Kristin, either, but she's here.

I don't believe in ghosts, Paine thinks. Not in the traditional sense. Not even after what he's read so far, which was almost—*almost*—convincing in the wee hours of the night.

But he has to admit, Kristin's ghost lives on in his mind, especially here, and now. Everywhere he turns, he sees her.

Less than five minutes later, he's standing in front of the three-story pale yellow wooden dormitory where he lived that summer.

Was it really only a decade ago?

He turns, looking down the leafy street for the private house where Kristin stayed, renting a room from the elderly owners. It, too, looks very much the same, although it has been painted a green instead of the peeling white paint he remembers.

She didn't want to live in a dorm. Kristin needed her own space. She had been raised as an only child, her half brother never having lived with her, and she couldn't stand the thought of sharing a closet, a room, a bathroom. Paine, too, is an only child. But he was in Chautauqua courtesy of loans and scholarships and part-time jobs. His parents couldn't afford the astronomical cost of renting private quarters. Anson could. Only the best for his baby girl. That's what he liked to say—as Kristin reminded Paine more than once.

Would she have married me if I had money?

This isn't the first time Paine has wondered about that. And it isn't the first time he's concluded that Kristin's issues with marriage went beyond money. Beyond him, even. She was a free spirit.

Even then, he sensed it. She was wild and carefree—ready for anything. She loved to go out dancing at a dive bar down the highway. She liked to drink, and she smoked long menthol cigarettes, and she probably did coke more than the one or two times he witnessed. She slept with him on their first date—though it wasn't even a date. It was later that first night he kissed her by the water. He told himself then—and countless times after—that she wasn't a slut. That she slept with him because she was already falling for him. That they were destined to be together.

They used to meet under the sprawling branches of an oak tree midway between the two houses.

Paine looks for it now, as he stands in the street where they once lived, but he can't find it.

It's gone.

So something—one thing—has changed here.

Considering how Paine's life has been altered since he was a carefree young theater student, it seems fitting that the grassy spot where the massive old tree once stood bears no evidence that it was ever there at all.

"Oh, my God. Is that you, Paine?"

Startled to hear his name, he spins around to see a tall man gaping at him from the steps of the residence hall. At first glance, he is unfamiliar, an ungainly stranger whose sharp features are framed by a goatee and a receding hairline.

Then he draws closer and something in the man's eyes triggers a surge of memories in Paine. In a rush he sees the man's face as it once was, with a full head of hair and none on the chin.

"Stan!" Paine exclaims, delighted. "You're still here?"

"Still here," Stan Mundy, Paine's former acting instructor, strides forward to shake Paine's hand. "I'm on the faculty at Juilliard now, but this is still where I spend my summers."

"That's wonderful. I can't believe it's you!"

"Likewise. Not that you don't look exactly the same, but . . . what are you doing back here, Paine? When you left here you said you were headed back to California for good. The East Coast didn't agree with you."

"Still doesn't, really," Paine says, though that isn't entirely true. He can do without the chilly gray weather, and without the spook-hunters who populate Lily Dale, but he can't help feeling a little more at home now . . . especially here, in Chautauqua.

"What are you doing these days?"

Paine tells him, briefly, about the television commercial acting class he teaches in L.A., and the minor success he's had in commercials and industrials. He leaves out the catering and classifieds jobs. He also leaves out any mention of Dulcie. Or Kristin.

"So you're just back here visiting, then?" Stan asks.

Paine nods, not about to go into the subject of Iris's death and the house in Lily Dale, either. "Strolling down memory lane, basically. You know, I'm surprised you remember me."

"Believe it or not, I never forget a student. It's not as though I'm a physics professor, droning on in a lecture hall that seats three hundred, Paine. I get to know my students. I pull their rawest emotions from them.''

"That, you do," Paine says, remembering what it was like to work with Stan. The man is a genius. Flamboyant, over-the-top, a pain in the ass, yes. But a genius, too.

"You were particularly memorable, Paine. Not only did I have a little crush on you—which I am long since over, by the way—but I still commend myself for the performance I got out of you. *Man of La Mancha.* Your work in that show was phenomenal. Of course, I had no idea at the time that you and Christine were—''

"It was Kristin," Paine cuts in, feeling as though a fist has clamped around his heart at Stan's mention of her name. Even the wrong name. "Not Christine."

"Ah, Kristin. That's right. She was a beautiful girl. A decent actress, too, although in my opinion she wouldn't have gotten in here if her father hadn't pulled strings with the admissions office. I have to admit, now that you and I are long past our instructor-student relationship, that I was somewhat jealous of her back then, once I realized—I mean, I wasn't entirely convinced you were straight until I saw the two of you together.''

Paine offers a tight smile. In his line of work, he's accustomed to homosexual men assuming he's one of them—and to fending off advances. And of course he knew back then that Stan was interested in him. Kristin used to tease him about it.

"I was sad to hear about her death a few summers back," Stan goes on. "It was in all the local papers. You did know about that, didn't you?" he adds as an afterthought. "She drowned.''

Paine manages a nod and a single word. "Yes."

The newspapers never mentioned him. Nor did her obituary in the *Evening Observer* list his name. Only Dulcie's,

Iris's, and Edward's. After all, Paine wasn't married to her. Technically, he isn't Kristin's survivor. Technically, the half brother she never saw is.

"It was a tragic accident," Stan says. "She apparently fell off a boat into Lake Erie."

No. It was Cassadaga Lake. But Paine doesn't bother to correct Stan. He tries to swallow the bitterness; tries not to think about what happened even as he realizes the name of the lake isn't the only detail that escaped Stan when he read the printed accounts of Kristin's death. Apparently, the man never noticed that her daughter's last name is the same as Paine's, and is unaware that Paine and Kristin continued their relationship after leaving Chautauqua.

Paine isn't about to tell him.

"Listen—how long are you staying in the area, Paine?" Stan asks, discarding the subject of Kristin's tragic death as casually as someone shedding one shirt and trying on another.

"I'm not sure, Stan."

"Because I'd love it if you'd sit in on a group session tomorrow or Tuesday. You might find it interesting. And one of our faculty members has been delayed in Europe on a movie set, so we're a bit short-handed."

"You want me to help you teach?"

"Not per se. But you're welcome to poke your head in if you like."

"That might be fun," Paine says slowly. It would get him away from Lily Dale for a few hours. Maybe Julia will stay with Dulcie.

"Terrific." Stan tells him when and where to find the session, then heads off down the street, sashaying a bit.

Paine watches him absently.

Once again, he's seeing Kristin.

Hearing Stan's words.

You did know that she drowned, didn't you?

It was a tragic accident.

Was it?

He and Julia haven't discussed the topic since Friday night.

But she, like Paine, thinks there might have been more to Kristin's death.

Oh, Christ. Maybe I should just turn the damned house over to Rupert Biddle, get the hell out of here tomorrow with Dulcie, and forget all about it.

But if he does that, will it really be over? Will he be able to sever all ties with Lily Dale—with Kristin's death? Will he ever be able to forget? To stop wondering?

He knows the answer.

So.

Is that the real reason he turned down Rupert Biddle's offer?

Not just because the old man rubbed him the wrong way, or reminds him of his domineering father . . .

But because Iris's house is Paine's last remaining tangible tie to Kristin. His last chance to find out what really happened to her.

And he's not going to leave Lily Dale until he knows the truth.

Pilar presses the brake, drawing to a stop in front of the listing roadside mailbox that bears the name REYNOLDS.

Sinclairville is small enough that there are only two listings under that fairly common name in the phone book, both with full first names.

This is it, Pilar thinks, looking ahead down a long, open gravel lane toward the beige farmhouse with brown shutters. Even from here, across a broad expanse of field, she can see that the place sorely needs a paint job, and the straggly flower beds beneath the porch could stand to be weeded. The air of shabby desolation seems suited to the gray landscape.

Why am I doing this?

This isn't the first time since she left home that the thought has crossed Pilar's mind. Each time, she has answered it with less conviction.

She's here because of Nan. She owes it to her friend to track down her daughter and make sure they are able to see each other one last time, before it's too late. Rupert doesn't realize how little time Nan has left. But he—and Katherine, too—will be grateful to Pilar later.

What if Lincoln Reynolds has no idea how to reach Katherine?

That's fairly likely, Pilar supposes. All she knows is that Rupert sent his daughter away to boarding school to get her away from this man. But Katherine has been back to the area since. Surely she looked up her first love, now that so many years have passed. Myra said Lincoln married someone else.

Yet the place doesn't seem to have a woman's touch about it, Pilar notices as she drives down the lane toward the house. There are window boxes beneath the windows, but they're bare of flowers. Despite the lack of a breeze, the clothesline in the side yard is strung with a man's white sleeveless undershirts and boxers and socks, and a few large pairs of jeans and denim work shirts.

Pilar pulls to a stop behind a dusty blue pickup truck. It occurs to her that she should probably have phoned first— or instead. But her instinct, upon finding Lincoln Reynolds listed in the white pages, was to see him face-to-face. Maybe in part it's her own curiosity. She wants to see the man Rupert Biddle despised so much that he sent his only child to live somewhere else just to keep her away from him.

"Can I help you with something?"

Pilar looks up with a start. A large man is standing beside her open window, clutching an empty plastic laundry basket. He's well over six feet tall and barrel-chested, with a stomach that protrudes beneath a plain gray T-shirt and sticks out above the waistband of his worn Levi's.

She finds her voice. "Are you Lincoln Reynolds?"

"That's me."

He must have once been handsome, she thinks, studying his weathered, sunburnt face. He has nice brown eyes and thick gray hair with the kind of sideburns that keep coming in and out of fashion. Pilar suspects his have been there since his youth, rather than a conscious effort to be hip. Everything about the man says hick farmer.

Is that why Rupert didn't like him?

"My name is Pilar Velazquez. I live over in Lily Dale."

"Lily Dale?"

She watches him carefully, expecting to see recognition, but not the stark emotion that flits into his eyes. Is he thinking of Katherine?

She removes the keys from the ignition and makes a move to open her door. He does it for her, setting the plastic laundry basket on the ground and muttering something.

"Pardon?" Pilar says, getting out of the car.

"Said I might as well leave the laundry awhile longer. It's been there two days already. Got soaked yesterday morning and I had to let it dry all over again."

She smiles faintly. "It's supposed to rain tonight, too. And it's not going to stop until later in the day tomorrow. Don't leave it too long."

He shrugs. "It'll dry again."

Curious about his marital status, she looks down at his hand. There's no wedding band on his ring finger, but a circular pale mark on his tanned knuckle shows that there was one there recently.

He catches her looking. "My wife died about a year ago," he says simply. "I just took off the ring a few weeks back. Thought it was time."

"I'm so sorry."

"I didn't ever like wearing it anyway. But she thought I should. So I did."

Pilar nods. She opens her mouth to tell him what she's doing here, but he beats her to it, posing that very question in his straightforward way.

"I wondered if you could spare a few minutes to talk to me, Mr. Reynolds. I thought you might have some information that I need."

"If it's about farming, I can probably help you. Otherwise, you've probably come to the wrong place. I don't know much about anything else."

She smiles. He's likeably charming. Again, she wonders why Rupert loathed him so much. Maybe there's more to Lincoln Reynolds than meets the eye—or maybe he was a different person way back when he was dating the Biddles' daughter.

"I actually wanted to ask you about someone you used to know in Lily Dale, Mr. Reynolds," Pilar says.

A shadow crosses his face.

He knows, she thinks. *He knows I'm going to ask about Katherine.*

Still, his tone is light when he says, "Is that so? Then you must be going back quite a few years, ma'am. I haven't known anyone over in that area for a long, long time. Haven't even been there in years."

"It was a long time ago," she agrees, wishing she had never come. Here's a widower who hasn't even shed his wedding ring long enough to erase its mark on his finger, and a total stranger comes poking around, dredging up his romantic past, asking him about an old flame he'd probably rather forget.

Unless he's still in touch with her.

That hope—and the thought of Nan Biddle wasting away in that dim back bedroom—allows Pilar to push forward with her query. "I heard you used to date a girl named Katherine Biddle, Mr. Reynolds."

"Yup." He smiles, but there's no mirth in it. "How did I know you were going to say that? Maybe I'm psychic, like Kathy's old man said he was."

Lincoln's phrasing and his tone indicate to Pilar that he's skeptical about Rupert's mediumship. Okay, well, perhaps that's how he alienated Rupert.

"How did you hear about me and Kathy, if you don't mind my asking?"

"One of the Lily Dale old-timers mentioned it."

"Then it sure as hell wasn't Rupert or Nan. I wouldn't be surprised if they've never mentioned my name again."

"No, it wasn't them." Pilar hesitates. "I take it you didn't get along with Katherine's parents?"

Lincoln Reynolds doesn't mince words. "They hated me. Especially her old man. They're the reason I lost Kathy."

"Why?"

"Because I was dirt poor. Always was, and pretty likely always would be. But Kathy didn't care. There I was, getting shipped off to Vietnam, with her promising to wait for me so we could get married the second I get back. I even gave her an engagement ring. I was too broke to buy one, but my mom had an antique platinum and diamond ring she had inherited from her aunt. It was the one nice piece of jewelry she ever had. I never even saw her wear it—she was afraid she'd lose it, she said. But she offered it to me to give to Kathy. She said we could have it reset, and that's what I told Kathy when I gave it to her. But she was thrilled with the ring just the way it was. Told me she'd never take it off. Next thing I know, I'm sitting in some stinking jungle reading a Dear John letter from her.''

Pilar doesn't know what to say, other than to repeat her earlier murmured apology.

"I'm sorry, too," Lincoln tells her, sending a small chunk of rock skittering across the dirt driveway with the toe of his work boot.

"Did she send the ring back to you?"

"No. She didn't mention it at all, in the letter. When I got home, years later, I asked my mother if she wanted me to try and get the ring back from Kathy. It was worth a lot of money—and we never had any. But she said to forget about it. She knew I would never give it to anyone else, and that it would only bring back bad memories.''

"I'm surprised Katherine didn't return the ring to your family.''

"So am I. I loved her. She said she loved me. I believed her when she said she'd wait for me. And you know what?''

"What?''

"I still think she really did love me. A girl can't fake that. When we were together, she acted the same way Corinne did, later, when I met her—Corinne is my wife. *Was,*'' he amends, looking down at his boots.

Pilar's heart aches for this man. But she can't lose sight of why she's here. She needs to get to the point, and get out of here, leaving him to his laundry and his losses.

"Mr. Reynolds, do you know where I can find Katherine Biddle?''

He looks up, clearly surprised. "Do I know where you

can find her? Hell, no. You think she ever got in touch with me again?''

''She never did?''

He shakes his head. ''I wrote to her a bunch of times. The letters always came back, stamped *Refused*. One of my buddies who stayed around here told me he heard Kathy's parents sent her off to some big fancy boarding school in New York City. When I got back from 'Nam, I went over there to Lily Dale, to talk to them. Figured maybe I could get them to at least tell me where she was, so I could talk to her. I guess by that time I knew it was a lost cause, me and her. But I needed—what do they call it? Closure.'' He snorts. ''Closure. Her old man gave me closure, all right. He closed the door in my face.''

''And the only reason he didn't like you was that you were poor?'' Pilar finds that hard to believe. Rupert isn't the warmest man in the world, but his standoffishness never struck her as snobbery.

''Yup. He thought I wasn't good enough for her. My family was dirt poor. He thought his daughter deserved better than a local yokel farmer. Told me that to my face more than once. Kathy told me not to let it bother me. Said she'd do what she pleased. But once I was gone, they got to her.''

''So she's never tried to see you, when she comes back from New York to visit Nan and Rupert? Not even after all these years?''

''Nah.'' He shakes his head. ''Would you? Look around you. This is all I ever had to offer her. It wasn't enough. Not for her.''

Again, Pilar finds herself at a loss for words in the face of his stark pain.

''It was different with Corinne. Her parents were farmers, too, over in Cherry Creek. She never expected anything more than I could give her. Lost her in an accident last July.

We were driving on a back road late at night. We never went out at night. I told her I was too tired, but she wanted to go visit her sister. I fell asleep at the wheel and rammed the car into a tree. I walked away without a scratch."

"My God," Pilar murmurs, suddenly struck by an image. Looking at Lincoln Reynolds, she sees the figure of a woman standing beside him. She has tired eyes, and blond hair with dark roots, pulled back in a ponytail. She's holding something toward him. It's a white box with writing on it. Pilar strains to see what it is.

"What's the matter?" Lincoln asks, watching Pilar. He turns to look where she's looking. There's nothing there but the empty laundry basket.

"I'm just wondering ... do you like those chocolate Hostess cupcakes, Mr. Reynolds? The kind with the squiggly white lines in the frosting?"

"How'd you know that?" He frowns. "I was just thinking about those last night. My wife used to buy them for me."

"I thought so." Pilar closes her eyes, tuned in to the energy of Corinne Reynolds.

"What are you doing? Are you okay?"

Puzzled, Pilar looks at him again. "I'm a medium, Mr. Reynolds." Catching the expression on his face, she quickly says, "Before you interrupt, can I just pass something along to you? It doesn't make sense to me, but ... anyway, your wife says you shouldn't have thrown away the cinnamon. The other stuff was okay to toss, but not the cinnamon. Do you understand that?"

His jaw drops.

"She's saying that you could probably manage to make yourself cinnamon toast, at least." Pilar smiles. "My guess is that she's joking around with you, Mr. Reynolds. I get the impression you're not much of a cook?"

He shakes his head, speechless.

Pilar watches the image of his wife fade away as her energy evaporates simultaneously.

"She's still with you, Mr. Reynolds," she says softly.

"I . . . I don't know what to say." He pauses. "I never believed in that stuff."

"Do you believe it now?"

"I don't know what to think."

There's a long silence. *It's peaceful here,* Pilar thinks, looking around. Nothing around but the farmhouse and the barn and a couple of old sheds, and acres of farmland. Not another house in sight.

"Do you want to come in?" the man asks suddenly, as though he should have thought of it before. "I don't have any . . . lemonade, or anything . . . but if you want . . ."

She shakes her head at his awkward invitation, thinking about what Christina and Tom would say about that. They're always saying she has to be careful now that she's alone. They wouldn't approve of her going into an isolated house with a stranger, especially when she didn't bother to tell a soul where she's gone this afternoon.

Not that there's anything the least bit sinister about Lincoln Reynolds, but you never know. She still isn't clear on exactly what happened between him and Katherine in the past. For all she knows, he was abusive to the girl and that's the reason Rupert went to such extremes to keep them apart.

Lincoln looks disappointed. "Are you sure you don't want to stay?"

"I should go. I have some appointments scheduled this afternoon." She jangles her keys, turning back toward the car door.

"Can I ask you something before you leave?"

"Sure." Pilar pauses with her hand on the door handle.

"Why are you trying to get in touch with Kathy?"

"Because her mother is seriously ill. Terminally ill. I thought Katherine might want to know."

He doesn't seem particularly disturbed by that news. There is clearly no love lost between him and Nan, whether or not she was as instrumental to the breakup as her husband was.

"Don't Rupert and Nan know where she is, then?" Lincoln asks.

"It's complicated," Pilar says, not wanting to go into it. "I thought maybe I could find her through you. Nobody else in Lily Dale seems to know exactly where she is."

"Do me a favor, Ms. Velazquez. If you find Kathy, tell her where I am. Tell her I wouldn't mind hearing from her."

Pilar gets into her car and gives him a little wave. "I'll do that."

She can see Lincoln Reynolds in her rearview mirror, standing absolutely still as he watches her drive away.

Julia runs the brush through Dulcie's long hair, crimped from the braids she just removed. "Do you want me to put it up in a bun, sweetie?"

"Whatever you want," Dulcie tells her, sitting absolutely still beside Julia on the bed.

It was her idea to have Julia do her hair again, while Paine works on the shower head in the bathroom. They can hear him clanking away on the pipes down the hall. Julia wonders why he's so determined to install it if he's only going to sell the house anyway, but she hasn't asked him that.

He was pretty quiet on the ride home from Chautauqua just now. Dulcie did most of the talking, asking Julia to come back to their house with them so that she could read her the storybooks they bought yesterday at the Book Nook.

Only now that they're home, she claims she doesn't feel like reading.

"Can you stay for dinner, Julia?" Dulcie asks as Julia gently untangles a snarled strand of silky blond hair.

"I don't think so, sweetie."

"Do you have another date with that guy, Andy?"

Andy. He hasn't entered Julia's mind all afternoon. Now the thought of him fills her with apprehension.

Their date last night went smoothly despite her misgivings. But she could feel her grandmother's presence all night; could sense her displeasure that Julia went ahead with dating Andy after all. Why? What is it about him that Grandma doesn't like?

It isn't that Julia's head over heels for him—but maybe she can be, if she lets herself.

If Grandma lets me.

It's hard enough for a young, single medium to have a love life around here without input from a nagging grandmother on the Other Side.

"No, Dulcie, I don't have a date with Andy tonight," Julia says. He's giving a workshop all day. She planned to go to it until Paine and Dulcie invited her to Chautauqua. She knows Andy doesn't mind that she's not there. He says he's more comfortable in front of an audience full of strangers, that seeing familiar faces is a distraction.

"Good," Dulcie says. "Then you can stay for dinner."

"Actually, I can't. I have to be at a message service in a little while, and I have an appointment scheduled after that." It's for a group reading—a trio of neighbors from Erie, all of them widows. They do this several times each season, and Julia has managed to connect with all of their husbands at one time or another.

"But you're coming tomorrow, right?" Dulcie asks. "When Daddy goes back to Chautauqua?"

"I'll be here," Julia says. She was a bit taken aback when Paine asked her to baby-sit. She really should be working. But she only has appointments scheduled in the morning, and he isn't leaving until after lunch. Besides, there really isn't anybody else he can ask.

"Maybe I'll have your bracelet finished by then," Dulcie says. "I worked on it for a little while this morning."

Julia smiles.

For a few seconds, the room is silent.

Then Julia hears the scream.

The burst of music.

They aren't alone.

Julia stiffens, the brush poised at the bottom of a strand of Dulcie's hair.

She can feel the familiar presence seeping into the room, this time more powerful than ever before.

Who are you? Julia demands silently, willing herself to receive the energy. *Why are you here?*

It comes to her in a rush.

But, as often happens, she doesn't get the whole thing. Only a fragment. The beginning and the ending.

Just enough to realize that the name starts with a *K* sound and ends with an *N*.

"Katherine. . . ."

Seated beside the bed, Rupert looks up sharply from the *Sunday Times*. Nan's head is turned toward the open window. He suddenly notices a strong fragrance in the room— flowers wafting in on the breeze. Something must be in bloom right outside the window, Rupert thinks vaguely as he rises and touches Nan's hand gently.

"It's okay, Nan," he says, unable to see from this angle

whether his wife's eyes are open, but certain she's not awake. "Shhh."

"Katherine . . ." Nan's head thrashes right and left.

He was right. She's asleep.

"Shhh," he says again. "It's only a nightmare. It isn't real. Wake up, darling. Everything is all right."

Nan's eyes open, drift closed again, open. This time they stay focused widely on Rupert's face.

"It's all right," he repeats in a soothing voice. "I'm here. I'm with you."

"Katherine." This time, it's a sigh.

"What about her, Nan?"

"Need to . . . see her . . ."

"She's not here, darling."

Nan's eyes are already fluttering closed again.

Rupert strokes the turban above her forehead, where her blond hair once was. She had the most beautiful hair. It was like sunlight. Even after it mixed with gray and she took to having it dyed at the beauty parlor. Somehow, the stylist managed to recapture her natural color.

Nan was so proud of her hair. Of her looks. The first time Rupert saw her, out on the stoop in front of the building on Stratford Avenue, he was captivated by her air of sophistication. Everything about her was classy. Only later did he find out that she made her own clothes—some of them from scraps—hand-stitching the seams in the bedroom she shared with three younger sisters and a colicky infant brother.

Rupert wonders whatever became of the rest of them—Nan's siblings, and her mother. Nothing much, he'd be willing to bet. Nan never regretted the choice her mother had forced her to make. She and Rupert have had a good life together.

And it's not over yet.

He's got to call his broker first thing on Monday morning and see about cashing out some of his investments. Maybe Paine Landry will budge if he offers a cash bonus . . . .

Nan's hands make a restless motion on top of the extra blanket Rupert threw over her a while ago.

Rupert stares at the repetitive movement. It looks as if she were holding a shovel. Digging.

"Are you in your garden, darling?" he whispers softly, stroking her head. "Is that where you are?"

The reply is a single word, faintly whispered.

"Katherine."

Miranda is one of the last to leave the auditorium.

The workshop on past-life regression was utterly fascinating. Given her background in parapsychology, she has seen such presentations before. But never has she seen a speaker so captivating as Andrew Doyle.

Kent would have loved this, she thinks, as she finally rises from her seat and heads toward the exit, where a few people still linger, speaking with Mr. Doyle. But something Kent ate for breakfast didn't agree with him, and he decided to go back to the hotel and sleep for a while.

Hopefully he's feeling better. But just in case he isn't, Miranda decides to stop and buy a can of ginger ale to take back to him.

She's a few steps from the cluster of people by the door when suddenly the crowd breaks up and several people depart at once, leaving Andrew Doyle standing alone.

Miranda smiles at him. "That was incredible," she says, on her way out.

"I'm glad it moved you," he replies easily.

She notices—not for the first time since she first glimpsed him on stage—that he's handsome. Not traditionally so, with his russet hair and almost elfin, upturned nose, but there's a definite appeal. And judging by the way his Irish green eyes are twinkling at Miranda, the appreciation is mutual.

If Kent were here, he'd tell me to run away from this guy as fast as I can, she notes. But Kent worries too much. And his protective big-brother act is getting awfully tiresome. He never approves of anyone Miranda finds attractive.

"I've seen other presenters explore the topic," Miranda tells Andrew Doyle, who seems to want to hear more from her, judging by the way he's not hurrying away. "But not the way you have. Obviously, you're passionate about your work."

"I'm passionate about a lot of things," is his provocative response. He holds out his hand. "You already know who I am. How about making things even?"

"I'm Miranda Cleary."

"What brings you to Lily Dale?"

She finds herself telling him the whole story—about Kent and the New England Ghost Society and the book they're planning to write. She goes into detail about their successful investigation the night before, and about the lilac tree and the house on Summer Street whose owner won't give them permission to access the grounds.

He listens intently to all of it. Which sets him apart from Michael right away, because Michael was never interested in her work. But then, this man is in the field of parapsychology, too.

He's too good to be true, Miranda finds herself thinking.

His emerald gaze fixed on her, Andrew asks, "Does anyone call you Mandy?"

"No."

"That's hard to believe." He leans closer to her, unmistakably flirting.

Her heart skips a beat. "Why . . . why is that?" she asks him. It's been a long time since a man has talked to her in this way.

"Because you happen to look like a Mandy," he says, reaching into his pocket and putting on his sunglasses. Now she can't see his eyes. "And it happens to rhyme with Andy . . . which is what you can call me."

"Then I guess you can feel free to call me Mandy."

"In that case . . . how about joining me for a bite to eat, Mandy?"

Miranda shoves aside an irritating echo of Kent's voice saying, "The trouble with you, Miranda, is that you can't spot trouble when it's looking you in the face."

She looks at Andy Doyle and smiles. "I'd love to join you for a bite to eat."

As the lady's presence fades from the room, Dulcie reaches for Julia, finding and clasping her arm.

"What is it, Dulcie?" Julia asks, her voice shaking. "What's the matter?"

"It's . . . her. You know she was here too, don't you? You got all quiet when she came, and you stopped brushing my hair. That's why, isn't it?"

For a moment Julia doesn't say anything. When she does, Dulcie notices that her voice sounds strange. But not surprised.

"You can feel her, Dulcie?"

"Yes. And I can see her. Can you?"

"You can *see* her?"

"You can't?"

"No." Julia puts both her hands on Dulcie's shoulders

and turns her around so that they're facing each other. Dulcie can feel Julia looking at her. "What did you see, Dulcie? Describe her."

"But . . . Julia . . . if you can't see her, how do you know she's here?"

"I feel her. And . . . I hear her."

"Her voice?"

"I hear her voice. And music."

"I heard it too! Music. And a scream."

Dulcie hears Julia letting out a long breath.

Then she asks, "She's been here before, Dulcie?"

Dulcie nods. "A few times. Up here in my room, and down by the bottom of the stairs, too."

"That's where I've felt her, too. But I can't see her."

"She talks to me. She took my book."

"*Where the Wild Things Are*?"

"Yes. She laughed about it, like it was a joke. But it wasn't funny. Why do you think she did that?"

"Because she wanted to get your attention. *Our* attention. They do that sometimes—move things around. Flicker lights. Change television stations—but, Dulcie, what does she look like?" Julia presses again, in a non-Julia-like voice.

"She isn't very clear, but I can tell she has blond hair. And her eyes are blue."

"How do you know? Are you sure?"

"I remember colors, Julia. I remember faces."

"Do you remember your mommy's face?"

Dulcie feels as if she's going to cry, thinking about that. "No. I try. I should remember what she looked like, shouldn't I, Julia? But I can't."

"You were so small when you last saw her . . ."

"I want to remember her, Julia. But I can never see her when I think about her. Unless . . ." Dulcie takes a deep breath. "Do you think the lady who keeps coming is my mom?"

Julia holds Dulcie close, stroking her hair. She's quiet for a long time before she says, "Yes, Dulcie. I think it might be her."

Chapter Nine

Early on Monday morning, Pilar drives through a warm rain down to Fredonia to buy sunscreen and several other items she'll need for her upcoming cruise. She stops at the Upper Crust bakery on the college town's bustling Main Street before heading back to Lily Dale. There, she buys more chocolate volcanos and a half dozen cinnamon rolls.

The chocolate volcanos—all but the one Pilar plans to eat after lunch—are for Iris's little granddaughter. She hasn't seen the little girl since the day she and her dad arrived, but she's heard them coming and going through the open screens. It's time she paid another neighborly visit.

As for the enormous, decadent sticky swirls laced with cinnamon and icing—those are for Rupert and Nan.

She drives straight to their place upon returning to Lily Dale, dismissing the notion that she should have called first. Rupert might still be smarting from the other night and tell her not to come over. If she simply shows up on the doorstep with a bakery box, he can hardly turn her away, can he?

Well, yes.

If anyone can, it's straight-talking Rupert.

But he doesn't. When he opens the door to find Pilar standing there in the drizzle, he almost looks happy to see her.

"Hi, Rupert. I brought you a little treat from town." Pilar thrusts the white string-tied bakery box into his hands. "They're cinnamon rolls from the Upper Crust. How is Nan?"

He purses his lips, as though he'd rather not say.

She waits, sympathetic, beneath her dripping umbrella. A car splashes by in the street behind her.

"She's asleep," Rupert tells Pilar. "Been sleeping all morning."

"Has she eaten anything?"

"I brought her yogurt for breakfast. She said she didn't want it. I put it back in the refrigerator. Maybe she'll have it later."

"Maybe she will."

But she won't.

Pilar pushes away an image of Raul those last days of his life. His organs shutting down, no longer requiring food. But Pilar's instinct was to keep plying him with nourishment, bringing spoonfuls of hot broth to his dry lips, frustrated when he resisted. Finally a hospice worker saw what was going on and gently convinced her to stop trying to feed her husband, explaining that Raul no longer had the stamina for digestion, that Pilar's efforts were putting unnecessary strain on his failing body. That was one of the most difficult moments in a week that was filled with them.

"Is she breathing any easier now that you've got the

oxygen for her?'' Pilar asks Rupert, expertly ignoring her flood of memories.

"How did you know about that?"

"I guess I heard it from somebody," she murmurs vaguely, wishing she hadn't brought it up. The last thing she wants is to have him worry about the neighbors' gossip. That sort of thing goes with the territory in a small town, but Rupert and Nan have always kept the locals at arm's length—perhaps for that very reason.

"Rupert, I was down at Kmart earlier, and I picked up a few new paperback romances for Nan. Can I stay and read to her a bit when she wakes up?"

"I'd like that," he says unexpectedly, glancing at his watch. "I do have an errand to run, and I didn't want to leave her alone while she was sleeping. She might be frightened if she wakes up and finds that I've left, and she might need something . . ."

"I'll stay with her," Pilar quickly assures him, biting back the impulse to tell him that he should have called her. "You go ahead. Take your time. Get some fresh air. I don't have any readings scheduled until after lunch today."

"I don't need fresh air," he says sharply, holding the door wide open so that she can step inside the still, dim house. All the shades are drawn. *He probably figures there's no sense in opening them on a dreary morning.*

How many days, dreary or not, did Pilar spend in Raul's sickroom with the curtains closed? Later, the hospice workers would come and go, opening things up, letting in light and air. But somehow, Pilar found that unlit cocoon comforting; there, she could hold the world at bay—along, perhaps, with the inevitable.

But there were times, even then, when she couldn't deny what was happening. Especially as Raul seemed less and less aware of her presence. Often, his gaze was focused on something over her shoulder, or in a far corner of the room. Occasionally, he seemed to be talking to an invisible person. As a medium, Pilar sensed that there was spirit energy in the room, but she wasn't able to connect with it. Whoever it was, was there for Raul.

When she told one of the hospice workers about it, the man gave a knowing nod. He told Pilar that the dying often interact with unseen visitors, seeming to be in the presence of someone who has passed on. He asked whether Raul mentioned any names.

He didn't.

Not until the last hours of his life. Pilar remembers how that day was the same and yet different, somehow, than the ones before. Something changed just before Raul died, something she couldn't put her finger on. But when she called the hospice worker and mentioned that something seemed to be changing in some subtle way, she was told, again, that this was something he had seen many times before. He said the families of dying people often reported the sense that some subtle, barely perceptible transition was taking place.

He gently cautioned Pilar that it might mean Raul's time might be drawing near.

She never left his side that morning, not even for a moment.

She simply stayed with him, watched him, memorizing everything about his face, so that she could keep him with her always. And she listened, too. Listened as his breathing grew shallow and erratic. As he muttered to that same presence that she could feel but couldn't see or hear. At last, Raul referred to the person by name.

Bobby.

Bobby, Pilar knew, was an old friend of her husband's. They were inseparable all their lives, but Pilar never had the chance to meet Bobby. He was killed in a terrible car accident just weeks before Pilar's path crossed Raul's for the first time. He always liked to say that Bobby sent her to him because he knew Raul would be terribly lonely without him.

Pilar found solace in the fact that Bobby was there to accompany Raul on his final journey, comforted that he didn't have to make it alone.

"There's something I have to go out and do," Rupert is telling her, bending to trade his suede moccasin-style slippers for a pair of shoes that are neatly aligned on the mat beside the door. "I won't be long."

She nods, suppressing her own memories, her heart aching for the old man. She closes her dripping umbrella, opens the door again, and props it on the step just outside.

Rupert needs help. If she hadn't happened to come along now, he'd have sat here waiting for his wife to awaken. He'd have to feel guilty, leaving her alone, worrying about her the whole time he's out.

Pilar is glad for the opportunity to be here for him, and for Nan.

But she's leaving town. Who will help while she's gone? Will Nan even last until she gets back?

He has no idea, she thinks, watching Rupert stride across the small foyer to a rolltop desk nearby, where he was obviously working before she arrived. *It's so easy to fool yourself when you're in his position.*

So easy to convince yourself that the worst isn't really about to happen. That time isn't running out. That you still have weeks, even months with your loved one.

Rupert sets the bakery box on the leather swivel chair and quickly straightens the papers on the desk.

Idly watching him, Pilar sees a yellow legal pad scribbled with columns of numbers, and beside it, what looks like a bank statement. She realizes, as he lifts the pad from the desk and folds the paper, sticking it between the pages, that he seems to be trying to conceal it from her. He must think she's as bad as the rest of the local snoops.

"I'll take those cinnamon rolls into the kitchen for you," she offers tactfully, wanting to leave him alone with what are obviously financial documents.

As she crosses to the chair and picks up the box, Rupert reaches up to bring down the top on the desk. In that moment, Pilar feels a rush of energy electrifying the air around her.

She hears Rupert curse and glimpses something falling off the desk, landing at her feet.

Then the energy is gone, and Rupert is quickly bending to retrieve the item.

But not before Pilar sees that it's a worn black leather-bound book stamped *Addresses* in gold lettering.

"I can feel his energy pulling back now, Mrs. Mackowinski," Julia says, opening her eyes and looking at the attractive, middle-aged brunette sitting across from her. "Is there anything you want to ask before we end this session?"

"Just . . . do you think Mikey's okay where he is?" the woman asks tearfully, blotting at her mascara-stained eyes with a soggy tissue.

"I feel like he wants you to know that he's just fine," Julia says softly, offering her a fresh tissue from the box at her elbow. "He's assured you that he's with your husband's parents, and that he was with your family in spirit when his sister got married. His bringing up the caterer's mix-up with the cake was his way of validating his presence there for you."

"I know." The woman smiles through her tears. "I believed that he was there even before you told me that. I felt him that day. I thought he would be laughing about the cake being chocolate instead of the vanilla his sister had ordered. He always loved chocolate.''

Julia smiles back at her.

"Thank you so much.'' Mrs. Mackowinski rises and smooths her rumpled rayon floral-print romper, picking up her oversize brown leather pocketbook from the floor beside the chair. "It's been hell since we lost Mikey. This is the first time I've felt close to him since the accident.''

"I'm glad.''

"I want to come back here, and bring my husband and daughter. They didn't want to come today . . . but when I tell them what you've said, they'll believe he was here. They'll want to come back with me and hear it for themselves.''

Julia nods, but cautions, "I can't guarantee your son will come through again, Mrs. Mackowinski.''

"Oh, he will.''

"Well, I'll be glad to do a group reading for the three of you as long as you keep in mind that I can't promise you anything. Just be sure to schedule the session in advance, because I tend to get busier as the summer goes on.''

"I will.'' The woman reaches out and stuffs several bills into the basket on a nearby table marked *Donations*. "I want you to know that I'll always be grateful to you. This has been just amazing.''

As she leaves, Julia watches her, taking a moment to bask in the knowledge that she has helped to ease a mother's grief. This is the main reason she remains committed to mediumship.

Still seated in her armchair, listening to the sound of Mrs. Mackowinski's footsteps on the front steps outside her window, Julia finds herself thinking again about the incident in Dulcie's bedroom yesterday. The apprehension she's managed to hold at bay throughout the busy morning returns full force.

Was it Kristin's troubled spirit she sensed in the house?

The garbled sound she heard when she asked for the spirit's identity would seem to indicate that. She got the *K* and *N* sounds clearly.

But she didn't feel her friend's energy in the room. Not the way she should. There was something darker attached to the energy, and no sense of the familiarity she would expect if she were receiving the energy of someone who had been so dear to her.

That doesn't mean it wasn't Kristin. Spirits are unpredictable.

Yet there are other possibilities. Perhaps the K-N sound didn't represent a name, but some other word, a part of some message the spirit wanted to pass on.

There's no way of knowing.

Dulcie mentioned seeing ''the lady'' several times in the stair hall, around the foot of the steps. That's where Julia most strongly sensed her presence, too. And that's where Kristin saw whatever it was that she saw that Halloween night—which could explain why her spirit, if it is indeed her spirit, is drawn to that spot.

Eager to share all of this with another medium—somebody she trusts—Julia left a message for Lorraine this morning. So far, her friend hasn't called back. Perhaps tonight, after the message service at the Medium's League building, she'll be able to speak privately with Lorraine or with another medium who might be able to shed light on the situation.

You can always call Andy, she reminds herself. She hasn't spoken to him since he brought her home Saturday night, depositing her on her doorstep with a kiss. She didn't bother to invite him inside.

If Andy sensed that she was more withdrawn than usual,

he didn't comment. In fact, he seemed a bit distanced himself. He was probably preoccupied with the workshop, which would be a full five-hour session instead of his usual three.

In any case, if it weren't for the nagging doubt placed in her mind because of her grandmother's intervention from the Other Side, Julia would probably confide in Andy about the presence in Iris's house. But, having learned to trust her instincts and the feelings given to her by those who have crossed over, something tells Julia that won't be a good idea.

Julia rises and lifts the lace curtain that covers the window in the small front parlor she uses to conduct business. Peering out into the street, she sees that the drizzle that fell all morning has stopped. But the sky remains cloudy. The house is usually fairly cool, but today warm, muggy air has filtered through the screens, leaving Julia's hair damp around her forehead.

It's time to drag the window fans down from the attic, she thinks, closing the parlor door behind her.

Deciding she needs a cold drink before getting ready to head over to Paine's, she walks into the kitchen. There, in the portion of the room that juts out from the back of the house with its own section of roof, an array of strategically positioned buckets remind her of the imminent home-improvement project. The contractor she consulted over the weekend initially said he couldn't begin work for a few weeks, but called back this morning to say that another job has been postponed. He can start tomorrow.

It's not a moment too soon, either. Last night, her bedroom ceiling leaked so badly she couldn't sleep, thanks to the steady plopping of water droplets into buckets.

Julia wonders how distracting the roof project will be. She can't expect to conduct readings in the parlor with workmen overhead, pounding nails and using power tools.

Well, hopefully the job won't last long. In the meantime, she'll have plenty of time to spend with Dulcie.

And to connect again with the entity—whether it's Kristin who's trying to communicate, or another troubled soul. One thing is certain: the spirit's persistence and the urgent undercurrent Julia has repeatedly associated with its presence indicates a strong need to get a message across. Somebody is trying to tell her—or Dulcie—something.

After pouring herself a glass of iced tea from the plastic pitcher in the fridge in the kitchen, Julia picks up the telephone and dials Andy's cell phone number. The least she can do is see how his workshop went yesterday, and thank him again for Saturday evening.

Just when she thinks the call is going to go into voice mail, he picks up, sounding surprised to hear from her.

"I just thought I'd call and say hello," she says casually. "How did it go yesterday?"

"How did what go?"

"The workshop . . . what else?"

"Oh, that . . . pretty well, thanks. You know, I saw you leaving the message service last night, but you didn't see me. I was across Melrose Park."

"No, I didn't see you." Julia sips her iced tea.

"I called your name but you didn't hear."

Is he making a statement? Or is there accusation in his tone?

Julia frowns, suddenly on edge. "No, I didn't hear you. I guess I had a lot on my mind. I'm in the middle of this roofing project . . ."

And there's a troubled entity in Iris's house, and it scares me. And maybe you're starting to scare me, too.

But of course, that's ridiculous.

Just because Andy was acquainted with Kristin, and was here in Lily Dale when she died . . .

Well, that doesn't mean Julia should even consider that he might have had anything to do with her death.

Of course not!

She's surprised at where her thoughts have led her. This is ridiculous. She shoves away the unwelcome notion her imagination has conjured, trying to focus on the conversation.

Andy asks her about the roofers, and whether she'll be attending the Medium's League message circle scheduled for eight tonight in the auditorium.

"I'll be there," she says. Monday message circles are part of the weekly rhythm of life in Lily Dale during the summer season.

"So will I. Maybe we can go out afterward for coffee, Julia."

She barely allows herself to hesitate before saying, "Sure, that would be nice."

Yet, even as she speaks, she again senses her grandmother's presence, discerning a faint aura of disapproval. It isn't as strong now as it was Saturday night, but it's tangible enough to cast a shadow of trepidation over her end of the conversation.

Frustrated, she traces a cold bead of condensation on the outside of her glass, swirling it with her fingertip, listening to his voice making small talk without hearing what he's saying.

Then she's jarred out of her reverie by a single word.

Kristin.

"What did you say, Andy?"

"I said, I bumped into Kristin's boyfriend and her daughter this morning at the cafeteria. They stopped there for breakfast. They were on their way to Tops to get groceries. That guy doesn't like me."

"What makes you say that?"

"I can feel it, Julia. Maybe he's just jealous, but . . ." Andy trails off, the implication clear.

"That's ridiculous." Her voice sounds higher than usual, and nervous, even to her own ears. "He's not jealous. Why would he be jealous?"

"Forget I said anything. But—look, he doesn't like me. I'm positive about that."

He's probably right. Paine wouldn't like Andy. He wouldn't like anyone in the field of paranormal research. Look at how he reacted to the two parapsychologists who requested permission for access to his backyard.

"It's just that he's a skeptic, Andy," Julia explains. "He doesn't even trust me, because I'm a medium. And when it comes to Dulcie—"

She breaks off, thinking better of telling Andy that Dulcie is spiritually gifted.

"When it comes to Dulcie, what?"

"Never mind. I'll see you tonight, okay?"

There's a long pause. Then Andy says, "Okay."

But I'm almost positive he knows what I was going to say about Dulcie, Julia thinks. And maybe she's just jumpy and irrational, but that bothers her.

"Can Julia take me down to the playground while you're gone, Daddy?"

Paine considers Dulcie's question as he munches a potato chip from the open bag on the counter. "I guess so," he agrees. "If the weather clears."

"It's still raining, isn't it? I can hear it."

"Yup, it's still raining." He sighs, thinking of California sunshine as he pulls a five-pound package of sugar from the paper grocery bag at his feet.

Five pounds?

What was he thinking? He just plopped it into the cart at the Tops supermarket when Dulcie reminded him that he needs it for his coffee. But he could have bought a smaller container of it. They would have to be in Lily Dale for a year for him to use up all this sugar.

And they won't be here for a year, that's for damn sure. Just as soon as they can clean out this house . . .

Just as soon as I figure out what the hell happened to Kristin . . .

They'll go home.

He shoves the package of sugar into an overhead cupboard, not bothering to pour it into the canister Iris used. That would be too permanent.

"Does it always rain here?" Dulcie wants to know.

"Looks that way, doesn't it?"

"Here, Daddy." Dulcie hands him two cans she's taken from the bag she's been emptying. "It's Campbell's soup, right?"

He smiles. "How did you know?"

"The size of the cans. Way too small for peaches. Way too tall for tuna. And you don't buy anything else in cans."

"I don't?"

She's right. He doesn't.

He really should learn how to cook. Little girls can't live on chicken noodle soup and tuna fish sandwiches alone.

She's gotten along fine so far on that diet, he reminds himself.

But he can't help thinking about how he grew up. His mother cooked dinner every night. Meat loaf, roasted chicken, mashed potatoes with homemade gravy, the kind you made from drippings and a little of that flour-water thickener his mother would let him shake up in a jar, when he was in the mood to help her. He usually only ventured into the kitchen when she was cooking if he thought he could filch a snack to hold him over when she wasn't looking.

When his father came home from work, the three of them sat down in the dining room and ate their meal, Paine's parents chatting about their days, and Paine chowing down and then wishing he could be excused to get back outside and play with his friends on the block. But his mother always made him stay put until the meal was over and they had coffee and dessert. She said it was good manners.

What about Dulcie's manners? Paine wonders, glancing at his daughter. She doesn't have a mother to teach her about things like that. It's all up to him.

It would have been, anyway. He can't quite picture Kristin presiding over a family dinner table, much less cooking a meal. With her, you were lucky if she remembered to call and order takeout. Even that was Paine's department.

Dulcie stops rattling bags and goes still, her head tilted. "Somebody's here, Daddy. At the door."

Of course she's right. There's a knock as soon as she finishes speaking.

Paine groans inwardly when he finds Rupert Biddle standing on the porch.

"We need to talk," the older man says, not wasting time on a greeting.

"I told you the other day, I'm not interested in selling you the house yet," Paine says.

"I know what you said the other day. But you didn't hear me out." The old man's piercing gray eyes bore into his. "May I please come in?"

Paine hesitates, considering.

Then, with a sigh of resignation, he opens the door.

* * *

"Kent, can I borrow the keys to the Jeep? I want to go out to get some lunch," Miranda says, poking her head into his room.

"They're on the dresser."

"Do you want me to bring back anything for you?"

"Don't even talk about food to me," he says with a groan.

"How about more ginger ale, then?" She crosses the room to the dresser, where the keys are surrounded by a litter of fallen pastel petals from the balding wildflowers in the glass.

"I still haven't finished the can you brought me this morning." Kent's face is as white as the pillowcase behind his head.

"That'll teach you to order biscuits with sausage gravy in a greasy spoon," she says, shaking her head. "You should have stuck with plain old waffles, like I did."

"You're talking about food," he groans, his arms folded across his stomach. "Stop."

"Kent, you've been sick for twenty-four hours now. I'm worried about you."

"Don't be. It's obviously food poisoning."

"I know, but if you aren't better by this afternoon, I think I should take you to a doctor."

"Fine. But leave me alone for now. I just want to sleep."

Miranda stops by the bed and pats his head. "Okay. I won't be gone long."

"Is it still raining out there?"

"Yup. We wouldn't have been able to do an investigation last night anyway."

"What did you do with yourself yesterday while I was here, barfing my guts out?"

"Went to that workshop on past-life regression. Wound up chatting with the presenter. We had dinner afterward at this nice Italian restaurant about fifteen minutes away from here. I'll show you where it is when you're better. They had amazing lasagna.''

"There she goes again," Kent says, mustering the strength to roll his eyes.

"Sorry."

"Get out of here before I throw up on you."

"I'll see you later," Miranda says, closing the door behind her and heading down the corridor.

Kent is so wrapped up in being sick that he didn't bat an eye at the news that she had dinner with someone.

Good.

She isn't in the mood for the usual Kent interrogation. After all, she's just had one date with Andy.

One date . . . enough to know that he could be dangerous.

Charming Andy is one of those men she finds too damn hard to resist. No wonder she found her way into his arms when they went for a walk by the lake after dinner.

He was kissing her, really knocking her socks off, when he suddenly broke off, looking disturbed.

When she asked him what was wrong, he told her that he had just spotted someone across the park—a woman he's been dating.

Naturally, disappointment coursed through Miranda, followed swiftly by elation when Andy said not to worry—that it wasn't a serious thing.

Then he asked her if she's free for lunch today . . .

Which is where she's headed now.

Andy said it would be better if they met somewhere off the grounds. He doesn't want to chance running into that woman he's been seeing.

"I'm going to cool it with her," he said, "but I just haven't had a chance to talk to her about it yet. We've both been busy."

"It's okay," Miranda told him, against her better judgment. "It'll be good to get away from Lily Dale for a little while. I'm going a little stir-crazy here."

"That's understandable." He gave her directions to the restaurant, saying she should meet him there.

As she hurries toward Kent's Jeep, smoothing her suitcase-rumpled flowered rayon summer dress over her broad hips, she tells herself that she's only having lunch with Andy out of boredom. She certainly isn't thinking anything can possibly come of it. Neither of them is in Lily Dale permanently, and even if they were . . .

Miranda has learned the hard way not to fall for a man like him. For all she knows, he has no intention of dumping his girlfriend.

But even if he is about to become available, Miranda's insecurities have her wondering . . .

Why on earth would someone like Andy want to be with me?

Lincoln always breaks for lunch early.

When you have breakfast at dawn and spend the morning working in the field, you're famished long before the noon hour. When Corinne was alive, she cooked their main meal to be served midday. She had a Crock-Pot, and used it to make pot roasts, spaghetti sauce with meatballs—you name it. She'd just dump the ingredients in when they got up, and by late morning, the house was filled with the mouthwatering aroma of a hot meal. For supper, they usually had lighter fare—soup and sandwiches, maybe an omelet.

Today, it isn't quite eleven o'clock when Lincoln heads from the barn to the house and opens a can of ravioli in the kitchen. He dumps the contents into a chipped bowl and puts it into the microwave, not bothering to cover it with a paper towel, the way Corinne liked him to do. That way, she said, she didn't have to scrub out the microwave all the time.

Lincoln doesn't mind the food spatters that are building up inside. He figures sooner or later, he'll clean the thing. That, or get a new one. This one's pretty ancient, like the rest of their appliances. Money isn't as low as it used to be, since he got the life insurance settlement. Besides, there's always the Sears charge. Corinne didn't like to use it unless it was absolutely necessary. But Lincoln figures one of these days, he'll drive down to Jamestown and replace the microwave and the toaster and the Mr. Coffee that drips so slowly he's taken to starting it before he takes his shower in the mornings.

As he waits for the three minutes to pass before his ravioli will be ready, he uses the small bathroom off the kitchen, then scrubs his filthy hands. There's no towel to dry them on—he has yet to fold the clean laundry heaped in bushels in the dining room. But at least he got it off the line before the rain started falling.

Thinking of the laundry reminds Lincoln of yesterday's unexpected visitor. Pilar.

Why did she have to barge in and stir up old memories?

It's not as if he doesn't think about Kathy every damn day of his life as it is. But having that woman here talking about it has left Lincoln feeling raw. He didn't sleep well last night; kept thinking about Kathy, and Rupert, and Nan, and all that happened so many years ago.

Back in the kitchen, he spreads three slices of Wonder Bread with a thick layer of margarine. He gobbles the bread and his ravioli in less than five minutes, seated at the wobbly wooden table in the corner by the window.

Corinne liked to call it the "breakfast nook," but that was just wishful thinking. The rooms in this old farmhouse his grandfather built are rectangular and unadorned by nooks or alcoves or even moldings, unlike some of those fancy gingerbread houses over in Lily Dale.

On only two occasions was Lincoln ever inside the house where Kathy grew up. The first was when she brought him home to meet her parents after they had been dating for a few months.

Lincoln's mother—who adored Kathy—bought him a new shirt for the occasion: a short-sleeved cotton one with buttons and a collar. She said he could wear it again a month later, for his high-school graduation. She even ironed his least-worn pair of jeans before he dressed for the dinner at the Biddles, and assured him that he looked fit to meet President Nixon.

But not fit to meet Rupert Biddle, he thinks now, stung even three-plus decades later by Kathy's father's obvious and immediate rejection. Though his wife at least attempted to be civil, if stiff, Rupert was cold to Lincoln from the start. Lincoln could feel the man's assessing gaze traveling over him from head to toe; could see in his eyes that he didn't approve. As they all picked at the elaborate dinner Nan prepared, only Kathy chattered—nervously, almost desperately, trying to find common ground between her father and Lincoln.

There was none.

What did a farmer's son who had never been more than thirty miles away from Sinclairville have in common with a middle-aged, well-known, well-off medium?

Absolutely nothing.

Before the evening was over, as Kathy helped her mother clear the table, Rupert managed to pull Lincoln aside and warn him not to get too attached to his daughter.

"She has big plans for her life," the man said.

Plans that don't include you.

He left that part unspoken, but the meaning was clear.

"She's not going to be around Lily Dale much longer," Rupert told him.

"I know she'll be going to college in less than two years," Lincoln replied. "I would never want to take that away from her."

"No, you won't be taking that away from her," Rupert said, almost in a warning tone. "But I'm not talking about college. Katherine may be finishing her high-school education elsewhere. The local school system isn't challenging enough for her. She deserves the best education we can give her. The best of everything."

"Yes, she does."

"Then we understand each other," Rupert said evenly.

Lincoln nodded, his gut twisting at what Kathy's father implied.

When he later questioned Kathy about her leaving Lily Dale before she went away to college, she brushed it off, telling him her father was always talking about sending her to a fancy boarding school. Her parents were both from New York City, she said, and even after all these years in Lily Dale, they were a bit snobbish about certain things.

Anyway, Kathy assured Lincoln that she had no intention of leaving Lily Dale. Not now, and not ever. She said she wanted to go to college at the state university over in Fredonia. They had an excellent school of music, and that was what she wanted to study. She loved to play the guitar, especially folk music.

Simon and Garfunkel.

They were her favorites. She could play all of their music, but Lincoln always requested the same song.

"Kathy's Song," it was called.

There hasn't been a rainy night since when, lying in bed listening to the drops hitting the roof overhead, Lincoln doesn't hear her sweet voice, singing the soulful lyrics for his ears alone.

I hear the drizzle of the rain . . . falling like a memory . . .

"I wouldn't be able to stand being more than a few miles away from you, Lincoln," she once whispered into his ear, resting her head on his shoulder. "I won't ever leave you."

No. But he left her.

Right after his eighteenth birthday, his number came up in the birthday lottery. He was shipped to Vietnam. The only thing that kept him going in that hellish jungle was the knowledge that Kathy would marry him when he returned.

After he got the letter saying she was leaving him, he didn't care whether he lived or died. He took foolish risks and was awarded a silver star medal. When his time was up he remained on active duty.

Finally, the war was wound to a close and he made his way home to Sinclairville, to the farm where his parents still toiled. There, he began to heal. And there, he met Corinne, at a barn dance one clear May evening when the sky was filled with stars.

He never forgot Kathy Biddle.

But he never stopped trying.

Glancing one more time at Nan to make sure she's asleep, Pilar rises from the chair beside the bed, her heart pounding.

As she moves through the room, she vaguely notices a faint, familiar scent wafting in the air. She assumes it's from something blooming outside the window . . . but the window is closed, and the scent seems to permeate the room from within.

That's odd, Pilar thinks, standing still and looking around for a source to the floral perfume. There's nothing she can see—not potpourri, or cut flowers, or cologne.

Stop wasting time. Rupert might be home any minute, she reminds herself. She hurriedly leaves the back bedroom and makes her way toward the front of the house. He didn't say where he was going, but he did tell her he wouldn't be long.

There's a wide window in the front door and the desk is in full view of it. If he comes home now, he'll spot her and realize what she's up to before he even steps inside.

He left on foot, which means he's stayed right here in Lily Dale.

Pilar steps out onto the porch, vaguely noticing that the rain has stopped at last. She glances in either direction down the street to see if he's coming. He isn't visible from here, but that doesn't mean he isn't nearby. You can't see very far down the narrow street, and several trees obstruct the view.

She'll have to move fast. There might not be another opportunity.

Scurrying to the desk, she tugs on the rolltop, half expecting to find it locked.

To her surprise, it isn't.

She lifts the top and rummages swiftly but carefully through the contents, quickly locating the address book.

Is Katherine married? What's her last name?

Pilar has no way of knowing.

She quickly flips the pages to the *B*s, assuming the Biddles' daughter might be listed under her maiden name.

She isn't.

Pilar will have to go through the book page by page until she finds it.

Luckily, there aren't many entries on each alphabetized page, and many of them are for area professionals: doctors, accountants, insurance agencies. It seems Rupert and Nan limit their friends and acquaintances to those Pilar recognizes as being from Lily Dale. Though they traveled frequently before Nan became ill, they don't seem to have been visiting far-flung relatives or friends. Nobody's address is outside the local area . . .

Until Pilar comes to the first one on the *J* page.

Katherine Jergins.

This is it, she realizes. It has to be. The name is followed by a New York address. The town is Garden City.

That's on Long Island. Pilar is almost certain of it.

There's a phone number, too.

I can pick up the phone and call her right now, Pilar tells herself. She's tempted to do it, but something is stopping her.

She can almost hear Raul's voice warning her not to be impulsive—not to stick her nose where it doesn't belong. Yet this time, it's more intuition than Pilar actually making contact with his energy. Her husband was a cautious person, that's all. He always told her not to make hasty decisions.

Anyway, now that she has actually found the information, she can call any time. It doesn't have to be now. Or even today.

Or maybe Rupert has already called her, she thinks hopefully. *Maybe she'll be here any day.*

Pilar finds a pen and a scrap of paper in the desk and hastily scribbles Katherine's name and address. She tucks it carefully into the pocket of her khaki slacks and puts the address book back where she found it, closing the desk lid.

Then she returns to Nan's bedside to watch her sleep. The floral essence still wafts in the back bedroom. Remembering Nan's love of gardening and her fondness for aromatic flowers, Pilar crosses to the window. Pressing her face against the glass, she peers out, certain she'll find a garden in full bloom. There's nothing but a patch of well-watered grass and a maple sapling ringed by red geraniums and impatiens, and yellow marigolds.

Rupert must have planted those, Pilar thinks. Nan never liked marigolds, and she doesn't care for bright, primary colors when it comes to flowers. She loves soft shades, mostly pinks and purples, and fragrant old-fashioned perennials. Nan doesn't bother with scent-free, lackluster annuals—like impatiens—that come in black plastic cell packs at the supermarket and Kmart.

As she turns away from the window, sniffing, Pilar notices that the aroma is distinctly familiar. Which flower smells like this? She can't place the scent—nor the source for it in the room.

Maybe Rupert spilled some kind of cologne in here earlier, she thinks, sitting by Nan's bed again. Her thoughts drift back to Katherine's phone number tucked securely into her pocket.

Another fifteen minutes passes before Nan begins to stir.

She mutters something, turning her head fitfully on the pillow.

Pilar frowns, rising and standing over the bed. The scent of flowers seems to be getting stronger still. She reaches out and touches Nan's thin shoulder. "Are you calling Rupert, Nan? He'll be right back. I'm here. It's me, Pilar."

Nan doesn't seem to hear her. Her eyes remain closed and she seems to rest more easily for a few moments.

Then her head turns abruptly to one side again and she calls out.

This time, her speech isn't the least bit muffled. Pilar clearly hears the one word that spills from her lips.

"Katherine."

She's calling for her daughter.

"It's okay, Nan," Pilar says softly, stroking her friend's arm. "It's okay. She's coming."

Nan opens her eyes. "Katherine . . . is coming." It's not a question. It's a statement.

"Yes, Nan. Katherine is coming." Pilar watches her, unable to tell whether she's lucid. She's almost staring through Pilar, rather than at her. "She loves you. Don't worry. She'll be here. I'll make sure of it."

The rain has stopped at last, but Julia leaves the hood of her neon orange raincoat over her head to protect her hair from the dripping trees overhead. This isn't her favorite thing to wear—she doesn't like the bright color. But her mother—with her usual disregard for Julia's personal taste—sent it to her on her last birthday, and it's the only rain jacket she has.

The air is scented with the pungent, earthy after-rain scent, and even the dingiest cottages, freshly washed, glisten in the yellow rays that poke through a hole in the dense clouds overhead.

She has almost reached the house she still finds herself referring to as Iris's when she spots a figure descending the porch steps.

Rupert Biddle.

The man turns in her direction.

She waves to him, calling out, "Hello, Rupert."

He looks almost startled to see her, as though he'd been lost in his thoughts even though he was heading straight for her.

"Julia," he says, barely slowing his pace as he approaches. "How are you?"

"I'm fine. How's Nan? I've been thinking of her."

"She has good days and bad days," Rupert tells her with obvious reluctance, coming to a halt where the gravel walk meets the street.

She can sense that Rupert doesn't want to stop and chat. He must be hurrying back home to his wife. Wondering idly what he was doing at Paine's place, she asks Rupert, "Is there anything I can do? Maybe I can run some errands for you, or pick up some groceries?"

"No, thank you. I get around pretty well."

Julia glances up at the house, and it occurs to her that he might be the person to ask about the energy she and Dulcie have recently sensed inside. After all, he lived here for most of his life.

Years ago, when she was a teenager, still haunted by Kristin's strange reaction to whatever she saw at the foot of the Biddles' stairs, Julia considered telling Rupert or Nan about the incident. But she never found the opportunity.

Or maybe it was more that she never quite felt comfortable with Rupert, who is a far more intimidating person than his wife. But Nan—well, Nan isn't a medium. She would be less likely to shed light on the issue than Rupert would.

It's now or never, Julia tells herself, and finds herself blurting, before he can continue on his way, "Rupert, can I speak to you about something, please?"

He's clearly taken aback, puzzled. They have never had more than a polite, distant conversation. "Speak to *me*? About what? Are you all right, Julia?"

"I'm fine, but . . . I've been spending some time in Iris's house these past few days. Far more time than I ever spent there when she was alive. And I've felt a rather troubled soul lingering there. So has Dulcie."

"Dulcie?" Rupert frowns, as though trying to place the name.

"Paine Landry's little girl. Kristin's daughter."

Briefly, she explains about the experience in Dulcie's bedroom last night, and about the presence she and Dulcie have encountered on various occasions in the house. She tells him that she got the perception that the name begins with a *K* sound and ends in an *N* sound, but that she doesn't feel that it's attached to Kristin.

"There are lots of words that begin with the letters *K-N*," Rupert points out, almost impatiently. "Know, and Knee, and Knock . . ."

Knock.

Julia frowns. Dulcie and her knock, knock jokes. But what does that have to do with anything?

"I don't think that's it, Rupert. I'm almost certain I was given the letters phonetically. I got a *K* sound. Not just an *N* sound, like Know and Knee . . ."

And knock, knock.

Again, Julia considers it. She sighs. In truth, she is certain of only one thing: the spirit has a compelling reason for making repeated visits.

She goes on, "I thought I would talk to you about it because you lived there for so long, Rupert—and because you're a far more experienced medium than I am. I was wondering if you ever sensed the energy I'm talking about."

"No, I never felt anything like that."

She decides not to bring up the Halloween incident. She gets the feeling Rupert finds this a waste of time and is anxious to be on his way.

"I guess that if the spirit wasn't attached to the house when you were there, maybe the person passed more recently. Do you think it might be Kristin? Because for some reason I'm not fully connecting with her, and the energy doesn't feel as familiar as I think it should."

"It could be her," he says, looking off down the street, seeming distracted. "Or maybe you're getting something else. As I said, maybe the *K-N* you heard isn't even a name. And if it is, it might be a reference to somebody else. Somebody you've never met."

"It might be," she agrees, frustrated as much by the spirit

as by Rupert's almost dismissive attitude. "But I can't help feeling like there's a reason the energy is there, a reason that I'm connecting with it regularly now, and so is Dulcie. Somebody is desperately trying to tell us something."

"Perhaps," Rupert agrees, looking anxiously at his wristwatch. "I'd be happy to speak more about this with you, Julia, but I'm afraid it can't be right now. I have to get home to Nan."

"I'm sorry," Julia says quickly. "Of course you do. Please give her my best. I'll bring her some flowers in a day or two. I know how much she must miss her garden, and it was always so beautiful at this time of year."

"Yes," Rupert says, "it certainly was."

She doesn't miss his pointed glance at the tangled bed of weeds on either side of the front steps.

"Iris wasn't much of a gardener," Julia feels obliged to say, almost apologetically.

"No, she wasn't."

"I'll help Paine get the beds into shape."

"I doubt that will be necessary," Rupert says, with a faint smile. "He's agreed to sell the house back to me. He and his daughter will be leaving Lily Dale by the end of the week."

Concealed in the shadows of the lilac hedge behind the porch, Edward goes absolutely still, absorbing the shocking detail.

Paine is going to sell the house back to Rupert? And he's going to do it this week?

That doesn't give you much time, Edward tells himself, looking up through narrowed eyes at the house where he should have grown up. *Not much time at all.*

So intent is he on formulating his accelerated plans that

he doesn't notice the small tape recorder propped in the branches above his head, still whirring softly, having recorded every word he just overheard between Rupert Biddle and Julia Garrity.

Chapter Ten

On Tuesday morning, after checking his voice mail back home and finding no messages from his agent, as usual, Paine takes his first shower in nearly a week. It feels so good, standing beneath the spray of the newly installed shower head, that he lingers there for well over fifteen minutes.

His thoughts wander back to yesterday afternoon, when he sat in on Stan's acting workshop at Chautauqua. It was invigorating, just being in a musical theater environment again after all these years. In California, his career has taken a far different path than he ever anticipated. Back when he was a theater student, learning and honing his craft, he never imagined himself doing commercials and industrials, or being a lowly stand-in on a movie set.

No, he'd always thought he was Broadway bound.

Then he met Kristin. She wanted nothing to do with Broadway. Hollywood was where she was headed.

Whither thou goest, I shall go . . .

He always planned that they would have that Bible passage read at their wedding.

Paine sighs, tilting his head back into the hot spray to rinse the lather of shampoo from his hair.

He planned a lot of things that never came true.

When he finally turns off the water and emerges into the steamy bathroom to towel off, he looks around for a switch that might turn on some kind of fan. There isn't one.

No wonder the yellow floral wallpaper is peeling at the seams, he thinks, glancing at it as he quickly slips into a pair of boxer shorts. Too much humidity.

His first instinct is that he needs to see about having a fan installed —and that it's a job he won't attempt to do himself. The shower head took him until well after midnight last night, and he's certain he kept Dulcie awake with all the noise.

But she's still asleep, he notes now, hearing nothing but silence in the old house as he leaves the bathroom and makes his way past her room to the top of the stairs.

There, it hits him that he won't have to worry about installing a fan, or doing anything else to fix the place up and capture a buyer's interest.

After all, he's selling it to Rupert Biddle, and he's selling it just as it is.

He hasn't yet broken the news to Dulcie.

He sent her upstairs to work on her bead bracelet while he and Rupert talked. When he told her she could play a tape on her Walkman, it was so that she wouldn't be able to eavesdrop on the conversation. But it wasn't because he wanted to keep the news of the sale from her.

He had no intention of giving in to Rupert's demands when they started talking.

No, he simply figured they were headed for a very vocal disagreement, and he didn't want Dulcie to overhear.

But what Rupert said changed everything.

How can Paine possibly refuse to return the place to an old man who only wants to bring his wife home to die?

On paper, Paine isn't a widower.

In his heart, he is.

He can't help but relate to Rupert Biddle's sorrow. And he won't stand in his way.

Somehow, the tragic reality of Nan Biddle's impending death has diminished Paine's own need to stay in this house, and to find out exactly what happened to Kristin.

Rupert is right.

The sooner he gets Dulcie back home and severs his ties to Lily Dale, the sooner they'll both be able to heal. Staying in this house will only prolong their pain.

Yes, Kristin lived here. And yes, she died here.

But she isn't here now, Paine reminds himself firmly, trailing his fingertips on the polished wooden banister as he arrives at the foot of the stairs.

Pilar pours steaming coffee into a blue ceramic mug and pauses, standing there beside the counter, to take a sip.

And then another.

Then, knowing she can put it off no longer, she carries the mug into the front room and sets it on the desk that holds the telephone. Beside it is the packet containing her airline tickets for tomorrow morning's flight to New York City.

Too nervous to lower herself into a chair, she stands as she lifts the receiver, holding it to her ear.

There's the dial tone.

How many times did she hear this sound last night, when she was finally alone in the house after she finished her final appointment?

How many times—before she finally sank into bed at midnight—did she stand in this very spot, frozen, until the dial tone gave way to the operator's recorded voice: "If you'd like to make a call, please hang up and try again. If you need help, hang up and dial your operator"?

Every time that happened, she put the phone down and walked away.

She never got far.

Yet nor did she ever go through with the call when she invariably found her way back to the phone.

Now, after a restless night, haunted by Nan's words—*Katherine is coming*—she knows what she must do. It's now or never. She'll be tied up with appointments and message services for the rest of the day.

Clutching the receiver in one hand and the scrap of paper from Rupert's desk in the other, Pilar begins to dial.

What if the phone has been disconnected?

What if that number in Rupert's address book belongs to a different Katherine in the metropolitan New York area?

She holds her breath as the phone rings on the other end.

And exhales it slowly as it rings . . .

And rings . . .

And rings.

No answer.

No machine.

I'll try again, Pilar decides, carefully putting the scrap of paper back under the heavy crystal heart-shaped paperweight Raul once gave her for their anniversary.

She glances at the open window nearby, where a slight draft flutters the curtains. Then she tucks the paper more securely beneath the weight. *I'll keep trying until I reach Katherine and tell her what she needs to know about her mom.*

The sweet smell of flowers drifts into the room on the breeze. Pilar inhales deeply. It's coming from the window box directly outside, the one she filled with aromatic annuals and herbs: purple stock, lavender, and nicotiana.

As she breathes in the delicious fragrance, she is reminded of yesterday, in Nan's bedroom. She forgot to ask Rupert about it when he returned. By then, the scent was gone anyway.

Now, all at once, Pilar recalls which flowers bear that particular fragrance.

The scent couldn't have been coming from something blossoming outside, Pilar realizes.

After all . . . lilacs are only in bloom at the beginning of May.

The telephone rings just as Rupert is turning off the flame beneath the whistling teakettle. He hurries to answer it, wondering whether it might be his investment broker calling back. Rupert left a message earlier. He's going to have to cash out several funds and take a big loss. But it will be worth it to buy back his house.

Paine said he would speak with the attorney about the sale. He's agreed to allow Rupert and Nan to take immediate occupancy, but it will take some time to sort through the legal paperwork and make the transaction official.

When Rupert lifts the receiver with an eager "Biddle residence," the answering voice doesn't belong to his broker. The accent—a perfect blend of Texas twang and East Coast aristocrat—is unmistakable.

"Hello, Rupert, this is Virginia Wainwright."

His heart sinks. "Virginia. How are you?"

"Back from Palm Beach and simply exhausted now that I've spent a full week getting the cottage into order again."

The cottage, Rupert knows, is a four-tiered lakefront house on the grounds of Chautauqua Institution, where Virginia's late husband, Harrison, was once on the board of trustees. Rupert also knows that Virginia didn't lift a finger getting the place into order again. She employs a full household staff, complete with a part-time nanny for occasions when her three small great-grandchildren visit.

"Rupert, I would like to see you as soon as possible," Virginia says. "It's been such a long winter and I've missed Harrison. I'm sure he's wondering where I've been."

"Virginia, we've talked about that. Harrison himself has let you know that he's always with you, wherever you are."

"Yes, but I've missed our weekly chats. One-sided conversations with him are so frustrating. When can you see me, Rupert?"

He hesitates. He wasn't planning on giving readings this season. At least, not now. Not with Nan so ill.

But one session with Virginia Wainwright, heiress to a Houston oil fortune, will be well worth his while. The woman, a regular summer client for years, always presents an exorbitant "donation" in exchange for Rupert's channeling the late Harrison. It would mean Rupert might not have to touch his retirement investments for a down payment after all.

"I'm busy today and tomorrow," Rupert informs Virginia. "How about later in the week? Thursday or Friday?"

"Wait until Thursday? That's out of the question, Rupert."

"Virginia, I'm afraid I can't see you sooner. I'm in the midst of packing up the house and taking care of some real estate business. Nan and I are moving in a few days."

She gasps. "Please tell me you're not leaving Lily Dale?"

"Of course not. We're just moving back to our old place on Summer Street."

"Don't frighten me like that, Rupert. I don't know what I'd do without you. You're the only person who has ever been able to put me in touch with Harrison."

"And I'll be happy to do so . . . on *Thursday,* Virginia."

After a few more attempts to change his mind, Virginia grudgingly agrees to the appointment later in the week.

Rupert hangs up the phone, satisfied. Cash is on the way. Everything has fallen into place.

He returns to the kitchen, where he quickly finishes making a cup of herbal tea for Nan. He places it on a tray, and, as an afterthought, adds a container of yogurt with a spoon. It's plain vanilla. Maybe it will appeal to her more than the fruited flavors do. She hasn't eaten much of anything in days. She isn't thirsty, either, though Rupert has gently insisted on spooning cool water and warm tea to moisten her parched lips and mouth.

Carrying the tray into the bedroom, he finds her asleep, just as she was when he left the room fifteen minutes earlier. He notices a fragrant floral aroma that seems to come and go in this room and absently wonders where it's coming from.

The puzzling thought vanishes as he realizes that Nan's breathing is irregular again. That keeps happening. Sometimes, her respiration speeds up, so that her breaths are almost coming in pants. Other times, it's so slow and faint that Rupert can barely hear it, and he has to keep checking her in dread.

Now Nan stirs, as though the movement in the room has disturbed her slumber.

"Nan, I've brought you some tea and a light snack, sweetheart," Rupert says gently as he sets the tray on the bedside table beside numerous orange plastic prescription bottles and the stacked paperback novels Pilar placed there yesterday.

There is no response from his wife, yet she turns her head away from him, her eyes still closed.

"Nan, sweetheart, wake up." Rupert bends toward her, stroking her head.

She mutters something incoherent.

Her arms, elbows bent, are on top of the quilt in the warm room. Suddenly, her hands come together, thumb on her right hand to pinky on her left, palms upward, fingers curled as though they've closed around something.

The handle of a shovel.

Her arms begin to move in familiar rhythm.

She's digging again.

"You're in your garden again, sweetheart," he says softly. "Aren't you? You're in your garden."

He swallows hard, watching her.

The air in the basement beneath Iris's house must be twenty degrees cooler than the sunny yard, Julia thinks as she descends the creaky stairs. Something brushes across her face. She lets out a little cry.

Ick.

Cobwebs everywhere.

At the foot of the steps, she eyes the old bureau, wondering if she can possibly move it up to the yard herself. Paine has gone back to Chautauqua to sit in on another acting class. Dulcie—happily settled with her beads on a blanket on the grass just outside the basement door—certainly can't help Julia carry this ancient thing.

For the moment, she has no choice but to work on it down here.

She opens the bag containing the furniture-stripping solution Paine bought for her, taking it out and reading the label carefully.

"Julia?" Dulcie's voice carries down through the open doorway.

"Yes, Dulcie?"

"Are you sure I can't come down there with you?"

"It's really dirty down here, Dulcie, and the stairway is too steep. I won't stay here long. I just want to get started on the dresser . . ."

Before your dad tells Rupert he can have it along with the rest of Iris's stuff he's selling with the house.

Paine said that was part of the agreement he made with Rupert. If the Biddles can't wait to move in, they'll have to dispose of Iris's belongings themselves. He said Rupert readily agreed.

Julia sighs, opening the plastic lid covering the nozzle on the rectangular metal can.

Paine and Dulcie really are leaving Lily Dale in just a few days, after the memorial service for Iris on Thursday. Howard Menkin will handle the details of the real estate sale. Paine said Julia can have Iris's old VW Bug if she wants, to keep or sell.

She'll keep it, of course. For sentimental reasons.

Part of her thinks that Paine has done the noble thing, turning over the house to Rupert for immediate occupancy so that he can bring Nan home before she dies.

Part of her thinks it's a cop-out.

Didn't Paine tell her that he was determined to find out what happened to Kristin here? Didn't he say he wanted Julia to help Dulcie deal with her clairvoyance? Well, not in so many words. But they both know what Dulcie is dealing with. They both know Julia is in a position to help the little girl.

Now he's brushed that aside in favor of fleeing Lily Dale

at the earliest opportunity—before the house is even officially sold to Rupert.

When Paine returned from Chautauqua yesterday and told
Julia about the move, there was no opportunity for discus-
sion. For one thing, Pilar had stopped by with a treat for
Dulcie, and was still on the porch chatting with Julia about
poor Nan Biddle when Paine arrived.

For another, he was late getting back. Julia had to rush
right off to her Medium's League Message Circle. As Julia
left, glancing at Dulcie's wistful expression, she found herself offering to come and spend time with the little girl again
this afternoon since a small brigade of workmen have taken
over her house with their noisy tools.

Dulcie's face lit up, of course, and Paine was only too
eager to take Julia up on the offer. He apparently enjoys
being back at Chautauqua, even if his first visit there on
Sunday obviously triggered haunting memories of the summer he met Kristin.

*If he would just stick around longer this summer, he
can get involved in Chautauqua's musical theater program
again,* Julia thinks, pouring the vile-smelling stripper into
a small plastic bucket and recapping the bottle tightly.

She should point that out to Paine in case he hasn't thought
of it.

Yes.

*And if he stays—at least through some or all of July—I
won't have to say good-bye to Dulcie so soon. She needs
me.*

But where can Paine and Dulcie stay? He's promised
Rupert the house.

And I guess I can't blame him for that.

It was the right thing to do.

The only thing a decent human being would do.

Besides, there's nothing holding Paine and Dulcie in Lily Dale.

Nothing but painful memories of Kristin and Iris.

Nothing but Julia . . .

Who has no business even entertaining the ridiculous notions that keep flitting into her mind.

Notions about Paine . . .

And herself.

He's off-limits, she reminds herself firmly, setting to work rubbing the stripper onto the old, dark-stained wood. *I would never get along with a man who thinks that what I do for a living is bogus.*

Didn't she say exactly that to Lorraine when she called Julia this morning? Her friend insists on insinuating that romance is brewing between Julia and Paine, refusing to believe that Julia is spending so much time here merely because of Dulcie.

Julia grew impatient with Lorraine's annoying tangent, about to hang up when Lorraine finally got around to the real reason for her call.

"You forgot your raincoat at the auditorium last night after the Message Circle," Lorraine told her. "I saw it on a seat as I was leaving and I knew it was yours."

"Ah, yes, the lovely shade of neon orange gave it away, right?"

"Exactly. I picked it up for you and tried to catch up with you and Andy, but you guys were obviously in a big hurry to get somewhere."

"Hardly. We were only going out for coffee."

"So, Jules, tell me . . . what does Andy think about your spending so much time with Paine Landry?"

"Why would he care?" Julia asked, trying to forget Andy's comment yesterday morning about Paine being jealous. "It's not as if Andy and I are a committed couple.

We've gone out on a few dates. And like I said, Paine and I are only friends—if that. Get it through your head, Lorraine."

But Lorraine only laughed.

Why doesn't she get it?

Even if Julia were to foolishly allow herself to fall for Paine, his heart obviously still belongs to Kristin.

And Julia would be wise to acknowledge that it always will.

"Edward? Is that you?"

"Yeah, Ma." Edward bends to pick up the Jamestown *Post Journal* from the worn mat in front of the door to the trailer before stepping inside. He blinks, his eyes adjusting to the dim interior.

His mother, wrapped in a faded terry cloth robe that was once blue, is smoking a cigarette and watching one of those televised court shows she's so fond of. As usual, neither she nor Edward bothered to fold up the pullout couch where he sleeps. Jocelyn Shuttleworth spends most of her days on it, doing exactly what she's doing now.

"How are you, baby?" she asks in her low-pitched smoker's voice as Edward plods over to the short strip of counter space and deposits his metal lunch bucket amid a clutter of dirty dishes, open food containers, and overflowing ashtrays.

"I'm too damned hot," he tells her, wiping a trickle of sweat from his brow. "That's how I am. What's up with this weather? Either rainy or humid as hell."

"It's going to rain again later," his mother says, her gaze fixed on the TV. "That should cool things off."

"It should, but it won't."

"You're in a good mood," she observes dryly, glancing at him. She pushes a strand of dyed red hair back from her once pretty face, prematurely wrinkled thanks to years of cigarettes and exposure to the elements. As Edward does now, Jocelyn worked on a road construction crew after the divorce from Anson Shuttleworth, for more than a decade until a back injury sidelined her on disability. There was a time when Edward was embarrassed, having a mother who wore a hard hat and tool belt. His friends teased him mercilessly about it when he was in elementary school.

They didn't pull that once he was in junior high though. He grew quite a few inches and pounds over one memorable summer, and nobody pushed him around after that. Those who tried found out the hard way that you didn't mess with Edward Shuttleworth.

You still don't, he thinks with self-satisfied pride.

"What's to eat, Ma?"

She shrugs, taking a drink from the plastic tumbler on the newspaper-littered table beside the couch. Edward knows his mother well enough to be aware that the amber liquid ain't lemonade.

"You know I can't go to the supermarket till after the first of the month, when my check comes, Edward."

"That sure as hell hasn't stopped you from shopping at the liquor store," he mutters under his breath.

Either she doesn't hear, or she chooses to ignore him.

He forages in the cupboard and finds an almost empty box of saltines. Biting into one, he finds that it's limp and soggy. With a grunt, he tosses the stale cracker, and the rest of the box, into the heaping trash bag in a plastic can under the sink. It topples off the pile and lands beside a can of Ajax that hasn't been used in a good month.

"You going back out later?" his mother calls after him as he heads into the bathroom.

"Yeah. Not till after dark. Why?"

"I need more cigarettes."

He closes the door after him and lifts the toilet seat, muttering, "Get 'em yourself."

Smoking.

That's one bad habit he never expected to pick up from his mother. As a child he never could stand the stale smell cigarettes leave on your clothes, your hair, your skin, your breath.

His father couldn't stand it, either. He doesn't recall much about the first few years of his life, when he and his mother lived with Anson Shuttleworth over in Lily Dale. But he does remember the big fights his parents had. Many of those arguments were about her smoking. She would try to quit, and then she'd sneak cigarettes, and Anson would find out.

"You can't hide anything from that man," his mother always said. "That's what I get for marrying a medium."

Yeah.

That's what she got. A man who quickly caught on to all her secrets—especially when she had an affair with an auto mechanic who lived down in Jamestown. Not that Anson hadn't had affairs of his own, his mother bitterly told Edward later.

But when Anson found out about his wife's indiscretion, he threw her out of the house. Edward was just a preschooler then, but he clearly remembers his mother telling him that his father hadn't even fought to keep custody of him.

He's always wondered if it's true.

Not everything Jocelyn told him is.

Edward found out later—much, much later—that his father really did pay her alimony. Child support, too.

What his mother didn't give to the mechanic—who lived with them on and off for a few years—she spent on booze, or gambled it away at OTB.

Just another of her damaging little habits.

Edward flushes the toilet and washes his hands, staring at his face in the mirror above the sink. Black hair already receding at the temples, close-set brown eyes, aquiline nose . . .

I look just like him, he thinks, recalling the father who drifted further and further from his life.

The father who died unexpectedly, dropping dead of a heart attack in his fifties . . . without a will.

Everything he had went to his second wife.

Iris.

The bitch.

Edward stares into his own angry gaze.

If it weren't for Iris, Edward and Jocelyn wouldn't still be living in this miserable trailer park.

And now that Iris is dead—and Kristin, too—everything that should have gone to Edward belongs to some little blind kid.

But not for long, Edward thinks with a scowl. And the sooner he gets his ass over to Lily Dale and inside that house, the better. Then he can put his plan in motion and everything will fall into place at last.

What if they're home again tonight?

They were, all yesterday afternoon, and last night. They never freakin' left the place. He thought of waiting around to sneak inside until the lights went off and they were asleep, but that was risky. Besides, he was exhausted, having spent hours lurking in the shadows near the porch, waiting for an opportune moment.

Hopefully, when Edward gets over there tonight, the house will be dark and empty.

If it isn't . . .

He'll worry about that when the time comes.

*   *   *

It's going to rain again. Soon. Standing on his porch, the mail he just retrieved from the roadside box in his hands, Lincoln can smell it in the air, sense it in the tree branches overhead, as they rustle in a slight breeze, turning their leaves upward.

All this rainy, gloomy weather has been good for his vegetable crops.

Bad for the soul, though.

Makes a man dwell on the dark things in his past.

And there are plenty of those in Lincoln's.

He opens the squeaky screen door and steps inside. He's been listening to it squeak for a lifetime. His mother always asked his father when he was going to oil the spring, just as Corinne used to ask Lincoln.

No sense oiling it now. Not when we're used to the sound. The squeak lets us know when somebody's comin' in.

That was his father's reply to his mother, and Lincoln's to Corinne.

He lets the screen door bang behind him.

In the living room, he dumps the mail on the coffee table and turns to survey the cardboard carton on the floor beside it. A musty smell fills the room. The thing has been stuck in a corner of the attic for decades, along with years' worth of clutter accumulated by Lincoln's parents.

Corinne never went up there. Said she couldn't stand to look at piles of junk.

Lincoln rarely went up, either. Not unless a squirrel got in, or he had to retrieve the Christmas lights or stash them away under the eaves again . . .

Or he wanted to open this box, to go through the contents and allow them to carry him back, over the years, to a time he'd usually rather not think about.

He never brought the box downstairs until now.

He didn't want Corinne asking all kinds of questions.

Lincoln reaches into the box and takes out a record album. Simon and Garfunkel. Kathy gave it to him for his birthday. "This way, you can play my song all the time," she told him.

Her song.

He carries the album over to the old record player on top of the dining-room sideboard. *It's probably warped,* he thinks, as he sets the old-fashioned black vinyl disk on the turntable.

He doesn't need to check the album sleeve for the song number. He knows it by heart, even after all these years. He sets the needle in the right groove and closes his eyes as the familiar guitar strains and soulful lyrics fill the room.

I hear the drizzle of the rain . . . falling like a memory . . .

Miraculously, the record isn't warped after all. He plays "Kathy's Song" all the way through, standing there, eyes closed, remembering.

Then he lifts the needle and carefully places it at the beginning again.

As the song starts over, he returns to the box and takes out several photographs. The rubber band that once held the stack together has long since grown brittle and snapped. Lincoln flips through the pictures, his mind drifting back over the years.

There's Kathy, perched on top of Lincoln's father's tractor, waving at the camera.

There's Kathy, blowing out the sixteen candles on the devil's food birthday cake Lincoln's mom made to surprise her.

There's Kathy, her long blond hair in pigtails. That was the style then. Kathy usually wore her long, straight hair parted in the middle, hanging down her back. But Lincoln talked her into the pigtails that day, saying she'd look cute. And she did. She tied them with blue ribbons that exactly matched the shade of her eyes.

Outside, the wind picks up, noisily swaying branches overhead.

Lincoln reaches into the box again.

He takes out the small stuffed red dog he won for her playing skee ball at the midway arcade the summer before he was drafted. He and Kathy used to trade it back and forth, giving it to each other whenever one of them needed cheering up. Lincoln was the last one to get it. Kathy gave it to him to take to Vietnam. He slept with it under his pillow the whole time he was away.

On nights when he had a pillow to sleep on.

Lincoln pushes away the memories of steamy, perilous nights in the jungle. He's not willing to go there now. That's a whole other chapter in his painful past.

Tonight belongs to Kathy.

Lincoln is taking the last thing from the box when he hears an unexpected sound from the next room, barely audible over the wind outside and the guitar music spilling from the stereo.

The squeak lets us know when somebody's comin' in.

"Who's there?" he calls, frowning. He wasn't expecting anyone.

There's no reply.

Maybe it was just the wind in the trees, he thinks, listening.

But there is no wind.

No squeaking.

He can hear only "Kathy's Song," winding to a bitter-sweet conclusion.

I know that I am like the rain . . . There but for the grace of you go I...

From where Lincoln sits on the living-room floor, the door in the small front hallway isn't visible.

Now the last guitar strains have faded and the room is silent, but for the scratching of the needle on vinyl and a soft pattering on the roof far above.

The rain has begun.

"Anybody there?" he calls.

For some reason, he remembers that woman, Pilar. How she told him she made contact with Corinne's spirit.

Do you believe in ghosts? Lincoln asks himself.

There's no answer to that question, nor to the one he asked aloud.

Lincoln leans forward.

A long shadow lurks on the wall in the hallway, cast by the glow of the porch light outside.

"Who's there?" Lincoln asks again, dread slowly seeping in as he gets clumsily to his feet.

"It's me," a hauntingly familiar voice says, followed by the unmistakable sound that throws Lincoln back to his military days.

The sound of a gun being cocked to fire.

Lincoln Reynolds's last thought, as he falls, mortally wounded, to the floor, still clutching the yellowed envelope bearing Kathy's Dear John letter, is that he never should have made that phone call this afternoon.

At dusk, turning away from the open, half-filled suitcase on the bed, Pilar looks at the phone.

She left Katherine's number downstairs on the desk, after trying it intermittently throughout the day. Maybe someone will be home now.

If not, she won't have another chance to call until she gets back from tonight's Thought Exchange session over at the auditorium. By then, it will be too late to phone a total stranger.

After quickly tossing a few more items into the suitcase—an extra pair of sandals, another sweater for cool shipboard evenings, a novel she's been meaning to read—Pilar heads downstairs. On the landing, she hears voices and glances out the screened window at the house next door.

Julia, Paine, and Dulcie are ducking through the rain, going from the front steps to the red car parked at the curb.

They look like a family, Pilar thinks, smiling as she watches Paine hurriedly open the passenger's-side door and help his little girl into the backseat.

He says something to Julia as she gets into the front, and she laughs, the frothy sound reaching Pilar's ears.

She sounds so happy, Pilar thinks, watching the three of them drive away.

Maybe Julia and Paine will fall in love, and they'll live happily ever after in Iris's old house.

You would have loved that, wouldn't you, Iris?

Pilar won't be able to attend Iris's memorial service on Thursday. She would have liked to go. She sighs, missing her friend. And now she's going to lose another. Nan.

She turns abruptly away from the window and continues down the steps to the living room, where she picks up the telephone and dials the number she now nearly knows by heart.

It rings once.

Twice.

And then, unexpectedly, there's a click.

Somebody is picking up.

Pilar's breath catches in her throat. She was so certain nobody would be home yet again that everything she intends to say to Katherine flies right out of her head.

"Hello?"

It's a man.

Katherine's husband?

Pilar finds her voice, heart pounding as she asks, managing to sound perfectly normal, "Hello, is Katherine there, please?"

For a moment she thinks he's going to tell her she has the wrong number. That no such person is at this listing.

But he doesn't.

He only says, pleasantly, "No, she isn't. Can I take a message?"

A message.

Pilar can't possibly explain who she is and why she's calling.

"No, that's all right," she says slowly. "Can you please tell me when she'll be back?"

"I don't expect her until late. She's in the city." There's a pause. "Who is this?"

"Just a friend. I'll . . . I'll call her tomorrow," Pilar says, hanging up before the man can ask another question.

But first thing tomorrow, Pilar will be flying to La Guardia Airport. And after killing several hours in New York City, she'll be meeting Christina, Tom, and the children and boarding a cruise ship.

You'll have to call her from a pay phone while you're in the city, Pilar tells herself. *It's probably not even considered a long-distance call from there.*

Or . . .

Or you can go to see her in person.

You have the address.

Pilar frowns, considering it.

It seems like a crazy idea, and yet . . .

The news she bears is disturbing. Far too disturbing to be blurted on a pay phone in a public place.

It would be better if she goes to see the Biddles' daughter.

She'll have plenty of time. Her plane lands before eight o'clock in the morning. Christina put her on the first flight out of Buffalo, explaining that even if there are delays—as often happens at La Guardia—Pilar will still most likely be in New York in time to board the ship.

Christina and Tom are flying into New York tonight. Tomorrow, matinee day on Broadway, they're taking the kids to see a musical. They invited Pilar to go, too, but she told them she'd much rather spend the day shopping and seeing the sights. She plans to check her luggage with the cruise line when she lands, and go off on her own, meeting her family back at the pier before departure.

Now, instead of going to Saks, Bloomingdales, and the Empire State Building, she'll find a car service to drive her to Garden City. It isn't that far from the airport in Queens. She already looked it up on a map yesterday after she returned from the Biddles'.

Pilar is so intent on her revised plan as she walks back up the stairs to get ready for the Thought Exchange that she doesn't even glance toward the window on the landing.

Thus, she doesn't see the dark figure slipping through the shadows beside the lilac tree toward the back of the house.

"Sorry I'm late."

"It's okay," Miranda says frostily as Andy hurries to the small table by the fireplace where she's been waiting for well over an hour.

And it isn't okay.

She should have known better than to get involved with someone like him. Everything about him should have set off warning signals in her, but if they sounded, she managed to ignore them until now.

"I got hung up with a few things that couldn't wait."

Andy takes off his dripping navy rain slicker and drapes it over the back of a chair. "Please don't hold it against me. I came as soon as I could."

Unreliable.

Unfaithful.

Unforgivable . . . right?

Right?

Miranda looks at Andy.

He flashes a sweet, little-boy smile. "Please don't be mad, Mandy."

How many times did Michael pull this on her? How many times did she fall for it, giving him just one more chance?

Too many times.

She pushes back her chair.

He reaches out to encircle her wrist with his strong, warm fingers. "Don't go. Stay and have another glass of wine with me. Please?"

She hesitates, looking anywhere but at him, knowing that if she allows herself to glance into those green eyes of his, she'll do anything he pleases.

She looks around the room. Few other tables are occupied here in the cozy lounge of the White Inn, a charming, upscale establishment in Fredonia. On a night like this, no one in their right mind would risk life and limb to go out for a drink.

Obviously, Miranda isn't in her right mind. She was terrified, driving down Route 60 in Kent's Jeep. He has no idea where she's gone, of course. He probably forgot that she never returned the keys to him the last time she used the Jeep. He's back at the hotel, in bed, most likely sound asleep. He blames his exhaustion on the medication prescribed by the doctor Miranda dragged him to yesterday afternoon. According to the doctor, the pharmacist, and the label warning, the medication wasn't supposed to make him groggy, but Kent claims he's ultra-sensitive to drugs. Mr. Dramatic. Miranda can only tolerate so much of him when he's not feeling well.

Hopefully, he'll be back to normal tomorrow.

And hopefully, this rain will end tomorrow.

Then Miranda and Kent can get on with their investigation, and move on to their next destination so that Miranda can put Andy out of her thoughts—and out of her life—for good.

It would be a hell of a lot easier if he wasn't so damned charismatic.

And a hell of a lot easier if she hadn't slept with him last night.

It was late when he came by the hotel looking for her. But she was still up, bored out of her mind, playing solitaire on her bed. It seemed natural to invite Andy to stay and play cards. And just as natural to respond when he kissed her . . . and then seduced her.

Not that it took much effort. It's been so long since she slept with anyone that it was actually a mutual seduction. When he got dressed in the wee hours, prepared to slip back through the deserted, rainy streets to his rented room, Miranda found herself asking if she could see him again tonight.

She had to prove to herself that she wasn't being foolish. That he wasn't just using her.

He hesitated before agreeing. He suggested that they meet late, here, outside of town.

She didn't want to ask him, then, what was going on with his girlfriend; whether he's broken up with her yet.

She doesn't want to ask him now, either.

"I can't stay," she tells him. But she doesn't pull her wrist from his grasp.

"Why not? It's a crummy night. You can't conduct an investigation in this weather."

"No, but . . ."

"Don't be mad, Mandy. I told you, I couldn't help it. What's the big deal? I was a little late—"

"More than an hour late."

"Let me buy you another glass of wine."

She shakes her head.

Yet still, she doesn't pull away.

"Let me make it up to you, Mandy."

Miranda knows what she should do.

She should get up right now and walk out the door.

Kent was right all along about men like Andy Doyle. She was a fool to have gotten involved with him.

It's nearly ten-thirty when Julia lets herself into her house, turning on lights as she walks from the living room through the dining room to the kitchen. What began earlier as a light summer rain has become a full-fledged thunderstorm that knocked out power in the Italian Fisherman, the quaint lakeside restaurant over in Bemus Point where Paine invited her to dine with him and Dulcie.

The staff hurried around lighting extra votive candles, and Paine and Julia reassured Dulcie, who nearly bolted out of her seat every time there was a deafening clap of thunder.

The harrowing drive home to Lily Dale took more than an hour, over wet back roads littered with fallen branches and an occasional downed wire. Julia sat in the backseat with Dulcie, her arm around the frightened little girl, who eventually relaxed and drifted off to sleep with her head on Julia's shoulder. She didn't even wake up when Julia gently pulled away from her just now as Paine dropped her off.

In the kitchen, the rain makes a strange sound on the

plastic tarp the workers have draped overhead. Looking up, Julia can see patches of sky through gaping holes that have been ripped between the rafters. For some reason, that makes her feel uneasy. As though somebody can use the opening to look in.

Or get in.

I'm just anxious because of the storm, she tells herself, going to the refrigerator for the pitcher of iced tea. She pours herself a glass and takes a sip, kicking off her wet sandals as she stands leaning against the fridge.

She certainly isn't dressed for weather like this. When she left home early this afternoon, the sun was shining. Now her navy shorts and white T-shirt are soaked through, just from the quick run from the car to the house. Paine was going to accompany her, but she told him not to leave the sleeping Dulcie in the car alone.

"At least take my jacket," he urged her, but she refused.

"Use it to put over Dulcie's head when you bring her in," she told him.

Now, she makes a mental note to get her raincoat back from Lorraine. Either that, or buy a new one in a more suitable color. With the way this summer's weather has been shaping up so far, she's going to need one.

Julia finishes her iced tea in a few more thirsty gulps, then puts the glass in the sink. Time to get out of these wet clothes, into some dry pajamas, and sink into bed.

There, she'll be able to think about what Paine said when she asked him how he can turn his back on Lily Dale so quickly and with such finality.

"I thought you wanted to know more about what happened to Kristin here, Paine," Julia said from the backseat of the car as Dulcie dozed on her shoulder and Paine steered through the treacherous storm.

"I thought I did, too," he told her. "But now I realize

that it's pointless. Being here, and speculating about what happened to her . . . well, how can that be healthy? Not so much for me, but for Dulcie? I've got to take her home, Julia. We need to make a fresh start. For three years, I've been a zombie. Like Rupert is now.''

"What do you mean?''

"Seeing him, realizing what he's going through, hearing his pain—that really shook me up, Julia. It's hell to live like that . . . immersed in pain and loss every second of the day. Rupert has a chance to do some of his grieving and to accept reality before his wife dies. I didn't get that chance. Instead, I've spent the past three years trying to accept the shock of what's happened. It's time for me to stop being haunted by Kristin's death and figure out how to live again. For Dulcie's sake.''

"I understand what you're saying,'' Julia said quietly, staring out the rain-spattered window into black nothingness.

She also understands that her reasons for wanting Paine and Dulcie to stay are purely selfish. These past few days with Dulcie have given her a taste of what it would be like if she ever has a child of her own. Her whole life, she has instinctively been a nurturer. Having somebody who needs her—somebody who so desperately needs to be cared for—has awakened a fierce longing in Julia.

She wants a child of her own. A family, a husband of her own.

Her mental image of Paine is replaced with one of Andy. Before they parted last night, she happened to mention needing to find somebody with a boat to take her out on the lake to scatter Iris's ashes on Thursday. Andy immediately offered to do it. Until that moment, she forgot that Andy, an avid fisherman, rented a small motorboat to use while he's here this summer. It was sweet of him to offer to help her with such a somber task.

Julia turns off the kitchen light and walks into the living room, pressing the wall switch that plunges the living room into darkness again. As she does, a flashing red light catches her eye.

The answering machine.

She's tempted to leave the messages until morning.

But sheer force of habit makes her cross the room in the dark and press the button.

The tape rewinds. Julia wonders if it was Andy who called.

If it was, I might as well call him back tonight, she thinks wearily. *I'll just get it over with, and I'll tell him I'm tired and can't talk.*

The tape stops whirring.

Myra Nixon's recorded voice fills the room.

"Hello, Julia, this is Myra. It's almost ten on Tuesday evening. If you haven't heard about Lorraine, please call me when you get in, no matter what time it is."

Lorraine?

Has something happened to Lorraine?

Her hand trembling, Julia dials Myra's number.

Hearing the phone ring, Rupert rises from the chair at Nan's bedside.

She's sleeping again, peacefully, for a change. No calling for Katherine. No digging.

He hurries into the kitchen to answer it, glancing at the clock as he picks up the receiver. It's nearly eleven o'clock. Who could be calling at this hour?

"Rupert? It's Pilar. I hope I didn't wake you . . ."

"No. No, I was up."

"I thought so. I just spoke to Myra Nixon and she happened to mention that your lights were still on. Is everything all right?''

Myra Nixon. Leave it to that busybody to see to it that everyone in Lily Dale knows his business. Being out of her sight range is another plus to the move back to Ten Summer Street, he thinks grimly.

"Everything is fine. I was just about to go to bed," Rupert tells Pilar brusquely, not in the mood for chatter.

"I just wanted to let you know that I'm leaving tomorrow morning. For my cruise."

"Yes. Yes, that's right. Well, have a good time, Pilar."

"I will. But, Rupert, please know that you and Nan are in my prayers."

"Thank you."

There's a pause. Then Pilar says, in a rush, "Please ask for help, Rupert, if you need it. There are so many people around who would be happy to help you. Nan is such a wonderful person, everybody around here is just aching to do something for her, or for you."

Tears sting Rupert's eyes and he reaches for a paper napkin from the holder on the counter, wiping them away before they can fall.

"I'll be gone a week, and then I'll be over to visit," Pilar promises. "Please tell Nan I'll read to her when I come."

He clears his throat. "I'll tell her."

"Oh, and, Rupert, did you hear about Lorraine?"

"Yes. I heard earlier, when I went out for milk."

"It's tragic, isn't it?"

Yes, he murmurs, it certainly is tragic.

A lot of things are tragic, Rupert thinks as he hangs up, alone in the silent kitchen as thunder rumbles in the distance.

* * *

An enormous tree has fallen across Route 60 just south of Sinclairville, blocking the road leading to Jamestown. The vast mountain of leafy branches is surrounded by police cars with flashing red lights. Officers in reflective orange uniforms stand in the roadway, directing cars to take turns creeping around it as the rain continues to fall.

It isn't coming down as heavily now as it was earlier. The thunder has long since faded into the distance, the deluge giving way to a steady drizzle.

Waiting for the cops to wave him around the downed tree, Edward finds it hard to be annoyed by the delay.

Usually brimming with impatience, especially when it comes to driving, tonight Edward is feeling almost serene.

He can sit here all night, for all he cares. He's in no hurry to get back home to Jamestown. He's content just to sit here, alone in the dark, savoring the moment—and digesting the little added surprise he stumbled across.

But nobody will ever have to know about that part. He'll see to that.

At last, things are about to fall into place for him.

At last, he has what he needs to make it happen.

He lips curve into a faint smile as he pats the envelope safely tucked into his T-shirt pocket.

Lying in bed, her hand resting reassuringly on *Where the Wild Things Are* under her pillow, Dulcie stiffens at the sound of soft footsteps in the hall outside her room.

Is it Daddy?

No.

No, she's almost positive it's not.

She's been lying here, wide awake, since well before he

climbed the stairs and went to bed a long time ago. She heard him close his door at the far end of the hall, and she hasn't heard him open it since.

For some reason, Dulcie can't sleep tonight. Yes, she slept in the car on the way home from the restaurant, so soundly that she didn't even get to say good-bye to Julia. And she slept right through Daddy carrying her up to bed, which is the only way she could have gotten here. He even remembered to change her into the new pink flowered pajamas she and Julia picked out in T.J. Maxx, and to take the ponytail scrunchy out of her hair, and to put her book under her pillow. Somehow, Dulcie slept through all of that.

But she didn't stay asleep. She doesn't know what woke her up earlier, or what kept her awake despite her exhaustion. She only knows that she's been lying here for a long time, almost as if she's been waiting for something.

Almost as if she's been expecting something, and now, at last, here it is:

Footsteps.

Somebody creeping through the old house in the dead of night.

Is it her again?

The lady who Julia says might be my mommy?

Her heart pounding, Dulcie considers the possibility.

There are two things wrong with it.

The first is that she doesn't feel the now-familiar presence of the ghost lady who has visited before.

The second is that whenever the lady came, Dulcie never heard her approach. It was more as though she came and went in a rush, appearing and disappearing in the blink of an eye.

Not like this, creeping in one sneaky step at a time.

Outside Dulcie's window, the overflowing gutter drips

rhythmically, sending one droplet after another to plunk onto the driveway below.

Inside the house, in the hallway outside Dulcie's room, a floorboard creaks.

The little girl holds her breath.

The footsteps have stopped.

Somebody is lurking there, just outside her door. She can feel it.

Is it Daddy?

Is it the ghost lady?

Is it Mommy?

Dulcie lies very still, her eyes open to nothing but the usual blackness, her whole body tense as she listens. She tries to tell herself not to be afraid, that it might really be her mommy's spirit, as Julia said. And she shouldn't be afraid of her mommy . . . should she?

There is a slight rustling outside her door, followed by a faint, telltale *click*.

Dulcie recognizes the sound.

It means somebody is turning the knob.

Then, all at once, the face appears in front of Dulcie—the face she saw before. The face of the beautiful golden-haired lady. Her blue eyes are wide, as if she's afraid. She's waving her hands frantically at Dulcie and her mouth is open wide, lips moving.

With the vision comes a rush of sound in Dulcie's ears, drowning out anything else. It's a frantic jumble of words, screeched in a phantom voice that Dulcie can hardly understand.

But one word is clear.

Danger.

In the instant before the spirit's energy dissolves, Dulcie gets a closer look at her. That's when she sees it—the grotesque crack in her skull, above her right ear. The blood that covers one side of her head, matting her hair, smearing her cheek red.

Then she's gone, leaving Dulcie in the dark once again.

But not alone, and not in silence.

She can hear the door softly opening, inch by inch.

Danger.

The beautiful woman isn't outside Dulcie's room, trying to get in.

She was right here, inside already, trying to warn Dulcie about whoever is on the other side of the door.

Danger.

Dulcie opens her mouth.

Her voice seems to catch in her throat as she hears a quiet footstep crossing the threshold.

Then she finds her voice and lets loose with a bloodcurdling scream.

"Daddy!"

She hears immediate commotion. Running footsteps in the doorway, in the hall, on the stairs before the front door closes with a distant click.

Then Daddy is rushing into the room. "What is it? Dulcie? What's wrong?"

He's too late.

Too late to catch the intruder.

But just in time to save me, Dulcie thinks, trying to catch her breath.

"Somebody was here, Daddy," she says, tears spilling down her cheeks as Daddy puts his arms around her and holds her close. "I'm scared. Somebody was in my room."

"It was just a bad dream, Dulc—"

"No! No, it wasn't, Daddy. Didn't you hear it?"

"Hear what?"

"Footsteps. Whoever was here—they ran out of my room and down the stairs."

Daddy doesn't say anything for a long time.

When he does speak, he doesn't say what Dulcie wants to hear. Actually, she doesn't know what she wants to hear, but she knows what she doesn't.

"Dulcie, don't worry. Whatever you think you heard . . . it wasn't anything that can hurt you. Nothing is ever going to hurt you again, because I'm here, and I'm going to take care of you. I'm going to take you home."

"Home?" she echoes, bewildered. "You mean, to California?"

"Yes. We only have to stay here another day, maybe two, while I wrap things up. Then we'll get out of here, and we'll never come back."

"But . . . what about Julia?"

Again, Daddy says nothing for a long time. Then he says, "Maybe Julia can visit."

He says it in that way adults have of telling kids something just to keep them quiet. To keep them from asking too many questions.

Dulcie leans her head against her daddy's chest, listening to his heartbeat.

"Don't leave me in here alone, Daddy," she says, wiping at her eyes, realizing she's crying.

"I won't, sweetheart. Come on." He stands and scoops her into his arms, carrying her down the hall. "You can come sleep in my room. I promise there are no ghosts in there and nightmares aren't allowed."

Ghosts.

Nightmares.

He thinks it was all in her head.

He doesn't believe that somebody was here, in the house, in Dulcie's room.

And she has no way of proving it to him.
Whoever it was has fled into the night.
But what did they want?
And what if they come back?
And how did the lady get covered in blood?

Chapter Eleven

Julia hurries down the corridor, a bouquet of flowers in her hand. She didn't take the time to cut them from her garden before leaving home first thing this morning—they're from the Garden Gate florist shop a few blocks away from Brooks Memorial Hospital in Dunkirk.

She's left her sunglasses on to hide her eyes, red and bloodshot from a sleepless night and teary morning.

Suddenly, a nurse in pink scrubs materializes in her path. "Excuse me, can I help you?"

"Yes, I'm here to see Lorraine Kingsley. She's a patient here."

"I'm sorry, she isn't able to have visitors yet," the nurse says, wearing a sympathetic expression. "She's in intensive care."

Julia swallows over a lump in her throat. "How is she?"

"It's been touch and go all night, and she's still critical, but her condition seems to be stabilizing. Her mother is flying in later this morning and the surgeon will consult with her then. Are you a friend of hers?''

Julia nods, unable to speak.

"Would you like to leave the flowers for her? I can put them by her bed so that she'll see them when she wakes up.''

Encouraged by the fact that the nurse said *when* and not *if*, Julia manages a smile and hands over the bouquet.

"Do you know if . . . are her daughters here?" Julia asks.

"They were here earlier, with their aunt.''

That would be Lorraine's older sister Laura, who lives in Buffalo.

"This is such a shock,'' Julia murmurs, wondering how the girls are coping. Their mom is all they have. She *has* to recover. Feeling tears spring to her eyes again, Julia reaches into her pocket for a tissue. She finds only a handful of soggy ones she used up during the ride over.

The kind nurse reaches for a box of tissues on a nearby counter and offers it to Julia, asking, "Have you heard anything about the police investigation? They told us it was a hit and run down in Lily Dale during that awful storm last night.''

"That's all I know,'' Julia tells her, dabbing at her damp, sore eyes.

She has been picturing what happened ever since Myra Nixon described the accident last night on the phone. She told Julia that Lorraine was struck as she was walking along the road on her way back from a healing temple service. The car mowed her down and kept going.

I can't believe the driver didn't see her, Myra said. *Somebody mentioned she was wearing that bright orange raincoat you must have loaned her. Everybody in town is always*

*saying you can see that coat of yours from a mile away—
no offense, Julia.*

Julia looks at the nurse. "When you see Lorraine's sister
again, would you please tell her Julia was here, and that I'd
be happy to help if she or the girls need anything? They're
teenagers, but I know they must be devastated by this.
They're very close to their mom."

And so am I, Julia thinks as she walks slowly back down
the corridor toward the elevator bank. She still can't quite
believe what's happened to Lorraine. She didn't sleep most
of the night, drifting off only when the first light of dawn
slipped through a crack in the blinds. The alarm went off
half an hour after that. She set it early so that she could be
at the hospital first thing.

Elevator doors slide open the moment Julia presses the
down button. She finds herself face-to-face with Lorraine's
sister, Laura.

After a tearful hug, Julia asks, "Where are the girls?"

"I brought them over to one of their friend's houses to
rest for a while. They've both been up all night."

"Is there anything I can do, Laura? Do you want me to
get anything from Lorraine's house to bring here? I have
the keys."

"Not yet. I don't know what she'll need when she comes
out of this . . ." Laura rakes a distracted hand through her
dyed red hair. "I can't believe this is happening, Julia. Just
when things were finally falling into place for her, and she'd
finally unloaded that bastard Bruce."

"I know. This feels like a nightmare. What a horrible
accident."

"If it was an accident," Laura says darkly.

"What do you mean?" Julia asks, startled.

"The police said she was wearing a neon orange coat
with the hood up, and she was right under a streetlight when

she was hit, well off the side of the road. The car swerved into her. There were tire marks on the grass, Julia. It was almost as if somebody was out to get her."

"But . . . who would do something like that?"

"I can only think of one person. Bruce."

Julia considers that. After an abusive marriage and bitter divorce, Lorraine's ex has been evading court-ordered alimony and child-support payments. Lorraine threatened him more than once with legal action for the money he owes. He's a loser, yes. But would he go this far to get her off his back?

"I have to get back in there," Laura says, glancing at her watch. "I've been gone more than an hour. I want to be there when the doctor comes in."

"Will you keep me posted, Laura? Call me later and let me know how she is."

Lorraine's sister promises to do so, then hurries off toward the intensive care unit.

Julia presses the down button again.

As she stands waiting for the elevator, she thinks about what Laura said. Was somebody really trying to hit Lorraine?

And if it wasn't Bruce . . . then who?

Lorraine doesn't have another enemy in the world.

Maybe it really was an accident, Julia thinks as the elevator arrives. *Thank God she's alive. It could have been worse. You never know. Maybe it* would *have been worse, if Lorraine hadn't been wearing my orange coat . . .*

Bright morning sunlight filters across the attic floor, illuminating a thick layer of dust and a smattering of bat droppings. Standing at the top of the steep flight of stairs, Paine surveys the stacks of cardboard boxes, the rickety-looking nursery furniture, the trunks he's already checked and found filled with cast-off clothing dating back a good forty years.

What am I going to do with all of this crap? What are the chances Dulcie will ever want any of it?

He sighs. With any luck, she'll stay asleep downstairs for another hour, giving him time to look through the cardboard boxes for any belongings of Iris's or Kristin's that might have sentimental value. Everything else, he'll leave for Rupert to sort through.

Paine makes his way over to the first cluster of cartons and lifts the interfolded flaps of the nearest one. The box is filled with old newspapers and magazines. The musty smell of yellowing paper wafts up. Rifling through them, glancing at the datelines, Paine sees that they were collected throughout the seventies. None of them seem to have any particular historical relevance. God only knows why Iris saved them. She was one hell of a pack rat.

Paine wonders whether Iris and Anson were as mismatched as he senses they were. He knows little about their relationship, aside from what Kristin told him. They met during what she described as her father's "midlife crisis," after he dumped his alcoholic spendthrift of a first wife and got back into the singles scene. Pretty, free-spirited Iris, who dabbled in pottery—and pot—and ran a health-food store in Fredonia, caught his eye. There were undoubtedly others, but to know Iris was to love her. Her marriage to Anson lasted nearly two decades, until the day he collapsed and died of a heart attack in her arms.

Paine shoves the first box aside and reaches for the next. This one is filled with baby clothes. Pastel little-girl dresses, ruffled bonnets, rumpled satin hair ribbons, lace-trimmed once-white anklets mellowed to ivory. Paine smiles, recognizing a little blue sailor dress with a red tie as having belonged to Kristin; she's wearing it in one of the baby photos on the mantel downstairs.

Dulcie might want to keep these things, he thinks, carefully tucking the flaps in again and carrying the box over to place it at the top of the stairs. If Dulcie ever has a daughter, she might want her to wear Kristin's baby clothes.

Dulcie as a mother . . . now there's an amazing image. With it comes the usual pang of regret as Paine realizes that Kristin will never see their daughter all grown up . . .

Or will she?

Right before Dulcie drifted off to sleep last night in his arms, she murmured something about having been visited again by the pretty lady—and that the lady's visited Julia, too, when Julia was here. Dulcie said Julia thinks the lady might be her mommy.

"I don't think she's here to hurt me, Daddy," Dulcie said sleepily. "I think she's here to watch over me. But, Daddy . . . I think somebody hurt her. When she was alive. I think she wants to tell me about that."

"Why do you think that?"

"Because she keeps coming back. And she has blood on her face. She keeps trying to tell me something. But I can't hear her."

"Then how do you know she's trying to talk to you?"

"I *sort of* hear her. It's like when we're in the car, Daddy, and you press that seek button on the radio and it skips over the stations that aren't coming in so well. That's what it sounds like when she talks to me. The words are never clear."

Paine lay awake long after Dulcie's breathing became steady and her little body settled into slumber at last. He kept thinking about what she said, about the lady.

Blood on her face?

Kristin wouldn't have blood on her face. She drowned. And anyway . . .

He doesn't believe in ghosts. He never has, damn it. But . . .

Can Kristin's spirit possibly be in this house?

"Why can't *I* feel you if you're here?" he whispers aloud now, standing still in the deserted attic. "Why won't you let me see you? Just one more time. If it's possible, babe, please. If you're here, let me see you . . ."

He waits, listening, watching . . .

Hoping.

"All I want is to see you again, babe," he says softly, wiping tears from his eyes with the hem of his T-shirt. "I never got to say good-bye. All I want is to say good-bye. . . ."

There is nothing.

Nobody here.

Just Paine, alone, heartbroken, same as always. He stares into space, remembering Kristin, absently watching a tiny, floating speck of dust as it glints in the sunlight before finally drifting to the floor.

Clad in a hard hat, orange work vest over a T-shirt, jeans, and steel-toed boots, Edward lifts his mirrored sunglasses to wipe a trickle of sweat from his brow. *Damn the sun,* he thinks, and is struck by the irony. Just yesterday, he was damning the rain.

Well, this work sucks in any kind of weather.

Good thing Edward won't be doing it much longer.

"Hey, Shuttleworth," his supervisor calls. "Get to it!"

"Yeah, yeah," he mutters, hoisting his square-point shovel again. They're following the truck that is grading the thick new layer of stones, preparing the roadbed for paving.

After a few more minutes, Edward glances around to see

if anybody is watching him. The others are concentrating on the job at hand, eager to complete this grueling part of the job and break for lunch.

Turning his back to the rest of the crew, Edward slips something out of his pocket and quickly drops it onto the roadbed in front of him. Moments later, he's shoveled a pile of gravel over it.

There. It won't be long before the spot will be sealed with layers of oily tar and asphalt.

Then there will be no chance of anybody stumbling across the letter, as Edward did. Lucky thing he happened to find it. If it fell into the wrong hands after all these years, it could ruin everything.

At first, it surprised him that Anson would save something like this. Now he's grown certain that his father wasn't the one who saved the letter. It had to have been Iris. The freaking pack rat saved everything: every art project Kristin ever made, every button that ever fell off a shirt, even old twist ties. It's no wonder that she regained possession of perhaps the most significant letter she ever wrote to her husband, and decided to save it just in case . . .

Well, who knows why she did it?

The important thing is that Edward found it with several other papers—most of them important family documents such as Kristin's birth certificate and the title to the VW, sealed in a large manila envelope in a locked drawer of the desk in the upstairs study. It was surprisingly easy for Edward to pick the lock.

Now nobody else will ever read Iris's heartfelt plea to her new husband, forgiving Anson's brief indiscretion and telling him that he was welcome to come back home again after all—that she and their infant daughter needed him. Iris also pointed out that they could put the affair behind them for good; that although Lily Dale might be the smallest of small towns, only three people in it knew Anson's deep, dark secret: Iris, Anson himself, and the woman with whom he'd had a one-night stand.

Even Edward, as much as he has always resented Iris, grudgingly respects his stepmother's ability to forgive the old dog.

Not many wives would take their husband back after something like that. His temperamental, insecure mother certainly wouldn't have.

Not many wives would urge their husband to pay the requested hush money to ensure that the other woman would never reveal to another living soul that he fathered her new-born child.

And not many wives would later allow their husband's illegitimate daughter to befriend their own little girl a few years later.

In his youth, Edward spent enough time with his father's new family to know that Iris apparently got over any lingering resentment.

After all, he remembers noticing that Kristin's friend Julia Garrity was more at home in the Shuttleworth household than he ever felt. Now he alone is left to appreciate the irony that it was the presumably unwitting Julia who looked out for Iris until her dying day.

"Is this it?" the turbaned driver asks Pilar, as he pulls to a stop in front of a two-story raised ranch on a quiet, leafy suburban street.

She checks the address on the curbside mailbox. "I guess so."

"You want me to wait, right?"

"Please," she says, gathering her purse and her navy blazer from the seat. "I won't be long."

"No problem." The driver turns up the radio a bit and the distinct strains of sitar music fill the car. He settles back in his seat and opens today's edition of the *New York Daily News*.

Pilar opens the door and steps out into the sunshine. A sprinkler a few feet away spurts water in an arc across the thick green lawn in front of the house. A straight walk leads up to the door, bordered by blooming marigolds.

Nan doesn't like marigolds, Pilar remembers as she starts up the walk. *She says the orangey color is too harsh.*

One glance around the yard shows that Nan's daughter doesn't take after her when it comes to gardening. There's no sign here of pretty pastels and old-fashioned blooming perennials. Katherine obviously likes a splashier, more conventional look. The foundation of her house is bordered by a clipped juniper hedge fronted by heavily mulched beds containing a few thatches of ornamental grass, smallish red geraniums, and more marigolds.

Pilar mounts the three concrete steps to a small stoop edged by a black wrought-iron railing. The inner wooden door stands open, and the sound of a game show on television filters through the outer white vinyl screen door. Pilar hesitates, wondering if she should knock on the door, or ring the bell.

It's not so much that she can't decide as that she isn't quite sure she's ready for this confrontation. Now that she's actually here, at Nan and Rupert's daughter's house, she wonders if this is such a good idea after all. She's about to meddle in a family's private matters at the most difficult time in their lives. Maybe she should just let well enough alone.

Besides, what if this Katherine Jergins isn't even Rupert and Nan's daughter?

True, she was the only Katherine in their address book. But that doesn't mean Pilar has come to the right place.

It's a strong possibility, yes. But what if Rupert and Nan haven't bothered to write down their daughter's address?

You know Christina's and Peter's addresses off the top of your head. Do you even have them written in your address book? Pilar wonders belatedly.

This is insanity. She doesn't belong here. Whether this Katherine Jergins is the Biddles' daughter or not.

She's about to turn around and retreat to the car waiting at the curb when she hears footsteps inside, followed by a startled gasp.

"Oh! You scared me!" a woman's voice says. "Did you knock? I didn't hear you."

Any doubt that Katherine Jergins is the Biddles' daughter evaporates when Pilar lifts her head to find a familiar face— the very picture of a younger, healthier Nan—looking back at her through the screen.

"You seem quiet. Are you all right?"

Miranda looks up at Kent, seated across the small table. They're in the shady outdoor cafeteria having lunch. Rather, Kent is heartily munching his order of Buffalo wings. Miranda hasn't touched her grilled cheese sandwich.

"I'm fine," she says, poking at a sliver of pale green pickle. Her stomach is churning. "I'm just a little tired." And hungover. And miserable.

"Late night?"

"Mmm-mmm," she says noncommittally.

"Who is he, Miranda?"

She looks up sharply. "Who is whom?"

"Your latest obsession? The guy you were with last night."

Her jaw drops.

"Look, I happened to wake up—Lord knows I've been sleeping enough with this medication—and I looked out the window and there you were, sneaking back into the inn."

Miranda says nothing. *I wasn't "sneaking,"* she thinks defensively.

"Was it a one-night stand?"

"No! Of course it wasn't. You know I wouldn't do something like that, Kent."

"But you would spend the night with somebody you've known for less than a week."

She lifts her chin stubbornly. "Maybe I was out taking a walk."

"Wearing a black dress and heels? At night? In the rain? Okay, whatever."

Miranda watches Kent dunk a miniature drumstick into blue cheese, then, in a few bites, strip it of its spicy red skin and fragments of dark meat.

"For someone who's been deathly ill, you've gotten your appetite back pretty quickly," she observes.

"I haven't eaten in days."

"I'd think you'd want to start with something bland."

"You'd think wrong." He tosses the bone aside, reaches for another wing, and regards her thoughtfully. "Look, Miranda, you don't have to tell me who he is. Just be careful, okay? And remember—we're out of here in a few days. With all the rain and my being sick, we're behind schedule as it is."

"I know."

"So don't start getting any thoughts about hanging around here longer."

"Believe me, I won't." *The sooner we get out of here, the better.*

"I'm getting the idea you aren't going to tell me what

you've been up to, or who he is. You think it's none of my damn business.''

''Exactly.'' She gives up on her sandwich. She has no appetite. She keeps thinking about last night, with Andy. She should never have had that second glass of wine with him. Or the third. She should have walked out when she intended to—right after he arrived.

Instead, she stayed long enough to get a little tipsy—okay, flat-out wasted—and make a fool of herself. She told him about her failed marriage and string of broken relationships. She told him all she wanted was to find someone who would love her, and settle down to have a couple of kids. She told him she was incredibly attracted to him, and that she wanted to see him again. That she hoped he would visit her in Boston.

He couldn't get out of there fast enough, leaving her to drive drunkenly back to Lily Dale in Kent's Jeep. She's lucky she managed to keep the car on the road and make it back in one piece.

Having picked the last wing clean, Kent tosses it onto the plate and looks at her. ''What's the plan for the rest of the afternoon?''

''I think I'm going to go back to my room and lie down,'' Miranda says. ''I've got a raging headache.''

It's the truth.

But Kent looks at her for a long moment, as though he doesn't believe her. ''Fine. But don't back out on me tonight. We're doing Leolyn Woods, right?''

''Right.''

''And did you want to see if you can talk to the owner of that house on Summer Street again and see if he'll give us permission to check out his property?''

''No,'' Miranda says hastily. ''That's okay. I'm over that.''

Again, Kent gives her a long look as though he doesn't believe her.

Then he shrugs. "Good. I don't think the guy is going to change his mind."

Her hands clenched on her lap, under the table, Miranda lets out a breath she didn't even realize she was holding.

Rupert hurries in the front door and goes straight to the kitchen, depositing his paper grocery bag on the counter. He woke up this morning to find that they've run out of milk. He forgot that he used the last of it yesterday afternoon in the instant vanilla pudding he made for Nan, hoping to entice her appetite.

He wound up tossing the pudding into the trash can. She wouldn't touch it, and Rupert never has liked vanilla.

Now, he hurriedly places the new carton of milk in the refrigerator and opens the bread box to put away the fresh loaf of whole-wheat bread. Already inside is an identical loaf he bought only a day or two ago.

I'm losing my mind, he thinks, noticing that both loaves bear the same expiration date. Oh, well. He'll feed the extra to the birds.

Seeing the unopened box of shredded-wheat cereal still on the counter where he left it earlier, he puts it back into the cupboard, his own appetite for breakfast long gone.

At last, he hurries into the bedroom to check on Nan, certain he'll find her asleep, as always.

To his shock, she's awake. Her weary blue eyes stare up at him from the pillow.

"Are you all right, darling?" Rupert asks, going to sit beside her on the bed. He picks up her skeletal hand. The skin is almost transparent, crepe draped over bones.

"I'm . . . tired . . ." Nan says. "So . . . tired . . ."

He nods, stroking her hand.

The only sound in the room is the sound of her breathing, the air making a rattling sound as it passes over the mucus collecting in her mouth and throat.

"I have news for you, darling," Rupert says abruptly.

This can't wait any longer. He was waiting to surprise her, but looking into her sunken face, he fears that she might not be able to hold on much longer without something to keep her going.

She looks at him, expectant, too exhausted to voice a question.

"You're going home, darling," Rupert tells her.

The expression that filters into her eyes isn't the spark of joy he was anticipating. Rather, it is a somber, knowing look. He realizes, in horror, what she thinks he's telling her.

"No, Nan . . ." He shakes his head, his voice catching in his throat. "I mean . . . I mean, I'm taking you home. To Summer Street. To our home, darling. You'll be much more comfortable there."

Still it doesn't come . . . the spark of joy.

She moves her head slightly on the pillow, a negative gesture.

"What's wrong, darling? Don't you want to go home?"

"Can't . . ." She fights for breath. Tries again. "Can't . . ."

He leans down and kisses her forehead gently, holding back the emotion that threatens to rise and take over, to make him lose control.

"Of course you can, darling. I'm going to make it happen. Just wait another day, Nan, maybe two, and then I'm going to bring you home."

Another day.

Maybe two.

Rupert strokes his wife's forehead beneath the turban. *Wait, Nan. Please, wait . . .*

* * *

When Julia walks up the front steps at Iris's, she can hear Paine's voice coming from the parlor inside. He sounds angry.

She knocks on the screen door, then steps inside.

"Julia? Is that you?" There's Dulcie, standing in the hallway in front of the kitchen doorway.

"Yes, it's me, Dulcie."

"I heard you coming." She stifles a yawn, gesturing at the parlor. "Daddy's in there, on the phone with somebody. He's really mad."

That's obvious. Julia hears Paine's voice harshly asking, "Well, how long do you think it might take?"

A pause.

"That's unacceptable!" Paine says. "I plan to be long gone by then."

Another pause.

"Fine. Fine. See what you can do and call me back."

Julia hears the beep of a cordless phone being hung up, followed by a muttered curse.

"Daddy, Julia's here," Dulcie calls sweetly, childishly unfazed.

Paine appears on the threshold of the parlor.

"Is everything all right?" Julia asks. He looks as bad as she feels—as though he didn't get much sleep last night, either.

"Is everything all right? Not really," he says shortly. "In fact, things couldn't be more *not* all right."

"What's wrong?"

"Howard Menkin just called. There's been an unexpected complication."

"What kind of complication?"

"Apparently, he just heard from a lawyer representing Edward Shuttleworth."

"Kristin's half brother?"

Paine nods, saying grimly, "He's contesting Iris's will."

"But how can he do that? He and Iris were barely on speaking terms."

"Exactly. But apparently, Anson Shuttleworth died without a will. Since Edward was of legal age when it happened, under New York State law, Iris inherited everything he had. She, in turn, left it to Dulcie since Kristin predeceased her."

"How can Edward contest that?" Julia asks, aware of Dulcie standing between them, listening intently. "And why only now?"

"Anybody can contest a will," Paine tells her. "But apparently, Edward has stumbled across some relevant information that might threaten Dulcie's inheritance."

"What kind of information? Did he find that Anson had a will after all?"

"The lawyer confirmed for Howard that it wasn't that, but he wouldn't tell Howard anything else. He wants to meet with us tomorrow. I don't have time for this," Paine bites out, shaking his head. "*Rupert* doesn't have time for this."

Julia rubs her tired eyes with the fingertips of both hands. This is shaping up to be the worst day she's had since . . . since . . .

Since you found Iris's body.

Which wasn't all that long ago.

What's happening around here?

Why do I suddenly feel as though Lily Dale isn't safe? As though nobody in it is safe? As though I'm not safe?

She only wants to go home and crawl back into bed. And she would have, after stopping to run a few errands in Fredonia on her way back from the hospital, if her house weren't crawling with tool-wielding men in work boots.

Instead, uncertain where else to go, she came here. Now she wonders if this was such a good idea. Being here might help to take her mind off what happened to Lorraine, but everywhere she turns in this house, there are reminders of Iris, and Kristin.

"Julia? Do you want to see what Daddy found in the attic?" Dulcie pipes up.

Julia snaps out of her dismal thoughts, glancing at the little girl's sweet face. "Sure, Dulcie," she says, telling herself that this is why she's here. For Dulcie. Because Dulcie needs her. "What is it?"

"It's an old"—Dulcie pauses around a huge yawn—"doll. Daddy says she probably belonged to Mommy."

"You're exhausted, Dulcie," Julia says. "Didn't you sleep well last night?"

"No." Dulcie hesitates, as though she wants to say something more. She glances at her father. Paine's eyes are concerned, but he says nothing.

"Daddy found the doll on the floor in the attic," Dulcie goes on, "wrapped in a blanket, way back in a corner under the . . . under the . . . what is it called, Daddy?"

"Eaves," Paine supplies.

Dulcie is already leading the way to the kitchen, her hand clasping Julia's as Paine trails behind, still clutching the phone.

"A doll, hmm?" Julia is trying to quell her doubts. "Let's see her."

Kristin never played with dolls. Never. She said dolls were for sissies. Julia never played with dolls, either. She was too much of a tomboy. As the only two girls in the elementary school who weren't into dolls, Julia and Kristin found their first common ground when they initially bonded so many years ago.

Dulcie feels around on the kitchen counter, her fingers

closing over a pink-wrapped bundle. She hands it over to Julia. "Here she is. See?"

Julia unwraps the blanket and peeks at the doll inside. It has a porcelain face, not vinyl, as did most of the dolls that were around when she and Kristin were kids. Julia can easily see what Paine, as a male, obviously did not: this doll is part of an earlier era.

"I don't think that was your mommy's doll, Dulcie," she says. "It must have belonged to some other little girl who lived in this house."

"Oh." Dulcie sounds disappointed. Julia is prepared to offer solace, but Dulcie quickly recovers, saying, "Well, Daddy found lots of baby clothes that for sure belonged to my mommy, and a bunch of pictures of her, too. Plus some of her old board games. I get to keep all of it and bring it back to California with me when we go."

"That's great, Dulcie."

"Knock, knock, Julia."

"Who's there, Dulcie?"

"Rupert and Nan have a daughter, don't they?" Paine asks abruptly, behind them.

"Daddy! I'm in the middle of a knock, knock joke," Dulcie admonishes.

Paine falls silent.

Dulcie turns back to Julia. "Say 'who's there?' again, Julia."

"Who's there?"

"Ozzie."

"Ozzie who?"

"Ozzie you around." Dulcie cracks up. "Get it, Julia? Ozzie you around. I'll see you around."

Julia forces a laugh but her eyes are on Paine, who is preoccupied.

"Rupert and Nan have a daughter," she tells him. "Why?"

"Do you think that's where the doll came from?"

"Maybe."

"Will you stay with Dulcie for a little while, Julia? I was going to bring her with me—I'm going over to Chautauqua to say good-bye to Stan. She could come along, but she's so tired and I thought if she stayed here she could take a nap . . ."

Even as he speaks, Dulcie yawns again, and rubs her eyes sleepily.

"It's okay," Julia says. "I'll watch her."

"Can I have the doll?" Paine holds out his hands. "I have to stop by Rupert's on my way and tell him what Howard said. I'll bring the doll along. He'll probably want to give it back to his daughter if it was hers."

"You don't know me," Pilar tells Katherine Jergins. "I realize this is a bit awkward. But I have something very important to tell you."

"Is it about my husband? Or my sons?" Katherine's gray eyes are worried. Behind her, framed on the walls, are a series of portraits. A boy and a girl. Obviously Katherine's daughter and son, progressing from toothless infants to gap-toothed schoolkids to slightly gawky teenagers. At least, the boy is gawky. The girl, a pretty blond, looks like her mother. And—Nan, again—her grandmother.

"No, it's . . ." Pilar clears her throat. She shouldn't have come. Oh, why did she come? She casts a longing glance at the car waiting at the curb. But it's too late to back out and leave now. She turns back to Katherine. "Can I . . . Would it be possible for me to come in so that we can talk?"

The woman is hesitant, toying with a pair of glasses

hanging on a chain around her neck. She, too, looks at the car at the curb, then shoots a questioning expression at Pilar.

"That's the car service I hired to drive me here from the city," Pilar explains. "He's going to take me back when I'm finished speaking to you."

Katherine nods. Yet she doesn't move to open the screen door.

Pilar reminds herself that this isn't Lily Dale, nor is it the Deep South, where she spends her winters. Here in the metropolitan New York area, people are more cautious. Less likely to open their doors to strangers.

"Listen, I can understand that you don't want to invite a complete stranger in," Pilar says. She looks around, her mind racing, her gaze settling on a couple of green resin Adirondack chairs in the sunny side yard. "Maybe you can come out and we can sit there and talk?"

"All right." Katherine pauses to poke her bare feet into a pair of leather sandals by the door.

Pilar watches her, noticing her trim and attractive figure in cropped beige pants and a raspberry-colored short-sleeved sweater. She's built like Nan. Even dressed like Nan, in well-tailored clothing. Everything about her reminds Pilar of her friend—except Katherine's sharp, slate-colored eyes. Those are the mirror image of Rupert's, as is their wary expression.

Curious, Pilar peeks again at the inside of the house. From here, she can see most of the living room and a sliver of the kitchen. Chintz slipcovers, wall unit, coffee table stacked with newspapers and magazines, magnet-covered fridge dotted with coupons, flyers, clippings.

The picture of middle-class suburbia. Comfortable. Lived-in.

So different from Rupert and Nan's place, Pilar finds herself thinking, glancing again at the framed photographs.

It strikes her that there are no such personal touches in the Biddles' home. Their refrigerator is bare of magnets. The surfaces are clutter-free. There are no framed family photos on the walls or anywhere, for that matter. In fact, Pilar realizes, she never even heard either of them mention having grandchildren.

Looking apprehensive, Katherine steps outside and walks with Pilar to the chairs. They sit. Katherine is expectant. Dubious, too.

"What did you say your name was?"

"It's Pilar. Pilar Velazquez." Pilar reaches into the pocket of her blazer and takes out a business card, handing it to Katherine.

The woman glances at it as Pilar searches her mind for the right thing to say.

How should she start? By saying that she's a friend of Katherine's parents?

A *friend?*

Pilar considers the word. Friends share intimate details of their lives. She and Nan have never been close in that way. Though less guarded than Rupert, Nan has maintained a polite distance exacerbated by the seasonal nature of their acquaintance.

Pilar settles on, "Katherine, I've known your parents for years."

"My *parents?*"

"Yes . . . my cottage in Lily Dale is right next door to theirs."

Katherine's rapidly chilling expression sends a chill down Pilar's spine.

So do her words, spoken bluntly in a flat tone. "My parents are dead."

* * *

Paine knocks three times, about to leave when Rupert appears at the door. The old man's eyes, behind his glasses, are shadowed by bluish circles and a telltale red swelling.

He's been crying, Paine realizes, his fingers tightening on the blanket-wrapped bundle tucked under his arm.

"What can I do for you?" Rupert asks, sounding a bit harsh.

He's entitled. Paine wishes he had opted to call instead. But it's too late now.

"I'm on my way over to Chautauqua, but I just wanted to stop and talk to you for a moment, about the house," Paine says.

"What about the house?" the old man asks sharply.

"I'm afraid we've got a hitch in the plan." He quickly explains what Howard Menkin said, watching the already grim expression in Rupert's bloodshot eyes grow even darker.

"I can't have this," Rupert says. "You and I have made all the arrangements. Nan and I are moving in before the end of the week. We can't wait any longer."

"Believe me, Rupert, I don't want to hold off either. The sooner I can get back to California and get back to normal, the better. I've got to get my daughter the hell out of here."

Rupert's gaze suddenly focuses on Paine. "Why is that?"

Paine hesitates. Should he tell the old man the house is apparently haunted? What if he changes his mind about moving back in?

Well, if the place is haunted, Rupert must know. He lived there for years. It probably didn't bother him. After all, he makes his living talking to ghosts. Living in a spook-filled house is probably good for business.

If there really is such a thing as ghosts, Paine reminds himself out of habit.

Oh, hell. Who am I kidding?

There's something in that house. Dulcie isn't making this stuff up. It's time Paine admitted—at least to himself—that he can no longer cling to his pragmatic disbelief in spiritualism.

"Rupert," he says cautiously, "my daughter has been seeing things. Hearing things. She seems to think there's a ghost there. Somebody who died violently. A woman. And she's trying to tell Dulcie something. Julia, too. Were you ever aware of this spirit when you lived there?"

"No," Rupert tells him, letting a heavy sigh escape. "But this isn't the first I've heard about it. Is your daughter frightened?"

"She woke up screaming in the middle of the night. Said there was somebody in her room. She tried to tell me that it was a real person—a prowler."

"A prowler?" Rupert's eyes widen. "Around here? That's not likely. Lily Dale is a safe place. Most people don't even lock their doors at night, and many who do keep a key under the mat—which I personally believe is foolish anywhere in this day and age. Anyway, what has your daughter told you about the spirit?"

Paine quickly tells Rupert about Dulcie's latest encounter. The old man listens intently.

"What do you think?" Paine asks him.

"I think that either your daughter has a very active imagination, or she's truly involved in something supernatural. In which case I would advise you to be very careful, Mr. Landry. This is nothing to take lightly."

"I don't take it lightly. I just . . . tell me what you see as the worst-case scenario."

"You could be dealing with a powerful negative energy.

An experienced medium knows how to invoke protection against questionable entities, who are capable of not only haunting, but possessing. Your daughter wouldn't know how to bar the threshold.''

Paine swallows, uncertain what to believe. The skeptic in him wants to write it all off as a lot of B.S., yet as a concerned father, he can't simply disregard his fears.

''I have to get back to my wife,'' Rupert says. ''And I believe you said you were on your way out of town?'' He glances over Paine's shoulder, at the red rental car parked at the curb. ''You're not bringing your daughter with you?''

''No, she's back at the house, hopefully taking a nap. I left her with Julia. She's baby-sitting.''

''That's nice,'' the man says in the expressionless manner of somebody who's just being polite. ''Please let me know what Howard says when you meet with him tomorrow evening. What time is the meeting?''

''Not until seven. Would you like to come along?''

''I can't leave Nan,'' the man says simply.

With a sympathetic nod, Paine turns to go. Then, remembering the doll, he turns back to Rupert, who is about to shut the door again.

''I found this in the attic,'' he says, unwrapping the blanket. ''Julia says it wasn't Kristin's. I know you have a daughter. I thought it might have belonged to her.''

''It might have,'' Rupert murmurs, taking the doll, looking down at it.

''Keep it,'' Paine says.

''I will. I'll ask Nan about it. She'll remember if it was Katherine's.''

Paine nods. ''I'll speak to you tomorrow.''

Still studying the old doll, apparently lost in thought, Rupert shuts the door without a reply.

* * *

Dulcie smiles as Julia pulls a blanket up to her chin and gives her head a pat.

"Got your book?" Julia asks.

"It's right here under my pillow."

"Are you comfy?"

"Mmm-hmm." Dulcie yawns. "But don't let me sleep all afternoon, Julia. I want to go down to the playground with you before Daddy comes back."

"Okay. I'll come up to check on you every little while. If you do wake up, don't try to come down the stairs alone. Just wait here for me. Okay?"

"Okay."

Dulcie feels Julia's weight rising from the mattress, hears her footsteps moving to the door.

"Julia?" she calls sleepily.

"Hmm?"

Dulcie wants to tell her what happened last night. About the person coming into her room. About the lady covered in blood. But she's too tired. So tired that she's not even afraid anymore. Not the way she was last night.

After all, it's the middle of the day. She can hear the birds singing outside her window. She can feel warm sunlight on her hair. And Julia is here to keep her safe.

"Never mind," Dulcie says with another deep yawn.

She'll tell Julia about everything later, she thinks, drifting off to sleep, glad nothing bad can happen when the sun is shining and the birds are singing and Julia is here.

Pilar stares out the window as the car creeps forward, inch by inch. There is nothing to see but the tiled walls of the Queens Midtown Tunnel, and a string of red taillights in front of them.

The driver mutters something about the traffic.

Pilar murmurs a suitable reply, but her mind isn't on the traffic.

She keeps picturing Katherine Jergins's blank stare when she told her about Rupert and Nan. She keeps hearing Katherine say that her parents are dead. That she's never heard of the Biddles. That Pilar must have her mixed up with somebody else.

Mortified, Pilar made a vague apology for disturbing Katherine. She fled without a backward glance, hurrying to the car waiting at the curb.

Now that she's had time to go over what happened, she's left feeling even more unsettled than she did back in Katherine Jergins's yard.

If the woman has never heard of Nan and Rupert, why is her address in their address book?

And why does she look exactly like them?

She has to be lying, Pilar thinks, shivering a little in the chilly air-conditioning.

Pilar leans her head back against the cool leather seat and goes over it again.

And again.

Each time, she comes to the same conclusion.

For whatever reason, Katherine is unwilling to admit to Pilar that she's the Biddles' daughter.

My parents are dead.

Maybe they are, as far as she's concerned.

They must have had a falling-out, Pilar concludes. That must be why Rupert hasn't called her about Nan. Or maybe he has called her. Maybe she knows what's going on, and chooses not to come.

But what could Rupert and Nan have done that was horrible enough to cause a rift like this? What could Katherine have done? How could families turn their backs on each other this way?

Did the problem have anything to do with Rupert and Nan's rejection of Lincoln? They sent Katherine away to boarding school in New York to get her away so that she wouldn't be there waiting when he got back from Vietnam. But she obviously eventually came around to their way of thinking, or she fell in love with somebody else. After all, she sent Lincoln that Dear John letter. It doesn't make sense that in adulthood, she would feel so much renewed anger toward her parents for manipulating a youthful romance that she would cut off all relations with them.

Besides, if that were the case, wouldn't she have contacted her lost love, hoping for a reconciliation?

Lincoln said he never heard from her again.

And both had happy marriages to other people, as far as Pilar can tell.

"It's about time," the driver says in his accented English.

Glancing up, through the windshield, Pilar sees that the end of the tunnel is finally in sight.

It won't be long before they reach the west side pier where the cruise ship is docked. Christina won't be there yet, but she'll grab some lunch or a cup of coffee and wait. Suddenly she's anxious to hug her daughter.

In the kitchen, Julia dials Andy's number. She's been meaning to call him all day. Lorraine's accident is all anyone was talking about around town when Julia stopped to do a few errands on her way over here, but there's a chance Andy hasn't heard yet. He'll want to know. He likes Lorraine.

Everyone likes Lorraine, Julia realizes. *Everyone except Bruce . . .*

"Hello?" Andy's voice sounds harried.

"Hi. It's me, Julia."

"Julia! How are you?"

"Worried sick," she says. She tells him about Lorraine. Of course, he's already heard. He says that the accident was a terrible shame.

"If it was an accident," Julia says.

"What do you mean by that?"

She tells him what Laura said about somebody hitting Lorraine on purpose. "She thinks it was Lorraine's ex-husband."

As Julia speaks, the mantel clock chimes in the parlor.

Hearing it, Andy asks, "Where are you?"

"I'm over at Paine's—at Iris's," she amends, realizing this is the first time she hasn't subconsciously referred to the place as belonging to its previous occupant.

"Oh. What are you doing there?"

"Baby-sitting Dulcie. Paine had to go to Chautauqua this afternoon, and Dulcie was exhausted, so I'm staying with her while she takes a nap."

"That's nice of you." Andy doesn't sound thrilled about it. "Do you want to have dinner later?"

Julia hesitates. "I can't. I'm not sure when Paine will be back. It won't be for at least a couple of hours, and then I want to go back to the hospital to see Lorraine . . ."

"Okay." Andy clears his throat. "I'm still seeing you tomorrow night, right?"

"Tomorrow night?" Belatedly, she remembers. Iris's ashes. He's taking her out on the lake to scatter them.

"Tomorrow night. Did you forget?"

"Of course I didn't forget. I guess I'll see you then."

"I guess you will." There seems to be a slight edge of sarcasm in his voice.

Julia hangs up, uncomfortable. She can't help feeling as

if she's using him, and wonders if he feels the same way. But she has to go through with it now. It's too late to find somebody else to take her out to scatter Iris's ashes on such short notice.

I should check on Dulcie, Julia decides, walking into the hall. *If she's asleep, I'll go down to the basement and spend some time working on the dresser.*

Standing at the bottom of the stairs, about to go up, she feels goose bumps rising on her arms.

She isn't alone.

Looking up, she glimpses a figure at the top of the stairs, her back to Julia. She has long blond hair.

Julia gasps.

And in the blink of an eye, she's gone.

Whoever she was.

Kristin?

Could it possibly have been Kristin?

Shaken, Julia stands for a long time at the bottom of the stairs, willing her to come back, waiting. She can hear the clock ticking in the parlor, birds singing in the yard, and the clicking of bicycle spokes as somebody pedals past the house. There's a session going on in the auditorium right now, and all is quiet in the streets.

At last, realizing the apparition isn't going to put in another appearance, Julia walks slowly up the stairs. Pausing outside Dulcie's room, she opens the door a crack and peeks inside.

The little girl is sound asleep, her even breathing audible from here.

Good.

She needs the rest, poor thing. She obviously had a restless night. Julia will ask Paine about it later.

She closes the door quietly. Dulcie is bound to sleep for at least an hour, maybe longer.

She might as well go down to the cellar to work on the

dresser for a little while. She'll have to see about having it moved to her place.

At the top of the steps, she pauses in the spot where she saw the apparition. It's empty now.

She moves forward and grasps the banister with a trembling hand, listening.

She half expects to hear something . . .

The music.

The scream.

There is only silence.

Yet Julia is suddenly filled with a terrible sense of foreboding.

In her room, Miranda lies on her bed, a pair of earphones on her head. They're plugged into the digital cassette recorder on the bedside table. She's been listening to the tape for the past hour, hoping to distract herself from thoughts of Andy. It isn't working. There's not much to hear.

It's about time that she got around to doing this, though. She has several tapes, made at various times over the past few days, whenever she managed to sneak back over to Ten Summer Street and pop a new tape into the recorder she planted there.

The first tape, which she just finished listening to, yielded nothing but the usual night noises: crickets, cars passing by, raindrops falling. With all the wet weather, she knew she was taking a risk with her equipment. Luckily, she managed to shelter the recorder well when she rigged it in the leafy boughs of the lilac shrub, keeping it dry but not muffled with a strategically placed plastic tarp.

Miranda knows what Kent would say if he knew she trespassed on that property after the owner denied them permission to conduct an investigation there. They agreed, when they first launched their business together, that it was something they would never do.

But somehow, Miranda couldn't help herself. When Andy suggested that she place some equipment there to monitor the property, she concluded it was a brilliant idea.

If she had thought of that herself, she most likely would have resisted temptation. But where Andy is concerned, there is no resisting temptation. As her therapist and Kent have so helpfully brought to her attention, when Miranda is infatuated—whether by a man, or a potential supernatural site—she is a woman with a mission.

Though, truth be told, the yard of the Summer Street house seemed much more important a few days ago, before Andy turned her life upside down. Now that he's ranked first among her so-called obsessions, it's all Miranda can do to make herself lie here and listen to the tapes, just in case she picked up anything.

She wonders idly what Andy is doing. Is he sitting in on the message service over in the auditorium? That's where Kent is.

Maybe Miranda should tell Kent what happened with Andy. She could use a shoulder to cry on—even if it means hearing Kent say "I told you so" for the gazillionth time in her life.

Sooner or later, Miranda is going to get it through her head that when it comes to men, she has a knack for choosing losers. Maybe all men aren't like Michael, but she can't seem to resist the ones who—

What was that?

Miranda sits up abruptly, frowning.

She reaches for the tape recorder and presses REWIND, then PLAY.

There it is again.

She barely noticed it.

Music.

The recorder has picked up the faint sound of guitar music.

It must be coming from a car passing by, Miranda tells herself, listening.

But no, that can't be. She can't hear a car, just the music. And it doesn't fade in and out, as it would with a car passing into the distance.

It simply spills out of nowhere, ghostly guitar strains for a familiar melody. It goes on for several seconds.

What is this song? I know it.

Miranda adjusts the volume, the balance, the tape speed. She presses REWIND again, then PLAY.

She frowns, listening to the familiar music, trying to identify it. The name of the song is elusive, dancing on the fringe of her consciousness.

Adjust the controls.

Rewind.

Play.

Where was the music coming from the night the tape was made?

An open window of a neighbor's house?

Adjust.

Rewind.

Play.

But why, if it was coming from somebody's house, did it start and end so abruptly, without the sound of a window or a door opening or closing? Why can't I hear other sounds that might spill out into the night with the music, like people's voices, footsteps, or a DJ's voice?

Adjust.

Rewind.

Play.

Okay, so maybe there's no natural explanation for it. Maybe a spirit is responsible for the music being on the tape. But what does it mean? And what the heck is it? I know I've heard it before.

Adjust.

Rewind.

Play.

Come on, Miranda. Concentrate! What song . . . ?

That's it!

Miranda smiles triumphantly, having placed the melody at last.

It's an old Simon and Garfunkel tune.

"Kathy's Song."

In the cellar, an old transistor radio of Iris's plays staticky music from an oldies station—the only one Julia can tune in. That's okay. The music reminds her of Grandma, who always claimed she was a jitterbug champion in her youth.

Julia uses the corner of a small scraper to strip loosened, gummy clumps of stain from the dresser's intricate antique scrollwork. It's tedious, mindless work, not nearly as enjoyable as she originally anticipated.

Oh, well.

Soon the roof will be done so she can work again, and Paine and Dulcie will be gone, and things will be back to normal.

Or will they?

The thought of Lorraine weighs heavily on her mind. There's been no word yet on her condition. When Julia last went up to check Dulcie about ten minutes ago, she called her own answering machine to check her messages. There were none. Then she called the hospital. All they would tell her was that her friend was in surgery.

As soon as Paine gets home, Julia intends to go back over

there. Even if she can't see Lorraine, she'll feel better just being nearby.

Julia goes absolutely still at the sound of a muffled thump.

What on earth is that?

She waits, poised, listening.

For a long time, there's nothing but silence.

Deciding it must have been her imagination, or perhaps a cat prowling around the cellar door, Julia uneasily begins to scrape the wood again.

Minutes later, a more distinct sound reaches her ears: a floorboard creaking overhead, on the first floor of the house.

"Dulcie?" Julia drops the scraper and hurries toward the stairway. She warned Dulcie not to try to come down the flight of stairs by herself. Maybe it's Paine. Maybe he's home early.

At the bottom of the steep, cobweb-draped stairway leading out of the cellar, Julia stops short, looking up in disbelief. The angled double doors at the top of the stairs are closed.

Fighting back a surge of panic, Julia swiftly mounts the stairs.

It must have been the wind.

Except . . .

What wind? It's a beautiful, calm day. There's not even a breeze.

And if the wind closed the doors, wouldn't I have heard them banging shut?

As she nears the top of the steps, Julia hurriedly reaches overhead to push open the doors.

They don't budge.

Reality sinks in, and with it, numbing terror.

Somebody has latched the doors from the outside, imprisoning Julia in the musty cellar.

* * *

"Paine!" Stan looks up from an issue of the *Chautauquan Daily*, obviously surprised to see him. "How did you know where to find me?"

"Hi, Stan. I looked for you at your office and somebody said you were here." *Here* being the wide porch that runs the length of the Athenaeum Hotel, a grand, wood-frame period structure with a distinct curved mansard roof.

"Have a seat. I'm just catching a break before my class starts."

Paine sits in one of the painted ladder-back rockers beside Stan and looks over the rail, admiring the view. The porch runs the length of the building, which sits high on a sloping lawn above the lake. Today, with the sky a brilliant blue and the sun dazzling overhead, the crystalline water is dotted with sailboats and speedboats towing skiers.

"I wanted to thank you for letting me sit in on your sessions this week," Paine tells Stan. "It's been invigorating."

"I'm glad." Stan looks thoughtfully at him. "Invigorating in the sense that you've changed your mind about live theater?"

Paine laughs. "I've got to make a living, Stan. Residuals from a chewing gum commercial pay more bills than being on stage ever could."

"Not necessarily. Not if you're on top. On Broadway. And it's not nearly as fulfilling."

Paine thinks about Margaret's son, the actor. For her last birthday, he sent her five dozen roses with a note that read *This is to make up for all the years I couldn't even afford to send you a card.*

Paine says slowly, "I can't afford to start over. I've got a daughter to raise."

Stan shrugs.

"What are you thinking?" Paine asks.

"That you're making excuses. But feel free. We all do it. I've got a million of them for why I haven't quit cigarettes yet. Speaking of which"—he checks his watch—"I've got to head back over to the classroom. I can smoke while I walk. Come on, walk with me."

Paine rises, and together they head down the broad wooden steps.

"I won't be back here again," Paine tells Stan. "I'm heading back to L.A. in a day or two."

He's made up his mind to go, no matter what's going on with the house. He can't afford to hang around waiting for the legal issues to be untangled. He'll handle the real estate transaction from afar if it turns out the house belongs to Dulcie. And if it doesn't . . .

Well, the money would have been nice, but they'll survive without it. They always have.

"Somehow, I can't see you living the rest of your life out there, Paine," Stan says, pulling a pack of Salems from his shirt pocket.

"Why not? L.A. is home for me and Dulcie. Everything is there."

"Everything. Huh. Good for you, then." Stan lights his cigarette and takes a drag.

They walk in silence up a steep, shady street beneath a canopy of old trees.

Everything is there?

What the hell is everything? A rented apartment? Uptight parents I never see? A couple of minimum-wage jobs and a half-assed teaching assignment?

"You can't think I should stay *here*," Paine says, frowning.

"Hmm? Did I say that?"

"You didn't have to. It's what you were thinking. That I should stay here in the East. Keep the house in Lily Dale. Teach at Chautauqua during the summers. Maybe even get back on stage. Start auditioning in New York, spend the rest of the year there, the way you do."

"Is that what you want, Paine?"

"No." He scowls. "That's not what I want."

The trouble is, he doesn't want his old life in L.A., either. Not anymore. Not now that . . .

Now that what? What's changed?

"Then what do you want, Paine?" Stan asks.

I want Kristin back. I want to be married. I want a real family. I want to live happily ever after, and I don't give a damn where, as long as I can shake this oppressive restlessness.

"I have no idea," he says glumly.

Dulcie . . .

Dulcie . . .

Abruptly awakened by the sound of someone calling her name, Dulcie groggily assumes that it's Julia. She sits up and pushes the blanket away, instinctively swinging her legs over the edge of the mattress, her feet onto the floor.

That's when she sees the lady, beckoning to her. The image isn't clear, but Dulcie can see her familiar blond hair, and her outstretched arms waving her forward. All around her is the black nothingness that is Dulcie's constant, whether her eyes are opened or closed.

Mesmerized, Dulcie moves toward the lady, somehow forgetting to feel her way along the furniture and the wall. Somehow, her steps are assured. Somehow, there are no obstacles in her path.

She moves in barefooted silence across the room and out

into the hallway, guided by the vision floating in front of her. A voice in the back of her mind reminds her that Julia said not to try to go downstairs alone, but another voice is louder.

The lady's voice, calling her name.

I must be dreaming, Dulcie thinks, dazed. *Otherwise I wouldn't be able to walk like this, without bumping into anything.*

In the hallway outside her room, Dulcie turns toward the stairway, but the lady wants her to go the other way.

A sound drifts up from the first floor.

Somebody is downstairs.

Dulcie opens her mouth, about to call out Julia's name.

No! Shhh . . .

She realizes that whoever is down there isn't walking across the floor like a regular person.

Dulcie can sense the stealthy movements of someone sneaking quietly through the house.

Somebody who shouldn't be here.

Just like last night.

Her heart pounding, she moves backward, away from the stairway, toward the lady. She can feel the pull, can feel the urgency in the lady's guidance.

Dulcie's outstretched hand encounters a doorknob.

Turn it.

She opens a door. Walks into a room. Disoriented, she has no idea which room it is; only knows that it isn't hers. She closes the door softly behind her.

She can hear the lower stairs creaking. Somebody is coming up.

The lady wants her to come farther into the room. Dulcie walks blindly, yet swiftly and strangely assured, moving forward until her outstretched hands encounter a window screen on the far end of the room.

Open it. Open the window. Get out of the house, Dulcie. Hurry.

She pushes the window upward. It isn't easy. The old wood barely moves a few inches, not enough of an opening for her to climb through above the screen. Dulcie's fingers find the edges of the screen, the old-fashioned kind that isn't built in, like the ones in the windows back home in L.A.

She can hear footsteps in the hall. One slow, steady step after another.

Dulcie shoves the screen until it contracts and falls forward, landing with a clatter on the hardwood floor at her feet.

The footsteps in the hall stop abruptly.

Then they start again, moving toward the door to this room.

Hurry, Dulcie. Get out.

Dulcie hesitates, reaching past the sill, feeling nothing on the other side but thin air. She tries desperately to remember Daddy's description of the outside of the house, struggles to remember which way she went in the hallway before coming into this room.

Is she at the front of the house, where the porch roof runs under the windows?

Or is she in the back, where it's a straight drop to the ground?

Get out, Dulcie. Get out. Hurry.

Her heart pounding, she raises a leg and straddles the windowsill. Her foot dangles into nothingness on the other side.

Trust me, Dulcie. Climb over the edge. You won't get hurt. Just get out. Yell for help. Get somebody's attention.

Her eyes squeezed tightly shut, the lady's outstretched arms beckoning, Dulcie holds her breath and hoists herself over the windowsill.

* * *

"Help! Somebody help!"

Her voice hoarse, Julia rams the cellar doors again with the broom handle. This time, it splinters in two.

She tosses it aside in bitter frustration and looks around once again in a futile attempt to find another way out of here. No windows, no other doors have magically appeared. She's been trying to get out of here for what seems like hours, yet she knows it can't have been longer than five minutes, maybe ten.

What if nobody finds her?

Exhausted, Julia slumps on the bottom step.

Dulcie doesn't know where she is.

Paine might not think to look for her here.

The old house is solidly built. Yet surely whoever was walking around upstairs could hear her thumping with the broom handle on the cellar doors, and, at one point, on the ceiling.

Julia feels sick inside as she allows herself to wonder who is up there with Dulcie—and whether that person deliberately locked her down here.

She's been telling herself that it had to be an accident. That perhaps Paine came home, saw the doors open, and closed them, thinking she had merely been careless.

But that doesn't make sense.

Paine would have seen the light, heard the radio, checked down here for Julia. He knows she's been working on the dresser.

Something tickles Julia's bare leg, just above her knee. She glances down.

A large brown spider with jointed, furry legs is crawling lazily upward there, toward the hem of her shorts.

With a piercing shriek, Julia bolts to her feet, flinging the loathsome creature away, not seeing where it lands.

Shuddering, wary, she brushes off her arms, her legs, her hair, feeling as though her skin were crawling with whatever lurks in the crevices of this musty old cellar. Spiders, centipedes, mice, bats . . .

Julia snatches up one half of the cracked broom handle and climbs back up the stairs. She has to get out of here. What if the lone lightbulb burns out and she's trapped here in pitch-blackness?

She lifts the splintered wood above her head, but before it makes contact, the door moves.

Stunned, Julia realizes that somebody's outside, opening it.

She's been saved!

Breathless, she watches as a crack of light falls through the opening. As it grows wider, blue sky and green branches appear, along with the silhouette of a person.

Julia blinks, momentarily dazzled by the sunlight.

Then she sees her rescuer's face looking down at her, his eyes masked by a familiar pair of sunglasses.

It's Andy.

Pilar paces in front of the bank of pay phones, one eye on the nearby set of glass doors. Any second now, Christina and her husband and children are going to burst through with their luggage. Then it will be time to board the massive ship that looms just outside, and set sail to the Caribbean.

With a disinterested glance at the dark-suited businessman barking orders into one phone and the pudgy, Hawaiian-shirt couple sharing the receiver of another, squealing farewells into it, Pilar walks, not for the first time, to the last phone in the bank, farthest away from the others.

She picks up the receiver, fumbling in her pocket for a plastic long-distance calling card paper-clipped to the small scrap of paper that bears the three numbers she's considering dialing.

Katherine Jergins's.

Lincoln Reynolds's.

The Biddles'.

Again, uncertainty seeps in.

Should she make a call?

Whom should she call?

What on earth should she say?

She settles on Lincoln's number. Perhaps there's something he didn't tell her, something he can share that might shed light on Katherine's reaction to the mention of her parents.

It seems to take an eternity to punch in the numbers on the calling card and wait for a line to open up so that she can dial.

When she finally does, the phone at the Reynolds residence rings . . . and rings . . . and rings . . .

With an anxious glance at her watch, and then at the glass doors, Pilar hangs up, consulting her list of numbers.

Katherine or Rupert?

Why can't you leave it alone? Just forget about it and go on your vacation. Stop meddling.

The paper trembles in her hand. Pilar thinks of Nan, lying—dying—in that small, unadorned room. Of Rupert, hovering at her side, anguished, alone. She has to help them.

Even if it means admitting to the old man that she's stolen his daughter's phone number from his address book and contacted her behind his back?

Pilar exhales heavily. He'll be furious.

Katherine or Rupert?

She makes up her mind and begins to dial again.

Katherine answers on the second ring.

She speaks in a rush. "Hello, this is Pilar Velazquez and we met earlier, when I stopped by your house. I'm so sorry to bother you again, but there's something that I think you should know."

The woman says, icily, "First of all, I told you, I have no idea what you're talking about. You must have me mixed up with someone el—"

"No, Katherine, please . . . I understand that you must have your reasons for denying—"

"Look, what are you? Some kind of scam artist?"

"Scam artist?" Pilar echoes incredulously. "No! I'm—"

"I saw your business card. I know what you people are like."

Her business card. *Pilar Velazquez, Registered Medium and Spiritual Counselor.*

"I have to go," Katherine says brusquely.

"No! Please don't hang up." In desperation, Pilar seizes the one name that might keep her on the line. "Please—I have a message for you from Lincoln. He says he wants to hear from you. Please don't—"

Too late.

The dial tone buzzes in her ear.

Driving slowly back through the gates of Lily Dale, Paine waves at the teenaged boy in the booth. He waves back with a grin.

Friendly kid. His name is Ben, and he always says hello to Dulcie when they pass. She shyly told him one of her favorite knock, knock jokes the day he introduced himself.

Knock, knock.

Who's there?

Ben.

Ben who?

Ben out here knocking forever, open the door!

To his credit, Ben that hilarious. Now he's Dulcie's local hero. And of course, Julia is her local heroine.

"Hey," Ben calls to Paine through the open car window, "where's Dulcie?"

"She's home."

"Tell her I've got a new knock, knock for her. It'll crack her up."

"I will." Smiling, Paine drives into the now-familiar maze of winding streets.

He waves at an elderly couple out with their poodle for an afternoon walk. The Coopers. They live a few houses down on Summer Street. Mrs. Cooper brought a handpicked bouquet and some homemade sugar cookies for Dulcie the second day they were here.

Funny how any place can start to feel like home, Paine muses. *If you let it.*

But he won't let Lily Dale feel like home. He doesn't want this. No matter what crazy thoughts might have flown into his head back there when he was talking to Stan, he doesn't want to stay here.

He slows the car to let two little girls on bicycles cross in front of him. He recognizes one of them from the playground. She invited Dulcie to teeter-totter with her.

Sweet kid, Paine thinks, rounding the corner onto Summer Street. Dulcie has never teeter-tottered before. She loved it.

And the little girl giggled at all of her knock, knock jokes, too.

Paine parks in the usual spot at the curb in front of the house. As he gets out of the car, he wonders idly whether Dulcie napped while he was gone. If not, he'll put her into bed extra early tonight. That'll give him a chance to finish going through the things in the attic and—

Halfway up the walk, Paine stops short.

"Daddy!"

Dulcie is calling him. He looks up to see her in the side yard, near the cellar doors. Julia is there, too. And that man she's been dating. Andy.

Paine frowns. What's he doing here? There's something about that guy that Paine doesn't like.

He strides across the grass toward the three of them. Something is wrong here. He can feel it. Can see it on Dulcie's face.

"What's going on?" he asks, giving his daughter a hug and looking at Julia. She, too, is obviously troubled.

She opens her mouth to speak, but Andy beats her to it. "Looks like you've had a prowler sneaking around here, Mr. Landry."

Mr. Landry? Paine's immediate reaction is that this guy is too young to be calling him Mr. Landry. There's a false aura of respect in the way he says it.

Damn, he rubs me the wrong way, Paine thinks.

Then he realizes what it is that Andy's telling him, and a chill slips down his spine. A prowler?

"That's what your daughter claims, anyway," Andy says. "But there aren't a lot of prowlers around here. It's pretty safe."

What she *claims?* Paine doesn't like the guy's insinuation. He looks at Julia, but Andy is still talking.

"I happened to stop by to see Julia, and I found your daughter out on the front porch roof, yelling her head off. She had climbed out the window and she was—"

"On the roof?" Paine thunders. "What the hell? Dulcie, what were you—" He turns on Julia, his heart pounding. "How could you let this happen?"

"I was trapped in the cellar." She is clearly shaken. "I was down there and somebody locked the—"

"You were down in the cellar and my daughter was climbing out *windows?*" Fury courses through Paine. He can barely see straight. "My God, she could have fallen. She—"

"Lucky for her, I came along," Andy cuts in heroically. "I told her not to move, and I raced into the house—all the doors were open—so I went upstairs and climbed out the window and got her."

Paine rakes a shaky hand through his hair, unable to digest the bizarre scenario. He turns to Dulcie. "Sweetheart, what were you doing on the roof? Why would you do a thing like that?"

"I was taking a nap," Dulcie says in a small voice, taking a step closer to Julia, "and then I—"

"Were you sleepwalking?" he asks incredulously. Dulcie has never sleepwalked, but . . .

"No." Her voice grows smaller still. She is almost cowering behind Julia as she says, "Somebody was sneaking around the house, and the lady told me to go out there."

Paine's heart seems to land with a thud.

For a long moment, all of them are silent.

Then Paine turns to Julia. "Can you please go now?"

She opens her mouth. Closes it again. He sees a streak of dirt on her cheek.

"Go," he repeats, and turns to Andy. "You, too. Just go."

"Daddy, please don't be mad at Julia," Dulcie begs in a choked voice.

"Go!" he bellows, reaching for his daughter. He pulls her against him, stroking her tousled blond hair.

She struggles in his grasp, her arms outstretched toward Julia, who looks almost dazed as she walks away, head bent.

Andy catches up to her, putting one arm around her shoulders and quietly saying something in her ear.

"No!" Dulcie cries, trying to break away.

Paine holds her fast against him. "It's okay, Dulcie. It's going to be okay. We're going to get away from here just as soon as—"

"I don't want to get out of here," Dulcie wails. "I want Julia. She takes care of me!"

"Yeah. She takes great care of you," he says flatly, shaking his head. He trusted Julia. How could she let this happen?

His scrambled thoughts run over the scenario again.

Prowler?

"Julia understands about the lady!" Dulcie sobs.

Paine freezes. The lady. Again.

He crouches beside his daughter, his arms still around her, holding her close. "Tell me about the lady, Dulcie," he says gently.

"I tried to tell you. You didn't listen, and you didn't believe me."

She's right.

She did try.

He didn't listen.

And he didn't believe her.

But maybe, he thinks with a shudder, looking up at the house, he should.

"Tell me again, Dulcie," he says resolutely, stroking her hair. "This time, I promise I'll listen."

Chapter Twelve

"Nan?" Stepping into the darkened room, Rupert leans close to his wife. A shaft of light from the kitchen illuminates her profile on the bed. She's completely motionless. Silent.

Rupert's stomach turns over.

"Nan!" He grabs one of her hands, folded on top of the quilt. "No, darling, please—"

He breaks off in sheer relief, realizing that her flesh is soft and warm. Bending closer still and putting his ear to her lips, he can hear the faint sound of air passing over the mucus in her lungs. He touches his mouth to hers. He rubbed lotion into them earlier, but her lips are again cracked and dry, a microscopic pink streak of blood escaping a split in the parched skin at the corner of her mouth.

"Oh, Nan," he whispers, a wave of sorrow breaking over him, threatening to sweep him into utter despair.

No.

He has to remain strong for her, until the end.

And this isn't the end. Not yet, he thinks stubbornly.

But it isn't the sheer force of Rupert's will alone that's keeping Nan here.

He walks to the bathroom, taking a clean, folded washcloth from a neatly organized drawer in the narrow linen closet. He runs water over it.

No, it isn't just that he isn't ready to let her go yet. *Her* will is keeping her here.

She isn't ready to go.

Physically, maybe. Physically, her body is shutting down, giving out on her.

But something is holding her here.

He knows what it is. But what can he do? He can't—

"Damn!" Burning his hand on the tap water that's suddenly running too hot, Rupert drops the washcloth and runs cold water over his fingers.

Terrible plumbing. That's just one of the things that's wrong with this house.

Irrational anger rises within him. For once, he doesn't squash it back. He allows the fury to vent through a shouted curse and a fierce kick at the pipe below the pedestal sink.

It's safe to be angry at the house, he realizes, fists clenched, breath coming in ragged pants.

Safer than being angry at other things. Things he can't control, no matter how he tries.

Rupert looks into the mirror over the sink. The frustration and weariness that have invaded his body are mirrored in his gray eyes, in the deep creases and dark trenches that line them.

This should be the last night he and Nan are spending in this house. Now Lord only knows how long it will be before they can move back home to Summer Street.

Rupert picks up the washcloth again, wrings it out, runs

warm water over it, and wrings it again. Then he takes the tube of cream from the vanity and carries it and the warm cloth carefully back to the bedroom.

He sits on the bed and looks at her.

Nan's eyelids are half open, but her pupils are glazed, unfocused. Alarm erupts within him again—until he realizes that she's asleep.

Rupert lets out a shaky breath, watching her.

This, too, is an odd physical symptom he's noticed increasingly these past few days—this strange way she has now of sleeping with slitted lids, a vacant stare. Even when her eyes are fully open and she's awake, Nan seems to be paying little attention to what's going on around her.

"I'm going to moisten your mouth for you, darling," Rupert says softly. "I'd do anything for you. You know that, don't you, Nan? Anything . . ."

He tenderly dabs at his wife's parched lips with the warm cloth as tears trickle down his weathered cheeks.

As Julia drives through the gates of Lily Dale, she notices that the moon is exceptionally bright tonight, the sky brilliant with stars.

If it had been like this last night, Lorraine would never have been hit by that car.

Or would she?

Of course not. It was definitely an accident. Laura told her that it turns out Bruce isn't even around—he's visiting a friend in Detroit and has been there for a week.

So it was an accident. But that doesn't change anything. Lorraine lies in a hospital bed, recovering from surgery, barely recognizable.

Julia tries to shut out an image of Lorraine's swollen bruised face. She couldn't speak because of the tubes in her throat, but when Julia gently squeezed her hand, Lorraine gazed intently at her and blinked several times as if to say *I know you're pulling for me.*

After spending the last four or five hours at the hospital with Lorraine's family, and being allowed that brief encounter with her friend, all Julia wants to do is go home and climb into bed, shutting out every horrible thing that's happened in the last twenty-four hours.

The winding streets of Lily Dale are almost deserted at this hour. Glancing at the clock on the dashboard, Julia sees that it's nearly nine-thirty. Driving past the turnoff to Summer Street, she is promptly attacked by the memory of what happened this afternoon.

Until now, she's almost managed to keep thoughts of Paine and Dulcie at bay. Now those thoughts rush in to assault her, filling her with guilt, and regret, and fear.

Julia doesn't blame Paine for being furious with her. He was right. Dulcie could have been badly hurt. But if Julia had any idea that she wouldn't stay in her bed . . . or that she would pull a stunt like that . . .

The lady told me to climb out the window.

Dulcie said it repeatedly as Julia grilled her for some explanation. She kept talking about someone sneaking up the stairs to get her, saying she was trying to get away and that the lady was helping her to escape.

Later, as they left, Andy made an infuriating comment, insinuating that Dulcie had made up the story about the prowler and an imaginary "lady" to explain why she disobeyed Julia.

"Dulcie isn't that kind of child!" Julia said fervently. "She doesn't misbehave that way."

"Calm down, Julia. I didn't mean anything by it. It's just that all kids are capable of bratty behavior once in a while, and of lying to cover it up."

"Well, Dulcie isn't lying about the lady," Julia retorted. "I've seen her, too."

His eyes widened. "What do you mean?"

Julia found herself spilling the whole story to Andy—about the presence she and Dulcie have encountered in the house, and the possible connection to Kristin.

Though Andy still expressed doubt that there was also a human prowler, as Dulcie claimed, he was willing to believe that she was telling the truth about being lured out of bed by the apparition. "It sounds to me as though there's some kind of malevolent energy in that house, Julia. The sooner Paine Landry gets his daughter out of there, the better. And you should stay away, too."

Ha.

Stay away? No problem. Judging by the way Paine looked at her when he told her to go, he'll probably run her off the property if she so much as sets foot on the grass.

Dulcie was crying for her as she left. That broke Julia's heart. But what could she do? Paine ordered her to leave, and he certainly won't welcome her back before they head to California.

I won't be able to say good-bye.

Julia tries to convince herself that maybe it will be better this way. Better for Dulcie. It isn't healthy for her to be so attached to someone she's never going to see again. A clean, immediate break would be best.

Still, Julia is planning on going to tomorrow morning's memorial service for Iris. And unless Paine has changed his mind, she intends to scatter Iris's ashes over the lake at dusk. She wants to do it, to honor the woman who, in her last years, was more of a mother figure to Julia than Deborah Garrity has been.

Julia sighs, turning onto her own quiet street as her thoughts wander back to this afternoon yet again.

She isn't inclined to agree with Andy—or Rupert Biddle—that the energy lurking in that house is dangerous. If Dulcie's perception was accurate, the spirit lured her out of her bed to help, not harm, her.

If only you didn't go down to the cellar and leave Dulcie alone in the house. What on earth were you thinking, Julia?

I was thinking that Dulcie was safe, sound asleep, and she promised not to leave her bed if she woke up. And I checked on her every fifteen minutes. This is Lily Dale, for Pete's sake. Nobody even locks their doors here.

But maybe they should.

As much as she's tried to consider Andy's pragmatic viewpoint and talk herself out of it, Julia is almost certain Dulcie was right about somebody prowling around the house. She herself thought she heard footsteps overhead, and she's not convinced they were Dulcie's. More frighteningly, she's inclined to believe that if there was a prowler, whoever it was knowingly locked her in the cellar. Those doors didn't close accidentally—no matter what Andy thinks.

Andy.

He seemed far more interested in recapping his heroic rescue of Dulcie from the roof and Julia from the cellar than he was in discussing the rest of it. He kept saying that it was a good thing he'd decided to drop in on her and say hello. Maybe he was just trying to distract her by avoiding the what-ifs. He probably just wanted to ease Julia's fears, reassure her, get her mind off what might have happened if he hadn't come along.

But now, as she pulls up in front of her house, safely home at last, Julia can think of nothing else.

Is Kristin's spirit trying to protect her daughter? If so, from whom?

Though reluctant to face a familiar, and far more troubling, likelihood, Julia can't keep the thought from seeping into her consciousness.

What if Kristin's death really wasn't accidental?

What if whoever killed her is after Dulcie?

Turning off the ignition, Julia is so caught up in her troubling thoughts that it takes a few moments for her to recognize the red car parked at the curb, in front of hers.

Startled, she glances up at the house.

There, on the front steps, sits Paine Landry, a sleeping Dulcie in his lap.

Standing at the ship's rail, Pilar stares down into the shimmering path of moonlight on black water. It's chilly out here on deck, but she can't bring herself to retreat to her cabin. Nor is she in the mood to return to the lounge, where her family is learning to line dance beneath dizzying strobe lights and a spinning silver disco ball.

Out here, beneath the canopy of starry sky, there is nothing but hushed, soothing salt air.

But the majestic serenity has yet to seep into Pilar.

Raul has been with her all night, so strong and unsettling a presence that she barely touched the succulent seafood feast in the dining room. She excused herself, telling her concerned daughter that she was feeling a little seasick.

The truth is, she's becoming increasingly uneasy about the Biddles' situation, and about her strange encounter with their daughter.

She senses that Raul wants her to do something—to act, somehow, on what she knows.

But what do I know? Nothing.

Obviously, there's been a rift in that family. Katherine Jergins has her reasons for considering her parents dead.

And okay, she's entitled to assume that Pilar—a total

stranger showing up on the woman's doorstep, claiming to have urgent news for her—is some kind of scam artist.

But I gave her my card. Seeing the Lily Dale address should have convinced her, Pilar thinks, not for the first time. Instead, the business card seemed to antagonize Katherine further.

Why? None of it makes sense.

Help me, Raul, Pilar begs silently, absently watching a strolling couple stop nearby to embrace in the moonlight. *I can feel that you don't want me to stay out of this, as you warned me to do last week. Now you want me to become even more involved. You want me to do something.*

But what?

And . . .

Why?

Is Raul urging her to somehow play intermediary and heal the relationship between Katherine and her parents? Is Pilar supposed to try to ease Nan's transition from this world, and Rupert's loneliness and grief, by reconciling them with their daughter?

That was her original plan.

Yet now she senses that there's more to it.

For some reason, Pilar is growing increasingly uneasy. Unless she's mistaken, Raul is trying to communicate some kind of threat—one that's somehow connected to Lily Dale, and the Biddles.

Maybe I should call and warn them that they're possibly in danger, Pilar thinks, walking slowly back to her cabin. *Maybe that's what Raul wants me to do.*

If so, it'll have to wait until tomorrow. It's too late to call now. Most likely, Rupert and Nan are both sleeping peacefully at this hour . . . if everything is still all right over there.

Acknowledging Nan's rapidly deteriorating condition, Pilar reminds herself that time is running out.

"It looks like nobody's home, or they're up in bed," Miranda tells Kent softly, standing beside him at the curb in front of the house at Ten Summer Street. Not a single light spills from the windows.

"Brilliant deduction," Kent says dryly. "Listen, if this ghost busting stuff doesn't pan out, you might want to think about detective work."

She ignores his quip, gazing across the shadowy yard at the moonlit lilac branches where her recorder picked up the ghostly strains of music.

Earlier, after dinner, when she played the tape for Kent, he was excited. He feels, as Miranda does, that there is no natural explanation for the sounds.

He also enthusiastically agreed to come back over here tonight with her to investigate further.

What he doesn't know is that Miranda lied to him about having gotten earlier permission from the owners. She couldn't help feeling guilty when he willingly accepted what she said, not even bothering to ask her for the signed release form.

If he knew there isn't one—and that she trespassed and planted the audio recorder here to get the tape . . .

But he won't have to know, she reminds herself, eyeing the deserted-looking house. *And we aren't hurting anyone. This is our business. We're scientists conducting important research. Who knows what else we'll find if we check out that spot?*

"Let's go, Kent," she says. "Come on."

As they move quietly across the damp grass, lugging their equipment, guided by the beams of their flashlights, Miranda wonders if they should have waited until later. After midnight, there will be even less chance of being discovered here.

But here, in the side yard, they're well concealed by the overgrown landscaping. Fortuitously, the blue-painted house next door, whose yard borders this one, is also dark and seemingly deserted. There's no one around to see Miranda and Kent setting up their tripods and cameras.

Miranda takes her Trifield meter from her vest pocket and turns it on.

"Everything set?" Kent asks quietly.

She nods.

With that, they begin to do what they always do, beginning an investigation.

They watch, and they listen, and they wait.

The bed is too small for both of them, but Rupert has climbed in anyway. He doesn't want to be on the other side of the house, alone in the big, empty master bedroom. He wants to be with his wife.

Nan is everything to him.

Lying here in the dark beside her, holding her as she sleeps, he is carried back, over the years. Back to so many nights, just like this one—summer nights, with the windows open to chirping crickets and the distant lapping of waves on the lake.

It wasn't always this serene, though.

There were nights in the city, steamy summer nights when street noises filtered up: traffic, sirens, kids playing in open hydrants, people playing cards on stoops.

It was like that the first time he ever slept all night with Nan. They lay on his lumpy mattress in his small, rented room, entwined in each other's arms, soaked from the humidity and the exertion of making love. Long after the mothers below had noisily called their children inside and the raucous card games had given way to quiet chatter punctuated by occasional bursts of laughter, Rupert asked Nan if she should be getting home.

He'll never forget her reply.

"I *am* home," she said with a sigh of contentment, snuggling against him.

"Your mother is probably frantic," he pointed out, smiling in the dark.

"So?"

As it turned out, her mother was frantic. Had the police looking for Nan. When she showed up the next morning, instead of being grateful to see her daughter alive, Nan's mother threatened to disown her.

Of course, Nan made up some story. She didn't dare tell her mother that she was in love with an older man.

Rupert smiles, remembering what an issue it had been back then—the few years separating their ages. It doesn't matter now. It hasn't mattered in years. They're soul mates.

He smiles, reaching out to stroke Nan's head. His fingers encounter fabric where her hair should be.

It all comes back to him.

The chemo.

Her illness.

Harsh reality, slapping him in the face.

Well, it always does, doesn't it? Much as he tries to lose himself in dreams of the past, he can't fully escape what's happening today.

He never could. All his life, even in those early days with Nan, he's had the habit of transporting himself away from the present. But in his youth, he was always looking forward, not back—fantasizing about the future, making plans.

Rupert always had big plans.

His mother used to say he was like his father in that way.

Rupert has precious few memories of the man: He was always packing and unpacking, coming and going, taking care of "business." He always smelled good. He and Mother danced together sometimes, all around the apartment, to music from the radio. And he liked to do tricks.

He made handkerchiefs disappear into thin air, pulled pennies from Rupert's ears. Simple stunts for a career con man. Whenever he left, Rupert's mother cried, and his father told Rupert to take care of her until he came back.

And he always did come back from wherever he was. Sometimes it took a few days, and sometimes months, but he always walked through the door eventually, and he always brought presents. Shiny, expensive toys for Rupert, clothes and perfume for Mother. He was full of stories about where he had been, and plans for their future. He always said that someday, they were going to be rich. They were going to live in a fancy house, and have a car—maybe two cars. Rupert would go to a private school, and he would go to college. And someday, Rupert would have an important job, Father said. He would have a job at a desk in a towering office building in Manhattan, and he would never have to leave his family the way Father had to leave them.

But Father always came back.

Which is why Rupert didn't think much of it the time that he seemed to be away longer than ever before. At first, Mother didn't worry. Then she did worry. That was when Rupert worried, too.

But all that worrying never brought Father back.

There were no more presents. There was no more dancing. Pretty soon, there wasn't even an apartment. Rupert and Mother had to leave, because she couldn't pay the rent.

Rupert remembers telling Mother not to worry—that if Father didn't ever come back, he would get a job and take care of her. He was going to buy her gifts, and make her laugh the way Father did, and when he was tall enough, he was going to dance with her, too. Mother only hugged him and told him that he was full of big plans, just as his father always was.

And then she said his father was never coming back.

"How do you know?" Rupert asked. "Did he tell you? Did somebody tell you?"

"I just know," his mother said sadly.

They lived with friends for a while, and with an old aunt of Mother's who smelled bad and had a tiny apartment infested with cockroaches.

Then Mother got sick.

It's all a blur, Mother dying. Rupert knows the basics: she died one August night on his aunt's sofa, and he was with her when it happened.

He was there . . . but he doesn't remember. He has never let himself remember the details.

After Mother died, he was taken to a place for orphans. St. Bertrand's Home for Boys was a depressing, frightening, Gothic structure somewhere above the Hudson River—New Jersey, or Rockland County—Rupert never knew where, and later, when he was older, he never felt the need to find out.

Wade came along when Rupert was on the verge of adolescence, long since resigned to the fact that he would spend the rest of his childhood in that gloomy institution.

Wade was an old friend of Father's. He told Rupert that his father was dead. And Rupert realized he had already known that.

Father was murdered, Wade said, by somebody who thought Father had stolen money from him.

Rupert never asked Wade whether his father really had stolen the money. He knew the truth about that, too. Instinctively, he understood that his father's "business" was shady, conducted on the fringes of legality.

Father was a con man, and so was Wade.

Later, Rupert learned why Wade didn't track him down earlier. It was because he was in prison for several years, serving time on a swindling charge.

But all that ever mattered to Rupert was that Wade finally came, and that he said Rupert could live with him.

Wade took him away from St. Bertrand's. He didn't bring him home, because Wade didn't have a home. He lived on the road. Rupert didn't mind that at first. Not for a long time. Not until he felt the urge to settle down, and went back to the Bronx, moved into that tiny apartment, and met Nan.

Clinging to her now, awash in grief, Rupert can no longer hold it in. He's being strangled by emotion, feels it rising in his throat, threatening to spill over.

And then it does.

A choked sob escapes him.

The foreign, guttural sound startles him into awareness. He clamps his mouth shut, takes a deep breath. And then another.

He will not cry.

He will not let go.

He will be strong, and he will do what has to be done, just as he always has.

Paine gently lays Dulcie on the bed in Julia's room. He covers her with the afghan Julia gave him—a heavy yarn one that somebody undoubtedly crocheted by hand. As he tiptoes out of the room, he finds himself looking around, out of curiosity. There is little to see in the light that spills in from the hall: old, mismatched furniture, sheer curtains, a couple of braided rugs on the scarred hardwood floor.

Beside the door is an old-fashioned high bureau. Julia's grandmother's dresser, he remembers. The one she says reeks of mothballs. Paine inhales deeply, but all he can smell is the faint herbal fragrance he has come to associate with Julia. He smiles. He likes the scent.

A white lace-edged scarf is draped across the dresser top, and on it are several framed photographs.

As he glances idly at them, it occurs to Paine that all of the pictures show women: women alone, in posed portraits typical of a bygone era, and women in snapshots, standing together. He recalls Julia telling him that she was raised by her grandmother, who was widowed young, and by her mother, who never married her father—"whoever he was," Julia added, with a trace of bitterness.

"You mean you never knew your dad?"

"Let's just say that my mother has had quite a few boyfriends. Obviously one of them got her pregnant almost thirty years ago—and she decided that I'd be better off not even knowing who he was. In fact, I doubt he even knows I exist."

Paine remembers noticing the hurt on Julia's face when she said that. Now he's struck anew by how that must have hurt her growing up. Just looking at her collection of photos, anyone would be struck by the obvious absence of any male influence in Julia's life.

Aside from Andy, of course. Not that there are any photos of him in evidence.

For some reason, Paine is pleased by this. He doesn't think much of Andy Doyle and wonders, not for the first time, what Julia sees in him. There's an air of self-centered arrogance about him that turned Paine off the first time he met him. But he must have his good points.

After all, he most likely saved Dulcie's life. And I didn't even thank him, Paine realizes belatedly.

He glances again at the photographs, zeroing in on one that ostensibly shows all three generations together: Julia, her mother, and her grandmother. Julia looks about eighteen in the photo: carefree and casual in jeans and sneakers, her short dark hair windswept. Her grandmother, too—judging by her expression, her clothing, her no-frills appearance—appears to be laid-back and easygoing. But the woman between them bears no resemblance to either of them.

Julia's mother—assuming that's she—stands carefully posed, her face expertly made up, her hair so obviously teased and sprayed that it looks like cotton candy. She's dripping in costume jewelry and wears a bright pink suit with an ultrashort skirt that shows off a length of well-toned, stocking-clad leg in high-heeled pink pumps.

Paine doesn't like her on sight. No wonder Julia rarely seems to mention her—and when she does, it isn't with affection.

About to leave the room, Paine stops short, glimpsing a framed photo he didn't notice until now.

He picks it up, hands trembling slightly.

Julia and Kristin, not more than twelve or thirteen years old, sit on a wooden pier. Both wear bathing suits: Julia's athletic figure in a simple one-piece tank, Kristin's precocious curves already filling out a pink bikini. Julia's hair is damp and her legs dangle in the water; Kristin's sun-streaked tresses are dry and neatly combed. Her knees are bent, with her arms wrapped around them and her feet firmly on the weathered planks of the dock. Both girls are grinning, as though sharing a private joke.

Paine notices that Julia's arm is wrapped around Kristin's shoulders in an almost protective posture.

Then he sees the red depth marker floating in the water in the background. DEPTH: 6 FEET.

No wonder Kristin isn't damp, as Julia is. No wonder her feet are on dry ground. No wonder Julia looks as though she's poised to pull Kristin back on board if she should slip over the edge of the pier.

The old, familiar image assaults him again. Kristin, struggling underwater. Panic rising, lungs filling . . .

No. Stop.

Paine places the frame back on the dresser and looks back at Dulcie, asleep on the bed. She never even woke up when he carried her into the house and up the stairs, with Julia guiding the way in whispers.

He softly closes the door behind him and makes his way back down to the first floor. On this trip, he notices more about his surroundings—the peeling wallpaper, the water-stained ceiling, the shabby furniture. There is old-house charm, but the whole place could stand to be updated and renovated.

Julia waits in the kitchen, pouring two cups of coffee from the pot she's just brewed. She pours milk into both and hands him one, along with a sugar bowl.

He smiles. "You remembered."

"The sugar? I just hope there's enough in there. I don't use it very often."

"There's enough." He stirs some into his coffee.

"Let's go into the living room," Julia suggests, with a frustrated glance at the ceiling.

He follows her gaze. Where the roof should be, there's nothing but a length of plastic tarp. One corner flaps audibly in the slight breeze outside.

"How long is it going to be like that?"

"A few more days," she replies. "Which is fine . . . as long as it doesn't pour out again. Everything was damp in here this morning. Have you heard the weather forecast, by any chance?''

He shakes his head, following her into the front room. The weather is the last thing on his mind at this point.

He doesn't waste any time getting to the point. Seated beside her on an antique sofa, its seat too narrow to be comfortable, he says, ''I came over, Julia, for a couple of reasons. I guess the most important one is to apologize for the way I yelled at you this afternoon.''

She bows her head so that he can't see her expression.

''I didn't mean to lash out that way,'' he says. ''It's just that Dulcie . . . she's all I have. Nothing is more important to me than my daughter. And when I thought about what could have happened to her . . . well, I guess I went off the deep end.''

''I don't blame you. I didn't realize I shouldn't have left her up there asleep while I was in the basement. It didn't seem like that big a deal at the time. I kept checking on her, and she promised to stay in bed and wait for me if she woke up. Besides, I figured I could have heard her calling me if she needed me. I left the basement doors open, and her bedroom window was open, and it was almost directly above—''

He curtails her guilt-ridden tirade with a brisk ''I know all that. Look, Julia, it's not like I stand over her bed every time she's asleep. It's not like I don't let her out of my sight. I didn't mean to blame you for doing something I very likely would have done myself. And I'm sorry. But . . . that's not the only reason I'm here.''

''It's not?'' She looks up at him, her eyes expectant. ''Why are you here?''

''Because I talked to Dulcie after you left with your— with Andy.'' For some reason, he won't let himself label him her boyfriend. And anyway, she never has.

"Look, thank him for what he did when you see him, okay? For me. Thank him for me," Paine says. "Because I didn't think to do it when he was here, and the way I acted ... well, I'm sure I must have come across as ungrateful, and I'm not. If it hadn't been for that guy ..."

"I know." She gives a slight shudder, holding her coffee cup steady in her lap with both hands.

"Anyway," Paine goes on, "Dulcie told me some things, and I don't know what to make of them. I'm hoping ... I thought maybe you could help."

"What kinds of things did she tell you?"

He takes a deep breath. "Some of it I've heard before—the same stuff that I told you on Saturday. But now ... she says you think her mother's spirit is in the house. She says you think Kristin is there, and that you and Dulcie can see and hear—"

"I can't see her," Julia interrupts. "Only Dulcie can."

"But ... I just don't get it. She's blind, Julia. I know you tried to explain it before, and forgive me if I seem a little thick, because I'm trying really hard to understand. If all this spirit stuff is real—" Seeing her wary expression, he quickly shifts gears, asking simply, "How can she *see* anything?"

"The best way to explain it, Paine, is that I'm clairaudient, but I don't need my ears to hear what I hear. It comes from inside my head. The same is true with Dulcie's clairvoyance. Whatever she's seeing isn't necessarily there, in front of her. If you or I were beside her, we quite possibly wouldn't see the apparition."

"I've never seen a ghost in my life."

"And I have. But I don't often connect with energy in a visual way. Your daughter seems to."

"How do we know it isn't a figment of her imagination?"

"We don't." Julia looks him in the eye. "But I strongly

doubt that it is. I've felt the same energy, Paine, and I've heard it. I've seen her, too.''

"And was it her? Kristin?''

''The vision wasn't very clear, and it only lasted an instant, but I did see blond hair.''

"Did you hear anything?''

"Not then. But once, when I asked the spirit to give me a name, I got a strong *K* sound at the beginning and an *N* at the end. The rest was garbled. But that isn't unusual.''

"So it sounded like it was saying its name is Kristin.''

"It could have been. But I don't ... I can't tell. I keep asking myself why, if it's her, I can't feel a strong sense of her.''

"Why do you think that is?''

"Most likely because Kristin and I were virtual strangers in our adult lives, Paine. We once knew each other so intimately—more intimately than I've ever known another person in my life. She was like a sister to me.''

He nods, recalling the framed photo upstairs. "But you grew apart.''

"People do.'' A faraway expression in her eyes gives way to something else. Something darker. "What is it that you want from me, Paine? Why are you here?''

He opens his mouth to answer her, uncertain what he's even going to say, but she doesn't give him a chance. She goes on, "I've done everything you asked me to do. I stayed away from you after we first met. I came back when you asked me to, and I tried to assess Dulcie's gift. I could have told you lots of things about her, things that you obviously decided you didn't want to hear. Then I left today when you asked me to. Now you're back.'' Her voice wavers. "I just don't know what you want.''

"I'm sorry, Julia. I guess I want you to tell me that my daughter is okay. That she's going to be okay. That ...

Look, when she climbs out a second-story window because a ghost tells her to—and she insists that the ghost is trying to save her from somebody who's sneaking around our house—well, what the hell am I supposed to think? Either my daughter is losing her mind, or . . . or I am. Because that would mean that this is real. All of this stuff I never believed in. All of this stuff I swore was impossible."

"It's real, Paine," Julia says softly. She reaches out and touches his arm below the short sleeve of his T-shirt. "I'm positive it's real."

A shiver slips down his spine. Mostly, because of dread that steals over him yet again. But there's something else, too. Julia's warm fingertips on his bare skin . . .

When was the last time a woman touched him there? Anywhere?

Until now, Paine has barely noticed the unfulfilled needs left by three years of self-imposed celibacy. But now is not the time to be seeing Julia as anything other than a friend. A friend whose help he desperately needs.

"Julia," he says, "Dulcie told me that the lady—the apparition—had long blond hair. And that she was covered in blood. On one side of her face. If it was Kristin . . . what does it mean?"

"I don't think . . ." Julia takes a deep breath. "I tried to tell you this before. The first night you were back—that I don't think Kristin's death was an accident, Paine. The more I think about it, the more certain I am that she was murdered."

Hearing Julia speak the words aloud with such conviction, Paine feels something snap inside. For the first time, he allows himself to accept his own suspicions as a probability. Miraculously, he doesn't buckle beneath the weight. His voice is steady as he asks Julia, "But who here in Lily Dale would possibly want Kristin dead?"

"Maybe when she was here, she got tangled up with some drug dealer," Julia says. "I told you she changed right after she arrived. She was brooding about something."

Paine thinks back. "Maybe. But after rehab, she was committed to staying clean. She wanted to be a good mom to Dulcie. I can't believe that within a day or two of flying back East she slipped that far. She was an addict, but . . ."

Julia starts to speak, then breaks off, hesitating just long enough for Paine to look up sharply, realizing that she's about to share something significant. "It could have been something else, Paine."

"Like what?"

As he listens to Julia's account of a long-ago Halloween night, he finds himself picturing the two little girls in the photo on Julia's dresser. He can see them so clearly— Kristin, headstrong, yet oddly fragile; Julia, protective, sweetly nurturing.

Paine realizes that the first time Julia brought up the possibility that Kristin was psychically gifted, what bothered him most was that if it were true, Kristin kept it from him.

Damn it. She kept so much of herself from him. That there was one more hidden element—such a significant element— angered him. And Paine took his anger out on Julia, since she was there and Kristin wasn't.

Now . . .

Now that he's set aside his skepticism and opened his mind to a realm of new possibilities . . .

He finds himself treating Julia with new respect.

"I think it's important that Kristin said she saw something at the foot of the stairs, just where I have felt the energy strongest," Julia tells him. "If it's Kristin's energy I'm feeling there now, then it makes sense that she's drawn back to that spot because it had such an impact on her in life."

"What do you think she saw there?" Paine asks her.

"Something that scared the hell out of her."

"A ghost," he says flatly. "A lady ghost, since she asked you if you saw 'her.' "

"Most likely. My theory is that until that moment, Kristin never had a supernatural experience. Or if she did, there was nothing jarring enough to frighten her. But whatever she saw that night was disturbing enough for her to do her best to separate herself from Lily Dale and everyone in it."

"But she had no say in that. Her father bought a place in Florida when he made so much money off the book and became a celebrity. It wasn't Kristin's decision to go. And she came back here every summer with her parents."

Julia nods. "But it was never the same. She never seemed comfortable here again. I think maybe she was afraid of what would happen if she accepted her gift. I think she was afraid of what else she might see."

"She was upset when Iris bought the Biddles' house," Paine remembers suddenly. "Really upset. I remember her arguing with her mother on the phone when Iris told her about it, and when she hung up, she became really withdrawn. She didn't want her mother living there. She said it was because she didn't think Iris could keep up a place like that on her own—she wanted her to buy a condo in a retirement community somewhere."

"That sounds like Kristin." Julia smiles faintly.

"But maybe there was more to her reasoning. And she didn't want to fly back here to help Iris get settled in, either," Paine muses. "She only came because Iris asked her to, and there was nobody else to do it." He looks at Julia. "So you're thinking that something happened to Kristin in that house when she was back here that summer? That maybe she saw something there again?"

"Maybe." Julia nods slowly. "And if that's true, then maybe whatever it was somehow led to her death."

"How are we supposed to figure out what happened to her?"

Julia throws up her hands helplessly . . .

Just as Dulcie's terrified shriek pierces the air.

"Miranda . . . look!"

Startled by the sound of Kent's hushed, but urgent voice, she snaps out of her reverie about Andy to see her partner pointing at the small screen on one of their video cameras. This one is on a tripod and aimed toward the lilac tree.

"What is it?" she whispers to Kent, stepping closer to peer over his shoulder at the screen. Just moments ago, she was comfortable in a short-sleeved T-shirt with only her sleeveless khaki work vest over it. Now she becomes aware of an icy chill in the air, as though the temperature has suddenly dropped a good twenty degrees.

"See that ecto?" Kent asks softly.

She does. She sees it vividly on the screen.

She looks up at the tree itself. As expected, the ectoplasm is invisible to her naked eye. There's no sign of the spirit form captured by the camera's infrared lens.

"It's taking shape." Kent's voice is barely audible.

Miranda nods, watching the screen as a human form becomes visible. It's barely defined by arms, legs, a head, yet what she can see is distinctly female.

"It's all right," Kent calls softly to the apparition. "You can show yourself. We won't hurt you."

Miranda shivers, hugging herself, suddenly uneasy.

"Come closer," Kent coaxes. In a low voice, to Miranda, he asks, "Is your tape recorder on?"

"Of course."

"Good. Maybe we'll get that music again on tape."

"Well, you should shut up so that it'll be clear if we do," she hisses.

He scowls but falls silent.

Miranda listens to the steady chirping of the cicadas. A slight breeze stirs the air, rustling the leafy branches.

Then another sound reaches her ears.

Car tires on gravel.

Turning around, she sees the arc of headlights swinging over the yard and house as a car slows and stops at the curb just in front.

"Looks like we have visitors," Kent mutters.

Recognizing the car, Miranda tugs his sleeve. "Hurry—grab your stuff. Let's get out of here!"

Rupert is almost sound asleep when the harsh, abrupt ringing of the telephone pierces the air. He starts, sits up, rubs his eyes, disoriented until he sees Nan beside him. Oh. He's in the back bedroom with her.

The phone rings again.

Nan doesn't stir.

Rupert touches her cheek gently, in dread. It's still warm. She's just deeply asleep.

Rising, he hurries into the kitchen and lifts the receiver, glancing at the clock. It's late. Who would be calling at this hour?

"Rupert?" a vaguely familiar voice crackles over the line, as though crossing a great distance.

"Yes?"

"It's Pilar."

His heart sinks. Now what? "Pilar. Aren't you supposed to be on vacation?"

"I am. I'm on a cruise ship. This is a terrible connection, but I . . . can you hear me?"

"Barely." He catches sight of a pile of mail on the otherwise uncluttered countertop. He left it there after retrieving it from the box earlier, forgetting to even look through it, much less open it.

"I'll be quick," Pilar promises. Static crackles on the line. "How is Nan?"

"The same. Asleep. As I was," he adds irritably, fed up with her intrusions, well-meaning or not. He picks up the mail, flipping through it. "So if that's why you called . . ."

"Rupert, that isn't the only reason I called."

Rupert puts two utility bills into one pile, and makes another of the junk: store circulars, catalogues, credit card applications. He hesitates when he sees a catalogue addressed to Nan, from Breck's bulb company. She always places an order at this time of year for the bulbs she plants every fall: daffodils, tulips, crocuses.

"I've been feeling my husband's energy around me all day," Pilar says. "I feel as though he's trying to tell me something. I feel like it has to do with you and Nan, and I'm getting a strong sense of danger, Rupert."

"Danger?" Rupert echoes. His hand, clutching Nan's gardening catalogue, is trembling. Does it belong with the junk mail? Or with the bills? "What do you mean? What kind of danger?"

"I don't know, Rupert. Just . . . be careful. Please."

"I'm always careful," he snaps, the catalogue hovering over the pile destined for the trash can.

"I know you are. It's just that earlier today . . ." Pilar pauses.

She wants to say something else. Whatever it is, she apparently doesn't know how to phrase it—and he doesn't want to hear it.

"I really should be going," he says, placing the Breck's

catalogue neatly beneath the two utility bills. "I can hardly hear you. There's too much static."

"Yes, that's fine. Good-bye, Rupert. I'm sorry I woke you."

"It's all right," he lies.

Hanging up the phone, he picks up the sales flyers and credit card offers and marches over to the trash can. He lifts the lid and deposits the junk mail inside . . .

Right on top of the doll Paine Landry brought over this afternoon.

"Why are we hiding?" Kent demands, as he and Miranda, lugging their equipment, steal through the trees at the perimeter of the yard at Ten Summer Street.

"Shhh!"

He drops his voice to a whisper. "But I don't get it. Those were the owners getting out of that car. Why don't we want them to see us?"

"Because . . ." She turns guiltily to Kent, cursing the luck that brought the residents home just when the ectoplasm was beginning to take shape. Now she has to come clean to Kent.

Miranda looks through the trees at the house. Lights are going on all over the first floor, and she can see silhouettes in the windows.

"Because why?" Kent slaps at a mosquito buzzing around his ear. "You said they signed the release form. So what's the problem?"

"I lied about that. That's the problem."

"You lied?" He stares at her. His face is mostly cast in shadow, but what she can see is ominous enough to make her take a step backward. "You mean, they didn't give their permission for us to be on their property?"

Miranda only nods. But her remorse is tinged with exasperation. Irrational exasperation, yes—but she can't help feeling irked with Kent and his rules. He's such a stickler for details. With him, everything always has to be by the book. What harm would it cause if just once, they collected data on private property without permission?

"How could you, Miranda?"

"Because something is going on there, Kent. By that tree. Probably in the house, too. You heard the music on that tape. You saw that ecto just now."

"That doesn't mean—"

"I wanted to know more about it. I couldn't help myself. And Andy said it wouldn't hurt anything if I checked it out. In fact, he mentioned just yesterday that the guy who lives there doesn't even own the house. His daughter inherited it and he's about to sell it. So—"

"Who's Andy?" Kent asks flatly.

Too late, Miranda remembers that she never told him about that, either.

With her overnight bag over her shoulder, Julia stands in the doorway of the smallest bedroom on the second floor of the house at Ten Summer Street.

This, she realizes, is where Dulcie climbed out the window this afternoon. Now she sees that it's closed and locked, the screen propped against the baseboard beneath the sill.

"I'll find some sheets for the bed," Paine says, behind her.

Julia jumps, startled.

"Sorry." Paine touches her arm. "You okay?"

"I'm fine. It's just . . . it's been a hell of a day . . . and night."

"I know. That bat didn't help matters."

She shudders at the thought of it. When they raced up the stairs to her room, they found Dulcie cowering, her head under the pillow, screaming about something furry landing on her face. Sure enough, a bat was swooping around the room.

It must have gotten in through a hole in the plastic tarp. As Julia wrapped Dulcie in the afghan and whisked her into the next room, Paine tried to hit the winged black creature with a rolled-up newspaper. He missed several times—and then the bat vanished into the hallway. Paine searched for it for almost half an hour before concluding that it could be anywhere—and that Julia should come home with him and Dulcie.

"Thanks for letting me stay here tonight," Julia tells Paine. "I'll call the exterminator first thing in the morning, before we leave for the memorial service. I couldn't have slept in that house, knowing that thing was lurking some-where."

"It's no problem, Julia. I just tucked Dulcie into bed. She's thrilled, of course, that you're here."

I wish I could say the same thing, Julia thinks, looking around the room. It's larger than Iris's small study across the hall, but smaller than the other two second-floor bedrooms. There's room for little more than a full-sized iron bed, painted white, a nightstand, and a bookshelf crammed with paperbacks and old magazines.

Julia doesn't want to be here, in this house, after all that has happened.

Yet it's the lesser of two evils. She'd rather spend the night under this roof than under her own tarp, with a wayward bat poised to dive-bomb her bed again.

Paine disappears into the master bedroom, and returns a few minutes later with sheets and a quilt. He starts to make up the bed.

Julia, standing on the opposite side of the mattress, stops him. "I can do that." She pulls the edge of the fitted sheet and tucks it beneath the corner of the mattress.

"I'll help you." He slides an elasticized hem over his corner, too.

They work silently until the bed is ready.

Paine looks at her. "Guess you're all set."

"Guess I am."

"We never finished our conversation."

"No, we didn't," she agrees, reaching up to rub the aching, exhausted spot between her shoulders. She's sore all over, completely weary. All she wants to do is crawl into bed and fall into a dreamless sleep.

"We can talk tomorrow," Paine tells her. "After Iris's memorial."

"Can't. I have to do a message service at Inspiration Stump right afterward, and then I want to get to the hospital again while it's still visiting hours, to visit Lorraine." She told him about her friend's accident in the car on the short drive over to his place.

"Then tomorrow night," he says. "After my meeting with Howard and Tom Ogden, Edward Shuttleworth's lawyer. Which reminds me . . . would you mind watching Dulcie while I go to that? I was planning to bring her with me, but I'd rather not if I don't have to."

He trusts her with his daughter again. Julia smiles. "Sure, I'll be glad to watch her."

"Thanks. Well . . . good night."

"Good night."

She changes swiftly into her nightgown, then waits until she hears Paine come out of the bathroom. She hears his footsteps creaking down the hall, hesitating in front of Dulcie's doorway, then retreating to the master bedroom. Only when Julia hears the click that means he's closed his door does she slip out of her room.

In the bathroom, she turns on the light. She has avoided this room ever since she found Iris sprawled in front of the tub.

Now, as she busies herself getting ready for bed, she refuses to look in that direction.

It isn't until she's brushing her teeth at the sink that she feels the electricity in the air.

Someone is here with her.

She can hear the faint murmur of voices. Then a startled, high-pitched scream, abruptly cut off.

Julia turns off the tap and listens intently.

The faucet at the sink isn't even dripping.

Yet she can still hear water splashing.

She turns slowly toward the tub.

It has to be dry. Empty.

The sound has grown louder.

Wild sloshing. Sputtering. Gasping. Choking. It's as though somebody is struggling in the water.

Mesmerized, Julia takes a step closer to the tub. Leaning forward, peering over the edge, she glimpses a face looking up at her.

Iris's terror-filled face, being held underwater by a pair of hands that are clasped tightly around her neck.

In her room at the Summer Street Inn, Miranda puts the last pair of jeans into her canvas duffel bag and tugs the zipper closed.

There.

All packed.

First thing in the morning, she'll check out and head back to Boston. Alone.

Maybe it's not too late to get a summer waitressing job, she thinks hopefully, lugging the heavy bag across the floor. *Or a share in a beach house.*

She places the duffel by the door beside the one that holds her investigative equipment. It's going to be a pain, carrying that bag on board the plane, but she doesn't dare check it with the other one. Her brother Francis once worked for an airline and warned her never to place anything the least bit fragile in checked luggage. Meaning Miranda will probably have to explain the Trifield meter and night scope to a curious airline employee running the security scanner at the airport.

And what if the X-ray machine ruins the film and cassette tapes packed inside the bag?

With a sigh, Miranda realizes her only option is to turn the film and tapes over to Kent, who's driving back.

Which would be a good idea . . . if they were on speaking terms.

But he's so pissed at her that it'll be a miracle if they remain roommates when he gets back in late August from the cross-country trip he's continuing without her.

Walking restlessly back over to the bed, Miranda catches sight of a few things she forgot to pack. Her flashlight and her audio recorder. Terrific. How's she going to fit this stuff into an already crammed bag?

As she looks at the recorder, she realizes that she might as well listen to the tape she made tonight in the yard at Ten Summer Street. She'll never get to hear it if the airline ruins her tapes.

She rewinds the cassette and lets it run as she continues her nightly routine, removing her makeup with cold cream and changing into her pajamas.

As she's flossing her teeth, she hears Kent's excited whisper caught on tape.

"Miranda, look!"

"What is it?" comes her hushed reply.

"See that ecto?"

A long pause, marred by the sound of crickets . . . and something else.

Frowning, Miranda reaches for the recorder just as Kent's voice announces, "It's taking shape."

After adjusting the volume, and balance, she presses REWIND, and then PLAY again.

"See that ecto?"

There it is again.

The music.

"Kathy's Song."

This time, she can hear more of it than before. The familiar guitar strains are audible on the tape for several seconds, in the background as Kent asks, "See that ecto?"

Miranda keeps listening, sitting absolutely still on the bed, her head tilted in concentration as the tape plays on.

"It's all right," Kent's voice calls softly. "You can show yourself. We—"

Stunned, Miranda abruptly presses STOP.

She rewinds the tape briefly.

PLAY.

"It's all right . . . you can show yourself. We won't hurt you."

In the midst of Kent's soothing words to the spirit, the music gives way to a sudden, repetitive, scraping sound.

It goes on as the dialogue continues.

Miranda listens intently. She hears Kent crooning to the spirit, "Come closer."

Then, to her: "Is your tape recorder on?"

"Of course."

"Good. Maybe we'll get that music again on tape."

Throughout their conversation, the rhythm continues steadily.

Miranda recognizes the distinct, rasping thud even before she rewinds the tape to listen to the passage again. And again. And again, in growing dread, wondering what it means.

It's the dull sound of metal hitting rock and dirt. The sound that a shovel makes, digging into the ground.

Chapter Thirteen

It seems as though all of Lily Dale has turned out for Iris Shuttleworth's memorial service at Assembly Hall. Glancing around the packed meeting room, Julia sees plenty of familiar faces, but there are strangers, too.

Iris's stepson, Edward Shuttleworth, is notably absent.

So are Rupert and Nan Biddle. Not a good sign. Julia makes a mental note to stop over there the first chance she gets, to see how Nan is and if there's anything she can do. Paine said the situation is touch and go now.

Julia feels tears welling in her eyes, thinking of Rupert's heartfelt effort to bring his wife home to die in the house where they spent the bulk of their lives together. She wonders whether anybody will ever love her that much.

Her thoughts drift to Paine, still pining away for Kristin. He'll probably never know what really happened to her out on the lake that night.

Or will he?

Julia tries to allay the surge of fear that rises again within her at the thought of somebody killing Kristin . . . and Iris. She tries to persuade herself that what she saw last night in the bathroom was a figment of her imagination, but she knows better.

Most likely, she witnessed Iris's last moments of life. She witnessed Iris dying at the hands of an invisible murderer.

Who?

Who would want her dead?

Julia turns her head, not wanting to stare anymore at the urn containing Iris's ashes.

That's when she glimpses Andy sitting on the opposite end of the room.

How nice that he came.

Then it hits her—

Oh, no. I told Paine that I'd watch Dulcie tonight, but Andy is supposed to take me out on the lake to scatter Iris's ashes.

She'll have to catch up with him after the service and ask him if they can do it on a different night. She wants to spend these last few hours with Dulcie.

Finally, the service is almost over. The congregation chimes in singing one of Iris's favorite songs: "Will the Circle Be Unbroken?" Surprised that the song has been included, Julia glances at Paine.

He smiles at her over Dulcie's bowed head. Leaning toward Julia, he whispers, "I remembered that Kristin once told me her mother loved the Nitty Gritty Dirt Band's recording of this song."

"That's right. She did." Touched, Julia fights back a fresh swell of tears. Paine is a sweet man. A far better man than she ever suspected.

Dulcie sniffles loudly between them, her little body quivering with quiet sobs.

Julia presses a tissue into the little girl's hand. "It's okay, Dulcie," she whispers. "Your grandmother is still with you. She'll always be with you."

"I know she will, Julia," Dulcie says, wiping tears from her sightless eyes. "But you won't be."

Julia says nothing, just puts her arm around Kristin's daughter and holds her close.

Rupert clings to the telephone receiver, pacing across the kitchen floor to the back door that looks out on the sunny yard, and back again to the counter, where an untouched container of yogurt and a full cup of now-cold tea still sit on a tray.

An instrumental rendition of "Moon River" plays on the line, to his irritation. If he has to be on hold for this goddamn long, he'd rather listen to silence.

Outside, he can hear the usual afternoon sounds: cars rolling through the streets, birds chirping, dogs barking, the distant ripple of children's laughter. The sounds are as garish to Rupert's ears as the Muzak, both of which indicate that beyond this room, this house, everything is status quo. The world is spinning along as usual.

Remarkable.

"Moon River" gives way to "The Girl From Ipanema."

Rupert clenches his teeth so hard that his jaw hurts. He barely notices.

His thoughts drift back to another sunny afternoon, much hotter than this one . . .

The Bronx was in the throes of a terrible heat wave; open windows and electric fans did little to cool the tiny fourth-floor walk-up. Then, as now, Nan lay in bed in the next room, in agony, as Rupert, beside himself with worry, frantically tried to reach an elusive physician.

But back then, phones didn't have hold buttons.

There was no Muzak. He heard every word the nurse spoke on the other end of the line.

"Oh, good, there you are, Doctor Hayden ... I have Rupert Biddle on the line. His fiancée is in labor."

Back then, doctors made house calls. Dr. Hayden arrived just in time to usher Rupert and Nan's daughter into the world, place her in Nan's weary grasp, and announce that it was a girl. The baby was whisked from Nan's arms moments later—

"The Girl From Ipanema" is interrupted by an abrupt click in Rupert's ear, followed by the welcome sound of Dr. Klauber's voice. "Rupert, I'm sorry to have kept you waiting. What can I do for you?"

Rupert forces his thoughts back to the present. "Nan seems to be growing much worse, Doctor. She's been asleep since last night, but it isn't a peaceful sleep. She seems to be struggling to catch her breath, even with the oxygen. I ... I don't know how to help her. You have to come here, Doctor. You have to do something, and I can't possibly get her to your office."

The doctor is silent for a long moment. Then he says grimly, "I'm afraid there's nothing I can do for her now, Rupert. I'm so sorry. I'm going to give you the phone number of somebody who can help. Call it. Someone will come immediately."

The bottom has fallen out of Rupert's world. "Who will come?" he asks bleakly, trying to focus on the conversation.

There's nothing I can do for her now, Rupert. I'm so sorry.

"A hospice care worker. Do you have a pen and something to write on?"

"Yes."

"Good. The number is 555-3323. Did you get that?"

"I got it," he lies, nothing in his trembling hand but the telephone.

"I wish you well, Rupert," the doctor says with finality.

Rupert hangs up, numb.

His feet carry him back to the bedroom, where Nan's harsh, shallow breaths are coming rapidly. Her eyes are open, but unfocused.

He read somewhere, once, that the hearing is the last sense to fade. That people have awakened from comas to give verbatim accounts of conversations that took place at their bedsides while they were unconscious.

Rupert clears his throat, swallowing hard over the tight lump that has risen there.

"Nan, darling, can you hear me? I love you. I'm here with you. I won't leave, Nan. I'll be with you. And, Nan, you'll always be with me. Even if you have to go . . ."

A choked sob escapes him. He inhales shakily, holds his breath, exhales with a shudder. He can do this. He can do whatever needs to be done.

"You can go, darling. Whenever you're ready."

Suddenly, her expression is lucid. Her eyes seem to focus on his.

He gazes down at her, whispering, "I know you've been hanging on, fighting it so hard, but, Nan . . . it's time to rest. Stop fighting."

She turns her head fitfully on the pillow, her mouth working, as though trying to muster the strength to speak.

"Shh," he says, taking her clammy hand, squeezing her limp fingers. "It's okay. Don't say it. I know what's holding you back. But, Nan, it's okay. You can go. It's okay to go."

Her breath makes a horrible gasping sound in her throat.

Rupert steels himself against the flood of tears that threaten to sweep him into hysteria.

A single word spills from Nan's cracked lips. "Can't . . ."

"Yes, Nan. You can. You can let go. Please, darling, I can't bear to see you this way. Everything is all right. Everything has always been all right. I love you."

"Can't . . ."

"Shhh."

"Kath . . ."

"Katherine. No, Nan. Don't think about Katherine. It's too late now. Just rest," he croons, stroking her cheek, tears spilling down his own. "Just rest."

"Daddy? Is that you?"

His arms laden, Paine peeks into his daughter's room. "I'm just bringing some boxes downstairs, Dulcie."

"Oh." She sighs. "I wish we didn't have to leave tomorrow morning."

Paine says nothing. He wishes they could have left *this* morning, right after Julia told him about the nightmarish vision she'd had in the bathroom last night.

If there's anything to it, then Iris was murdered.

But who the hell could possibly have wanted an eccentric old woman dead?

Hey, bub, who are you calling old?

Paine has to grin. That's exactly what Iris would have said. She clung fiercely to her youth, keeping her hair long and straight, and cramming her oversize figure into tie dye long before—and after—the retro look was in fashion again. She was nothing but an overgrown flower child who still listened to the Nitty Gritty Dirt band and the Grateful Dead, and whose VW remains covered with two eras' worth of bumper stickers for a variety of causes.

Well, at least the memorial service did her justice, Paine thinks. Iris would have been pleased at the turnout, and at the beautiful eulogy that captured her in all her quirky glory.

"What time is Julia coming back, Daddy?" Dulcie calls after Paine as he heads down the hall toward the stairway with the boxes.

"Not until later, sweetie. After supper."

"Can she come earlier?"

Paine musters as much patience as possible to reply, "No, she's busy this afternoon."

They've been over this several times already in the past few hours since they returned from Assembly Hall. He certainly has his work cut out for him after they leave here. Dulcie won't soon get over missing Julia.

Paine descends the stairs gingerly, unable to see his feet on the treads in front of him. The boxes are heavy, filled with old family photo albums he discovered in the attic. Dulcie might never be able to see them for herself, but he can't leave behind the pictures of Kristin's birth, and her childhood, even a couple of faded snapshots of Iris and Anson's wedding day.

Paine recalls Kristin once telling him that her parents were married barefoot on the shore of Lake Erie by some kind of hippie holy man. Now he has evidence. The happy bride wore a headband across her forehead, a psychedelic-print minidress, and strands of beads. The groom wore vertically striped purple and orange bell-bottoms and sideburns that reached his chin.

As Paine sets the box carefully beside the front door next to the one containing Kristin's baby clothes, he wonders whether he should load the stuff into the car tonight before his meeting, or come back and do it afterward.

He wants to get an early start in the morning and put as much distance between Dulcie and Lily Dale as possible.

One thing is certain: no matter what happens at that meeting with the lawyers later, they're leaving here in less than twenty-four hours, and they're never coming back.

Even Julia agrees that is the safest thing to do.

If it's true that somebody killed Iris—and Kristin— nobody is safe in Lily Dale. Especially not in this house.

Which is why Julia is picking up Dulcie later and bringing her over to Julia's place until Paine gets home. She called a little while ago from a pay phone at the hospital to report that the exterminator caught the bat, and the roofers have sealed the gaps in the tarp. She invited Paine and Dulcie to sleep at her place tonight, just to be safe.

So this is it. In a few hours, he'll be done packing, and Julia will be here. The last day here, in this house, will draw to an end.

If I leave now, I'll probably never know what really happened to Kristin and Iris, Paine realizes.

But if he doesn't leave now . . .

He shakes his head, thinking of Dulcie.

All that really matters is keeping her safe.

At last, Miranda spots Andy hurrying toward the auditorium, where he's scheduled to begin a lecture in five minutes. He's not alone. Nor is he with Julia.

At his side is a pretty brunette with a spectacular figure. She's wearing strappy sandals and a black tank top tucked into white shorts.

Miranda, clad in sneakers and an untucked polo shirt over longish khaki walking shorts meant to hide her lumpy thighs, hesitates. Yes, she's been trying to track down Andy all day. But does she really want him to see her in such an unflattering getup, especially when he's with a woman who could have stepped out of J. Crew's summer catalogue?

What does it matter?

She's leaving Lily Dale. If she'd been able to get a flight first thing as planned, she'd already be gone. Good thing she thought to call the airline before leaving here earlier. It turned out the flight she planned on taking was canceled. She was able to go back to bed and get a few more hours of much-needed sleep. The emotional turmoil of the last few days has finally caught up with her.

Well, soon enough, she'll be back home with nothing to do *but* rest. A cab will be here within the hour to take her and her luggage to the Buffalo airport for a six o'clock flight back to Boston.

But she couldn't leave without seeing Andy one last time. Taking a deep breath, she calls his name.

He looks up, startled, glancing around.

"Andy!" She waves at him.

Is he frowning, or just squinting into the sun despite his ever-present sunglasses?

It's hard to tell from here. Miranda walks toward him, watching him say something in the brunette's ear. She looks disappointed, but heads into the auditorium, casting a look over her shoulder.

Miranda ignores her.

"Hi, Mandy. What are you doing here?" Andy is clearly surprised, but perhaps not pleasantly so. "I got your voice mail message last night."

"You didn't call me back," she says, hating the accusing tone in her voice but unable to extinguish her emotions.

"I had a memorial service to go to."

"Last night?" She wonders who died. He doesn't look very broken up about it.

"This morning. And you said you were leaving first thing."

"I was supposed to. I couldn't get a flight. I'm going in a little while."

"You're flying? Weren't you supposed to be driving cross-country with your partner?"

"We had a falling-out last night."

Andy looks impatient. "Why?"

Irritated by the sense that he's not the least bit interested, Miranda gives him a detailed reply. She tells him about the investigation at Ten Summer Street last night, and the owner coming home, and Kent being angry that she lied about the release form.

"The thing is, if he weren't so uptight about formalities, he would have been interested to hear what I got on the tape I made last night, before we were interrupted."

Andy asks, "What did you get?" She can't see his eyes behind the opaque black lenses but she's willing to bet that he's bored stiff with this conversation. After all, it isn't about him.

She decides to prolong it, telling him about the music she heard on the tape, and about the shoveling sounds at the end.

"What do you make of that?" she asks him.

He checks his watch. "I have no idea. But I'm going to be late for my lecture, Mandy. I'd better run."

"Yeah, you'd better."

He reaches out and gives her a quick squeeze that's utterly devoid of affection.

"Good luck," Andy calls over his shoulder as he heads to the auditorium. "I hope I'll see you again sometime."

"No, you don't," she mutters when he's out of earshot. "Good riddance to you, Andy Doyle. You're nothing but a phony loser."

* * *

Dulcie stands in the doorway of her room, listening for Daddy's footsteps below. He said he was carrying a few boxes out to the car and he'd be right back, but he hasn't yet.

"Daddy?" she calls, loudly enough to carry through the open second-floor windows.

"What's wrong, Dulc? Are you okay?" His voice, concerned, floats back up.

"I'm fine. I just have to go to the bathroom!"

"I'll be right there to help you down the hall. Don't move."

Dulcie sighs, crossing her legs. She really has to go.

Putting a hand on the wall just outside her door, she takes a cautious step down the hall. And then another.

She can do this. The bathroom isn't far from her room. She's made the trip often enough with Daddy or Julia to know how many steps it takes.

She feels her way along the corridor, counting steps.

She's almost there when she hears it.

The music.

The scream.

"No," Dulcie whispers, her eyes squeezed shut.

She doesn't want to hear it.

She doesn't want to see it.

But it's there all around her, and then in front of her: the lady's face.

This time, it's much clearer than before.

And she isn't looking at Dulcie. She's looking past Dulcie, over her head, as if someone tall is standing behind her. Her blue eyes are full of tears, and she looks furious.

"You can't do this to me!" she screams, taking a step backward. "I'm leaving!"

At first, Dulcie, bewildered, thinks the lady is talking to her.

Then she hears a roar in response—an angry burst of sound that Dulcie doesn't recognize, at first, as words. But she quickly realizes that it's a man's voice, yelling. Yelling so loud the lady keeps flinching, and backing away. Her left hand is clasped in a fist against her neck, her right hand covering it.

"Be careful!" Dulcie calls, as the lady edges close to the top of the stairs. "What are you doing? You're going to fall!"

The lady takes another step backward.

The roar grows louder.

Another step . . .

"Look out!" Dulcie shrieks.

Too late.

The lady plunges backward, down the steps. There's an awful commotion—screams, and thuds. And then nothing. Just . . . an awful silence.

Dulcie realizes she's been holding her breath.

She lets it out slowly, trembling as she leans against the wall for support.

Suddenly a face pops up in front of her.

Dulcie cries out.

It's the lady's face. Now one side of her head is cracked open. Her hair is caked with blood.

"What do you want?" Dulcie whimpers, her eyes shut tightly in vain. There's no escaping the gory image there, in front of her.

Leave . . .

"What?" Her jaw is quivering so that she can barely speak.

Leave . . . Don't let him—

"Dulcie?" That's Daddy's voice calling up to her, Daddy's footsteps pounding up the stairs.

"Don't let him what?" Dulcie echoes desperately, but then Daddy is here, and the lady is gone.

Chapter Fourteen

Lugging her carry-on bag toward the security checkpoint, Miranda wonders yet again about the cassette tapes and film she packed in her other bag, the one that she checked. Do airports X-ray all luggage, or just the carry-on? If they X-ray the bag holding the tapes and film, will the data be destroyed?

There's a long line at the security checkpoint. Miranda takes her place at the end, checking her watch. She was hoping to get here soon enough to grab something to eat, but there was an accident on the thruway and it delayed her arrival by more than half an hour.

Oh, well. Maybe they'll hand out peanuts on the plane. Do airlines still do that?

Miranda tries to remember the last time she flew and realizes that she hasn't been on a plane since she and Michael went to Cancun on their honeymoon.

You really have to start learning how to live a little, she scolds herself, inching her way forward as the line moves up. *You should make some new friends, plan a trip to Europe, maybe join some kind of club . . .*

Especially if she's no longer going to have Kent in her life. The thought of losing his friendship stings more now that she's left Lily Dale—and Andy—behind for good.

Kent has his faults. Who doesn't? But he's the only other person who would have been fascinated by what she captured on that tape in the yard of the house at Ten Summer Street. Now she'll never know what's buried under the lilac tree.

The only thing that's certain is that something is there. What else could the recorded digging sounds have meant?

"Miranda!"

Startled, she turns to see Kent hurrying off the escalator, waving at her.

"Oh, my God . . . what are you doing here, Kent?"

"Don't go back to Boston. Please."

She scowls. "Why shouldn't I?"

"We have the whole summer ahead of us, Miranda. It's going to be great. And I didn't mean to freak out on you. It's just that—"

"I screwed up, Kent. I know it was wrong to lie to you. And I'm really sorry."

"I've been trying to understand why you did it."

She only shrugs.

"I guess you got caught up in your—" He pauses meaningfully, and manages to avoid the word *obsession*. "*Curiosity* about that place, huh, Miranda?"

She offers a tight smile. "I got caught up in a lot of things while we were in Lily Dale."

Kent gives her a questioning look.

"His name was Andy. I'll tell you about him later," Miranda says. "The important thing is that—"

"Excuse me." Somebody taps her on the shoulder. "The line is moving."

She looks up to see a wide gap opening between her and the man in front of her. She automatically moves to close it, but Kent puts his hand on her arm, holding her back.

"Come on, Miranda. Don't get on the plane. Come back to Lily Dale with me. I can't make this trip and write this book without you."

"Yes, you can."

"You're right, I can." Kent grins. "But it won't be as much fun alone."

"You got that right." Miranda hands him her bag. "This is heavy. You carry it."

"Let's go."

"Yeah, and let's hurry. I have to get my luggage back from the baggage check. You'll never believe what I picked up on tape last night."

"Are you all right, Dulcie?" Julia asks, her hand clutching the little girl's arm as she leads her up the front steps. "You've been quiet all the way over here, and you didn't even get excited when I said we could have pizza. I thought you loved pizza."

"I do. It's just . . ." She trails off.

Julia glances at her. Her vacant blue eyes are troubled.

"Just what?" Julia prods, fishing for her key in her pocket. She opens the front door and leads Dulcie inside.

"Something happened this afternoon," Dulcie tells her, toying with the end of one of the blond pigtails Julia braided for her before she left this morning.

"What happened, Dulcie?" Julia absently reaches out to tuck a wayward wisp of hair more securely into the elastic at the bottom of the braid. "You can sit down," she adds, guiding Dulcie to the sofa.

Dulcie sits. "When I was alone upstairs . . ."

"Your father left you alone upstairs?" Julia finds that surprising. Paine said he wasn't going to let Dulcie out of his sight all day, and cautioned Julia to do the same tonight.

"He was just outside the front door, loading stuff in the car. He was only gone for a minute, and he could hear me the whole time," Dulcie says defensively. "And I was fine . . . except . . ."

"What happened?" Julia asks again, studying the little girl intently as she kneels beside her.

She listens intently as Dulcie tells her about the latest vision of the lady. How she was crying and arguing with somebody. How she fell down the stairs, presumably to her death. How she tried to warn Dulcie.

Don't let him . . .

Don't let who what?

What does it mean? Kristin wasn't killed in a fall down the stairs. She drowned.

Maybe the lady isn't Kristin.

But if not . . .

Who is she?

"Did you tell your dad about this?" Julia asks Dulcie.

Paine didn't say anything about it, but he rushed off the moment she got there. She was late getting back from her message session, and he had to drive all the way down to Jamestown for the meeting.

"Yes, I told him. He said not to worry. He said we're leaving first thing in the morning, and that I don't have to go back to the house ever again."

"You don't," Julia says firmly. "You're staying here tonight. Your dad will be back later, and in the meantime we'll—"

She breaks off suddenly, hearing a knock on the front door.

"Oh, great," she mutters.

"What was that?" Dulcie asks.

"Somebody's at the door. I'll be right back."

Certain it's a passerby wanting a reading, Julia decides she should probably take down her medium shingle until she's able to get back to work.

But when she arrives in the hall, it isn't a potential customer on the other side of the screen door.

"Andy!" Belatedly, she realizes that she never told him to come later. She got caught up in the crowd of mourners after the service and by the time she had a moment to look for Andy, he was gone. She meant to call him after the Stump service, but was in such a rush to get to the hospital—and from the hospital back to Paine's—that she completely forgot.

"Weren't you expecting me?" As usual, Andy's eyes are obscured by his sunglasses, but she can hear the confusion in his voice. "I thought we said that on Thursday we would—"

"I'm baby-sitting for Paine's daughter right now. I meant to ask you earlier if we could go out on the lake some other time, but I completely forgot about it. I'm so sorry."

"Oh." He seems hesitant. "The thing is, Julia, I only have the boat for the rest of this week. I'm not getting as much use out of it as I expected, and I canceled the lease for July."

"Don't worry. I can get somebody else to take me out—"

"Or I can take you now, like we planned. It's a beautiful night. The water is so calm it's like glass."

"But Dulcie—"

"She can come, too. Iris was her grandmother. It would be fitting if she was there, too, don't you think?"

"I guess." Julia considers that. It *would* be meaningful.

"What's holding you back, Julia?"

"It's just . . . I'm not sure Paine would want me to take her out on the lake without his permission."

"But I want to go."

Startled, Julia turns to see Dulcie standing in the doorway behind her, obviously eavesdropping.

"I want to scatter Gram's ashes," Dulcie says firmly. "It's not fair that you were going to do it without me."

Julia and Andy exchange a glance.

"I've got kid-sized life preservers on board," he says in a low voice.

Still, Julia is reluctant to agree.

"Please, Julia," Dulcie begs. "It's the last chance I'll have to do something for Gram. My mom would have wanted me to be there, no matter what my dad thinks."

"We don't have to be out long," Andy points out. "Like I said, the water is perfectly calm. Not a wave in sight. And when we get back to shore, I'll take both of you out for pizza."

"That would be great," Dulcie pipes up. "I'm starving."

Julia glances at the urn she earlier placed carefully on a small table just inside the door.

Dulcie is Iris's last living relative. She—and not Julia— should carry out Iris's last wishes. She should scatter her grandmother's ashes on the water where her mother died. Then the two of them, mother and daughter, will truly be together for eternity. And Dulcie will carry the memory of this last journey with her long after she leaves this place. It might even bring her peace, a sense of closure, in years to come.

"What do you say, Julia?" Andy asks, jingling his keys in his hand.

"Okay."

* * *

"Forget? No! No, Virginia, of course I didn't forget," Rupert lies, holding the door wide open. "Come right in."

As Rupert struggles to get hold of himself, Virginia Wainwright sweeps into the room, bringing with her a cloud of expensive perfume. She's dripping in diamonds and silk, and her hair is sprayed into a snowy mound of tendrils high above her unnaturally tight-skinned forehead.

Rupert happens to know that Mrs. Wainwright is no stranger to plastic surgery.

In fact, that was one of the first messages he ever gave her from her late husband.

"Forgive me if this sounds blunt, but . . . Harrison wants you to know that he loves your face-lift, Virginia," Rupert recalls saying.

She was stunned, of course. Convinced that information could only have come from beyond the grave. After all, she hadn't told a soul about her surgery. Nobody knew—except, of course, for her doctors back in Houston, and her loyal maid who nursed her through the ordeal.

"Rupert? Are you all right?"

He looks up, blinking. Mrs. Wainwright is looking at him with an expression that comes as close to concern as he's ever seen on her self-involved face.

"Yes . . . I'm fine."

Another lie.

He glances toward the back of the house. Nan is sleeping in the bedroom. He isn't sure whether her breathing is still as frighteningly shallow as it was earlier, or if he's merely become accustomed to the desolate sound after an entire day spent at her side.

You can send Mrs. Wainwright on her way, he reminds

himself. *You don't even have to explain why you can't do a reading for her right now. You don't owe her anything.*

Except . . .

Except that he'd be giving up a small fortune if he sends her on her way.

But at this point, it goes beyond the money. The truth is, Rupert can't bear to return alone to that back bedroom to resume his vigil. Despite his earlier, heartfelt promise to Nan, he needs a moment away, to regroup—to prepare himself for the long night ahead.

Nan is so out of it that she certainly has no idea he's left. And he can carry the baby monitor into his study with him, so that he'll hear if anything changes.

Rupert escorts Mrs. Wainwright into his study off the living room. "I'll be right with you, Virginia. Please bear with me for a moment."

"Don't be long. I'm so anxious to contact Harrison."

"I won't be long."

Rupert returns to the back bedroom, where he finds Nan just as he left her, deeply asleep, her eyes closed. Her breathing is still rapid and shallow, but there have been no changes.

"I'll be in the other room if you need me, darling," Rupert whispers, planting a gentle kiss on her forehead.

He turns on the base monitor, still in its usual location on the nightstand, and picks up the receiver.

In his study, he finds Virginia Wainwright anxiously tapping the toe of her designer shoe on the carpet. She stops tapping when she sees him, her gaze going directly to the baby monitor. "What on earth is that? Don't tell me you're baby-sitting. Do you have grandchildren?"

He shrugs, loathing her. He turns on the monitor and sets it on a nearby table.

"That's going to interfere with the spirit energy," Mrs. Wainwright informs him. "I read that—"

"It won't interfere," he interrupts brusquely. "Now let's get started."

She gives the monitor another wary glance, but settles into her seat.

Rupert closes his eyes.

Over the monitor, he can hear the faint sound of Nan's breathing.

Mrs. Wainwright swallows audibly, seeming to swish the saliva around in her mouth. Disgusted, he fights the urge to send her on her way.

But that will mean giving up the money.

And it will mean returning to the grim reality of the back bedroom.

Rupert takes several deep breaths, pretending to sink into a meditative state. In truth, he's forcing himself to move aside, for now, the tremendous weight of grief and stress. He has a job to do, a job that, after so many years, nearly comes naturally to him.

At last, Rupert plunges in, eyes closed, voice trancelike. "Harrison is here," he announces.

"Yes!" Mrs. Wainwright's voice is hushed. "I can feel his energy."

"He wants to know why it took you so long to get in touch with him. He says he's disappointed."

"I'm so sorry, Harrison!" Mrs. Wainwright says.

"He tells me that he wants you to stop flirting so much, Virginia. He's showing me some kind of social event—I can see waiters in black tuxedos with trays of hors d'oeuvres, and out the window there are palm trees, and you're all dressed up . . ."

"Yes! The hospital ball. It was a black tie affair . . ."

"You're wearing some kind of heirloom piece of jewelry . . ."

She gasps, clutching her hands to her breast. "Yes! Yes,

I know what he's talking about. My grandmother's diamond brooch.''

''Yes, he says that's it. And he sees you flirting.''

''Flirting? I wouldn't call it—''

''Harrison says you were flirting with several gentlemen.''

''*Several?* Are you sure?''

''One in particular. Harrison says he was dapper.''

''Oh, Harrison, he meant nothing to me!'' Mrs. Wainwright exclaims. ''It was just a harmless flirtation. We didn't even kiss.''

''No . . .'' Rupert sighs. ''But Harrison tells me the idea entered your head.''

''Yes. Yes, it did. But then I pushed it right back out again. I'm so sorry, Harrison.''

''He's saying that he understands. He's telling me that he knows you've been lonely. And he says . . .'' Rupert puckers his brows, as though trying to discern the spirit's message more clearly. ''He says that the nights are the hardest for you. That's when you miss him most.''

Mrs. Wainwright sniffles. ''That's right. I can't bear the nights. Even after so many years . . .''

''Harrison says not to forget that he's always with you. He was there in Florida with you when you received that disturbing phone call a few months ago . . .''

''Disturbing phone call?'' She frowns.

Rupert's eyes are open now, surreptitiously watching her ponder his words. ''Yes, he's saying you were very aggravated by something the caller told you, and that he was by your side.''

''I don't—''

''He says it was long distance,'' Rupert prods. ''I'm not getting the origin very clearly but I feel that it was from somewhere north . . .''

''The pushy telemarketer! That's it! Yes, my dear Harrison, I was so very disturbed by that call. The man was selling magazine subscriptions and he had that awful New York accent. He simply wouldn't take no for an answer.''

Rupert smiles, triumph momentarily obliterating everything else.

Tonight, it's almost too easy.

"Mom, please promise me that you're not going to check your answering machine back home every single day we're away,'' Christina says in the passageway outside the dining room. "Ship-to-shore calls cost a fortune.''

"So? It's my nickel.'' Pilar is already hurrying toward the sign marked BUSINESS CENTER. She calls back to her family, "I promise I'll meet you at the table in a few minutes. Go ahead and start if you want to.''

As she makes her way to the public telephones, she wonders why she hasn't been able to relax all day. She can't seem to let go of her worries about the Biddles.

After dialing her home telephone number and the password to access her voice mail, Pilar hears a mechanical voice announce in its unique staccato cadence, "You have one new message. Please press *one* to hear your message.''

It's got to be about the Biddles, Pilar thinks, pressing 1. She wonders, with a sinking heart, whether she's about to hear that Nan has passed away. It's what she's expecting.

"Hello ... this is Katherine Jergins. I'm just calling because ... well, because I realized that I was pretty rude to you earlier. I thought maybe we should talk.''

"This is incredible,'' Paine tells Howard Menkin as the two of them descend the wide cement steps leading away from the law offices of Anderson and Ogden. "How is it that this never popped up until now?"

Swinging his briefcase in one hand and rubbing his mustache thoughtfully with the other, Howard agrees, "The timing *is* pretty fortuitous. And I find it interesting that Ogden failed to tell us exactly where his client got this so-called evidence."

They've reached the sidewalk of one of Jamestown's busiest streets—which, in a city this size, on a Thursday evening, is fairly deserted. Paine finds the ghost-town aura almost as depressing as the news Tom Ogden just delivered.

"Where are you parked, Paine?" Howard asks.

"Just down the block."

"I'll walk you to your car."

"Thanks."

They walk in silence. Paine is still reeling from Ogden's bombshell.

Apparently, Iris and Anson Shuttleworth were never legally married.

According to the newly produced evidence—a marriage license bearing the name of the officiant—the Jerry Garcia look-alike who presided over their barefoot nuptials was a fraud. In flagrant violation with Section 11 of the New York State Domestic Relations Law, the so-called Reverend Toby Bombeck was never ordained as a minister of any sort. In fact, he spent the better part of the last three decades in prison on various drug and criminal charges.

Ogden, infuriatingly closemouthed when pressed for further details, did reveal how Edward Shuttleworth happened to run into Bombeck, a complete stranger, after all these years. It happened in some dive bar one fateful night not long after Iris died. They got to talking, Bombeck recognized Edward's last name, and connected it with Iris, whose obituary had just appeared in the local paper. At some point that evening, Bombeck drunkenly confided that when he married Edward's father and stepmother, he wasn't legally qualified to perform weddings. He found it hilarious that the unsuspecting bride and groom never realized they weren't really married.

Clearly, Edward found it more intriguing than hilarious.

"Let me ask you something," Paine says suddenly to Howard, brooding beside him as they walk along.

"What's that?"

"How *do* you think Edward got his hands on that marriage license? Assuming his father didn't just hand him a copy sometime in his childhood—"

"Which is certainly a far-fetched scenario." The lawyer shrugs. "Anyone other than the bride or groom can write to Vital Records in Albany and request a copy, but they need to include a letter from an office or agency that is requiring the document."

"In other words, some joe off the street can't just get a copy of somebody else's marriage license."

"Right. And anyway, that was no recent copy, Paine. That was an original document. The paper was yellowed."

"That's what I thought. So how did Edward get it?"

"He's a shady character. My guess is as good as yours, but—"

"Do you think he could have broken into Iris's house to find it?"

Howard shrugs. "I wouldn't put it past him. Why?"

Paine falls silent, musing. What if Edward was Dulcie's prowler?

The only thing is . . .

Last night? That doesn't make sense. Ogden called a couple of days ago to call this meeting. He must have had the marriage license in his possession before today . . .

But not necessarily, Paine thinks. Maybe Edward told the lawyer that he could produce it before their meeting tonight?

"What's the matter?" Howard asks, watching him. "Think that creep has been snooping around your place when you weren't home?"

"Or maybe when I was home. Dulcie thought she heard someone creeping around the house a couple of times."

"My God, Paine . . ."

"I know. But it doesn't matter at this point. I'm leaving in the morning with Dulcie, Howard. It doesn't make sense for us to stay, especially now. This is one big tangled legal mess. It's going to take months to sort it all out. Whether there's a chance that it can somehow come out in our favor, or not, I'll handle everything from California."

"I don't blame you," Howard says as they come to a stop in front of Paine's rental car. "You know that I'll keep you apprised of the developments, but if that license proves to be legitimate, I think we both know the implications are clear."

"Absolutely."

Anson died without a will. Under New York State law, his estate went to Iris under the presumption that she was his wife. If, however, Anson and Iris weren't legally wed, she wouldn't have a legal claim to his inheritance and the estate should have been divided between Anson's children.

Kristin's death—assuming she was actually fathered by Anson, for which, as Ogden ominously pointed out, there is no proof—leaves Edward as Anson's sole surviving child and primary heir.

"Look, Paine, I'm not going to give up on this without a fight. We have a good case. You know that I'm prepared to argue that your daughter is entitled to at least half of her grandfather's estate—"

"I know you are," Paine says. "But . . ."

"But what?"

Something snaps inside Paine as he stands there, his car keys poised in front of the lock. He's had it. It's too much. All of it.

"Look, I'm grateful, Howard—"

"Well, it's my job, Paine, to see that—"

"I know, but this is really about the house, isn't it?"

"The house?"

"Ten Summer Street. I mean, that's all we're talking about here, right? It's all there is to Iris's estate. And at this point, as far as I'm concerned, Edward Shuttleworth can freaking have the place with my blessings."

"What do you see, Julia? Tell me," Dulcie says breathlessly above the steady hum of the outboard motor.

Seated beside her on the narrow bench at the back of the boat, Julia wonders if she can possibly capture the surrounding beauty in mere words.

"The sun is sinking low in the west," she begins, "and it's streaking the sky with pink and orange, and it's reflected in the lake. Andy was right—the water is so calm that it's like glass. I can see lots of trees, and the silhouettes of the cottages at Lily Dale on one side of the lake, and some of them have lights on inside now. Oh, and there are two swans floating over by the shore. They're so pretty, Dulcie. Their bills are touching, as though they're kissing."

"Do swans fall in love with each other like people do?"

Julia smiles, glancing at Andy. But he doesn't seem to have heard Dulcie's question. He's intent on steering the boat, looking straight out over the water.

Somewhere in the back of Julia's mind, a shred of anxiety takes hold. All day—no, she realizes, for *days*—she's been trying to keep certain thoughts at bay. Thoughts about Andy. Now they rush at her, bringing a tide of fear.

Andy was here the summer Kristin died.

Andy is here again . . . and now Iris is dead.

Andy was there yesterday, when Dulcie was out on the roof.

"Julia? Do swans fall in love?"

"Maybe they do, Dulcie." There is a waver of tension in Julia's voice.

"I wish you would fall in love with my dad," Dulcie says.

Out of the corner of her eye, Julia sees Andy stiffen. So he is listening.

Caught off guard by the little girl's words, she doesn't know what to say. She can't even think clearly.

"Dulcie . . ." Julia begins, trailing off, her mind whirling. *Oh, Christ. Andy? Could Andy possibly be the one who killed Kristin and Iris? It doesn't make sense, but . . .*

"If you fell in love with my dad and he fell in love with you, we wouldn't have to leave Lily Dale," Dulcie is saying. "Or else you could come with us, back to California. Then I would have a mommy."

"You had a mommy who loved you very much, Dulcie," Julia tells her softly, keeping a wary eye on the man steering the boat.

"But my mommy is dead," Dulcie says. "And now my gram is dead, too."

Julia's grasp tightens on the handles of the urn in her lap. She doesn't know what to say.

"I don't want me and Daddy to be alone anymore." There is a sob in Dulcie's voice now. "I want you to be with us, Julia. Please. Please love my daddy."

"Dulcie, I—"

"Please love me."

"I do love you, Dulcie," Julia says helplessly. "I *do* love you."

Her words seem to echo off the water.

Noticing the sudden silence, Julia realizes that they've reached the middle of the lake, and Andy has cut the motor.

Rupert tucks Mrs. Wainwright's substantial check into the appropriate slot on his rolltop desk, then closes the top. As an afterthought, he locks it. There's no telling how long it will be before he can get down to Lakeshore Savings and Loan in Fredonia to deposit the money.

Still clutching the receiver for the baby monitor, he hurries back to the bedroom. There, he finds Nan still unconscious. She seems to be gasping for breath now, her parched lips parted slightly, fluid rattling ominously in her throat.

Rupert sinks to the mattress beside her, clutching both her hands in his as guilt overtakes him. He shouldn't have left her. Why did he leave her alone? He promised he wouldn't.

"Nan," he says softly, a sob in his voice. "Nan, I'm sorry. I shouldn't have—oh, Nan. Why is this happening to us?"

The only reply is the harsh sound of her respiration as she drags oxygen into her tortured lungs. Rupert leans his head against her ribs where her breasts used to be, before the cancer began its slow, lethal raid on her body.

Cancer.

Nan.

Mama.

The dam bursts.

A flood of repressed memories rushes toward him.

"All I ever wanted was to be with you. Don't leave me." His plea is hollow in the silent room; it's not his voice at all, but that of the little boy left behind in a dingy Bronx apartment a lifetime ago.

"Please don't leave me. Please, Mama . . ."

His tears are soaking the blanket; the blanket is muffling the sound of her heartbeat but he knows it's still there, can feel her chest rising and falling beneath his cheek. He tries to memorize everything about her, so that after she's gone, and he's alone, he can remember what it was like, being with her. Not being alone.

"If you stay I promise I'll take care of you."

Oh, Nan.

Oh, Mama . . .

"I'll work hard and I'll earn money, and I'll get us a nice place to live. A real home. I promise . . ."

The stark rasping of breath is drowned out by the sudden piercing ring of the doorbell.

As she dials Katherine Jergins's number with a trembling finger, Pilar prays that the woman will be home to answer her call. According to the voice mail, the message was left hours earlier.

She deflates a bit when a male voice answers the phone. It isn't the man who answered when she called the other night. This voice is younger. More impatient.

Pilar asks for Katherine.

"Yeah, she's here, but I'm on the other line. Can she call you back?"

"I . . . Actually, this is a ship-to-shore call, and . . . I'm sorry, but can I please speak to her now?" Pilar can't stand the thought of prolonging the conversation with Katherine even another minute.

"Yeah, hang on. Mom!" the voice hollers, just before a click.

For a second, Pilar thinks she's been disconnected. Then she realizes that the boy—Katherine's son—must have picked up on call waiting and is hanging up the other line.

Sure enough, after an agonizing few moments, there's another click, and then Katherine's voice is tentatively saying, "Hello?"

"Katherine, this is Pilar. I just got your message."

"My son says you're calling from a ship?"

"That's right. I'm on a cruise and I—I'm very anxious to speak to you about your parents."

"I realized after you called again the other day that you might not be—" Katherine takes a deep, audible breath, then continues, "What I mean is, I thought you were some kind of scam artist until it occurred to me that you might have been talking about my other parents."

Pilar frowns. "Your 'other parents'?"

"Ms. Velazquez, my adoptive parents are both dead. But I realized that maybe you meant my birth parents—and that they might be alive, and looking for me."

Standing on Rupert's doorstep, Paine presses the doorbell again. Somebody has to be home. Rupert's car is parked in the driveway in front of Paine's rental, and there are lights on inside.

Paine shifts his weight impatiently, wanting to leave, but deciding to give Rupert another minute to get to the door. He promised to let the old man know what happened during the meeting with Ogden . . .

A faint sound reaches Paine's ears.

He listens in worried disbelief.

Somebody is crying. Loudly. It's an odd, eerie sound, and it's coming from inside the house.

Paine reaches out and turns the knob. It's unlocked.

"Rupert?" he calls, stepping into the house.

All he can hear is the blood-chilling sound of a grown man wailing.

"Okay, Dulcie. Here it is." Standing behind the little girl, Julia passes the urn to Dulcie, wondering if Andy can see her hands trembling.

Dulcie flinches beneath the weight. "It's heavy!"

Her abrupt movement rocks the boat.

"Careful!" Julia quickly steadies Dulcie, placing her hands on the orange life vest that seems too large for her small shoulders.

She returns her uneasy gaze to Andy, standing behind them. He's wearing sunglasses; it's impossible to read his expression.

The sun is almost down, Julia thinks, panic building within her. Why is he wearing sunglasses?

He does that a lot. Maybe it's just a habit. Or maybe . . .

Maybe he's trying to hide behind the dark lenses.

Let's get this over with and get back to shore, Julia tells herself, trying to subdue another swell of panic. She tugs at the top of the urn, removes the cover.

"What do I do?" Dulcie asks in a hushed tone.

"I guess you . . . I don't know." Julia looks over her shoulder again at Andy. "Should we say something, or just . . . ?"

He merely shrugs. "Whatever you think."

"Maybe we can sing," Dulcie suggests. "That circle song, from the service this morning. I liked that song."

"I did too," Julia says softly. "It was one of her favorites."

"Can we sing it?"

Julia swallows audibly, looking out over the water. Her

voice wavers as she sings, "I was standing by my window on one cold and cloudy day . . . when I saw that hearse come rolling for to carry my mother away . . ."

"Mom? Are you all right?" Christina asks, setting down her champagne flute as Pilar sinks into her chair at the table. Her daughter's dark eyes are concerned.

"I . . . I'm not sure what I am." Pilar looks around. "Where are Tom and the kids?"

"Up at the buffet. Again. You're scaring me, Mom. What happened when you called home?"

"I got a message from somebody I never expected to hear from." Pilar quickly explains about the Biddles' situation, and that she took it upon herself to track down their daughter, thinking she should be at her dying mother's bedside.

"But as it turns out, Christina, Katherine Jergins never even knew Rupert and Nan Biddle. They gave her up for adoption when she was born. Katherine's adoptive parents never even told her the truth before she died. She found out a few years ago when she needed a medical procedure and found out that her younger brother's blood was incompatible with hers—and that they couldn't possibly be related. She remembered her mother's pregnancy and knew that her brother was her parents' biological child. That was when she figured out that she must have been adopted."

"Well, it isn't unusual for parents to keep something like that from a child," Christina points out.

"No, but it's unusual for people to claim that they've raised a daughter, as the Biddles did." Pilar is troubled. "I don't understand why Rupert and Nan would lie. They convinced everyone in Lily Dale that their daughter Katherine was raised there, and that they sent her away to boarding school. They've also convinced everyone that she still visits them. Off-season. When the place is deserted. No wonder nobody I've ever spoken to has mentioned meeting Katherine. Except for one person . . .''

''Who?''

''Lincoln Reynolds,'' Pilar says uneasily.

In the bedroom, Paine finds Rupert huddled over his wife, sobbing like a child.

''Oh, Rupert . . .'' Paine goes to him, laying a hand on his shoulder.

Rupert spins around with a start. ''What are you doing here?''

''The door was open, so I—''

''Go away,'' Rupert bellows. ''Leave us alone.''

Paine can hear the woman in the bed struggling for breath.

''She's in agony, Rupert,'' he says softly. ''Shouldn't we call a doctor, or an ambulance?''

''I called the doctor. He says there's nothing he can do.''

''I'm so sorry . . .''

''Oh, Mama,'' Rupert sobs, as though Paine weren't even in the room.

Mama? Paine's blood runs cold.

''Rupert,'' he says gently, ''that's Nan. Your wife.''

''Nan . . .''

''Your wife.'' Paine realizes that Rupert isn't all there right now. He simply can't handle the anguish of losing Nan. His mind must be playing tricks on him. ''Rupert, isn't there somebody I can call? You shouldn't be alone. What about . . . don't you have a daughter? Can I call her?''

''Kath . . . erine . . .'' The word spills from Nan's lips.

The woman's eyes are open now, focused on Paine's. There is an air of desperation about her.

"Katherine," Paine echoes. "She's your daughter? Can I call her for you?"

Nan gasps, erupts in a choking sound.

"No!" Rupert stands, wild-eyed, looking from his wife to Paine and back again. "No!"

"She's trying to speak, Rupert," Paine says, reaching for Nan's hand, squeezing it. "Do you want Katherine, Nan? I'll call—where is she?"

It seems to take every ounce of Nan's strength to force the final words past her lips.

"Kath . . . dead."

With darkness, a hush has fallen over the lake.

Dulcie sits on the seat, clasping the empty urn against her chest, her face turned toward the sky, her eyes closed.

"Can we go back now?" Julia asks Andy, struggling to keep her growing urgency at bay. As she moves toward the seat, she catches her heel on a fishing pole and nearly falls.

Andy reaches toward her.

Swiftly regaining her balance, Julia instinctively jerks away from him.

He freezes, his hand hovering in midair, inches above her arm. "What's the matter?"

"I just . . . I'm sorry. I thought you . . ."

"You thought I what?"

"Why are you wearing sunglasses?" she asks, her heart pounding loudly in her ears. "Can't you take them off now? It's dark out."

Dulcie has turned toward them, a curious expression on her face.

"Julia?" she asks. "Is everything okay?"

Andy slowly removes his sunglasses. His eyes meet Julia's. In his intent green gaze, she sees concern. Confusion.

But nothing more.

Nothing threatening.

Julia exhales in relief. "Everything's fine, Dulcie. Let's go back to shore."

"Your daughter is dead?" Paine asks in sorrowful surprise, turning to Rupert.

"No!" Rupert protests. "No! Darling, please . . . don't . . ."

On the bed, Nan gasps for breath, looking up at them, both of them, her blue eyes pleading.

Katherine had the same blue eyes, Rupert remembers.

Big blue eyes that followed him everywhere from the moment she was born.

She adores her daddy, Nan used to say.

Katherine was Daddy's girl, all right. Rupert wanted to give her everything. Everything his father couldn't give him . . .

And everything Rupert couldn't give to her sister.

The first Katherine.

The baby girl who was born on a sweltering August day less than a year after he met Nan.

The baby girl who was born after Nan's mother told her pregnant teenaged daughter to leave and never come back; after Rupert struggled to support them with a couple of Wade's tried-and-true scams and succeeded only in getting himself arrested.

It was in jail that Rupert learned of the underground operation that arranged fast, illegal adoptions for wealthy suburban couples who were willing to pay big money for healthy newborns. If they signed the papers agreeing to give up the child, there would be enough money up front, before the baby was born, for Rupert to post bail. And afterward, when they handed over the child, there would be more than enough money to allow Rupert and Nan to make a fresh start somewhere else. . . .

What choice did they have? They were penniless. There was no one to help them. Nan's mother had disowned her. Wade was in prison.

Eventually, Rupert convinced Nan that they had no business bringing a baby into the world until they were able to get married and raise it together. She was devastated, but she realized he was right. She trusted him.

"We did what we had to do . . ." he murmurs.

"Rupert?"

The voice jars him back to the present.

"Is Katherine dead?"

He stares at Paine Landry, trying to decipher the question. His mind is muddled.

Katherine?

Dead?

He shakes his head slowly, remembering.

Nan never got over the loss of her firstborn child. Giving up that baby for adoption broke her heart. And Rupert's too. But he was better equipped to cope. He was accustomed to heartache.

It was Nan who insisted on keeping track of their first child. An old friend of Wade's was willing to keep them posted—for a fee, of course. For years, Nan cherished the sporadic progress reports, the furtively snapped photos from a distance, of a blond little girl with Rupert's gray eyes. Her adoptive parents named her Katherine.

When Rupert and Nan were finally married and Nan delivered their second daughter, she insisted that they name her after the sister she would never know existed. It didn't seem like a good idea, but Rupert agreed. Nan wanted so much to recapture the child she had lost. Whatever Nan wanted, he tried to give her. Always.

That was why they came here to Lily Dale in the first place. Nan wanted to live in a small town. She didn't want Rupert to travel to make a living, the way his father had, and the way Rupert himself had, with Wade. There must be something he could do close to home . . .

There was.

Putting people in touch with the spirits of their dead loved ones turned out to be the easiest con of all. He always marveled at their willingness to believe, at their eagerness to dismiss anything that didn't ring true. In time, he had more hits than misses, thanks to shrewd research into his clients' backgrounds, luck, and a true knack for studying human nature.

Wade had taught him well. It was simple for Rupert to perfect his skills over the years, simple to trick his clients— especially lonely widows—into thinking he was giving them information courtesy of the great beyond. They never realized he was simply performing one of the world's oldest parlor tricks.

"Rupert . . ." Paine Landry's hands are reaching toward him. Coming to rest on his shoulder.

Rupert shakes off the gentle grip, dazed, lost in memories.

"I know this is traumatic for you, Rupert," Paine is saying. "What can I do? How can I help? I'm so sorry I didn't realize that your daughter was dead. For some reason I had the impression—"

"Stop talking about her!" Rupert roars.

"All right . . . I'm sorry," Paine says helplessly. "Should I go? I don't know what to—Look, I don't want to leave you alone, Rupert . . . I don't want to leave you and Nan . . . not now. I don't think she has much time, and she needs to talk . . . Maybe if you talk to her about your daughter . . ."

Rupert's gaze settles on Paine. In the maelstrom of anger

and fear swirling through Rupert's mind, one terrifying thought touches down.

He knows.

With that knowledge comes the eye of the storm. A sudden calm settles over Rupert. Raw instinct takes over.

He swiftly turns and leaves the room without a word.

"I think Dulcie and I will walk back to my place," Julia tells Andy as the three of them walk away from the pier toward Andy's car.

Andy doesn't argue. Nor does he mention seeing her again. He looks up at the twilight sky and observes, "Lots of stars. It's going to be a nice day tomorrow."

No, it isn't, Julia thinks. *Dulcie and Paine are leaving.*

They've reached Andy's car.

Julia begins, "Thanks for taking us—"

She's cut off by the sound of somebody calling Andy's name.

She turns to see an attractive woman strolling toward them. She's tanned and pretty, and Julia notices that Andy's face lights up at the sight of her.

"Hey, Heather," he says, shooting a wary glance at Julia, as if he's suddenly wishing she would get lost. "How's it going?"

"Not bad." The woman licks the pink ice cream cone in her hand, her eyes flicking over Julia.

"Heather, this is Julia. Julia, Heather," Andy says, obviously uncomfortable.

"And I'm Dulcie."

"Oh, right, that's Dulcie."

Julia checks to see whether Heather has any reaction to Dulcie's blindness, but she doesn't even glance at the little girl. She has eyes only for Andy.

And she can have him, Julia thinks, realizing she isn't the least bit jealous. She wonders only fleetingly whether Andy has been dating other women—Heather included—since she started seeing him. It doesn't matter. They're completely wrong for each other.

That's what Grandma was trying to tell me.

Andy will never love Julia. Not the way Paine . . .

The way Paine loved Kristin.

"Thanks for taking us out on the boat, Andy," Julia says. How could she have convinced herself, out on the water, that Andy meant to harm her and Dulcie?

"No problem, Julia. I'm glad I could help. See you later."

He isn't even looking at her.

Holding Dulcie's hand, Julia leads the little girl away from the waterfront. The streetlights have come on and crickets have taken up their nightly chorus. People are strolling the streets or out on their porches, enjoying the warm summer evening.

"How far is it to your house, Julia?" Dulcie asks.

"Not far. Are you too tired to walk?" Maybe Julia should have let Andy drive them.

"No. I don't want to get there. Because Daddy will be there and he'll make me go to bed. And anyway, Andy was supposed to take us out for pizza. Remember?"

"I forgot all about that." Clearly Andy did too.

Julia realizes that she forgot something else: she left the empty urn on Andy's boat. She hesitates, looking back at the pier. Andy and Heather are already driving away in Andy's car, heading toward the gate leading out of Lily Dale.

He doesn't waste any time, she thinks, almost amused. Oh, well. She'll get the urn back later.

She turns back to Dulcie. "I'll tell you what, sweetie.

How about if we take the long way home? We can stop at the café to eat.''

Dulcie's face lights up. ''That would be great. Thanks, Julia.''

''Okay, then we need to head this way.'' Julia guides Dulcie across the road and turns up Green Street.

As they walk up the quiet block, a more cheerful Dulcie tells knock, knock jokes. Julia laughs at every one, but her thoughts are elsewhere.

Who killed Kristin and Iris?

And why?

It's a tired refrain, but Julia can't stop the persistent questions running through her mind.

Maybe she should go to the police.

But she has no evidence that her friends were murdered. Only a gut instinct—and disturbing psychic visions. Will the authorities take her seriously? Or will they dismiss her as a quack?

Julia is so caught up in her reverie that they've almost passed the Biddles' house before she notices that Paine's red car is parked in the driveway.

''Hey, Dulcie, your dad is here visiting Rupert Biddle.'' Julia backtracks a few steps to the front walk, pulling Dulcie gently along. ''Let's stop and tell him to meet us at the café.''

''I thought it was going to be just the two of us, Julia.''

''Your dad might be worried if he gets back to my place this late and we aren't there, Dulcie. Come on.''

''All right,'' she says reluctantly.

As they walk up the Biddles' front steps toward the screened outer door, Julia is surprised to see that the inner door is standing open. That's not like Rupert, who always seems to value his privacy. Maybe it's because Paine is on his way out.

Pressing her face close to the screen, Julia calls out, "Hello? Rupert? Paine? Is anybody . . ."

She trails off, her knees suddenly buckling beneath her.

Rupert Biddle is standing in the hallway, clutching a handgun.

Listening to Nan Biddle fight for every breath, Paine fights back panic. Rupert has left him alone with a dying woman, a total stranger. What should he do? Where the heck is Rupert?

Paine instinctively reaches out and strokes her arm. "There you go, it's all right," he murmurs, looking around the room for a phone.

He should call somebody. A doctor. Or the police. Somebody.

His heart pounding, Paine says gently, "I know you must be afraid, Mrs. Biddle. But I'm right here, and Rupert is . . . I'm sure he'll be right back."

A door slams somewhere at the front of the house. His first thought is that Rupert has fled in shock, unable to cope. Then he hears the sharp click of a dead bolt being turned, and footsteps in the kitchen.

"Get in there," Rupert's voice says harshly.

Paine looks up toward the doorway, half expecting to see Rupert ushering an EMT into the room.

His blood runs cold at the sight of the old man herding a terrified Julia and Dulcie in front of him, aiming a gun at their backs.

"They're obviously not home, Miranda," Kent says as she reaches out for the third time to press the old-fashioned doorbell at Ten Summer Street.

"I know, but . . ." She casts a longing glance at the lilac tree in the yard. "How are we going to wait any longer to find out what's buried there?"

"We'll have to. No way are we digging there without their permission."

"I know. But—"

"No way," he says again. "Let's go get coffee or something and we'll check back later. Hopefully somebody will be home then."

"Even if they are home, there's no guarantee that they'll listen to what we have to say this time," Miranda points out. "They thought we were a couple of crackpots before. What makes you think they're going to let us dig up their yard?"

"We'll play the tape for them," Kent says. "If that doesn't convince them, nothing will. And if nothing will . . . then we'll just have to forget about it."

Miranda sighs and follows him down the steps.

"Paine!" Julia cries out. Thank God he's alive. She was certain Rupert had already—

"Shut up!" Rupert pokes her in the back with the hard nose of the gun.

She can no longer see the mad glint in his eye, but she glimpsed it for a split second from the other side of the screen door, right before he aimed the gun directly at her and ordered her and Dulcie into the house.

Sick waves of fear and nausea course through Julia as she struggles to stay calm, her mind racing to make sense of the bizarre scenario.

"Rupert, put the gun down." Paine's voice is somehow steady. He stands deadly still, his gaze fixed on the old man behind Julia and Dulcie, who has begun to whimper as she grasps what's going on.

"Shut up! All of you! Just shut up!"

The room falls silent, but for Nan's agonized gasps for air.

"Nan, darling, please," Rupert's voice begs, behind Julia. "Please hold on. I'll be with you in just a few moments, as soon as I . . ."

He trails off, but his meaning is chillingly clear.

"Why are you doing this, Rupert?" Julia asks softly, afraid to raise her voice to him, afraid to move a muscle. Her eyes are locked on Paine's face; his eyes, in turn, are fixed warily on Rupert.

"He knows. The kid knows, too," Rupert says. "And you too, Julia. You know too, don't you?"

She finds her voice again, expecting it to come out small and frightened. But it doesn't. "I know *what*, Rupert?" Lord, how can she sound normal when she's feeling anything but?

"You know about Katherine . . ."

"Katherine. Your daughter?" Bewildered, Julia tries to stay on track, tries to make sense of what he's saying. "What about Katherine?"

"Don't pretend you don't know," he snaps. "And *you*—"

Julia hears Dulcie cry out, feels the child flinch at her side. Rupert must have jabbed her with the gun. A fierce, protective fury swoops through Julia. She wants to tell him to leave the little girl alone. But she doesn't dare open her mouth. Nor does Paine. Yet Julia realizes that he looks poised, ready to pounce.

No. Please. Don't take any chances, Paine. Julia attempts to catch his eye, but he's watching Rupert and Dulcie intently, his features a barren mask of dread.

"I heard you talking to her," Rupert is saying to Dulcie.

"On the stairway the other day, when you didn't even know I was there. You can't see anything, but you saw her, didn't you? What did she say to you?"

"Do you mean ... the lady?" Dulcie's tiny, terrified voice cuts right through to Julia's heart.

"Katherine." Rupert is impatient. "What did she say? How many times have you seen her?"

"A few times." Dulcie's voice quavers.

"What did you see?"

"She ... she was bleeding. She fell down the stairs because she was trying to get away from the bad man. He was yelling, and he was reaching toward her, and she fell ... She was bleeding in her head!"

"It's okay, Dulcie," Paine says in a soft, even tone.

"Shut up!" Rupert screams.

Julia's mind is whirling. Rupert's daughter Katherine is dead? It was her spirit on the stairs? Was Rupert—her own father—the "bad man" she was trying to escape?

"It was an accident, Rupert, wasn't it?" Julia is desperate to keep him talking, to keep his temper from careening out of control. If he starts firing that gun ...

"It was an accident!" the old man echoes with a sob in his voice. "Of course it was an accident! My daughter meant everything to me, and when I saw that she was ..."

"What happened then?" Paine asks, taking the slightest step forward.

"Nan and I ... we panicked. We didn't know what to do. We had to do something. And then Nan ... she collapsed. She couldn't take it. She fainted. And I ..."

"What did you do, Rupert?" Paine asks, moving another few inches away from the bed where Nan lies dying. Toward all of them—Julia, and Dulcie, and Rupert, and the gun ...

"There was already a hole," he says in a faraway voice. "I always wonder if things would have been the same if I hadn't dug that hole that afternoon. But I had dug it, because it was springtime, and Nan—she had bought some shrubs over at the garden center. Lilacs. Nan loves lilacs. They smell so sweet . . ."

Julia numbly tries to grasp the horror of what he's saying.

Rupert buried his dead daughter in the yard at Ten Summer Street.

It was springtime.

That meant Lily Dale was still virtually deserted. He told people that he had sent Katherine away to boarding school, and . . .

He and Nan have carried on the charade ever since? But that's impossible.

"If only Katherine had listened to me . . . I tried to tell her . . . Nan and I *both* tried to tell her. For months . . ."

How could they have pulled it off? Julia wonders, bewildered, as he rambles on. How could they have convinced an entire population that their daughter still existed? That she was coming and going, visiting her parents during the bleak off-season. And nobody ever suspected the truth.

Not even me. They even fooled the handful of us who were here year-round.

Julia thinks back, trying to recall any mention of the elusive Katherine Biddle. She can see herself running into Nan and Rupert around town, making small talk with them, hearing them make casual reference to their daughter.

"Katherine was here last week," Rupert might say, or "We're hoping Katherine will be able to come for Christmas."

There was never any hint that he wasn't telling the truth. Never any reason to suspect that Katherine didn't exist.

Rupert always did all the talking, she realizes. *He was so convincing.*

She glances at the woman in the bed, seeing her not like

this, but as she always was, right by Rupert's side, silently supporting her husband.

How could she have gone along with it? Julia wonders. In a macabre *Stepford-Wives* scenario, Nan blindly agreed to whatever he said, whatever he did . . .

Did she love her husband that much? Need him that much? The answer is clear, Julia thinks grimly.

"Katherine wouldn't have had any kind of life with that farmer." Rupert's voice is almost trancelike, as though he's repeating a familiar mantra. "She would have been turning her back on the life we worked so hard to give her. She said she wouldn't mind struggling, being poor, but she didn't know. She didn't know. Not like I know. When I saw that ring on her finger that night, I went out of my mind. I just . . . all I wanted was for her to take off the damned ring. To give it to me. I never knew . . . I never knew she'd fall . . ."

Julia hears the despair building in his voice and dares to speak up again. "It was an accident, Rupert."

But this time, her words don't soothe him. This time, he seems to snap out of a daze.

She can feel the sudden tension behind her as he barks, "Get over there." He pokes her in the back again with the gun. "Across the room. Against the wall. All of you. Go."

Dulcie whimpers. Julia reaches for her arm.

"Don't move!" Rupert snarls.

"I have to help her walk. She can't see."

"Really? She can see when she wants to. She saw my daughter. *Move.*"

Julia falters, glancing at Paine, who sends her a look that says, *Do exactly what he wants you to do.*

"Straight ahead, Dulcie," Julia says under her breath. "There's nothing in your way. Nothing between you and the wall. Just keep going."

"What's he going to do to us?" Dulcie asks, a tremor in her voice.

"Shut up!" the old man growls.

Julia wonders what happened to the Rupert Biddle she knew.

But you never knew him. All these years, you've seen him around town, talked to him, even admired him . . .

She never suspected what he was capable of doing . . . or the lengths he would go to in order to protect his secret.

He's going to kill us, all of us, to keep us quiet.

No. That can't happen. I won't let it. Not now. Not like this.

Is this what Kristin felt at the end? And Iris?

Julia has reached the wall. She darts a glance around the room as she turns gingerly to face her captor, checking for a possible escape. A door is ajar just a few feet away, leading to a bathroom. But she doesn't dare make a break for it. The three of them could never get inside before Rupert started shooting, and even if they could, he would shoot through the flimsy-looking wooden door.

There's a sudden sputtering, choking sound from the bed.

Rupert glances at Nan.

She's still struggling, damn it. Can't Rupert see that she needs him? Can't he forget about all the rest of it? Just drop the gun, and go to his wife, and take her into his arms?

Julia looks at Paine, who appears ready to seize the moment that Rupert's attention is diverted. But the old man looks sharply back at them, the gun still aimed in their direction.

"Please, Rupert, you have to think about what you're doing, here. You have to get hold of yourself and think about the consequences."

As Paine speaks, Julia finds herself taking strength from his presence, from the calm in his voice.

Dulcie is between them, quivering in fear. Julia knows that if Rupert raises the gun, Paine will shield his daughter with his body. And so will Julia.

Again, rage comes to mingle with her fright. This time, it grows stronger. How dare he threaten to hurt an innocent child? How dare he threaten any of them?

She thinks about Kristin. About Iris.

Rupert killed them. He must have. But why?

Then, in the blink of an eye, it all becomes clear.

"That's what Kristin saw, isn't it?"

Rupert jerks his head abruptly at the sound of Julia's voice. His gray gaze narrows.

Drawing courage from deep inside—from the place that still aches for the lost friend she loved like a sister—Julia takes a deep breath and lifts her chin, boldly facing Rupert. "Kristin saw Katherine on the stairs that Halloween night, didn't she? Covered in blood, like Dulcie said."

That's it. That has to be it.

"It scared the hell out of Kristin," Julia goes on, understanding for the first time what must have happened. "It made her afraid of her gift, afraid of that house, afraid of Lily Dale. And when she came back three years ago and her mother had moved into that house, she saw it again, didn't she? But . . . how did you know, Rupert? How did you know what she saw?"

Miraculously, he responds to the question. With a derisive snort, he asks, "How did I know? She asked me about it, that's how. Showed up on my doorstep one night right after she came back here, asking me questions. Questions that brought up a lot of bad memories that Nan didn't need. Not right then. She had enough to worry about . . . she was getting sicker, and the doctor kept telling me that stress would make her worse. When that Shuttleworth girl came here and started talking about what she saw on the stairs in our house ... Nan almost had a nervous breakdown. She just fell apart. *Damn* her. Damn that girl for what she did to Nan.''

He's insane, Julia thinks. He's blaming Kristin for his wife's being terminally ill. Is that what happened? He snapped? He snapped and he killed her?

"She was terrified of the water, Rupert," Paine says. "How did you get her out on a boat?"

"She couldn't have been that afraid." His words are laced with derision. "All I did was call her and tell her I needed to talk to her about what she saw. I said I had remembered something I thought might help. Told her we had to talk someplace private, where nobody could hear us. Made her promise not to tell anyone she was meeting me. Guess she never told."

No, Kristin never told.

And yes, she was afraid of the water. But not as afraid as she should have been.

And not as afraid as she was of what lurked in the house at Ten Summer Street.

Julia has to know the rest of it. "What about Iris?"

"She came to me for a reading. Said she wanted me to put her in touch with her daughter's spirit."

"When was this?"

"Maybe a month ago. All that time went by, and then she had to dredge things up. She said she didn't believe Kristin died accidentally, and that she wanted to contact her and find out what happened."

He trails off, shaking his head.

"Did Kristin's spirit come through?" Paine prods.

"It sure did. It told Iris to stop snooping around. Told her that she was better off leaving it alone. But she didn't want to listen." He snorts again.

Of course he never made contact with Kristin. He faked it. Did Iris see through him?

"What did she do, Rupert?" Julia asks, trying to keep her voice steady.

"I could tell she was suspicious. I couldn't let her go any further. I couldn't let her start talking to people, asking questions, trying to—"

"So you snuck into her house when she was getting ready to take a bath, and you drowned her!" Julia knows her voice is shrill, knows she's losing control, knows this is foolish, perilous. Yet she can't seem to help herself. She takes a step toward Rupert, her fists clenched, heedless of the gun in his hands. "You bastard! You made her death look like an accident, too! And you thought you were going to get away with it! And you thought you were going to get the house back, so that nobody else would ever know. Then, when you realized what was happening with Dulcie, you came after her, too, didn't you?"

He simply nods.

"There really was someone in the house yesterday," Julia realizes. "It was you. You locked me in the basement, and you went after Dulcie, and if Andy hadn't come along . . ."

She trails off, suddenly aware that Rupert has stiffened. He's glaring at her, murderous intention clear in his glittering gray eyes even before he raises the gun, holding it with both hands, taking aim at Julia.

The click as he cocks the weapon is followed by another sound. A horrible sound . . .

A loud, rattling sigh as Nan Biddle expels her last ragged breath.

The old man freezes. He seems to be listening, his features transforming into a mask of alarm.

"Noooo!" An unearthly howl escapes Rupert's lips, a

howl that chills Julia to the bone. He jerks around, facing the bed where his wife lies deathly still. "No! Nan!"

In that moment, Paine makes his move, rushing forward.

Julia grabs Dulcie and barrels toward the bathroom, hurtling inside the small room and slamming the door. She presses the button lock and looks frantically around for an escape. There's a small window above the toilet. It's too small for her to squeeze through, but Dulcie would fit.

"Listen, Dulcie," she hisses at the little girl as she scrambles on top of the toilet seat and tugs on the window lock. "There's a window here that I'm going to help you through. It isn't a far drop to the ground. As soon as you're out, Dulcie, I want you to . . . to . . ."

To what?

Julia can hear thumping and grunting as Paine and Rupert tussle in the next room. There's a loud crash, as though a piece of furniture has toppled over.

She can't send Dulcie blindly running into the yard with a sharp drop-off to the lake on one side and the road on the other. Nor can she tell her to start screaming for help. Not when there's a chance Rupert has already gotten the gun back and would go after the little girl.

Distraught, Julia tries to figure out how to save the little girl. She has to get her out of this house. Any second now, Rupert could start shooting through the bathroom door.

Maybe Dulcie's best bet is to hide in the shrubs close to the foundation . . .

Dulcie is sobbing, clinging to Julia's legs as she shoves the window open. "What about you, Julia? What about Daddy? I don't want to go out there alone!"

"You have to, Dulcie. Don't worry about us." Julia struggles to unlatch the screen. It comes free. Dulcie's escape route is clear.

"Come on, Dulcie." Julia swiftly pulls her up onto the toilet seat. "I want you to go legs first. I'll help you. Come on."

"No! Please, Julia, don't make me."

"Dulcie, you have to trust me. Please. I love you. I'm going to get you out of here so that he can't hurt—"

She breaks off at the sound of Paine's sudden shout from the next room.

"Rupert, no!"

Julia's breath catches in her throat.

"Rupert, please don't do it. Drop the—"

Paine's frantic plea is lost in the sudden blast of a single gunshot.

Seated at the outdoor café, about to bite into a thick roast beef sandwich on a salted kimmelweck roll, Miranda freezes.

Kent looks up from his own sandwich, startled. "What was *that?*"

"It must have been a firecracker. The Fourth of July is only a few days away." Miranda bites into her sandwich.

"Yeah, and by then, we should be finished with Cleveland and on to Cincinnati," Kent says around a mouthful. "Maybe we can spend the Fourth on one of those riverboat rides. I'll bet they have fantastic fireworks displays out there."

"I'll bet you're right. That sounds like fun."

But Miranda can't help thinking that she isn't ready to look ahead until she feels as though their work is done here. And it won't be until they find out what's under the lilac tree at Ten Summer Street.

* * *

"Paine? Paine?"

"Yes. I'm okay," he manages to call to Julia behind the bathroom door.

"Daddy!" Dulcie's voice shouts, over Julia's audible "Thank God."

Paine shudders, turning his back on the blood-splattered scene, closing his eyes to shut out the horror of what he just witnessed.

Forcing himself to move, he walks to the bathroom door. *It's over.* His body begins to shake. *It's over.*

He reaches out, tries to turn the knob. It's locked.

"Julia . . . ? It's okay. You can—"

She throws the door open. A tide of relief sweeps through Paine as he catches sight of his little girl standing there beside Julia, safe and sound. He hauls Dulcie into his arms, kissing her hair, holding her close.

His raises his gaze to meet Julia's above his daughter's head.

Her expression is somber. She has seen what lies behind him in the bedroom.

Rupert's body is draped across Nan's on the bed, most of his head blasted away by the shot he fired at close range into his own temple.

"I couldn't get the gun away from him," Paine says raggedly. "I tried . . ."

"I know."

Paine lifts Dulcie, cradling her against his side with one arm. With the other, he reaches for Julia.

"Come on," he says softly, taking her hand. Her skin is icy. He can feel her trembling.

"Can we go home, Daddy?" Dulcie whimpers, burying her face in his shoulder. "I want to go home now."

"Sure, Dulcie. We can go home. Let's all go home."

He hears Julia swallow hard. Sees her gazing past him, at Nan and Rupert.

"He didn't want to live without her," Paine says simply. Julia nods.

I didn't want to live without Kristin, either. But I had to go on. For Dulcie.

For three years, he's merely gone through the motions. But now . . .

Now it's over.

Now he knows what happened.

Now he can move on.

Alone, with Dulcie.

Just the two of them.

He looks at Julia.

Or maybe . . .

No.

He's not ready for that.

He doesn't know if he'll ever be ready for that again. What matters now is taking care of Dulcie, and learning how to live—really *live*—again.

Her head bent and eyes closed, Julia listens to the dull thud of metal slamming into dirt.

Sweat trickles down her temples. She wipes it away, praying for a breath of breeze to stir the hot, humid air.

Thunder rumbles in the distance.

The weather service is predicting a big storm this afternoon—one that's sure to break the muggy heat wave as well as ruin tonight's scheduled Fourth of July fireworks display over the lake. Julia figures that wouldn't have been any fun without Paine and Dulcie, anyway. They weren't planning to go down to the waterfront with her. They're leaving first thing tomorrow morning, their trip having been postponed several days already. Paine said he wants Dulcie to get a good night's sleep, and the fireworks wouldn't have started until almost ten o'clock.

Julia's eyes snap open at a sudden clanking sound.

A few feet away, a detective's shovel has struck something solid in the widening hole around the lilac tree in the yard at Ten Summer Street.

The man bends over to examine it.

Julia's breath catches in her throat.

"It's just a rock," a nearby police officer mutters.

The detective puts it aside and, with two other investigators, resumes digging.

A few minutes later, they finally manage to wrestle the lilac's root ball loose from the soil. It takes all three sweat-soaked detectives and several cops to carefully remove the large shrub from the spot where it has grown since that tragic, long ago April day.

Julia looks at Paine, standing beside her. He raises an eyebrow as if to ask, *Hanging in there?*

She nods slightly.

Beside them, Miranda Cleary whispers something into Kent Gilman's ear.

Julia is glad they were given permission by the police to be here, too. Granted, the cops still aren't convinced they're going to find anything buried under this tree. And they all but said Miranda's audiotapes were a hoax.

But an investigation into the Biddles' past confirmed that there is no trace of Katherine Biddle's existence after the April of her junior year in high school. Records show that she never returned from spring break, and that her parents transferred her to a boarding school. Nobody ever thought to confirm their story. And nobody ever saw her again.

Silence hangs over the yard, broken only by the steady

rhythm of the shovels sinking lower into the earth where the shrub once stood.

Julia's thoughts turn to Rupert Biddle. Even now, days later, she remains stunned at the discovery that her neighbor was capable of killing Kristin and Iris to protect his terrible secret.

He killed poor Lincoln Reynolds, too.

When the police went out to his Sinclairville farm to question him about Katherine Biddle's decades-old disappearance, they discovered his body. The bullets were traced to Rupert Biddle's gun, and Lincoln's telephone records revealed that he placed a call to the Biddle residence on what was probably the day he died. Nobody will ever know what was said during that conversation. But whatever it was infuriated Rupert enough to send him over to Lincoln's place to kill the man he still loathed.

A ripple of little-girl laughter drifts into the yard through Pilar's open window.

Julia looks up in that direction, and then over at Paine. A faint smile touches his lips.

Dulcie is in Pilar's kitchen, baking brownies. Pilar, who flew back from her cruise the moment she learned of the Biddles' deaths, volunteered to baby-sit the little girl while the digging takes place. "Don't worry, I'll distract her. She'll be busy and happy," Pilar said cheerfully.

The excavation wears on.

Heat lightning sizzles over the lake.

The air is oppressive, the sky ominously overcast.

All the world seems to be holding its breath.

Then . . .

"I've got something," the detective announces, dropping his shovel and crouching at the hole. He reaches in, carefully brushing dirt aside with a gloved hand as the others press closer.

"It looks like a bone," he announces grimly.

Julia's stomach turns over.

Miranda Cleary lets out a low wail.

It's what they were expecting, and yet . . .

Julia realizes that there was some part of her unwilling to believe that Rupert's story was true. That he buried his daughter's broken corpse in his own backyard.

Wiping tears that mingle with the perspiration on her face, Julia looks up at Paine. She's startled to see that his eyes, too, are glistening.

Side by side, they watch in bleak silence as Katherine Biddle's remains are unearthed, inch by agonizing inch.

"Hey, what's that shiny thing?" one of the detectives asks.

"It looks like jewelry," another replies. "Wipe some of that dirt off."

A moment later, somebody says, "Yeah, that's a ring on the finger. Looks like an engagement ring."

Julia gasps.

Paine reaches for her hand. "You okay?"

She looks up at him. "I don't know why . . . I guess I assumed he would have taken it off her before he buried her."

"Maybe he tried and couldn't get it off," Paine says softly. "Or maybe he overlooked it."

"Maybe."

Julia watches solemnly as the detectives resume their gruesome task, unearthing the remains of a young girl whose only crime was to fall in love with a poor boy.

A slight gust stirs the branches overhead.

There is a loud, close clap of thunder.

Finally, fat raindrops begin to fall.

As Paine's warm grasp squeezes her fingers reassuringly, Julia lifts her face to the weeping heavens, welcoming the cool moisture.

And wondering if Katherine Biddle and Lincoln Reynolds are together somewhere at last.

Epilogue

December
Lily Dale, New York

The snow begins to fall as Julia rounds the corner onto Summer Street.

Fat, lacy flakes drift down from the gray sky, the official start of the season's first blizzard. By tonight, if the Accuweather forecast is correct, Lily Dale will be buried under two feet of snow, with more on the way by daybreak and windchills well below zero.

It's perfect weather to stay inside by a warm fire, Julia thinks as she heads up the street, her head bent against the icy wind. Maybe later she can finally start writing out her Christmas cards.

Just yesterday, she received one from Pilar in Alabama. In it, she wrote that she was already looking forward to getting back to Lily Dale in June, and promised to send Julia a postcard from her spring trip to Japan to visit her son.

There was a card from Lorraine, too. She's been staying with her sister in Buffalo while she goes through rigorous daily physical therapy sessions. But she's making tremendous progress, and she, too, expects to be back in Lily Dale in time for the summer season. She's going to make a full recovery, thank God. She even managed to crack a weak joke the last time Julia spoke to her on the phone.

"I've definitely learned my lesson. This has taught me not to borrow your clothes anymore without asking, Jul."

Julia barely managed to smile. After all, Lorraine was almost killed because she was wearing Julia's jacket. Rupert must have seen her walking that night, recognized the distinct orange color of the raincoat, and mowed her down, thinking it was Julia. The police later found evidence on his car's bumper that he had hit something.

The flakes are falling faster now, swirling through the air, clinging to rooftops and bare tree branches overhead. Julia has almost reached Ten Summer Street.

She walks past it every day on her late afternoon stroll. She tells herself that she needs to check on things while the house is empty, just as she used to do when Iris was away for the winter.

If only Paine and Dulcie were just away for the winter. If only Julia could look forward to their return with the spring.

But that isn't going to happen. According to Paine's mid-November update on the legal tug-of-war over the house, it looks like things are finally winding down. Most likely, Edward's lawyer is going to settle. They're going to sell the house and split the proceeds down the middle, with half going to Dulcie and half to Edward, who is only interested in cash, and not the old house.

The lawyers and Realtors will handle the sale. There is no need for Paine and Dulcie to come back to Lily Dale again.

Julia has known all along that she would never see them again after that heart-wrenching good-bye before they drove off on that last rainy July morning.

That didn't stop her from spending the last five months pretending. Hoping. Wishing . . .

At least they keep in touch fairly often. Rather, they did.

Dulcie called Julia almost daily when she first got back to California. Then the calls tapered off a bit. Finally, a few weeks ago, they stopped altogether.

When Julia called Paine and Dulcie to wish them a happy Thanksgiving, the operator informed her that the number had been disconnected. There was no forwarding information.

Stopping on the sidewalk in front of Ten Summer Street, Julia finds her gaze drawn, as always to the spot just behind the porch where the lilac once stood.

Poor Katherine Biddle.

At least now perhaps she can rest in peace. She was given a decent burial soon after the coroner's office released her body. Julia attended the service with Pilar.

Later Pilar took it upon herself to hire a landscaper to plant the shrub again in a different spot on the property at Ten Summer Street. But the shovels' blows had badly damaged the roots. The shrub eventually wilted and died. There will be no fragrant blooms this spring.

Maybe it's better that way.

Julia lifts her gaze to the house.

The house that might have been hers . . .

If things were different.

But it's better this way, Julia reminds herself.

After all, Iris died here.

Katherine died here.

Kristin's fate was sealed here.

Kristin . . .

My sister.

Even now, all these months after her mother blurted the bombshell during a long-distance phone call, Julia is struck by renewed surprise.

Kristin was my sister.

Anson was my father.

Dulcie is my niece.

Every time that shocking reality drifts into her mind, she has to fight back the urge to call someone—no, to call *Paine*—and tell him the astounding news. But she promised her mother she would never tell a soul, and she won't.

Even if keeping the secret means never claiming a share of the house at Ten Summer Street.

Even if it means never being acknowledged as Dulcie's blood relative.

Hungry for more information about the past, Julia tried to get Deborah Garrity to reveal more.

"Oh, I knew I never should have told you," was her mother's wailed response.

And she probably wouldn't have told, if she hadn't happened to call Julia a few hours after Katherine Biddle's skeleton was unearthed. Her emotions raw, Julia sobbed the whole tragic story of Katherine's death, and Iris's and Kristin's murders, to her mother. Uncharacteristically quiet on her end, Deborah listened intently, then said slowly, "Julia, there's something you should know about the Shuttleworths . . ."

So. Now she knows. Her mother had an affair with Kristin's father right around the time Iris got pregnant with Kristin. Both Anson and Iris knew that Anson was Julia's father. Kristin, presumably, did not.

Julia can't help feeling hurt, even now, by Anson's detached attitude toward her all those years ago, whenever she visited the Shuttleworth household. No wonder he locked himself in his study when she was around. It wasn't that he disliked children. He just couldn't stand the sight of a little girl he had no intention of acknowledging as his own.

Yet the pain of his rejection is tempered by the memory of Iris's willingness to tolerate the unwitting friendship between her daughter and Julia. It must have been heart-wrenching for her to welcome Julia into her home back when the pain of her husband's betrayal was still fresh. That she was kind to Julia back then is as remarkable, in retrospect as the fact that she treated Julia as a surrogate daughter in recent years.

How Julia aches to hug Iris to thank her for her friendship—and for allowing Kristin's.

No wonder . . .

The words keep running through her mind. Now it all makes sense. The indestructible lifelong bond between her and Kristin. Julia's fierce sense of responsibility toward Dulcie. Her acute longing, even now, for both of them.

No wonder . . .

And yet . . .

Would Julia have felt any less attached to Kristin if there weren't a blood bond between them?

Would she feel any less deprived by Dulcie's absence now?

She's spent a lifetime it seems hungering for family. Not just for the family she's lost—her grandmother, and the father she assumed she never knew—but for the family she's always longed for: siblings, a husband, children of her own.

She might never marry or become a mother.

But at least I had a sister . . . wherever you are, Kristin.

At least I have a niece . . . wherever you are, Dulcie.

As she stands staring at the house at Ten Summer Street, lost in thought, Julia is suddenly struck by the realization that something is different.

Startled, she gapes at the front door, adorned by a simple pine wreath with a red velvet bow.

Julia frowns. Who could have put that there?

Maybe the Realtors are already preparing the place for sale, trying to make it look homey again.

The snow is coming down hard now. She should get back home. Turning away from the house, Julia takes a deep breath . . .

And realizes that the chilly air is tinged with woodsmoke.

She turns again slowly, looking up at the old house.

A thin tendril of smoke wafts from the chimney.

Stunned, Julia walks slowly up the steps.

She lifts her hand to knock.

"Julia!" The front door is thrown open. "Daddy saw you through the window. Are you surprised to see us?"

Framed in the doorway, Dulcie is neatly dressed in a black velvet jumper with a lacy white blouse and polished little black Mary Jane shoes. There's even a ribbon in her hair— tied a little lopsided, but Paine is getting much better.

The little girl launches herself at Julia, throwing her arms around her.

Julia hugs Dulcie back, opening her mouth to speak, but her voice seems to have vanished.

Paine appears in the stair hall. His hair is neatly trimmed, she realizes, looking up at him over the top of Dulcie's head. He's clean shaven, too. And something else is different . . .

"Dulcie, let Julia come in and close the door. I just got the fire going and you're letting all the heat out."

It's his eyes, Julia realizes. They're no longer overcast with worry. Now they're twinkling at her, with no sign of bruise-colored trenches beneath them.

Julia finds her voice at last. "What . . . what are you guys doing here?"

"We came back," Dulcie says simply.

"To sell the house?"

"To buy it," Paine says with a grin. "I got a few decent jobs over the last few months—after I cut my hair and made myself presentable," he adds with a laugh. "They were only commercials, but the money was good. Enough so that we can buy out Edward's half and—"

"We're going to fix up the house so we can come back in the summer," Dulcie cuts in excitedly. "And we might live in New York City, too, in the spring. Daddy's friend Stan is going to—"

"Slow down, Dulcie," Paine cuts in, laughing. "There's a lot to tell Julia. There's no rush. We're sticking around for awhile."

Over his shoulder, she can see that the familiar stair hall is stacked with boxes.

Paine follows her gaze. "That's all our stuff," he says. "I rented a truck to get it here. This time we took our time driving across the country. I figured it might be awhile before we do it again."

"We went to the Grand Canyon, Julia," Dulcie says. "And we climbed down inside it. I could feel how big it was. It was awesome."

"That's great, Dulcie." Julia's gaze meets Paine's, finding unaccustomed warmth there.

"After we got back, I felt like we didn't belong in California anymore," he tells her. "I don't know where we do belong, but it wasn't there. Maybe it isn't here, either . . . but we're going to find out."

Julia ponders that.

She looks over at the familiar stairway, almost expecting, even now, to see or hear something there.

"What do you think of our plan?" Paine asks.

"I think . . . I think that Iris would have liked this plan," Julia says slowly.

Yes. Iris would have liked knowing that they're going to give this old house, and Lily Dale, a chance.

"What do *you* think?" Paine is watching her carefully.

"I think it's a good idea, too," Julia says honestly.

As for Kristin . . .

Well, Kristin would have liked to know that Dulcie is where Julia can keep an eye on her.

Somehow, it doesn't matter to Julia now that Dulcie and Paine might never know the whole truth. All that matters is that Kristin will always be a part of her. Now, so will Dulcie . . .

And maybe Paine, as well.

Julia glances from daughter to father, still barely able to believe her eyes. "I never expected to see you guys again."

"I thought of calling you to tell you we were coming back, but Dulcie wanted to surprise you."

"I thought it would be a good Christmas present for you," the little girl says, giggling.

"It definitely is, Dulcie. It's the best Christmas present ever."

As Julia speaks, she swears she can hear a faint ripple of joyous laughter echoing through the old house.

Afterword

This novel is pure fiction, but Lily Dale is a real place. It exists a few miles from my hometown of Dunkirk, New York, and it really is a gated Victorian-era resort community inhabited primarily by spiritualists.

When I reached my teen years, it became sort of a summer ritual for a group of us girls to head down Route 60 to Cassadaga Lake. We traipsed through Lily Dale, clutching our hard-earned baby-sitting cash and searching for mediums willing to "read" us. Back then our biggest hope wasn't that the spiritualist would make contact with some lost loved one. No, what we wanted to know was whom we were going to marry? We took this stuff seriously—we always wrote down copious notes during our sessions with the mediums, lest we later forget some relevant detail.

A few years ago, while browsing through a box of my old school-day clutter in my parents' attic, I came across some long-forgotten notes I had made during a teenaged visit to Lily

Dale. According to my loopy teen-girl handwriting, when I asked the medium the big question—who am I going to marry?—she responded that his name began with the letters *M-A*. At the time, I wrote this down with a heart beside it, convinced it meant I would marry a certain someone named Matt, who, as I recall, was my high-school crush at the time. Little did I know back then that I wouldn't meet and marry my soul mate—whose name happens to be *Mark*—for almost another decade. Coincidence? Maybe. Maybe not.

I have always been intrigued by paranormal phenomena. As a kid, I loved to read spooky stories. But I clearly remember the turning point—the precise event that convinced me that the dead don't just . . . *die*. That they're all around us, and that they can communicate.

It happened one Friday night when I was thirteen. I was baby-sitting, as I often did, for my two younger cousins, Michael and Katie, while my Aunt Mickey and Uncle Ron went out for the evening. Their house was big and old—no scarier, really, than countless similar houses in Dunkirk, New York, including my own. But that night, in my aunt and uncle's living room, something happened that would forever change what I thought about that house, and baby-sitting . . . and "ghosts."

It began with a cool breeze on the back of my neck as I sat—wide awake, mind you—watching television. The couch was in the middle of the room—behind it, a grand piano and grandfather clock (prone to chiming at regular intevals and waking snoozing sitters!), and beyond that, obscured from my view, the big wooden front door. Which, I realized that night, was suddenly standing wide open.

That was odd. I was pretty certain I had not only closed it, but turned the dead bolt and locked the chain. After all, I had just seen the movie *Halloween*, and unlike poor Jamie Lee Curtis and her doomed pals, I wasn't taking any chances while baby-sitting.

Puzzled, but not yet paralyzed with fear, I got up, closed the door, locked the bolt and the chain and returned to the couch.

A few minutes later, I again felt the cool air on the back of my neck.

Again, the door was standing wide open.

This time, I was terrified. I ran upstairs to check my cousins, suspecting a prank. They were both sound asleep in their beds.

Their plump black and white cat, Columbus, was acting strange. Granted, this particular feline *was* strange—but tonight, he seemed edgier than usual and he flat-out refused to budge from his spot on Katie's bed and come downstairs with me. When I dragged him down, all thirty pounds of him, he bolted right back up the stairs. Clearly, he didn't want be in the living room with me . . . and whoever was there with me.

I sat again to watch television, confident that the door was securely locked. I checked it and rechecked it.

But as soon as I started to relax, it happened again.

I didn't actually see it open.

It happened when I wasn't looking. All I know is that the big old wooden door unlocked itself—a dead bolt and a chain—and swung open.

Naturally, I freaked out. I called my parents, who were home at our house right around the corner. My mom was asleep. My dad answered the phone. To say that he was skeptical is a vast understatement. My father, a pragmatic Capricorn banker, basically informed me that it was simply my dramatic imagination (I was, after all, a budding author even then) playing tricks on me. He said my aunt and uncle would be home soon, and not to worry.

Even now, I must feel sorry for my jittery adolescent self. Anyway, I wound up calling my friend Bobby, whose parents were also out for the night. I made him stay on the phone with me until my aunt and uncle came home.

When my Aunt Mickey drove me home, I told her what had happened. She didn't seem to think much of it. I remember thinking she probably didn't believe me, either. I didn't have much time to discuss it with her, anyway—it was a fifteen-second drive.

Flash forward to a few Christmases ago. I was back in my hometown for the holidays with my husband and children. We gathered for Christmas dinner at my Aunt Mickey and Uncle Ron's new house—another big old potentially haunted Victorian. Anyway, the conversation drifted to the old days when I used to baby-sit for Michael and Katie, who are now grown with families of their own. I brought up the night the door kept opening on its own, and how my father didn't believe me and dash to my rescue. Nobody, in fact, had ever seemed to believe me on the many occasions that I repeated that story through the years.

That Christmas, however, my Aunt Mickey spoke up at last. "Oh, that was just the ghost," she told me.

"What ghost?"

"The ghost who lived in that house. Lots of nights when I was alone in that living room after everyone else had gone to bed, I would feel her there with me. She was mischievous, but she never scared me."

Well, she certainly had scared me!

When I asked my aunt why she didn't admit to me back then that the house was haunted, she said, "Because I knew the ghost was harmless, and I knew that if I told you about her, you'd never baby-sit for us again!"

She was right, of course. I might be a believer, but I'm also a chicken.

Anyway, at last I felt vindicated—because I always knew that the door unlocking and opening by itself wasn't my imagination.

If that incident sparked my interest in the supernatural, several recent encounters have only deepened my conviction that the dead can communicate. After tragically losing three close relatives—both my parental grandparents and my mother-in-law—in a little over a year, I visited a medium at Lily Dale under the guise of "research" for this book, yet searching for some respite from overwhelming grief. She new nothing about me, and asked that I not even reveal my name to her. Yet she managed to distinctly bring forth all three of my lost loved ones with details that convinced me they were there, talking to me through her. In fact, she relayed a message from my grandparents to their still stubbornly skeptical son. When I passed it along to my father, he was a little shaken, wide-eyed, and willing to admit that the medium had brought up a reference to something she couldn't have known.

Yes, there are fraudulent mediums. Yes, there are grief-stricken relatives who look for—and find—"proof" of a sign or message from their dearly departed where there is mere coincidence. Yes, there are cynics who refuse to acknowledge the possibility of another level of existence even in documented paranormal phenomena for which there is no logical scientific explanation.

But before and during the research process for this book, I have personally witnessed the work of many legitimate mediums—including several at Lily Dale, and the internationally acclaimed John Edward. For the open-minded, and for those who grieve the loss of precious family members, there is infinite comfort in knowing that a few gifted human beings can bridge the gap between our world and the next.

Wendy Corsi Staub
June 2001

Please read on for an exciting sneak peek at
Wendy Corsi Staub's next thriller,
DEAD BEFORE DARK,
coming in May 2009!

Attica, New York
June

They called him the Night Watchman.

Back in the late sixties, he stole into women's homes after dark on nights when the moon was full and they were alone. He slaughtered them—and always left an eerie calling card at the crime scene.

The authorities never publicly revealed what it was.

For over a year, the killer engaged in a deadly game of cat and mouse with the local police and the FBI, the press, and the jittery populations of cities he so sporadically struck beneath a full moon, claiming seemingly random female victims.

No one ever did manage to figure out how or why he chose the women he killed.

The only certainty was that he watched them closely in the days or weeks leading up to their deaths. Learned their routines. Knew precisely where and when to catch them alone at night, off guard and vulnerable.

Then, out of the blue, the killing stopped.

Months went by without a telltale murder. Then years.

The Night Watchman Murders joined a long list of legendary unsolved American crimes, perhaps the most notorious since the Borden axe murders almost a century before.

Unsolved? Of course Lizzie was guilty as hell. She was acquitted based only on the Victorian presumption that a homicidal monster couldn't possibly dwell within a genteel lady.

Back then, few suspected that pure evil was quite capable of lurking behind the most benign of facades.

A hundred years later, as the Night Watchman went about his gruesome business undetected, even those who knew him best had yet to catch on. He—like others who would come after him: Ted Bundy, John Wayne Gacy, Jeffrey Dahmer—was a monster masquerading as a gentleman.

Unlike the others, though, he was never apprehended. Not for the Night Watchman Murders, anyway.

A theory came to light, when the bloodbath was so suddenly curtailed, that the killer had either died himself, or been jailed for another crime.

As the decade drew to a close, the lingering public fascination with the Night Watchman faded and was finally eclipsed by interest in the elusive Zodiac Killer.

Years went by, decades dawned and waned, the nineteen-hundreds gave way to a shiny new millennium.

Once in a while, some Unsolved Crimes buff would turn the media spotlight on the Night Watchman.

For the most part, though, he remained shrouded in shadow, and has to this day.

Ah, well, the darkest night always gives way to dawn.

He emerges into the hot glare of summer sunlight on what happens to be the longest day of the year.

Fitting, isn't it?

He smiles at the final uniformed guard standing sentry over his path to freedom.

The guard doesn't smile back.

They never have. They simply keep a joyless, steady vigil, scrutinizing the most mundane human activities, day in and day out, night in and night out.

Night in and night out . . .

Ha. No joy in it for prison guards, anyway.

Street clothes are on his back for the first time in three and a half decades; bus fare home is stashed in his pocket . . . if he had a home to go to.

Thirty-five years is a long time.

But finding a place to live is the last thing on his mind as he walks toward the bus stop, free at last, with nightfall hours away.